THE ...
OF DR DALTON

BY

ROBIN GIANNA

RESISTING
HER REBEL HERO

BY

LUCY RYDER

MILLS &
BOON

THE LAST TEMPTATION OF DR DALTON

BY
ROBIN GIANNA

MILLS & BOON

Published in Great Britain 2014
by Mills & Boon, an imprint of Harlequin (UK) Limited,
Eton House, 18-24 Paradise Road, Richmond, Surrey, TW9 1SR

© 2014 Robin Gianakopoulos

ISBN: 978 0 263 90761 2

Harlequin (UK) Limited's policy is to use papers that are natural, renewable and recyclable products and made from wood grown in sustainable forests. The logging and manufacturing processes conform to the legal environmental regulations of the country of origin.

Printed and bound in Spain
by Blackprint CPI, Barcelona

Dear Reader

As I was writing my debut Medical Romance™, CHANGED BY HIS SON'S SMILE, I fell a little in love with a secondary character—charming playboy Dr Trent Dalton. Writing a book about him and how a certain spunky woman turns his life upside down was sure to be fun!

I chose Liberia as the setting for this story because of its unique ties to the United States, as well as its interesting West African culture. The civil wars the people of Liberia endured in the very recent past were horrific, with medical care nearly non-existent during the worst of it. Mission hospitals and schools like my fictional ones in this story are an important part of the country's healing and growth. I hope you enjoy learning a little about Liberia, too, as you read the story.

Trent travels the world working in mission hospitals, careful never to get tied to one place—or one woman—for very long. Beautiful Charlotte 'Charlie' Edwards certainly has to be determined and feisty to meet the challenges of running a mission hospital, and I knew she was the perfect heroine to tame him. But just when he finally realises she's the one worth sticking around for, he finds out she just might have been playing him all along.

Please drop me a line through my website, www. RobinGianna.com, if you enjoy Trent and Charlie's story. I'd love to hear from you!

Robin

Recent titles by Robin Gianna:

CHANGED BY HIS SON'S SMILE

DEDICATION

Mom, you always told me
how important writers are to the world.
This one's for you.

ACKNOWLEDGEMENTS

Many thanks to:

Critique partner, writer friend
and paediatric emergency physician Meta Carroll,
MD, for spending so much time walking me through
medical scenes and double-checking them for
accuracy. I appreciate it so, so much!

My sister-in-law, Trish Connor, MD,
for helping me figure out why my heroine
had needed plastic surgery as a child.

Cynthia Adams, piano teacher extraordinaire,
for the perfect music choices in the story.

CHAPTER ONE

IT WAS ALL she could do not to throw her stupid phone out of the car window.

Why wasn't he answering? Charlotte Edwards huffed out a breath and focused on driving as fast as she possibly could—not an easy task on the potholed dirt road that was just muddy enough to send her sliding into a tree if she wasn't careful.

Thank goodness it was only May in Liberia, West Africa, and just the beginning of the rainy season. Her battered four-by-four handled the terrible roads pretty well, but once they were inches deep with mud and water all bets were off.

Adrenaline surging, Charlie cautiously pressed harder on the gas pedal. No matter how uncomfortable it would make her feel, she absolutely had to catch Trent Dalton at the airport before he left—then tell him off for not answering his phone. If he had, she'd have paid for a taxi to bring him back stat to her little hospital, instead of wasting time making this trek both ways.

The sudden ringing of her phone made her jump and she snatched it up, hoping it was Trent, seeing she'd called a dozen times. "So you finally decided to look at your phone?"

"It's Thomas."

The hospital technician sounded surprised and no won-

der. Her stomach twisted with dread, hoping he wasn't de-
livering bad news. "Sorry. You calling with an update?"

"The boy is still holding his own. I pray he'll be okay
until Dr. Dalton gets back here. But I wanted to tell you
that Dr. Smith has offered to do the appendectomy."

"What? Tell him no way. I'm not having a liar and a
hack working on any of our patients—unless Trent's already gone, in which case we'll have no choice but to re-
consider. I'll let you know as soon as I get to the airport."

"Yes, Ma."

She hung up and shook her head, managing a little
smile. The word "Ma" was used as a sign of respect in Liberia, and no matter how many times she'd asked Thomas
just to call her Charlie, or Charlotte, he never did.

Dr. Smith had been sent by the Global Physicians Co-
alition to work at the Henry and Louisa Edwards Mission
Hospital for a one-year commission. But when his arrival
had been delayed they'd asked Trent to fill in for the five
days until Smith could get there. Though he'd just finished
a stint in India, Trent had thankfully not minded his vacation being delayed until Smith showed up.

Not long after Trent had left to start his vacation,
though, the GPC called to tell her they had discovered
that Smith had falsified his credentials. No way would she
have him work here now.

And, because problems came in multiples, they had a
very sick little boy whose life just might depend on getting surgery pronto. If only John Adams, her right-hand
man for everything to do with the hospital and school,
hadn't been off getting supplies today. Charlie would've
sent him to drag Trent back to take care of the little boy,
saving her from enduring an hour's drive in close quarters
with the man. That was, if he hadn't flown off to wherever
he was going next.

Anxiety ratcheting up another notch, Charlie almost

called Trent again, knowing there was little point. Then she spotted the airport in the distance. Shoving down the gas pedal, hands sweating, she slithered and bumped her way down the road, parked nearly sideways and ran inside.

Relief at seeing him still sitting there nearly made her knees weak. And, of course, that weakness had nothing to do with again seeing the gorgeous man she'd enjoyed a one-night stand with just hours ago. Memories of what they'd spent the night doing filled her cheeks with hot embarrassment, and she wished with all her being she'd known their last kiss this morning wouldn't really be good-bye. She wished she had known before she'd fallen into bed with him. If she had, she most definitely would have resisted the delicious taste of his mouth and the all too seductive smile.

He was slouched in a hard chair, his long legs stretched out in front of him, a Panama hat pulled over his face with just his sensuous lips visible. Lips that had touched every inch of her body, mortified heat rushed back to her face. Even sitting, his height made him stand out among the passengers sprawled everywhere in the airport. A battered leather bag sat next to his feet. His arms were folded across his chest and he looked sound asleep.

Dang it, this was all too awkward. She squirmed with discomfort at the very same time her nerve-endings tingled at the pleasure of seeing him again. Disgusted with herself, she took a deep breath, stepped closer and kicked his shoe. "Wake up. We need to talk."

She saw him stiffen, but other than that he didn't move, obviously pretending he hadn't heard her. What—he thought she'd come all this way just to kiss him goodbye again? Been there, done that and now it was over between them. This was about business, not pleasure. But with that thought instantly came other thoughts. Thoughts of all the pleasure she'd enjoyed with him last night, which made her even more annoyed with herself.

"I know you're not asleep, Trent Dalton. Look at me." She kicked him in the ankle this time, figuring that was sure to get his attention.

"Ow, damn it." He yanked back his leg and his finger inched up the brim of his hat until she could see the nearly black hair waving across his forehead. His light blue eyes looked at her, cautious and wary. "What are you doing here, Charlotte?"

"I'm here because you wouldn't answer your stupid cell phone."

"I turned it off. I'm on vacation."

"If you'd left it on, I wouldn't have had to spend an hour driving here, worried I wouldn't catch you before you left. We have to talk."

"Listen." His expression became pained. "It was great being with you, and moving on can be hard, you know? But going through a long-drawn-out goodbye will just make it all tougher."

"We can't say goodbye just yet."

"I'm sorry, Charlotte. I have to leave. I promise you'll be fine."

Of all the arrogant... Did he really think women had a hard time getting over him after one night of fun? Fabulous fun, admittedly, but still. She felt like conking him on the head. "Sorry, but you have to come back."

"I can't," he said in a soft and gentle voice, his blue eyes now full of pity and remorse. "We both knew we only had one night together. Tomorrow will be better. It will. In a few weeks, you'll forget all about me."

"You are so incredibly full of yourself." She couldn't control a laugh that ended in a little snort. The man was unbelievable. "Our fling was over the second you kissed me goodbye, tipped your hat and left with one of your adorable smiles and the "maybe see ya again sometime, babe" parting remark. What would make you think I had a problem with that? That's not why I'm here."

He stared at her, and she concentrated on keeping her expression nonchalant, even amused. She wasn't about to give him even a hint that she would think about him after he was gone.

"So why are you here, then?"

"I'm throwing out the new surgeon."

"Throwing him out?" Trent sat up straight. "What do you mean?"

"The GPC contacted me to tell me they found he'd falsified his credentials. That he'd had his license suspended in the U.S. for alcohol and drug use—over-prescribing of narcotics."

"Damn, so he's a loose cannon." He frowned. "But that doesn't mean he's not a good surgeon."

"Just because we're in the middle of West Africa doesn't mean our docs shouldn't be top notch. The GPC left it up to me whether I wanted him to work for us or not. And I refuse to have someone that unethical, maybe even doped up, working on our patients."

"So when is the GPC sending a new surgeon?"

"As soon as possible. They think they can get someone temporary like you were in a few days, no more than a week. Then they'll round up a doc who can be here for the year. All you have to do is come back until the temp gets here, or a day or two before."

"I can't. I just spent a solid year in India and I need a break before I start my new job in the Philippines. I have vacation plans I can't change."

She had to wonder what woman those plans might be with. "I don't believe your vacation is more important to you than your job."

"Hey, the only reason I worked twelve straight months was to pay for my vacation."

"Yeah, right." She made a rude sound in her throat. "Like you couldn't make tons more money as a surgeon in the U.S., paying for vacations and country club memberships and fancy cars. Nobody works in a mission hospital for the money."

"Maybe I couldn't get a job in the U.S." His normally laughing eyes were oddly serious.

"Mmm-hmm." She placed her hands on the arms of his seat and leaned forward, her nose nearly touching his. The clean, manly scent of him surrounded her, making her heart go into a stupid, accelerated pit-pat. But she wasn't about to back down. "So, I never did ask—why *do* you work exclusively in tiny hospitals all over the world, pulling up stakes every year? Most docs work for the GPC part-time."

"Running from the law." His lips were so close, his breath touching her skin, and more than anything she wanted to close that small gap and kiss him one more time. "Murdered my last girlfriend after she followed me to the airport."

She had to chuckle even as she watched his eyes darken, showing he still felt the same crazy attraction she felt. That she'd felt the first second she'd met him. "I always knew you were a dangerous man, Trent Dalton. I just didn't realize quite how dangerous."

Just as she felt herself leaning in, about to kiss his sexy mouth against her will, she managed to mentally smack herself. Straightening, she stepped back.

"So. We have an immediate problem that can't wait for you to think about whether playing golf or chasing skirts, or whatever you do on vacation, is more important than my little hospital."

"What problem?"

"We've got a seven-year-old boy who's got a hot appendix. Thomas is afraid it will rupture and says he doesn't have the skill to handle it."

"Why does he think it's his appendix? Even if it is, Thomas is a well-trained tech. I was impressed as hell at the great job he does on hernias."

"Hernias aren't the same thing as an appendix, which I think you know, Dr. Dalton. Thomas says he's sure that's what it is—that you're the only one who can do it. And to tell you that the last thing the kid needs is to get septic."

His brow lowered in thought before he spoke. "What are his symptoms?"

"His mother says he hasn't eaten for two days. He's been feverish—temp of one-hundred-point-four—and vomiting."

"Belly ache and vomiting? Maybe it's just the flu."

"The abdominal pain came first, then the vomiting."

"Has the pain moved?"

"From his umbilicus to right lower quadrant." She slapped her hands back onto the chair arms. Was the man going to ask questions all day in the hope of still getting away from here? "Listen, Trent. It's been thirty-six hours. If the appendix doesn't come out, it's going to rupture. I don't need to tell you the survival rates of peritonitis in this part of the world."

A slow smile spread across Trent's face before he laughed. "Maybe *you* should do the surgery. Why the hell didn't you become a doctor?"

"I can get doctors. I can't get somebody to run that hospital. So are you coming?"

He just looked at her, silent, his amusement now gone. The worry on his face touched her heart, because she was pretty sure it was on her behalf—that he didn't want to come back because she might get hurt, which she'd bet had happened often enough in his life as a vagabond doctor.

As though it had a mind of its own, her palm lifted to touch his cheek. "I've only known you a few days, but that's enough time to realize you're a man of honor. I'm sure you'll come take care of this little boy and stick it out until we can get someone else. A one-night fling was all it was meant to be for either of us—anything more would be pointless and messy. From now on, our relationship is strictly professional. So let's go before the boy gets sicker."

His hand pressed against the back of hers, held it a moment against his cheek then lowered it to gently set her away from him. "You're good, I'll give you that." He unfolded from the chair and stood, looking down at her. "But I can only stay a few more days, so don't be trying to guilt me into more than that. I mean it."

"Agreed." She stuck out her hand to seal the deal, and he wrapped his long, warm fingers around hers. She gave his hand a quick, brisk shake then yanked her own loose but didn't manage to erase the imprint of it.

It was going to be a long couple of days.

As the car bounced in and out of ruts on the way back to the hospital, Trent glanced at the fascinating woman next to him while she concentrated on her driving. The shock of seeing Charlotte's beautiful face at the airport had nearly knocked the wind out of him. The face he'd seen all morning as he'd waited to get away from it.

He stared at her strong, silky eyebrows, lowered in concentration over eyes as green as a Brazilian rainforest. Her thick brown hair touched with streaks of bronze flowed over her shoulders, which were exposed by the sleeveless shirts she liked to wear. He nearly reached to slide his fingers over that pretty skin, and to hell with distracting her from driving.

He sucked in a breath and turned his attention back to the road. How could one night of great sex have seemed like something more than the simple, pleasant diversion it was supposed to have been?

"The road is worst these last couple miles, so hang on to your hat," she said, a smile on the pink lips whose imprint he'd still been feeling against his own as he'd sat in that damned airport for hours.

"You want me to drive?"

"Uh, no. We'd probably end up around a tree. You stick with doctoring and let me handle everything else."

He chuckled. The woman sure took her role as hospital director seriously, and to his surprise he enjoyed it. How had he never known he liked bossy women?

"So, where were you headed?" Charlotte asked.

"Florence." But for once he hadn't known what the hell he was going to do with himself for the three weeks the GPC gave doctors off between jobs. Getting in touch with one of his old girlfriends and spending time with her, whoever it might be, in London, Thailand or Rio until his next job began was how he always spent his vacation.

"Alone? Never mind. Pretend I didn't ask."

"Yeah, alone." She probably wouldn't believe it, but it was true. He hadn't called anyone. He couldn't conjure the interest, which was damned annoying. So he'd be spending three weeks in Italy all by his lonesome, with too much time to think about the fiery woman sitting next to him. The woman with the sweet, feminine name who preferred going by the name of a man.

Charlotte. Charlie. If only he could have three weeks of warms days and nights filled with her in Florence, Rome and the Italian Riviera—with her sharp mind, sense of humor and gorgeous, touchable body. Last night had been… He huffed out a breath and stared out of the window. Not a good idea to let his thoughts go any further about *that* right now.

At least there hadn't been a big, dramatic goodbye. Seeing tears in those amazing green eyes of hers and a tremble on her kissable lips would have made him feel like crap. He had to make sure that during the next few days he kept his distance so there would be no chance of that happening. Which wouldn't be easy, since he'd like nothing more than to get her into bed again.

He looked out over the landscape of lush green hills and trees that led to the hospital compound and realized he hadn't got round to asking Charlotte how she'd ended up here. "You never did tell me how your family came to be missionaries in Liberia. To build all this."

"My great-grandparents were from North Carolina. My great-grandfather came from a family of schoolteachers and missionaries, and I'm told that when he and his new wife were barely twenty they decided to head to Africa to open a school. They came to Liberia because English is the primary language. Three generations later, we're still here."

"They built the whole compound at once?" The hard work and commitment so many missionaries had put into their projects around the world amazed him.

"The hospital came about twenty years after they built the house and school in 1932. I've always loved the design of that house." She gave him a smile. "Since Liberia was founded by freed slaves, my great-grandparents brought the Southern antebellum style with them. Did you know that antebellum isn't really an architectural style, though? That in Latin it means 'before war'? It refers to homes built before the U.S. Civil War. Sadly ironic, isn't it? That the same could be said for here in Liberia too." She was talking fast, then blushed cutely. "And you probably didn't want or need a history lesson."

"Ironic's the word," he said, shaking his head. "I've never worked here before. What the civil wars have done to this country is… Heck, you can't begin to measure it."

"I know. Unbelievable how many people died. What the rest have had to live with—the chaos and terror, the shambles left behind. The horrible, disfiguring injuries." Her voice shook with anger, her lips pressed in a tight line. "Anyway, nothing can fix the past. All we can do is try to make a difference now."

"So, your great-grandparents moved here?" he prompted.

A smile banished her obvious outrage. "Apparently my great-grandmother said she'd only move here if she could make it a little like home. They built the house, filled it with beautiful furniture and even got the piano that's still in the parlor."

"And Edwardses have been here since then? What about the wars?"

"The wars forced my parents to leave when I was little and go back to the U.S. Eventually we moved to Togo to start a new mission. The hospital and school here were badly damaged by gunfire and shrapnel, but the house was just in bad disrepair, stripped of things like the windows and sinks. John Adams and I have been fixing it up, but it's third on the list of priorities."

He couldn't imagine how much work—and money— it was taking to make that happen. "So what made you want to resurrect all this? It's not like you really remember living here."

"Just because I haven't lived here until now doesn't mean my roots aren't here, and John Adams's roots. They are. They're dug in deep through our ancestors, and I intend to keep them here. My plan is to grow them, expand them, no matter what it takes."

"No matter what it takes? That's a pretty strong statement." He'd met plenty of people committed to making things better for the underprivileged, but her attitude was damned impressive.

"These people deserve whatever it takes to get them the

help they need." Her grim tone lightened as they pulled in front of the one-story, painted cement hospital. "Let's get the boy fixed up. And, Trent…" Her green eyes turned all soft and sweet and he nearly reached for her. "Thanks for coming back. I promise you won't be sorry."

CHAPTER TWO

THOMAS HOVERED IN the clinic outside the door to the OR, looking anxious. "Where is the patient?" Trent asked. "Is he prepped and ready, or do you want me to examine him first?"

"I thought he should be examined again, to confirm my diagnosis. But he's in the OR. With Dr. Smith."

"Dr. Smith?" Charlie asked. What the heck was he doing in there? Hadn't she asked him to stay out of the hospital and away from patients? "Why? Did you tell him Dr. Dalton was coming back?"

"Said since he was here and the boy needs surgery fast he'd take care of it."

Anger welled up in Charlie's chest at the same time she fought it down. She supposed she should give Smith kudos for stepping up despite the circumstances, instead of being mad at her refusal to let him work there. "Well, that's... nice of him, but I'll tell him our other surgeon is here now."

"Give me a minute to scrub," Trent said as he grabbed a gown and mask and headed to the sink.

Charlie hurried into the OR to find Don Smith standing over the patient who was being attended to by the nurse anesthetist but not yet asleep. She stopped short and stared at the anxious-looking little boy. Could there be some confusion, and this wasn't the child with the hot appendix? His eyelid and eyebrow had a red, disfiguring, golf ball-sized lump that nearly concealed his eye completely. How in the world could he even see?

Her chest tightened and her stomach balled in a familiar pain that nearly made her sick. The poor child looked freakish and she knew all too well how horribly he must be teased about it. How terrible that must make him feel.

She lifted a hand to her ear, now nearly normal-looking after so many years of disfigurement. Her hand dropped to her side, balled into a fist. How wrong that he'd lived with this, when a kid in the States never would have. More proof that the project so dear to her heart was desperately needed here.

"Is this the child with appendicitis?" At Dr. Smith's nodded response, she continued. "I appreciate you being willing to take care of this emergency, but my other surgeon is here now. Help yourself to breakfast in the kitchen, if you haven't already."

"I'm here. Might as well let me operate. You'll see that I'm a capable and trustworthy surgeon. I want you to change your mind."

"I won't change my mind. Losing your license and falsifying your credentials is a serious matter, which frankly shows me you're *not* trustworthy."

"Damn it, I need this job." Smith turned to her, his face reddening with anger. "I told everyone I'd left to do humanitarian work. If I don't stay here, they'll know."

"So the only reason you want to work here is to save your reputation?" Charlie stared at him. "Hate to break it to you, but your drug addiction and loss of license is already public record in the States."

"For those who've looked. A lot of people I know haven't."

"I'm sorry, Dr. Smith, but you'll have to leave. Now."

"I'm doing this surgery and that's all there is to it. Nurse, get the anesthesia going." He turned to the patient and, without another word, began to swab the site while the child stared at him, his lip trembling.

Anger surged through her veins. Who did this guy think he was? The jerk wouldn't have spoken to her like this if she'd been a man. "Janice, don't listen to him. Stop this instant, Dr. Smith. I insist—"

Trent stepped between Charlie and Smith, grasping the man's wrist and yanking the cotton from his hand. "Maybe you didn't hear the director of this hospital. You're not doing surgery here."

"Who the hell are you?" Smith yanked his arm from Trent's grasp. "You can't tell me what to do."

"No, but she can. And I work for her." Trent had a good three inches on the man, and his posture was aggressive, his usually warm and laughing eyes a cold, steely blue. "I know your instincts as a doctor want what's best for this boy, which is immediate attention to his problem. Your being in here impedes that. So leave."

Smith began to sputter until his gaze met Trent's. He stepped back and looked away, ripping off his gown and mask and throwing them to the floor. "I can't believe a crappy little hospital in the middle of nowhere is too stupid to know how good I am. Your loss."

He stalked out and Charlie drew in a deep, slightly shaky breath of relief. She'd thought for a minute that Trent would have to physically take the guy out, and realized she'd completely trusted him to do exactly that. Then she pulled up short at the thought. She was in charge of this place and she couldn't rely on anyone else to deal with tough situations.

"Thanks, but you didn't need to do that. I had it handled."

Trent looked down at her with raised brows. "Did you, boss lady?"

"Yeah, I did."

He reached out, his long-fingered hand swiping across her shoulder, and she jerked, quickly looking down. "What, is there a bug on me?"

"No—a real big chip. I was wondering what put it there." His lips tipped up as his eyes met hers.

What? Ridiculous. "I don't have a chip on my shoulder. I'm just doing my job."

"Accepting help is part of being head honcho, you know." Those infuriatingly amused eyes lingered on her before he turned to the nurse. "Have you administered any anesthesia yet?"

"No, doctor."

"Good." He rolled a stool to the gurney and sat, that full smile now charmingly back on his face as he drew the sheet further down the child's hips. "So, buddy, where's it hurt?"

He pointed, and Trent gently pressed the top of the boy's stomach, slowly moving his hand downward to the right lower quadrant.

"Ow." The boy grimaced and Trent quit pressing his flesh to give the child's skinny chest a gentle pat.

"Okay. We're going to fix you up so it doesn't hurt any more. What's your name?"

"Lionel." The child, looking more relaxed than when Charlie had first come into the room, studied Trent. With his small index finger, Lionel pushed his bulging, droopy eyelid upward so he could see. "My belly will be all better? For true?"

"For true." Trent's smile deepened, his eyes crinkled at the corners as his gaze touched Charlie's for a moment before turning back to the child. "Inside your body, your appendix is about the size of your pinky finger. It's got a little sick and swollen, and that's what's making your belly hurt. I'm going to fix it all up while you sleep, and when you wake up it won't hurt any more. Okay?"

"Okay." Lionel nodded and smiled, showing a missing front tooth.

"But, before we take care of your sore belly, I want to talk about your eye." Trent gently moved the boy's hand before his own fingers carefully touched all around the protrusion on and above the eyelid. "Can you tell me how long it's been like this?"

Lionel shrugged. "I'nt know."

"I bet it's hard to see, huh?"

"Uh-huh. I can't see the football very well when we're kicking around. Sometimes Mommy has tape, though, and when she sticks it on there to hold it up that helps some."

"I'm sure you look tough that way. Scare your opponents." Trent grinned, and Lionel grinned back. "But I bet you could show how tough a player you are even more if you could see better."

Charlie marveled at the trusting expression on the child's face, how unquestioning he seemed as he nodded and smiled. She shifted her attention to Trent and saw that his demeanor wasn't just good bedside manner. The man truly liked kids, and that realization ratcheted the man's appeal even higher. And Lord knew he didn't need that appeal ratcheted up even a millimeter.

"Is your mother around? Or someone I can talk to about fixing it at the same time we fix your belly?"

"My mommy brought me. But I don't know where she is right now."

As his expression began to get anxious again, Trent leaned in close with a smile that would have reassured even the most nervous child. "Hey, we'll find her. Don't worry."

He stood and took a few steps away with a nod to Charlie. When they were out of hearing distance, he spoke in an undertone. "I want to take care of his hemangioma and we might as well do it while he's under for the appendix. There'll be a lot of bleeding to control, and I'll get him started on antibiotics first. After I remove the tumor, I'll decide if it's necessary to graft skin from his thigh to make it look good. In the States, you wouldn't do a clean surgery and an appendix at the same time, but I can do it with no problems."

"If it wouldn't be done in the States, we're not doing it here." Didn't he get that this was why she'd thrown Smith out?

"If you think mission doctors don't do things we wouldn't do in the U.S., you have a lot to learn." No longer amused, a hint of steel lurked within the blue of his eyes. "Here, I can follow my gut and do what's best for the patient, and only what's best for the patient. I don't have to worry about what an insurance company wants, or cover my ass with stupid protocol. You can either trust me to know I'm doing what's best for Lionel, or not. Your call."

Charlie glanced at the boy and knew better than anyone that they were talking about a tremendously skilled procedure, one that would require the kind of detailed work and suturing a general surgeon wouldn't be capable of. "I'm in the process of getting a plastic surgery center together. That's what the new wing of the hospital is for. How about we suggest to his mommy that she bring him back when it's operational?"

He shook his head. "First, there's a good chance they live far away and it won't be easy to get back here. Second, he's probably had this a long time. The longer we wait, the more likely the possibility of permanent blindness. Even if it is fixed later, if his brain gets used to not receiving signals from the eye that part of his brain will die, and that'll be it for his vision. Not to mention that in West Africa a person is more susceptible to getting river blindness or some other parasitic infection in the eye. What if that happened and he ended up blind in both eyes? Not worth the risk."

"But can you do it? Without him still looking...bad? The plastic surgery center will be open soon. And a plastic surgeon would know how to do stuff like this better than you would."

"You don't know who you're dealing with here." His eyes held a mocking laugh. "He'll look great, I promise."

She stared at him, at his ultra-confident expression, the lazy smile. Would she be making a mistake to let him fix the hemangioma when in just a few weeks she was supposed to have a plastics specialist on board?

She looked back at Lionel, his finger still poked into the disfiguring vascular tumor so he could see out of that eye as he watched them talk. She looked at the trusting and hopeful expression on his small face. A face marred by a horrible problem Trent promised he could fix.

"Okay. You've convinced me. Do it."

CHAPTER THREE

HOURS PASSED WHILE Trent worked on Lionel. Worry over whether or not she'd made the right decision made it difficult for Charlie to sit in her office and do paperwork, but she had to try. With creditors demanding a big payment in three weeks, getting that funding check in her pocket for the new wing from the Gilchrist Foundation was critical.

She made herself shuffle through everything one more time. It seemed the only things that had to happen to get the money were a final inspection from a Gilchrist Foundation representative and proof she had a plastic surgeon on board. Both of which would happen any day now, thank heavens.

So how, in the midst of this important stuff, could she let her attention wander? She was thinking instead about the moment five days ago when Trent had strolled into this office. Thinking about how she'd stared, open-mouthed, like a schoolgirl.

Tall and lean, with slightly long, nearly black hair starkly contrasting with the color of his eyes, he was the kind of man who made a woman stop and take a second look. And a third. Normally, eyes like his would be called ice-blue, but they'd been anything but cold; warm and intelligent, they'd glinted with a constant touch of amusement. A charming, lopsided smile had hovered on his lips. When she'd shaken his hand, he'd surprised her by tugging her against him in a warm embrace. Disarmed, she'd found herself wanting to stay there longer than the brief moment he'd held her close. She'd found her brain short-circuiting at the feel of his big hands pressed to her back; his lean, muscled body against hers; his distinctive masculine scent.

That same friendly embrace had been freely given to every woman working in the hospital, young and old, which had left all of them grinning, blushing and nearly swooning.

No doubt, the man was dynamite in human form, ready to blast any woman's heart to smithereens.

But not Charlie's. She'd known the second he'd greeted her with that genial hug that she would have to throw armor over that central organ. She'd cordially invited him to join her and John Adams for dinners, enjoying his intelligence, his amusing stories and, yes, his good looks and sophistication. She'd been sure she had everything under control.

But the night before he was to leave, when that embrace had grown longer and more intimate, when he'd finally touched his lips to hers, she hadn't resisted the desire to be with him, to enjoy a light and fun evening. An oh-so-brief diversion amidst the work that was her life. And, now that circumstances required they be in close contact for a little longer, there was no way she'd let him know that simply looking at him made her fantasize about just one more night. That was not going to happen—period.

Yes, their moment together was *so* last week. She smirked at the thought, even though a ridiculous part of her felt slightly ego-crushed that he, too, wanted to steer clear of any possible entanglement.

But that was a good thing. The man clearly loved women, all women. She'd known she was just one more notch in his travel bag, and he'd been just another notch in the fabric of her life too. Except that there hadn't been too many opportunities for "notching" since she'd finished grad school and come back to Africa.

She had to grin as she grabbed the info she wanted to share with the teachers at the school. Notching: now there was a funny euphemism for great sex if ever there was one.

She was so deep in thought about the great sex she'd enjoyed last night that she stepped into the hall without looking and nearly plowed her head into Trent's strong biceps.

"Whoa." His hands grasped her shoulders as she stumbled. "You late for lunch or something?"

Her heart sped up annoyingly as he held her just inches from his chest. "Is that a crack about how much I like to eat?"

"Not a crack. I've just observed that when you're hungry you don't let anything get between you and that plate."

She looked up into his twinkling blue eyes. "Hasn't anyone ever told you that women don't like people implying they're gluttons?"

"No negative implications from me. I like a woman who eats." His voice dropped lower. "I like the perfect and beautiful curves on your perfect and beautiful body."

As she stared up at him, the light in his eyes changed, amusement fading into something darker, more dangerous.

Desire. It hung between them, electric and heavy in the air, and Trent slowly tipped his head towards hers.

He was going to kiss her. The realization sent her heart into an accelerated tempo. A hot tingle slipped across her skin as his warm breath touched her mouth, and she lifted her hands to his chest, knowing she should push him away, but instead keeping her palms pressed to his hard pecs.

She couldn't let it happen, only to say goodbye again in a few more days. He'd made it clear he felt the same way. But, as she was thinking all that, she licked her lips in silent invitation.

His hands tightened on her arms as though he couldn't

decide whether to pull her close or push her away, then he released her. "Sorry. I shouldn't have said that. I forgot we're just casual acquaintances now." He shoved his hands in his pockets, his expression now impassive, all business. "I wanted to let you know it went well with Lionel."

She sucked in a breath, trying to be equally business-like, unaffected by his potent nearness and the need to feel his lips on hers one more time. "He's okay? You fixed the hemangioma? And he looks good?"

"You probably wouldn't think he looks good."

Her stomach dropped. "Why…? What, is it messed up?"

He laughed. "No. But right now it's sutured and swollen and would only look good to a zombie. Or a surgeon who knows what he's doing. We'll take the bandage off in a few days."

"Okay. Great." She pressed her hand to her chest, hoping to goodness it really had turned out all right. Hoping the hard beat of her heart was just from the scare, and not a lingering effect of the almost-kiss of a moment ago.

"Can you unlock your car for me? I need to get my stuff out and take it to my room."

"Of course. But I didn't tell you—even though I'm not happy with our Dr. Smith, I couldn't exactly throw him out on the streets until his flight leaves tomorrow. So he's going to be staying in the room you were in for just to-night."

"What? I'm not staying at your house again."

It was hard not to be insulted at the horror on his face. 'Goodbye, Charlie' took on a whole new meaning with Trent. "Sorry, but you're sleeping on a rollaway here in my office. I don't want you staying in my house, either."

"You do too." His lips quirked, obliterating his frown.

"Uh, no, I don't. Like I said before, you're an egomaniac. Somebody needs to bring you down a peg or two, and I guess it's going to be me."

"Thanks for your help. I appreciate it more than you know." That irritating little smile gave way to seriousness. "And it's good we're on the same page. Second goodbyes can get...sticky."

"Agreed. And you're welcome. I'll get my keys now before I head to the school." She turned, so glad she hadn't fallen into an embrace with the conceited guy. His long fingers grasped her elbow and the resulting tingle that sped up her arm had her jerking it away.

"Wait a second. You're going up to the school?"

"Yes. I have some things I want to go over with the teachers. I'm having lunch with them and the kids."

He was silent, just looking at her with a slight frown over those blue eyes, as though he couldn't decide something. He finally spoke. "Mind if I come along? I'd like to see it, and I'm not needed in the clinic right now."

"Sure. If you want." She shrugged casually. Did the man have to ponder whether seeing the school was worth being with her for a few hours? Or was she being hypersensitive?

She led the way down the short hall into the soupy, humid air, making sure to stand on Trent's left so her good ear would be closest to him. "The kids love visitors. But we'll be walking, so don't be surprised if you get a little muddy."

"Glad I'm not wearing my designer shoes today. Then again, I could've taken them off. Nothing like a little mud between the toes."

The thought of cool, squishy mud on bare feet, then playing a little footsie together, sounded strangely appealing, and she rolled her eyes at herself as they trudged up the road to the schoolhouse. Maybe she needed to try and find a local boyfriend to take off this edge she kept feeling around Trent. He reached for the binder of papers she was carrying and tucked it under his arm.

"So you were the boy who earned points by carrying a girl's books to school? Why doesn't that surprise me?"

"Hey, I looked for any way to earn points. Carrying books was just one of them."

"I can just imagine. So what other ways did you earn points?" And why couldn't she just keep her mouth shut? "You know, never mind. I don't think I want to know."

"You already know some of them." He leaned closer as they walked, the scent of him teasing her nose. "But a few things got me more points than others. For example, my famous shoulder-rubs always scored big."

The memory of that shoulder rub came in a rush of clarity—them naked in her bed, sated and relaxed, the ceiling fan sending cool whispers of air across their skin. Her breathing got a little shallow and she walked faster.

"One of the ground rules is to stop with the references to last night. Got it?"

"I wasn't referring to anything but the shoulder rub I gave you at your office desk. Can I help it if your mind wants to go other places?"

She scowled at the bland innocence on his face. The man was about as far from innocent as he could be. "Mmm-hmm. So, when you mention back rubs, you don't picture me naked?"

His slow smile, his blue eyes dancing as he leaned closer, made her feel a little weak at the knees. "Charlotte, you can bet I frequently picture you naked." His gaze held hers, then slid away to the road. "Again, I'm sorry. That was inappropriate. Let's talk about the school. Did you open it at the same time as the hospital?"

Phew; she had to stop just blurting out what she was thinking, though he seemed to have the same problem. Good thing he changed the subject, or she just might have melted down into the mud.

"John Adams concentrated on getting the school open

while I focused on the hospital. His daughter, Patience—I think you met her?—will be going to school next year, so he's been pretty excited about the project. They live in a small apartment attached to the school, so she'll probably be there today. She loves to hang out in the classrooms and pretend she can read and write."

"Patience is a cutie. She and I bonded over ice-cream." His eyes always turned such a warm blue when he talked about children; it filled her chest with some kind of feeling she didn't want to analyze. "So, is John from here?"

"Just so you know, he's always gone by both his first and last name. I'm not sure why." She smiled. "John Adams's parents both worked with my parents here. They left too when the war broke out. Their family and mine met up again in Togo and, since he's just a few years older than I am, he's kind of like a brother. And I love Patience like I would a niece."

"Where's her mother?"

"She died suddenly of meningitis. It was a terrible shock." She sighed. "Moving here with me to open this place has been a fresh start for John Adams and Patience, and hugely helpful to me. I couldn't have done it alone."

"I've been wondering where your funding is coming from. The GPC's been cutting back, so I know they can't be floating cash for the whole hospital."

"We've shaken down every possible donor, believe me. The school was as big a shambles as the hospital, and usually donor groups focus on one or the other. But we managed to get the building reasonably repaired and the basics in—desks and supplies and stuff. We opened with thirty primary-school-aged kids enrolled and have almost a hundred now." She shook her head. "It's not nearly enough, though, with half a million Liberian kids not attending school at all. And sixty percent of girls and women over fifteen can't read or write."

He frowned. "Is it as hard to raise cash for a school as it is for a hospital?"

"It's all hard. But I'm working on getting a donation from a church group in the States that'll help us hire a new teacher and have enough food for the kids' lunches. I'm excited. It looks like it's going to come through." Charlie smiled at Trent, but his expression stayed uncharacteristically serious. "We hate turning families away, but can't just endlessly accept kids into the program, you know? It's not fair to the teachers or the students to have classrooms so big nobody gets the attention they need. So I'm sure hoping it works out."

"How soon will you know?"

"In the next day or two, I think."

His expression was oddly inscrutable. "Be sure to tell me if the donation comes through or not, okay?"

"Okay." She had to wonder why he wanted to know, but appreciated his interest. "As for the hospital, I'm supposed to get a giant check from the Gilchrist Foundation as soon as the new wing is ready to go, thank heavens."

He stopped dead and stared at her. "The Gilchrist Foundation?"

"Yes. You've heard of them?"

"Yeah. You could say that."

CHAPTER FOUR

"HAS THE GILCHRIST Foundation donated to hospitals you've worked at before?" Charlotte asked. "Did they come through with their support? I'm a little worried, because we're scraping the bottom of the barrel just to get the wing finished."

Trent looked into her sweet, earnest face before turning his attention to the verdant landscape—not nearly as vivid and riveting as the color of her eyes. "They're a reputable organization."

"That's good to hear." She sounded slightly breathless, her footsteps squishing quickly in the mud, and he slowed his stride. He resisted the urge to grasp her arm to make sure she didn't slip and fall. "I heard they were, but they're making us jump through some hoops to get it."

He almost asked *what hoops?*, but decided to keep out of it. The last thing he wanted was to get involved with anything to do with the Gilchrist Foundation. Or for Charlotte to find out his connection to it. "It'll be fine, I'm sure. So, this is it." He looked up at the one-storey cement building painted a golden yellow, the windows and door trimmed in a brick color. "Looks like you've done a nice job restoring it."

"It took a lot of money and manpower. It was basically a shell, with nothing left inside. The windows were gone and there were bullet holes everywhere. John Adams and I are pretty proud of how it turned out."

As they reached the wooden door of the school he saw Charlotte glance up at the sky, now filling with dark-gray clouds. "Looks like rain's coming, and I wasn't smart enough to bring an umbrella. Sorry. We won't stay too long."

"I'm not made of sugar, you know. I won't melt," he teased. Then the thought of sugar made him think of her sweet lips and the taste of her skin. It took a serious effort to turn away, not to pull her close to take a taste.

They left their muddy shoes outside before she led the way in. Children dressed in white shirts with navy-blue pants or skirts streamed from classrooms, laughing and chattering.

"Mr. Trent!" Cute little Patience ran across the room, the only one in a sleeveless dress instead of a uniform. "Mr. Trent, you bring me candy?"

"Sorry, Miss Impatience, I don't have any left." She wrapped her arms around his leg and the crestfallen expression on her face made him wish he'd brought a whole lot more. Too bad he hadn't known he'd be here longer than a few days.

"How about gum?"

He laughed and swung her up into his arms. "Don't have any of that left either." He lowered his voice. "But, next time you're at the hospital, I'll sneak some pudding out of the pantry for you, okay?"

"I heard that." Charlotte's brows lifted. "Since when are you two best friends? Dr Trent just got here a few days ago."

"Mr. Trent and me are good friends, yes." The girl's arms tightened around his neck, which felt nice. Kids didn't want or expect anything from you but love. And maybe candy too, he thought with a smile. There weren't too many adults he could say that about.

"Patience and I share a fondness for that chocolate pudding."

"Hmm." A mock frown creased Charlotte's face as she leaned close to them. "I didn't know you were stealing supplies, Dr Dalton. I'm going to have to keep an eye on you."

"What's the punishment for stealing?" His gaze dropped from her amused eyes to her pink lips. Maybe if he stole a kiss he'd find out.

"I don't think you want to know." Her eyes were still smiling and he found himself riveted by the glow of gold and brown flecks deep within that beautiful green.

"Miss Edwards!" Several kids ran their way. "You coming to see our play this Wednesday? Please come, Miss Edwards!"

Charlotte wrapped her arms around their shoulders in hugs, one after another, talking and smiling, making it obvious she wasn't a distant director around here; that she put in a lot of face time, truly cared about these kids. That impressed the hell out of him. He'd seen a lot of hospital directors in his day, even some in mission hospitals, who were more focused on the bottom line and making donors happy than they were about helping the patients they existed for.

Trent set Patience back on her feet. "Have you been doing any more drawing? You know I like to see your art." Nodding enthusiastically, her short legs took off running back down a hall.

He watched Charlotte with the kids. He'd never worked at a mission hospital that included a school in its compound. He hadn't been able to resist a chance to peek at it and see what they were accomplishing, even when he knew it wasn't the best idea to spend much time with Charlotte. The whole reason he'd come was to see the school children, but he found it impossible to pull his attention from the smiling woman talking to them. He'd teased her about picturing her naked, but the truth was he couldn't get the vision of her out of his mind at all: clothed or unclothed, smiling and happy or ready to kick someone's ass.

Damn it.

Time to get his mind on the whole reason he was here—to find out what the kids were learning and how the school helped them. Charlotte patted a few of the children and turned her attention to him.

"Is this where we're going to eat?" he asked. The room was filled with folding tables that had seats attached, and some of the children were already sitting down.

"What, are you hungry? And you were making fun of me wanting lunch."

He grinned at her teasing expression. Man, she was something. A fascinating mix of energy, passion and determination all mixed in with a sweet, soft femininity. "I haven't eaten since five a.m. But I still wouldn't knock someone over in a hallway in search of a meal."

"As if I could knock you over, anyway." She took the binder from him and gestured to the tables. "Find a seat. I'll be right back."

Standing here, looking at all the bright-eyed and happy kids, he was annoyed with himself. Why hadn't it hadn't ever occurred to him to donate some of his fortune to this kind of school? He'd focused on giving most of his anonymous donations to the kind of hospitals he worked in. To those that medically served the neediest of humans in the world.

But that was going to change to include helping with education—a whole other kind of poverty. Not having access to learning was every bit as bad as having no access to health care.

"Here's my picture, Mr. Trent!" Patience ran up with a

piece of construction paper crayoned with smiling children sitting at desks, one of them a lot bigger than the others.

"Who's this student?" he asked, pointing at the large figure he suspected just might be a self-portrait of the artist.

"That's me." Patience gave him a huge smile. "I sit in class sometimes now. Miss Jones said I could."

"I bet you're really smart. You'll be reading and writing in no time." And to make that happen for a lot more kids, he'd be calling his financial manager pronto.

"Yes." She nodded vigorously. "I go to read right now."

She took off again and he chuckled at how cute she was, with her little dress and pigtails flying as she ran. He sat at one of the tables and saw the kids eyeing him, some shyly, others curious, a few bold enough to come close. Time for the tried and tested icebreaker. He pulled a pack of cards from his pocket and began to shuffle. "Anybody want to see a card trick?"

Faces lit, giggles began and a few children headed over, then more shoved their way in, until the table was full and the rest stood three-deep behind them.

"Okay." He fanned the cards face down and held them out to a grinning little girl with braids all over her head. "Pick a card. Any card." When she began to pull one out, he yanked the deck away. "Not that one!"

Startled, her grin faded and she stared at him.

"Just kidding." He gave her a teasing smile to let her know it was all in fun, and she giggled in relief as the other children hooted and laughed. He held out the fanned deck again. "Pick a card. I won't pull it away again, honest. Look at it, show it to a friend, but don't let me see it. Then stick it back in the deck."

The girl dutifully followed his directions. He did his sleight-of-hand shuffling before holding up a card. "Is this it?" He had to grin at how crestfallen they looked as they shook their heads. "Hmm. This it?"

"No, that's not it." She looked worried, like it would somehow be her fault if the trick didn't work.

"Well, you know third time's a charm, right? *This* is the one you picked." He held up what he knew would be the card she'd chosen, and everyone shrieked and whooped like he'd pulled a rabbit from a hat or held up a pot of gold.

"How you do that, mister?" a boy asked, craning his neck at the card deck as though the answer was written there.

"Magic." One of the best parts about doing the trick was showing the kids how to do it themselves. "How about we do it a few more times? Then I'll teach you exactly how it's done."

Before Charlie and the teachers even got back to the common room, the sound of loud talking and laughter swept through the school's hall. Mariam, the headmistress, pursed her lips and frowned. "I'm sorry, Miss Charlotte. I don't know why they're being so rowdy. I'll take care of it."

"It's fine. They're at lunch, after all." Though she was pretty sure it hadn't been served yet. Curious as to what was causing all the excitement, she walked into the room, only to stop in utter surprise at the scene.

Looking ridiculously large for it, Trent sat at a table completely surrounded by excited children, like some handsome Pied Piper. He was holding up cards, shuffling and flicking them, then handing them to kids who did the same, all the while talking and grinning. As she came farther into the room, she could hear the students bombarding him with questions that he patiently answered more than once.

She hadn't seen this side of Trent before. Yes, she'd seen his gentle bedside manner with Lionel, his obvious caring for the boy. Still, she couldn't help but be amazed at the connection she was witnessing. So many of the children in this school had been traumatized in one way or another and a number of them were orphaned. Yet, to watch this moment, you'd think none of them had a care in the world other than having a fun time with whatever Trent was sharing with them.

She moved closer to the table. "What's going on here?"

One of the older boys waved some cards. "Mr. Trent is showing us card tricks, Miss Edwards! See me do one!"

"I'd love to." Her eyes met Trent's and her heart fluttered a little at the grin and wink he gave her. "But you should call him Dr Trent. He's a physician working at the hospital for a few days."

"Dr Trent?" Anna, a girl in the highest grade they could currently offer, looked from Charlie to Trent, her expression instantly serious. "You a doctor? My baby brother is very sick with the malaria. Mama Grand has been treating him, but we're worried. Would you care if I go get him and bring him here for you to see?

"Can your mommy or grandmother bring him to the hospital?" Charlie asked.

Anna shook her head. "Mommy is away working in the rice fields. But I can get him and carry him there if that is better."

"How old is he?" Charlie asked.

"Six years old, Ma."

Charlie knew many of these kids walked miles to get to school, and didn't want Anna hauling an ill six-year-old that kind of distance. Not to mention that she could hear rain now drumming hard on the roof of the school. "How about if I drive and get him? You can show me where you live."

Trent stood. "It's pouring outside. I'll go back and get

the car and pick you two up, then we'll just see him at your home."

Charlie pulled her keys from her pocket and headed for the door. "It's okay, I'll just…"

In two strides, Trent intercepted her and snagged the keys from her hand. "Will you just let someone else help once in a while? Please? I'll be right back."

Charlie watched as he ducked out of the doorway into the heavy rain, all too aware of the silly surge of pleasure she felt at the way he insisted on taking on this problem, never mind that she could handle it herself. Well, not the medical part; she was thankful he'd be able to contribute his expertise as well as the nurses and techs at the hospital.

Her car pulled up in no time and, before she and Anna could come out, Trent had jogged to the door with an open umbrella and ushered Anna into the backseat. Water slid down his temples and dripped from his black hair as he opened the passenger door for Charlie. "You're riding shotgun this time, boss lady."

"It's my car. I know how to drive in this kind of weather."

He made an impatient sound. "Please just get in and stop arguing."

She opened her mouth to insist, but saw his set jaw and his intent blue eyes and found herself sliding into the seat, though why she let him tell her what to do she wasn't sure. It must have something to do with the man's overwhelming mojo.

She wasn't surprised that he proved more than competent at the wheel, despite the deepening mud and low visibility through the torrential rain. Even in good weather, this thinning road was barely more than a track through the bush. It couldn't really be called a road at all at the moment.

A group of crooked, heartbreakingly dilapidated zinc shacks appeared through the misty sheets of rain, and the distinctive smell of coal fires used for cooking touched Charlie's nose.

"It's up here. That one," Anna said, pointing.

The car slid to a stop. "Sit tight for a sec," Trent said. He again grabbed the umbrella and brought it to their side of the car before opening Charlie's door.

"I'm not made of sugar, you know. I won't melt," Charlie said, repeating what he'd said to her earlier as she climbed out to stand next to him.

"You sure about that? I remember you tasting pretty sweet." Beneath the umbrella, he was so close she could feel his warmth radiating against her skin. The smell of the rain, mud, coal fires and Trent's own distinctive and appealing scent swirled around her in a sensory overload. His head dipped and those blue eyes of his met hers and held. She realized she was holding her breath, struck by a feeling of the two of them being completely alone in the world as the rain pounded a timpani concerto on the fabric above their heads.

Her heart did a little dance as his warm breath touched her face. Blue eyes darker now, his head dipped closer still until his lips slipped across hers, whisper-soft, clinging for a moment. "Yeah. Like sugar and honey."

His lids lowered in a slow blink before he straightened, turning to open Anna's door.

The child led the way as they trudged up to a group of metal shacks, giving Charlie's heart rate a chance to slow. Why had he kissed her when they'd agreed not to go there? Probably for the same reason she'd wanted him to—that overwhelming chemistry between them that had caught fire the first day they'd met.

They approached a shack that looked as though it must be Anna's home. A cooking pot sat over a coal fire with what smelled like cassava simmering inside. The shack's crooked door was partially open, and Anna shoved it hard, scraping it along the muddy ground until they could step inside the dark interior.

A young child lay sleeping on a mat on the dirt floor and another was covered with a blanket, exposing only his or her outline. An older woman with a brightly patterned scarf on her head sat on a plastic chair, stitching some fabric.

"Mama Grand, I bring a doctor to see Prince."

The woman looked at them suspiciously. "No need, Anna. I use more healing herbs today and Prince will be fine soon."

Anna twisted her fingers and looked imploringly at her. "Please. The doctor is here, so let him see if Prince is getting better."

Trent stepped forward and gave one of his irresistibly charming smiles to the woman. "I'm sure you're doing a fine job taking care of Prince. But the boss lady, Miss Edwards here, will be mad at me if I don't have work to do today. She might not even pay me. Can I please just take a look at your fine little one while I'm here?"

The woman's stern expression softened slightly, and after a moment she inclined her head. Charlie had a hard time suppressing a smile. Trust Trent to turn it around to make Charlie look like the bad guy, and to know exactly how to twist it so his being there was no reflection on the older woman's treatments.

Trent crouched down and looked back at the woman. "Is this Prince hiding under the blanket? May I look at him?"

She nodded again, and Trent reached to pull the blanket from the small, huddled shape. He quickly jerked back when he saw the exposed child.

"What the…?" Trent's face swung towards Charlie, his eyebrows practically reaching his hair.

CHAPTER FIVE

THE LITTLE BOY looked like a ghost. Literally. He'd been covered head to toe in white paint. In all Trent's years of seeing crazy and unusual things around the world, he'd never seen this.

Charlotte covered a small smile with her fingertips, and he could tell she wanted to laugh at whatever the hell his expression was. Could he help it if it startled him to see the little guy looking like that?

"It's a common home remedy here for malaria. The sick person is painted white as part of the cure."

"Ah." Trent schooled his features into normal professionalism and turned back to the boy. He touched his knuckles to the sleeping child's cheeks, then pressed the child's throat, both of which were hot and sweaty. The boy barely opened his eyes to stare at him before becoming wracked by a prolonged, dry cough. When the cough finally died down, Trent leaned close to him with a smile he hoped would reassure him. "Hi, Prince. I'm Dr Dalton. How do you feel? Anything hurting?"

Prince didn't answer, just slid his gaze towards his sister. She knelt down next to him and touched her hand to the boy's thin shoulder. "It's okay, Prince. Dr Dalton is here to help you get better."

"Have you had belly pain or diarrhea?" The boy still just stared at him, looking scared, as though Trent was the

one who looked like a ghost. Maybe the child was deliri-
ous. "Anna, do you know about any belly pain? Has he
been confused or acting strange?"

She nodded. "He did complain about his tummy hurting. And he has been saying silly things. I think he seems
the same as when I had the malaria—shaking and feeling
very hot and cold."

"Trent, how about I drive back to the compound and
get the malaria medicine?" Even through the low light, he
could see the green of Charlotte's eyes focused intently on
his. "I'll bring it back here; maybe we won't have to scare
him by taking him to the hospital."

He shook his head, not at all sure this was malaria. "If
he has belly pain, it might be typhoid, which requires a
different kind of antibiotic. Hard to tell with a child who's
sick and obtunded like he is. The only way to know for
sure is if we take him back to the hospital and get a blood
test—see if it shows the parasites or not."

"No hospital." The older woman's lips thinned. "If de
boy go, he will never come back."

Obviously, the poor woman had lost someone she loved.
"I'll watch over him myself," Trent said. "I promise to
keep him safe."

"Mama Grand, no boys are kidnapped any more. For
true. The war is over a long time now."

Damn, so that was what she was worried about. He
could barely fathom that boys this young had been kidnapped to be soldiers, but knew it had happened so often
that some parents sent their children out of the country to
be safe, never to see them again.

He stood and reached for the woman's rough and
gnarled hand. "I understand your worries. But it's important that Prince have a test done that we can only do at the
hospital. I promise you that I will care for Prince and look

after him like I would if he were my own child, and return him to you when he's well. Will you trust me to do that?"

The suspicious look didn't completely leave the woman's face, but she finally nodded. Trent didn't want to give her a chance to change her mind and quickly gathered Prince in his arms, wrapping the blanket around him as best he could.

"You want to come with us, Anna? You don't have to, but it might make Prince feel more comfortable," Charlotte said.

"Yes. I will come."

"Are you going to hold Prince so I can drive, or do you want to take the wheel?" he asked Charlotte as they approached the car.

"You know the answer to that." Her gorgeous eyes glinted at him. "You're in the passenger seat, Dr. Dalton."

He had to grin. "You really should address this little controlling streak of yours, Ms. Edwards. Find out why relinquishing power scares you so much."

"It doesn't scare me. I just trust my own driving over anyone else's."

"Mm-hm. One of these days, trying to control the direction the world spins is going to weigh heavy on those pretty shoulders of yours. Drive on, boss lady."

Tests proved that Prince did indeed have typhoid, and after a couple days he'd recovered enough to return home. Charlie was glad that Trent's expertise had led him to insist the child be tested, instead of just assuming it was malaria, as she had.

She was also glad that, in the days that had passed since Trent had come back, she'd managed to stop thinking about him for hours at a time. Well, maybe not *hours*. Occasionally, the man sneaked into her thoughts. Not her fault, since she wasn't deaf and blind—okay, a little hard of hearing in that one ear of hers she was grateful to have it at all.

His voice, teasing and joking with the nurses and techs, sometimes drifted down the hall to her office. His distinctively tall form would occasionally stride in front of her office on his way from the clinic to the hospital ward until she decided just to shut the darn door.

She'd made a conscious effort to stay away from the hospital ward where she might run into him. She got dinner alone at home, or ate lunch at her desk so she wouldn't end up sitting with him in the kitchen. She spent time at the school instead of here, where thoughts of him kept invading her brain, knowing he was somewhere nearby.

It helped that Trent had kept their few interactions since the brief kiss in the rain short and professional. When the man said goodbye, he sure meant it, never mind that she felt the same way. Thank heavens he'd be leaving again in the next few days so she wouldn't have to suffer the embarrassment of thinking about all they'd done in their single night together.

Her door opened and her heart gave an irritating little kick of anticipation that it just might be his blue eyes she'd see when she looked up.

But it was John Adams standing there. "Any word yet on the funding for another teacher?"

She smiled and waved a paper. "Got the green light. I'm sending the final forms today, and they said we should get a check in about a month. Is the woman you've been training going to work out?"

"Yes, most definitely." He dramatically slapped a hand to his barrel chest. "She is smart and beautiful and I am in love with her. Thanks to God I can officially offer her a job."

"You're starting to remind me of ladies' man Dr Dalton. No mixing business with pleasure." A flush filled her cheeks as soon as the words were out of her mouth, since she'd done exactly that, and the pleasure had been all too spectacular.

"Yes, ma'am." He grinned. "Anyway, I also stopped to tell you to come look at our little patient this morning."

"What little patient?"

"Lionel. The one with appendicitis and the hemangioma—or who used to have a hemangioma. You won't believe what Trent's done with it."

Alarm made Charlie's heart jerk in her chest. She'd worried from the moment she'd agreed to let Trent take care of such a delicate procedure. Had he messed it up? She'd checked on the child a couple of times, but a patch had still covered his eye. "What do you mean? Is it going to have to be redone when we get a plastic surgeon in here?"

"Just come and see."

She rose and followed him to the hospital ward, her fears eased a bit by John Adams's relaxed and smiling expression. Still, she couldn't shake the feeling that she might have made a big mistake.

Lionel's head was turned towards his mother, who sat by his bedside, and Charlie found herself holding her breath as they came to stand beside him.

"Show Miss Charlotte how well you're seeing today, Lionel," John Adams said.

The boy turned his head and she stared in disbelief.

The patch had been removed and, considering he'd had surgery only days before, he looked shockingly, amazingly normal.

The angry red bulge that had been the vascular tumor was gone. His eyebrow and eyelid, other than still being bruised and slightly swollen from surgery, looked like any other child's. His big, brown eye, wide and lit with joy, was now completely visible, just like his other one.

"Oh, my. Lionel, you look wonderful!" She pressed her hands to her chest. "Can you see out of that eye?"

"I can see! Yes, I can! And Mommy show me in the mirror how handsome I look!"

"You even more handsome than your brothers now, boyo, and I told them so," his mother said with a wide smile.

Tears stung Charlie's eyes as she lifted her gaze to the child's mother and saw so many emotions on the woman's face: happiness; profound relief; deep gratitude.

All because of Trent.

Where was the man? Had he seen the amazing result of his work? She turned to a smiling John Adams. "Has Dr Dalton seen him since the patch was removed?"

"Oh, yes. He took it off himself this morning."

"Dr. Dalton told me he gave me special powers, too, like Superman." The child's face radiated excitement. "Said I have x-ray vision now."

His mother laughed. "Yes, but Dr. Dalton was just joking and you know it. Don't be going and telling everyone that, or they'll expect you to see through walls."

"I can see so good, I bet I can see through walls. I bet I can."

"Maybe you'll become a doctor, Superman, who can see people's bones before you operate." Trent's voice vibrated into the room from behind Charlie's back. "That would be pretty cool."

"I want to be a doctor like you. I want to fix people like you do, Dr. Trent."

Trent's smile deepened as he came to stand next to Charlie. "That's a good goal, Lionel. If you study hard in school, I bet you can do anything you set your mind to."

Charlie stared at Trent, looking so relaxed, like all this was no big deal. Maybe it wasn't to him, but it was to her, and to Lionel and to his mother. A very, very big deal.

"I can't believe the wonderful job you did," she said, resting her hand on his forearm. "You told me I didn't know who I was dealing with and you were sure right."

"Now she learns this, just before I'm ready to leave."

The twinkle in his eyes, and his beautifully shaped lips curved into that smile, were practically irresistible. She again was thankful that he would be heading out of her life very soon before she made a complete fool of herself. "Good thing you don't have x-ray vision too. Hate to think what you'd use it for."

"Checking for broken bones, of course." His smile widened. "What else?"

She wasn't going where her mind immediately went. "Probably to decipher a bank-vault combination, so you could go on vacation without working a solid year. Speaking of which, the GPC says a general surgeon should be here in a matter of days, so you can have them schedule your flight out of here soon."

"Great."

The relief on his face was obvious and she hated that it hurt a tiny bit to see it. "I can't help but wonder, though, why are you working as a general surgeon when you can do things like this?"

His smile faded. "You think plastic surgery has more value? More than saving someone's life? I don't."

"It's a different kind of value: changing lives; changing the way someone is viewed, the way they view themselves. You have an obvious gift for this, a skill many would envy." Did he not see how important all that was? "Your focus should be on plastic surgery. On helping people that way."

"The way other people view a person, what they expect them to be and who they expect them to be, shouldn't have anything to do with how they view themselves." He took a step back and pulled his arm away from her touch. She hadn't known those eyes of his were capable of becoming the chilly blue that stared back at her. "Excuse me, I have a few other patients to check on."

She frowned as she watched him walk through the hospital ward. What had she said to make him mad?

"I have things to do too," John Adams said. But, like her, his gaze followed Trent, his expression thoughtful. "Bye, Lionel. See you later, Charlie."

"Okay. Listen, can you come have dinner tonight at my house? I'd like to talk to you about some things."

He nodded and headed off. Charlie watched Trent examining another patient and could only hope John Adams came up with a good idea for how she could accomplish her newest goal—which was to encourage Trent to perform surgery on a few patients in the day or two he'd still be here, patients who'd needed reconstructive surgery long before the plastic surgery wing had even been conceived.

She knew how desperately some of these people needed to have their lives changed in that way. Not to mention that it wouldn't hurt for her to have a few "before and after" photos that would impress the Gilchrist Foundation with what they were already accomplishing. And, really, how could Trent object?

As she headed back to her office, her cell phone rang and she pulled it from her pocket. "Charlotte Edwards."

"Hey, Charlie! It's Colleen. How're things going with Trent Dalton?"

"With Trent?" What the heck? Did the gossip vine go all the way to GPC headquarters? Besides, nobody here knew she and Trent had briefly hooked up…did they? "What do you mean?"

"Is it working out that he came back until the new temp gets there?"

Phew. Thank heavens she really didn't have to answer the first question, though their moment together was history anyway. "He's doing a good job, but I know he wants to move on. Do you have a final arrival date for the new doc?"

"Perry Cantwell has agreed to come and we're finalizing his travel plans. Should be any day now." Her voice got lower, conspiratorial. "Just tell me. I've seen photos of Trent that make me salivate, but is he really as hunky as everyone says? Whenever I talk to him on the phone his voice makes me feel all tingly."

If just his voice made Colleen feel tingly, Charlie hated to think what would happen if she saw him in person. She wasn't about to confess to Colleen that, despite his reputation, she'd fallen into bed with him for one more than memorable night. While she felt embarrassed about that now, she still couldn't regret it, despite unexpectedly having to work with him again. "He's all right. If you like tall, good-looking surgeons who flirt with every woman in sight and think everything's amusing."

"Mmm. Sounds good to me if the surgeon in question has beautiful black hair and gorgeous eyes." The sound of a long sigh came through the phone and Charlie shook her head. She supposed she should feel smug that über-attractive Trent had wanted to spend a night with her. But, since he likely had a woman in every port, that didn't necessarily say much about her personal sex appeal. "I actually have his new release papers on my desk to send out today. Are you going to hit on him before he leaves?" Colleen asked. "Might be a fun diversion for a couple days."

Been there, done that. And, yes, it had been—very fun. Keeping it strictly professional now, though, was the agreed goal. "I've got tons to do with the new wing opening any time now. And my dad called to say he's coming some time soon to see how things are going with that."

"Actually, I have some bad news about the new wing,

I'm afraid." Colleen's voice went from light to serious in an instant.

Her heart jerked. "What bad news?"

"You know David Devor, the plastic surgeon we had lined up to work there?" Colleen asked. "He has a family emergency and can't come until it's resolved, which could be quite a while."

"Are you kidding me? You know I have to have someone here next week, Colleen! The Gilchrist Foundation made it clear we won't get the funding we need until I have at least one plastic surgeon on site."

"I know. I'm doing the best I can. But I'm having a hard time finding a plastic surgeon who wants to work in the field. I'm turning over every rock I can, but I can't promise anybody will be there until Dr. Devor is available. Sorry."

Lord, this was a disaster! Charlie swiped her hand across her forehead. The hospital was scarily deep in the red from getting the new wing built. It had to be opened pronto.

"Okay." She sucked in a calming breath. "But I have to have a plastic surgeon, like *now*."

"I know, but I just told you—"

"Listen. I need you to hold off a day or two before you send Trent's release papers. Give me time to talk to him about maybe staying on here. If he agrees, you can send Perry Cantwell somewhere else."

There was a long silence on the phone before Colleen spoke. "Why? Cantwell's expecting to come soon. And I can't just hold Trent's paperwork. He's already filled in for you twice and is way overdue for his vacation. I don't get it."

"I found out Trent's a plastic surgeon, not just a general surgeon." She gulped and forged on. "If Devor can't be here, I have to keep Trent here at least long enough to get the wing open and the funding in my hand. Otherwise

I won't be able to pay the bank, and who knows what'll happen?"

"Maybe he'll agree to stay."

"Maybe. Hopefully." But she doubted he would. Hadn't he made it more than clear that he wanted to head out ASAP? The only reason he'd come back for a few days was because of how sick Lionel had been. "All I'm asking is for you to hang onto his release papers until I can talk to him."

"Charlie." Colleen's voice was strained. "You're one of my best friends. Heck, you got me this job! But you're asking me to do something unethical here."

"Of course I don't want you to do anything you feel is unethical." This was her problem, not Colleen's, and it wouldn't be right to put her friend in the middle of it. "Just send them out tomorrow instead of today, address them to me and I'll make sure he gets them. That will give me time to contact the Gilchrist Foundation and see if they'll make an exception on their requirements before the donation check is sent. If they won't, I'll try to get their representative to come right now while Trent's still here. I'm pretty sure the guy is close—somewhere in West Africa. I'll go from there."

Colleen's resigned sigh was very different from the one when she'd been swooning over Trent earlier. "All right. I'll wait until tomorrow to send the release papers and finalize Perry's travel plans to give you time to talk to Trent. But that's it."

"Thanks, Colleen. You're the best." Charlie tried to feel relieved but the enormity of the problem twisted her gut. "Hopefully they'll send the funding check even if we don't have a plastic surgeon here yet and we'll be out of the woods. I'll keep you posted."

The second she hung up, she searched for the Gilchrist Foundation's number. What would she do if they flat out said the conditions of the contract had to be met, which would probably be their response? Or if they couldn't send their representative here immediately? If the GPC couldn't find a plastic surgeon to come in any reasonable period of time, the whole hospital could fold. Every dollar of the GPC's funding, and all the other donations she'd managed to round up, had been spent renovating the nearly destroyed building, buying expensive equipment and hiring all the nurses, techs and other employees needed to run the place. And the money she'd borrowed to build the new wing was already racking up interest charges.

Adrenaline rushed through her veins as she straightened in her seat. The end justified the means. The hospital absolutely could not close and the plastic surgery wing had to open. It had to be there to help all the people who had horrible, disfiguring injuries left from the war. It had to help all the kids living with congenital deformities, like cleft palates, which they'd never have had to live with if they'd been born somewhere else. Somewhere with the kind of healthcare access she was determined to offer.

If the Gilchrist Foundation insisted on sticking with the contract stipulations, she had no choice but somehow to make sure Trent stayed on until the money was in her hand.

CHAPTER SIX

TRENT HAD BEEN relieved that Charlotte wasn't in the hospital commons for dinner. He hadn't wanted to make small talk with her while pretending he didn't feel insulted by her words.

The book he tried to read didn't hold his attention, and he paced in the sparse little bedroom until he couldn't take the confinement anymore. He headed into the humid, oppressive air and strode down the edges of the road, avoiding the muddy ruts as best he could.

When he'd first met Charlotte, he'd been impressed with her enthusiastic commitment to this place, to her vision of what she wanted it to become. And, as they'd spent time together, she'd seemed interested in his life. She'd asked smart and genuine questions, and he'd found himself opening up, just a little—sharing a few stories he usually kept to himself, nearly talking to her about things he just plain didn't talk about.

But, when it came right down to it, she was like anyone else: a woman who questioned who he was and why he did what he did. Who didn't particularly care what he wanted from his own life. Had she asked him *why* he didn't do plastic surgery exclusively? Expressed any interest in his reasons?

No. She'd just made the same snap judgment others had made. She'd told him what he should do, convinced she knew. Exactly like the woman in his life he'd trusted completely to have his back, to know him, to care.

A trust he'd never give again.

It was disappointing as hell. Then again, maybe this was a good thing. Maybe it would help him feel less drawn to her.

He needed to see this as a positive, not a negative. And, when he left in just a day or two, maybe the peculiar closeness he felt to her would be gone. He'd leave and hope to hell his world would be back to normal.

He kept walking, not having any particular destination in mind, just feeling like he didn't want to go back to that room and smother, but not wanting to chit-chat with people in the hospital either. Maybe he should call up a buddy on the phone, one of the fraternity of mission doctors who understood his life and why he did what he did. They always made him laugh and put any personal troubles in perspective.

As he pulled his cell from his pocket, he noticed a light up ahead. Had he somehow got turned around? He peered through the darkness and realized he was practically at Charlotte's doorstep. Had his damned stupid feet unconsciously brought him here because he'd been thinking of her so intently?

About to turn off on a different path, he was surprised to see little Patience bound out the door, holding a rope with a tiny puppy attached, bringing it down the porch steps. It sniffed around before doing its business, and Trent wanted to laugh at the look of distaste on the little girl's face as she picked up a trowel from the steps.

He didn't want to scare her by appearing out of nowhere in the darkness. "You have a new dog, Patience? When did you get it?"

She looked up at him and smiled. "Hi, Mr. Trent! Yes, Daddy got me another doggie. After my poor Rex was killed by that ugly, wild dog, I been asking and asking. He finally said yes, and my friends at the school like having her to play with too."

"What's its name?"

"Lucky—cos I'm lucky to have her. Except for this part." The look of distaste returned, replacing the excitement as she gripped the trowel. "I promised Daddy I would do everything to take care of her."

He scratched the cute little pup behind the ears, chuckling at the way its entire hind end wagged in happiness before he reached for the trowel. A little doggie doo-doo was nothing compared to many of the things he'd dealt with. "Here. I'll do it for you this time." With a grateful smile, Patience let him dig a hole to bury the stuff. "What are you and your new pup doing here at Charlotte's house?"

"Miss Charlie fixed dinner for me and Daddy. They talking about work."

The door opened and the shadow of John Adams's big body came onto the porch. "Somebody out here with you, Patience?"

"Mr. Trent, Daddy. He's meeting Lucky."

"Trent. Come on inside. Charlie and I were just talking about you."

Damn. He didn't want to know what they were talking about and didn't particularly want to see Charlotte. But his feet headed up the steps, with Patience and the puppy trailing behind.

The warm glow of the quaint room, full of an odd mix of furniture styles and colorful rugs, embraced him as he stepped inside and he wondered what it was about this old house that gave it so much charm and appeal. An old upright piano against a wall had open sheet music leaning against the stand. Charlotte, dressed in sweatpants and a T-shirt, was curled on a sofa, and she looked up, her lips slightly parted.

The surprise in her green eyes gave way to a peculiar mix of wariness and warmth. As their gazes collided, as he took in the whole of her silken hair and lovely face, he was instantly taken back to earlier today. To their physical closeness beneath that umbrella. To the moment it had felt like it was just the two of them, alone and intimate. Despite all his promises to himself and to her, he'd found himself for that brief second leaning in to taste her mouth, to enjoy the sweetness of her lips.

Being in her house again sent his thoughts to the moment they'd sat on that sofa and kissed until both of them were breathless, ending up making love on the floor. Why did this woman make him feel this way every time he looked at her?

"Trent. I'm…surprised to see you."

Could she be thinking about their time together here too? "I was taking a walk. Then saw Patience and her new pup."

Patience ran to the piano and tapped on the keys, bobbing back and forth as the dog pranced around yapping. "Lucky likes to sing and dance, Mr. Trent, see?"

"She has a beautiful voice." As he smiled at the child, he was struck by a longing to go to the piano himself. To finger the keys as he'd done from the time he was six, until he'd left the U.S. for good. He hadn't realized until he'd first walked into this room with Charlotte a few days ago how much he'd missed playing.

"Miss Charlie has a very pretty voice," Patience enthused. "Please play for us, Miss Charlie. Play and sing something!"

Charlotte shook her head. "Not tonight. I'm sure Mr. Trent doesn't want a concert."

Her cheeks were filled with color. Surely the ultra-confident Charlotte Edwards wasn't feeling shy about performing for him? "Of course I'd like to hear you. What's your favorite thing she plays, Patience?" Surprised at how much he wanted to hear Charlotte sing, he settled himself into a chair, figuring there was no way she could say no to the cute kid.

"That song from church I like: *How Great Thou Art*. Please, Miss Charlie?" The child's hands were clasped together and for once she stood still, her eyes bright and excited.

As Trent had predicted, Charlotte gave a resigned sigh. "All right. But just the one song."

She moved to the piano, and his gaze slid from her thick hair to the curve of her rear, sexy even in sweatpants. Her fingers touched the keyboard, the beginning measures a short prelude to the simple arrangement before she began to sing. Trent forgot about listening to the resonance of the piano's sounding board and heard only the sweet, clear tones of Charlotte's voice, so moving and lovely his chest ached with the pleasure of it.

When the last piano note faded and the room became quiet, he was filled with a powerful desire for the moment to continue. To never end. Without thought, he found himself getting up from the chair to sit next to Charlotte, his hip nudging hers to scoot over on the bench.

"Let's sing a Beatles tune Patience might like," he said, his hands poised over the keys, his eyes fixed on the beautiful green of hers. He began to play *Lean On Me* and, when she didn't sing along, bumped his shoulder into hers. "Come on. I know you know it."

"Yes, Miss Charlie! Please sing!" Patience said, pressing her little body against Charlotte's leg.

John Adams began to sing in a slightly off-key baritone before Charlotte's voice joined in, the dulcet sound so pure it took Trent's breath away. When his hands dropped from the keyboard, he looked down into Charlotte's face, seeing Patience next to her, and he was struck with a bizarre and overwhelming vision of a life he hadn't even considered having: a special woman by his side, a family to love; the ultimate utopia.

"That was wonderful," she said, her eyes soft. "I didn't know you could play. Without music, even."

He drew in a breath to banish his disturbing thoughts. "I was shoved onto a piano bench from the time I was little, and had a very intimidating teacher who made sure I was classically trained." He grinned. "I complained like heck sometimes when I had to practice instead of throwing a football around with my friends, but I do enjoy it." He hadn't realized how much until just now, shoulder to shoulder with her, sharing this intimate moment.

"Play something classical. Simple modern songs are about it for my repertoire."

He thought about what he'd still have memorized from long ago and realized it shouldn't be Bach or Haydn. That it should be something romantic, for her. "All right, but don't be surprised if I'm a little rusty. I bet you know this one: Debussy's *Clair de Lune*."

When the last notes of the piece died away, the softness on her face only inches from his had him nearly leaning in for a kiss, forgetting everything but how much he wanted to, and the only thing that stopped him was Patience's little face staring up at him from next to the keyboard.

"I liked that, Mr. Trent!"

"Yes." Charlotte's voice was a near-whisper as she rested her palm on his arm. "That was…beautiful."

As he looked at the little girl, and stared into Charlotte's eyes filled with a deep admiration, the whole scene suddenly morphed from intimate and perfect to scary as hell. Why was he sitting here having fantasies about, almost a longing for, a life he absolutely did not want?

Abruptly, he stood. He needed to get out of there before he said or did something stupid.

Hadn't he, just earlier this evening, been annoyed and disappointed in her? Then one more hour with her and, bam, he was back to square one with all those uncomfortable and mixed feelings churning around inside. What the hell was wrong with him, he didn't want to try to figure out.

"You know, I need to head back to my quarters. I'm going to get most of my things packed up. I'm sure the GPC let you know the new temp is coming in just a day or two?"

"We need to talk about that." The softness that had been in her eyes was replaced by a cool and professional expression. He was damned if it didn't irritate him when he should be glad. "We have an issue."

"What issue?"

She glanced at John Adams before returning her attention to Trent. "Come sit down and we'll talk."

"I'm happy standing, thanks." Her words sounded ominous and he folded his arms across his chest, the disconcerting serenity he'd been feeling just a moment ago fading away like a mirage in the desert. He had a feeling this conversation had something to do with him staying longer, and that wasn't happening.

"The new temp is delayed. I'm not sure when he's going to get here." She licked those tempting lips of hers and, while her expression was neutral, her eyes looked strained and worried. As they should have.

"I told you not to try to guilt me into staying. I can't be here indefinitely." Except, damn it, as he said the words the memory of the comfort he'd felt a moment ago, that sense of belonging, made it sound scarily appealing.

"I'm not trying to guilt you into anything. I'm simply telling you the facts. Which are that, if you leave, there won't be another surgeon here for a while."

"The GPC does a good job finding docs to fill in when there's a gap. Especially when a place has nobody. Besides, you have Thomas here, and he does a great job on the hernias and other simple procedures."

"But what if we get another appendicitis case? Ectopic pregnancy? Something serious he can't handle?"

He shoved his hands into his pockets and turned to pace across the room, staring out the window at the heavy blackness of the night sky. Looking anywhere but into her pleading eyes.

"If there's one thing I've learned over the years, it's that one person can't save everybody who needs help, Charlotte. I'd be dead if I tried to be that person. Think about the ramifications of this for others, too: the longer I'm here, the more the snowball effect of docs having to fill in where I'm supposed to be next, which is the Philippines." He turned to her, hoping to see she understood what he was saying—not that the idea of staying here longer was both appealing and terrifying. "If the GPC hospital in the Philippines doesn't have anyone because I'm not there, is that okay? Better for patients there to die, instead of patients here?"

Her hands were clasped together so tightly her knuckles were white. "Just a couple of weeks, Trent. Maybe less, if it works out."

He shook his head. "I'm sorry, Charlotte. As soon as my release paperwork comes through from the GPC, I have to head out."

"Trent, all I'm asking is…"

The room that had felt so warm and welcoming now felt claustrophobic. He turned his attention to John Adams so he wouldn't have to look at her wide and worried eyes. "I have a few patients scheduled for surgery early, so I'm going to get to bed. If either of you know of patients needing surgery, you should schedule them in the next couple days before I leave." He scratched the dog behind the ears before he walked out the door, finding it impossible to completely stuff down the conflicting emotions that whirled within him.

As he walked through the darkness, a possible solution struck him that would assuage his guilt. Maybe a phone call to an old friend would solve all his problems and let him move on.

CHAPTER SEVEN

"How the hell are you, Trent?"

Trent smiled to hear Chase Bowen's voice on the phone. He'd worked with Chase for a number of years in different parts of the world, and the man had been the steadiest, most committed mission doctor he'd ever met. Until a certain wonderful woman had swept into the man's life, their little one in tow, and had changed him into a committed dad rooted in the States.

"I'm good. Decided to try to get hold of you during my lunch break before I see some patients in the clinic this afternoon. How's Drew doing?" When he'd heard the shocking news that Chase and Dani's little boy had cancer, it had scared the crap out of him. Thank goodness they'd caught it in time and the prognosis was excellent.

"He's doing great." The warmth and pride in Chase's voice came through loud and clear. "Completely healthy now, swimming like a fish and growing like crazy. So where are you working?"

"I'm filling in as a temp here in Liberia, hoping to head off on vacation soon, but there are some issues getting a new doc here." A problem he knew Chase was more than familiar with.

"So who's the lucky woman vacationing with you this time? Where are you going?"

"Still figuring all that out." No reason to tell Chase

about his weird feelings, that he hadn't been able to find an interest in calling anyone. The man would laugh his butt off, then suggest he see a shrink. "How's Dani?"

"Wonderful. I haven't told you that Drew's going to have a baby brother or sister."

"That's great news. Congratulations." Of all the people he knew, Chase was the last one he'd ever have expected mostly to leave mission work to have a family. But he had to admit, the man seemed happy as hell. "You doing any mission stints at all?"

"Dani and I have gone twice to Honduras together, then I stayed for another week after she headed home. It's worked out well."

"You have any interest in coming to Liberia for just a week or so to fill in for me until the new doc gets here? The GPC needs me to head to the Philippines as soon as possible." Which wasn't exactly true, but he was going with it anyway, damn it.

"I don't know." Chase was silent on the line for a moment. "I'd really like to, but I'm not sure now's a good time. Dani's been a little under the weather, and I wouldn't want to leave her alone with Drew if she's not up to it. Let me talk to her and I'll call you back."

"Great. Give her a hug for me, and tell her I'm happy for both of you. And Drew too."

"Will do. Talk to you soon."

Trent shoved the phone in his pocket and headed back into the hospital. He'd known it was a long shot to think Chase might be able to fill in for him, but with any luck maybe it could still be a win-win. Chase could enjoy a short stint in Africa and Trent could shake the clinging dust of this place off his feet and forget all about Charlotte and her work ethic, spunkiness and warmth.

He thought about Dani, Chase and Drew and their little family that was about to grow. A peculiar sensation filled his chest and he took a moment to wonder what exactly it was. Then he realized with a shock that it was envy.

Envy? Impossible. He'd never wanted that kind of life: a wife who would have expectations of who you should be and how you should live. Kids you were responsible for. A life rooted in one place.

But there was no mistaking that emotion for anything else, and he didn't understand where the hell it had come from. Though Chase had never wanted that kind of life either—until he'd met a woman who had changed how he viewed himself.

The thought set an alarm clanging in his brain. He didn't want to change how he viewed himself. He'd worked hard to be happy with who he was and what he wanted from his life, leaving behind those who hadn't agreed with that view. Now wasn't the time to second-guess all that.

Resolutely shaking off all those disturbing feelings, he continued down the hospital corridor, hoping Charlotte's office door was closed, as it often was, since he had to walk by to get to the clinic. Unfortunately, the door was wide open and her melodic voice drifted into the hallway as she talked with John Adams.

"I'll be fine. I know how to use a gun, remember?"

"I'm not okay with that, Charlie. Patience and I'll pack a bag and move in for a few days until we're sure it was a one-time thing."

A gun? What was a one-time thing? He stopped in the doorway and looked in to see John Adams standing with his arms folded across his chest, a deep frown creasing his brow, and Charlotte staring back with her mulish expression in place.

"Except somebody needs to be at the school too, you know. After all the work and money we've put into the place, we can't risk it being wrecked up and having things stolen."

"What are you talking about?" Trent asked.

"This is not your concern, Trent. John Adams, please close the door so we can talk."

Trent stretched his arm across the door to hold it open. "Uh-uh. You want me to be stuck here for a while longer, you need to include me. What's going on?"

"Somebody broke into her house early this morning after she came to work. When she went there at lunch to get something, she found the door jimmied open and some things gone."

Trent stared at John Adams then swung his gaze to Charlotte. She frowned at him, her lips pressed together, but couldn't hide the tinge of worry in the green depths of her eyes. "What the hell? What was stolen?"

"A radio. The folding chairs I keep in a closet. Weird stuff. Thankfully, I had my laptop with me at work. It's not a big deal."

"It is a big deal." The protectiveness for her that surged in his veins was sudden and intense. "You can't stay there alone, period. The obvious solution is for John Adams to stay in their quarters at the school, and for me to stay with you until I leave."

Had those words really come out of his mouth? It would be torture to stay in her house with her, knowing she was close by at night in her bed. Bringing back hot memories of their night together. Making him think of the unsettling closeness and connection he'd felt while they'd sat at the piano together singing.

But there was no other option. Keeping her safe was more important than protecting himself from the damned annoying feelings that kept resurfacing.

"That's ridiculous, Trent." Her eyes still looked alarmed, but he was pretty sure it wasn't just about the break-in. "I'll be fine. Whoever it was probably just hit the place once and isn't likely to come back."

"You have no idea if that's true or not." He stepped to her desk and pressed his palms on it, leaning across until his face was as close to hers as hers had been to his at the airport. She smelled so damned good, and the scent of her and the lip gloss she was wearing made him want to find out what flavor gloss it was. "So, you never did tell me," he said, mimicking what she'd said to him at the airport. "What makes you so damned stubborn and resistant to accepting help when you need it? Except when it comes to the hospital, that is?"

"I'm not stubborn. I just don't think this is worth getting all crazy about."

"Maybe not. But it's not a hardship for me to stay at your house so you're not alone until we see if this is a one-time thing or not." So, yeah, that wasn't true. It would be a hardship to be so close to her without taking advantage of it, but no way was he leaving her at risk.

"Good." John Adams spoke from behind him. "Thanks, Trent. I appreciate it. I'm going back to the school now. See you both later."

He straightened. "I've got patients to see in the clinic then I'll get my things. See you back here at six."

"Seriously, Trent—"

"Six."

As he headed to the clinic, he was aware of a ridiculous spring in his step, while at the same time his chest felt a little tight. Obviously, his attraction to Charlotte was keeping the smarter side of his brain from remembering why he needed to keep his distance. And how the hell he was going to keep that firmly in mind while sharing her roof was a question to which he had to find an answer.

"So, Colleen, I'm all set!" Charlie forced a cheerful and upbeat tone to her voice. "Trent has agreed to stay on until the Gilchrist rep does his evaluation. So you can wait to schedule Perry Cantwell until then."

"That's great news for you, Charlie! So all your worries were for nothing."

The warmth in her friend's voice twisted her stomach into a knot. Lying to her felt every bit as bad as lying to Trent, but what choice did she have? "Yes, no worries." Oh, if only that were true.

"I'll let Perry know so he can plan his schedule. After the Gilchrist rep comes, give me a call to tell me how it goes."

"Will do. Thanks, Colleen." Charlie hung up and dropped her head into her hands.

How had her life become a disaster?

As if it wasn't enough to have the bank breathing down her neck, the plastic surgeon indefinitely delayed, Gilchrist insisting on the original stipulations of their agreement and having to skulk around lying to Trent and Colleen, she had a burglar who might come back and a gorgeous man she couldn't stop thinking about spending the night in her bed.

No. Not in her bed. In her spare bedroom. But that was almost as bad. Knowing his long, lean, sexy body was just a few walls away would be tempting, to say the least. But now there was an even better reason to steer clear of getting it on with him again for the days he was here.

She was pretty sure that if he knew she was delaying Perry Cantwell's arrival and had shoved his release papers beneath a pile on her desk he wouldn't take it lightly. In fact, she was more than sure that his easygoing smile would disappear and a side she hadn't seen yet would emerge—a very angry side— and she wouldn't even be able to blame him for it.

Her throat tight, Charlie took inventory of the new supply delivery, trying not to look at the big invoice that came with it. This whole deception thing felt awful, even more than she'd expected. But she just couldn't see another so-lution. Thank heavens the Gilchrist Foundation had said their representative should be here within the week. After they gave their approval and she got the check, Trent could be on his way. No harm, no foul, right?

The end justifies the means, she reminded herself again.

With a box of syringes in her arms, she stepped on a stool, struggling to shove the box onto a supply shelf, when a tall body appeared next to her. Long-fingered hands took the box and tucked it in front of another.

"Why don't you just ask for help from someone who's not as vertically challenged as you are?" Trent asked, his eyes amused, grasping her hand as she stepped off the stool.

Looking at his handsome, smiling face so close to hers, a nasty squeeze of guilt made it a little hard to breathe. She didn't even want to think about how that affable ex-pression would change if he knew about her machinations.

"Just because I'm not tall doesn't mean I'm handi-capped. And I'm perfectly capable of getting off a stool by myself."

"I know. I only helped you to see those green eyes of yours flash in annoyance. Amuses me, for some reason."

"Everything amuses you." Except, probably, liars.

"Not true. Burglars don't amuse me. So are we eating here, or at your house to crack heads if anybody shows up?"

His low voice made her stomach feel squishy, even though he was talking about cracking heads. "Nobody's going to show up. And I still don't think you need to come. I have a gun, and I doubt you're very good at cracking heads anyway."

"Don't count on that." The curve of his lips flattened and his eyes looked a little hard. "Anybody tries breaking into your house, you'll find out exactly how good I am."

The thought of exactly how good she knew he was at a number of things left her a little breathless. "I just want to be clear about the ground rules—"

"Dr. Trent." Thomas appeared in the doorway and Charlie put a little distance between her and Trent, not wanting to give the gossip machine any more ammo than they might already have. "There's a boy in the clinic whose mother brought him in because he's not eating. I did a routine exam, but I don't see anything other than a slightly elevated temperature. He is acting a little odd, though, and his mother's sure something's wrong, so I thought you should come take a look."

"Not eating?" Trent's brows lowered. "That's not a very significant complaint. Did you look to see if he has strep or maybe tonsillitis?"

"His throat looks normal to me."

"Hmm. All right." He turned his baby blues to Charlie. "Don't be going home until I come back. I mean it."

"How about if I come along? I haven't had time to visit the clinic for a while." She might not be in medicine, but the way doctors and nurses figured out a diagnosis always fascinated her. And she had to admit she couldn't resist the chance to watch Trent in action again.

"Of course, Ma," Thomas said, turning to lead the way.

CHAPTER EIGHT

THE BOY, WHO looked to be about ten years old, was sitting on the exam table with a peculiar expression on his face, as though he was in pain. "Hey, buddy," Trent said, giving him a reassuring smile. "Your mommy tells us you're having trouble eating. Does your stomach hurt?"

The child shook his head without speaking. Checking his pulse, Trent noted that he was sweaty, then got a tiny whiff of an unpleasant odor. It could be just that the child smelled bad, or it could be a symptom of some infection.

"Let's take a look in your throat." Using a tongue depressor, he studied the boy's mouth, but didn't see any sign of an abscess or a bad tooth. No tonsil problem or strep. Once Trent was satisfied that none of those were the problem, the boy suddenly bit down on the stick and kept it clamped between his teeth. "Okay, I'm done looking in your mouth. Let go of the stick, please."

The boy didn't budge, then started to cry without opening his mouth. Trent gently pressed his thumb and fingers to the boy's jaw to encourage him to relax and unclamp his jaw. "Let me take the stick out now and we'll check some other things." The boy kept crying and it was all Trent could do to get him to open his mouth barely wide enough to remove the stick.

Damn. Trent thought of one of his professors long ago talking about giving the spatula test, and that sure seemed to be what had just happened with the stick. "Did you hurt yourself any time the past week or two? Did something poke into your skin?"

"I'nt know." The words were a mumble, the boy barely moving his lips, and Trent was now pretty sure he knew what was wrong.

"Thomas, can you get me a cup of water?"

"Yes, doctor."

When he returned with the cup, Trent held it to the boy's lips. "Take a sip of this for me, will you?" As he expected, the poor kid gagged on the water, unable to swallow.

"All right. I want you to lie down so I can check a few things." Trent tried to help him lie on the exam table, but it was difficult with the child's body so rigid. The simple movement sent the boy into severe muscle spasms. When the spasms eventually faded and Trent finally was able to get him prone, the child's arms flung up to hug his chest tightly while his legs stayed stiff and straight. He began crying again, his expression formed into a grimace.

Trent was aware of both Thomas and Charlotte standing by the table, staring with surprise and concern. He grasped the boy's wrist and tried to move his elbow. The arm resisted, pushing against his hand.

"What do you think is wrong, Trent?" Charlotte said, obviously alarmed.

He couldn't blame her for being unnerved, since this wasn't something you saw every day. It was damned disturbing how a patient was affected by this condition.

"Tetanus. I'm willing to bet he's had a puncture wound, probably in the foot, that maybe he didn't even notice happened. The infection, wherever it is, is causing his jaw to lock, as well as all the other symptoms we're seeing."

He released the child's arm and lifted his foot, noting it was slightly swollen. Bingo! There it was: a tiny wound oozing a small amount of smelly pus.

The poor kid was still crying, the sound pretty horrible through his clenched teeth. He placed the boy's foot back down and refocused his attention on calming him down. "You're going to be all right, I promise. I know this is scary and you feel very uncomfortable and strange. But I'm going to get rid of the infection in your foot and give you medicine to make you feel better. Okay?"

The brown eyes that stared back at him were terrified, and who could blame the poor little guy? With tetanus, painful spasms could be so severe they actually pulled ligaments apart or broke bones.

"What do you do for tetanus?" Charlotte asked. "Is it…?" She didn't finish the sentence, but he knew what she was asking.

"He'll recover fine, now that we've got him here. Thomas, can you get what we need for an IV drip of penicillin? And some valium, please."

"Penicillin?" Charlotte frowned and leaned up to speak softly in his ear. "Since he's so sick, shouldn't you give him something—I don't know—stronger?"

"Maybe it's a good thing you're not a doctor after all." He couldn't resist teasing her a little. "In the U.S., they'd probably use an antibiotic that costs four hundred dollars a day and kills practically every bacteria in your body instead of just the one causing the disease—kind of like killing an ant with a sledgehammer. But, believe me, penicillin is perfect for this. You can't kill bacteria deader than dead."

Her pretty lips and eyes smiled at him. "Okay. I believe you. So that's it? Penicillin? Do you need a test to confirm that's what it is?"

"No, his symptoms are clear. That's what it is." He found himself feeling pleased that she trusted him to make the right decision. Since when had he ever needed other people to appreciate what he did and what he'd learned over the years?

He reached to pat the child's stiffly folded arms. "Hang in there. I'll be right back." Grasping Charlotte's elbow, he walked far enough away that the boy couldn't hear them.

"Penicillin is just part of the treatment. We'll need to do complete support care. I have to get rid of the clostridium tetani, which is the bacteria in his foot that's giving off the toxin to the rest of his body. It's one of the most lethal toxins on earth, which is why it's a damned good thing his mother brought him in. He wouldn't have made it if it was left untreated."

She shuddered. "How do you get rid of the…whatever it was called…tetani toxin?"

"I'll have to open his foot to remove it and clean out the dead and devitalized tissue so it can heal. It'll give the penicillin a chance to work. I'll give him fluids and valium to keep him comfortable so he can rest. He'll have to stay here several days, kept very quiet, to give his body time to process the toxin."

She nodded and her eyes smiled at him again, her soft hand wrapping around his forearm. "Thank you again for coming back, Trent. I bet our lying Dr. Smith would never have been able to figure out what was wrong with this boy. You're…amazing."

He didn't know about all that. What he did know was that *she* was amazing. In here, looking at this boy, concerned and worried but not at all freaked out by the bizarre presentation of tetanus, despite not being in medicine herself. He'd bet a whole lot of his fortune that the women he'd dated back in the days of his old, privileged life in the States would have run hysterically from the room. Or, even more likely, would never been in there to begin with.

"I have to take care of his foot right now, which is going to take a little time. Promise you'll stay here in the hospital until I'm done?" He found himself reaching to touch her face, to stroke his knuckles against her cheek.

"I know you think you're all tough and can handle any big, bad burglar that might be ransacking your house as you walk in the door. But, for my peace of mind, will you please wait for me?"

"I'll wait for you." The beautiful green of her eyes, her small smile, her words, all seemed to settle inside his chest and expand it. "Since it'll be past time for dinner to be served here, I'll fix something for us when we get there."

"Sounds great." He wanted to lean down and kiss her, the way he had in the rain the other day. And the reasons for not doing that began to seem less and less important. Charlotte definitely didn't act like she'd be doing much pining after he was gone.

That was good news he hoped was really true, and the smart part of him knew it was best to keep it that way, to keep their relationship "strictly professional," and never mind that he'd be spending the night back in her house. The house in which, when the two of them *weren't* just colleagues, they hadn't gotten much sleep at all.

Despite the comfort of the double bed, with its wrought-iron headboard and soft, handmade quilt, Trent turned restlessly, finally flopping onto his back with his hands behind his head. The room was girly, with lace curtains, a pastel hooked rug and an odd mix of furniture. The femininity of it made him even more acutely aware that Charlotte was sleeping very close by.

Every time he closed his eyes, he saw her face: the woman who had fascinated him from the first second he'd walked into her office. That long, silky brown hair cascading down her back, her body with curves in all the right places on her petite frame and her full lips begging to be kissed were as ultra-feminine as the bedroom.

But her willful, no-nonsense personality proved that

a woman who oozed sexiness and femininity sure didn't have to be quiet and docile.

He'd guessed being here would be a challenge. How the hell was he going to get through the night keeping his word that their relationship would stay strictly professional? Get through the next few days?

Focusing on work seemed like a good plan. He'd tell her he wanted to head into the field to do immunizations, or whatever else patients might need, keeping close proximity to Charlotte at a minimum. The last thing he wanted to do was hurt her, and so far it seemed their brief time together hadn't negatively affected her at all. No point in risking it—not to mention that he didn't want to stir up that strange discomfort he'd felt at the airport when he'd tried to get out of there the first time.

A loud creak sent Trent sitting upright in bed, on high alert. Had someone broken in? Surely, lying there wide awake, he would have heard other sounds if that was the case?

Probably Charlotte wasn't sleeping well, either. He stared at the bedroom door, his pulse kicking up a notch at another creak that sounded like it was coming from the hall. Could she possibly be planning to come into his room?

He swung his legs to the floor and sat there for a few minutes, his ears straining to hear if it was her, or if he should get up to see if what he'd heard was an intruder. While it seemed unlikely someone could break in without making a lot of noise, he threw on his khaki shorts and decided he had to check the place out just to be sure.

He opened the bedroom door as quietly as possible and crept out in his bare feet, staring through the darkness of the hallway, looking for any movement. The scent of coffee touched his nose and he relaxed, since he was pretty sure no intruder would be taking a coffee break.

Charlotte was up; he should just go back to bed. But, before he knew what he was doing, he found himself padding down the narrow staircase to the kitchen.

"Did you have to make so much racket in here? I was sound asleep," he lied as he stepped into the cozy room. Seeing Charlotte standing at the counter in a thin, pink robe, her hair messy, her lips parted in surprise, almost obliterated his resolve to keep his distance. Nearly had him striding across the room to pull her into his arms, and to hell with all his resolutions to the contrary. But he forced himself to lean against the doorjamb and shove his hands in his pockets.

"I was quiet as a mouse. Your guilty conscience must be keeping you awake."

"Except for that 'murdering my old girlfriend' thing, my conscience is clean. I abandoned my vacation plans, didn't I? Came back here to work for you?"

She nodded and the way her gaze hovered on his bare chest for a moment reminded him why he hadn't been able to sleep, damn it.

"You did," she said, turning back to the percolator. "I'm grateful, and I know Lionel's family is grateful too. And the other patients you've taken care of since then." She reached into the cupboard to grab mugs. "Coffee?"

He should go back upstairs. Try to sleep. "Sure."

He settled into a chair at the table and she joined him, sliding his cup across the worn wood. His gaze slipped to the open vee of her robe. He looked at her smooth skin and hint of the lush breasts he knew were hidden there, pictured what kind of silky nightgown she might be wearing and quickly grabbed up his cup to take a swig, the burn of it on his tongue a welcome distraction.

Time for mundane conversation. "So, tell me about what you studied in school. Didn't you say you got an MBA?"

"Yes. I got a hospital administration degree, then went

to Georgetown for my masters. I knew I'd be coming here
to get the hospital open and running again, so all that was
good." She leaned closer, her eyes alight with enthusiasm. "I met a lot of people who shared their experiences
with me—about how they'd improved existing facilities
or started from scratch in various countries. I learned so
much, hearing the things they felt they did right or would
do differently."

He, too, leaned closer, wanting to study her, wanting
to know what made this fascinating and complex woman
tick. "I've been surprised more than once how much you
know about medicine. Tell me again, why didn't you become a doctor?"

"Somebody needs to run this place. Create new ways
to help people, to make a difference. Like I said before, I
can get doctors and nurses and trained techs. I focused my
training on how to do the rest of it. My parents encouraged
that; they've trusted me and John Adams with the job of
bringing this place back."

A surge of old and buried pain rose within him and he
firmly shoved it back down. It must be nice to have someone in your life who believed in you, who cared what you
wanted. It must be nice to have someone in your life who
didn't say one thing, all the while betraying you, betraying
your blind trust, with a deep stab in your back.

"I've worked at a lot of hospitals in the world. That experience might come in handy if you have any questions."

"Thanks. I might take you up on that."

Her beautiful eyes shone, her mouth curved in a pleased
smile, and the urge to grab her up and kiss her breathless
was nearly irresistible. Abruptly, he stood and downed the
last of his coffee, knowing that between the caffeine and
her close proximity there'd be no sleep for him tonight.

"I'm going to hit the hay. Try not to make a bunch of

noise again and wake me up. I don't want to fall asleep in the middle of a surgery tomorrow."

She stood too and the twist of her lips told him she knew exactly why he was awake. "Don't worry. The last thing I want to do is disturb your sleep."

"Liar." He had to smile, enjoying the pink that stained her cheeks at the word. "Anyway, you've already done that, so you owe me. Maybe you should disturb my sleep for a few more hours; help me relax."

Why did his mouth say one thing, when his brain told him to shut up and walk out? Until the slow blink of her eyes, the tip of her tongue licking her lips, the rise and fall of that tantalizing vee of skin beneath her robe, obliterated all regrets.

"I don't think your sleep is my responsibility," she said. "You're on your own."

She swayed closer, lids low, her lips parted, practically willing him to kiss her. What was the reason he'd been trying not to? Right now, he couldn't quite remember. Didn't want to.

"Seems to me we agreed you were in charge of my life while I'm here." Almost of their own accord, his feet brought him nearly flush with her body. Close enough to feel her warmth touch his bare chest; to feel her breath feather across his skin. "Got any ideas on a cure for insomnia?"

"Less coffee in the middle of the night? Maybe a hammer to the head? I've got one in the toolbox in the closet."

He reached for her and put his hands on her waist. "I know you said you couldn't promise not to hurt me, but that seems a little drastic." His head lowered because he had to feel her skin against his lips. He touched them softly to her cheek, beneath her ear. "Any other ideas?"

Her warm hands flattened against his chest. When they didn't push, he drew her close, her curves perfectly fitted to his body. Much as he knew he should back off right now, there was no way he could do it. He wanted her even more than the night they'd fallen into her bed together. And that night had knocked him flat in a way he couldn't remember ever having experienced before.

Her head tipped back as he moved his mouth to the hollow of her throat and could feel her pulse hammering beneath his lips. "We have morphine in the drug cupboard at the hospital," she said, her voice breathy, sexy. "A big dose of that might help."

"You're a much more powerful drug than morphine, much more addictive, and you know it." Her green eyes filled his vision before he lowered his mouth to hers and kissed her. He drew her warm tongue into his mouth, and the taste of her robbed him of any thoughts of taking it slow. Of kissing her then backing off.

Her hands roamed over his chest, sending heat racing across his flesh, and he sank deeper into the kiss, tasting the hint of coffee, cream and sweet sugar on his tongue. Her fingers continued on a shivery path down his ribs, to his sides and back, and he wrapped his arms around her and pulled her close, the swell of her breasts rising and falling against him.

His thigh nudged between her legs and, as she rocked against him, he let one hand drift to her rear, increasing the pressure, loving the gasp that left her mouth and swirled into his.

The rattling sound of a doorknob cut through the sensual fog in his brain and Trent pulled his mouth from Charlotte's. They stared at one another, little panting breaths between them, before her gaze cut toward the living room.

"What the hell? Are you expecting someone?"

Her eyes widened and she pulled away from him. "No," she whispered. "Darn, I left my gun upstairs. I'll have to go through the living room to get it. Should I run up there?

If he—or they—get in you could punch them or something till I get back down with it. Or maybe you shouldn't. Maybe *they* have a gun."

Metal scratched against metal then a creaking sound indicated the door had been opened, and Charlotte's hands flung to her chest as she stared out of the kitchen then swung her gaze back to Trent.

"The door was locked, wasn't it? Does someone have a key?" It hadn't sounded like forced entry to him. Maybe it was somebody she knew. And the thought that it could be a boyfriend twisted his gut in a way it shouldn't twist for a sweet but short interlude.

"No. The only other key is in my office at the hospital."

Her whisper grew louder, likely because she was afraid. He touched his finger to her lips and lowered his mouth to her ear. "Is there really a hammer in the closet?"

She nodded and silently padded to it in her bare feet, wincing as the door shuddered open creakily. She grabbed the head of a hammer and handed it to him, then pulled out a heavy wrench and lifted it in the air, ready to follow him.

What would she have done if he hadn't been here with her tonight? The thought brought a surge of the same protective anger he'd felt when he'd heard about the first break-in, which had made him more than ready to bust somebody's head.

"Stay here," he whispered. He slipped to the doorway and could see a shadowy figure with a bag standing near the base of the stairs.

CHAPTER NINE

HEART POUNDING, CHARLIE stepped close behind Trent, peeking around him as he stood poised to strike the intruder. Never would she have thought that the burglars would come back, especially at night when she was home. Thank goodness Trent was here. Much as she said she could look after herself—and she could; she was sure she could—having a big, strong man in the house definitely made her glad she wasn't alone as someone was breaking in.

She looked up to see Trent's jaw was taut, his eyes narrowed, his biceps flexed as he raised the hammer. He looked down at her, gave a quick nod, then burst across the room with a speed sure to surprise and overwhelm whoever had broken in.

The man was shorter than Trent, who slammed his shoulder into the intruder's chest like he was an American football linebacker. The intruder landed hard, flat on his back, and Trent stepped over him, one leg on either side of the man's prone figure. With one hand curled in a menacing fist, Trent's other held the hammer high.

"Who the hell are you? And you better answer fast before you can't answer at all," Trent growled.

"What the heck? Who are *you*? Charlie?" Her father's voice sounded scared and trembly and she tore across the room in a rush.

"Oh, heavens! Stop, Trent! It's okay. It's my dad." The wrench in her hand suddenly seemed to weigh twenty pounds and she nearly dropped it as she shook all over in shock and relief. She fell to her knees next to her father, placing the wrench on the floor so she could touch his chest and arms. "Dad, are you all right? Are you hurt?"

"I…I'm not sure." He stared up at Trent, who stepped off him to one side and lowered the hammer. "Next time I'll know to knock, seeing as you have a bodyguard."

"Sorry, sir." Trent crouched down and slipped his arm beneath her dad's shoulders, helping him to a sitting position. "You okay?"

"I think so. Except for the hell of a bruise I'm going to have in the morning." He stood with the help of Trent and Charlie and rubbed his hand across his chest, then offered it to Trent. "I'm Joseph Edwards. Thanks for looking out for my daughter."

"Uh, you're welcome. I guess. Though I think this is the first time I've been thanked for beating somebody up. I'm Trent Dalton."

Charlie glanced at Trent to see that charming, lopsided smile of his as he shook her dad's hand. The shock of it all, and the worry of whether her dad was okay or not, had worn off and left her with a hot annoyance throbbing in her head. "What are you doing here, Dad? I thought you weren't coming for a couple more nights. Why didn't you call? You're lucky you don't have a big lump on your head. Or a gunshot through your chest."

"I tried to call but couldn't get any cell service. After I met with Bob in Monrovia, I decided not to stay at his house like I'd planned, because his wife's not feeling well. Then I got the key from the hospital so I wouldn't wake you—though that obviously wasn't a problem." He raised his eyebrows. "I won't ask what you're doing up in the middle of the night."

"That wouldn't be any of your business," Charlie said, glaring at Trent as his smile grew wider. His grin definitely implied something it shouldn't, and it sure didn't help that the man had no shirt on. Though, as she thought back to what exactly they were doing when her dad had arrived, it wasn't too far off. It had, in fact, been quickly heading in the direction of hot and sweaty sex and she felt her cheeks warm. "But if you must know, Trent is doing surgeries at the hospital for a few days and, um, needed a place to stay. We were just talking about the hospital and stuff."

"She obviously doesn't want you to know, but that's not entirely the truth," Trent said.

She stared at him. Surely the man wasn't going to share the details of their relationship—or whatever you'd call their memorable night together—to her *father?*

"What is the truth?" her dad asked.

"The reason I'm spending the night here is because someone broke into the house yesterday. I didn't think she should be alone until it seemed unlikely the guy was coming back. Which is why I knocked you down first and asked questions later."

"Ah." Her father frowned. "I have to say, it's concerned me from the start that you were living here by yourself. Maybe we should rethink that—have a few hospital employees live here with you."

"I've been here two years, Dad, and nothing like this has happened before. I'm sure it's an isolated incident. I like living alone and don't want that to change."

"Maybe you should get a dog, then—one with a big, loud bark that would scare somebody off."

A dog? Hmm. It might be nice to have a dog around and she had to admit she might feel a touch safer. "If it will ease your mind, I'll consider it."

"We'll talk more about this later." Her dad lowered himself into a chair and rubbed his chest again, poor man.

Though she felt he'd brought it on himself by sneaking in. "I'm looking forward to hearing about how the new wing is coming along. Must be about finished, isn't it? When is the first plastic surgeon supposed to get here?"

"Um, soon." She glanced at Trent and saw his brows twitch together. This was her chance to ask him to stay until the Gilchrist rep got here, to do a few plastic surgery procedures, since the subject had come up. Maybe, with her dad there, he wouldn't be so quick to say no. She pulled the ties of her robe closer together, trying not to give off any vibes that said, *I'm desperate here.*

"Trent. Ever since I saw what a wonderful job you did on Lionel's eye, I've been meaning to ask." She licked her lips and forged on. "There are a few patients who've been waiting a long time to have a plastic surgery procedure done. Would you consider doing one or two before you leave?"

"You know, I'm not actually a board-certified plastic surgeon." His eyes were unusually flat and emotionless. "Better for you to wait until you have your whole setup ready and a permanent surgeon in place."

"You do plastic surgery?" Her father's eyebrows lifted in surprise. "I assumed you were a general surgeon, like the ones who usually rotate through the GPC-staffed hospitals."

"I am."

"Come on, Trent." Charlie tried for a cajoling tone that might soften him up. "I saw what you did for Lionel's eye. You told me, when you wanted to do it, that I didn't know who I was dealing with, remember? And you were right."

He looked at her silently for a moment before he spoke. "I'm leaving here any day now, Charlotte. It wouldn't make sense for me to perform any complex plastics procedures on patients, then take off before I could follow up with them."

"Please, Trent." Her hands grew cold. "Maybe you could even stay a few extra days, to help these patients who so desperately need it. When you see some of them, I think you'll want to."

"I can't stay longer. And it's not good medical practice for me to do a surgery like that, then leave. I'm sorry." He turned to her dad, the conversation clearly over by the tone of his voice. "Since you're here tonight, sir, I'm going to grab my things and head back to my quarters."

Charlie watched him disappear up the steps and listened to his footsteps fade away down the hall. Why was he so adamant about this? And what could she possibly do to convince him?

Trent managed to avoid Charlotte the entire following day. He took dinner to his room, and if she noticed she didn't say anything. When his phone rang and he saw it was Chase, a strange feeling came over him before he answered. A feeling that told him he'd miss this place when he left, whether it was tomorrow or days from now.

"So, I'm sorry, man, but it's just not going to work out," Chase said in his ear. "Wish I could sub for you. I'd love to head back to Africa for a week or so. But I'm pretty busy at work here and, like I said, Dani's not feeling great this month. Says she didn't have morning sickness with Drew, but she sure does now."

"Maybe it's you that's making her sick this time, and not her pregnancy," Trent said. "Which I could fully appreciate."

"Yeah, that could well be true." Chase chuckled. "Any chance you'll be coming to the States some time? Dani and I go to the occasional conference here. It would be great to catch up."

"No plans for that right now. I'll let you know if I do." He wouldn't mind a visit back to the States, so long as it wasn't New York City. It would be nice to see Chase and Dani, and maybe even cute little Drew and his new baby sibling. He hadn't been back for quite a while. "Who knows, maybe we can temp at the same time in Honduras when I'm between jobs. Let's see if we can make that happen."

"That would be great. Stay in touch, will you?

"Will do. Take care, and give your family a hug for me."

Well, damn. He shoved his phone in his pocket. So much for that great idea. But he'd known it was a long shot that Chase would be able to fill in for him here in Liberia until the new doctor arrived.

The uneasy feelings he had about being stuck here were peculiar and annoying. It wasn't like it was a big deal if he went on his vacation all by his lonesome tomorrow or a couple weeks from now. The GPC was used to delays like this, so they probably had a temp lined up for him in the Philippines until he got there.

But this tug and push he kept feeling around Charlotte was damned uncomfortable. One minute all he wanted was to kiss her breathless, knowing that was a bad idea for all kinds of reasons; the next, she was bugging him about doing plastic surgery that he plain didn't want to do, which put the distance between them he knew they should keep in place. That he knew he should welcome.

There had been a number of times his plastics skills had come in handy over the years, doing surgeries on a cleft palate, or a hemangioma like Lionel's, that were important to how the patient could function every day. But actually working in a plastic surgery hospital? One dedicated to procedures that mostly improve someone's looks? No, thank you. He'd rather keep people alive than just make them look better to the world.

He sat at the tiny desk in his room and went through the mail that had arrived this week. One was from the GPC and he tore it open, wondering if it was finally his release papers, or if they'd had to relocate his next job to somewhere other than the Philippines because of this delay.

Perplexed, he read through the letter twice. Clearly, there was some mess-up here. How come the director, Mike Hardy, thought the new doctor was already at the Edwards Hospital? Mike's letter advised him that, because of the imminent arrival of this doctor in Liberia, a temp filling in at his new job wouldn't be necessary and he could still take his full three weeks off. His revised arrival date in the Philippines was exactly three weeks from today.

He picked up his phone to call Mike, but figured it would make sense to talk to Charlotte first. Maybe she knew something he didn't.

He left his room and strode down the long hallway from the residence quarters into the hospital. Dinner had been over an hour ago, so she very well might be back at home. And he wasn't about to follow her over there. If she'd already left, he'd forget about talking to her and just call Mike.

A glance in her office showed she wasn't there, so he went to the dining hall. Her round, sexy rear was the only part of her he could see. With her head and torso inside a cupboard as she kneeled on the floor, he stopped to enjoy the view and had to resist the urge to shock her by going over and giving that sexy bottom of hers a playful spank.

"Does anyone know if the rest of Charlotte Edwards is in here?" he asked instead.

Her body unfolded and she straightened to look at him, still on her knees. "Very funny. I'm just trying to organize this kitchen equipment. Too many cooks in here are making it hard to find anything when you want it."

"When you have a minute, I need to talk to you about the new doc coming."

He had to wonder why her expression was instantly

alarmed. Was she worried there'd been an even longer delay? Thank goodness her dad was here now, so Trent wouldn't be spending any more tempting nights in her house.

She shoved to her feet and walked over. "What about the new doc?"

"I got a letter from Mike Hardy telling me all systems are go for my vacation. I'm wondering what the mix-up is. Or if someone is coming tomorrow and they somehow forgot to send my release papers."

She snatched the letter from his hand and looked it over, her fingers gripping it until they were practically white. "Um, I don't know. This is weird. Last I heard, there was nobody in place yet. Let me see what I can find out and I'll let you know. Believe me, I'm as anxious to get you out of here as you are to leave."

"Never mind." He tried to tug the paper from her hand, but she held on tight. It pissed him off that she wanted him out of there so badly, which was absolutely absurd, since he wanted the same thing. "I'll call Mike in the morning. Give me my letter back."

"I'm the director of this hospital and staffing is my responsibility."

Her green eyes were flashing irritation at him, as well as something else he couldn't figure out. The woman was like a pit bull sometimes. "Why are you so controlling? Technically, the GPC employs me, you know. And this is my job, my vacation and my life. Give me my letter."

"Fine. Take the letter." She let it go and spun on her heel toward the doorway. "But I'm going home, then calling Mike. I'm asking you to let me handle this; I'll let you know what he says. Hopefully this means you're on your way very soon."

His hand crumpled the letter slightly as he watched her

disappear into the hall. Why he wanted to storm after her and kiss her until she begged him to stay was something he wasn't going to try to understand.

CHAPTER TEN

CHARLIE HELD TRENT'S release papers in slightly shaky hands then shoved them deeper under the pile on her desk. She tried to draw a calming breath and remind herself that Colleen believed Trent had agreed to stay, so the new doctor wouldn't just show up on the doorstep and give Trent the green light to leave. But if Trent called Mike Hardy, who knew what would happen?

She prayed the Gilchrist representative would show up fast. Surely they'd be impressed with what a great job the hospital's plastic surgeon had done on Lionel's eye; they would never know the talented man would be out of there as soon as the rep left. Trent would charm them, even if he didn't know he was supposed to, because the man oozed charm just by breathing. And all would be well. It would.

Paying bills wasn't exactly the way to forget about the problem, but it had to be done. Charlie tore open the mail and grimly dropped every invoice into the box she kept for them. One thing she could do to relieve the stress of it all was work harder on other sources of funding besides Gilchrist. Her dad had always told her to never put all her eggs in one basket, so she tried to have multiple fundraising efforts going. Time to make some more calls and send more letters to previous donors. There was no way any of them would come close to what the Gilchrist Foundation had committed, but something was a whole lot better than nothing.

A letter with a postmark from New York City and the name of some financial organization caught her eye and made her heart accelerate. The Gilchrist Foundation was based in NYC. Could they possibly just have decided to send a check without worrying about the final approval?

She quickly ripped it open then sighed when she read the letterhead: not from the foundation. But her brief disappointment faded as she read the check that was enclosed with the letter. She stared, not quite believing what she was seeing.

Fifty thousand dollars, written to The Louisa Edwards Education Project. With slightly shaky hands, she scanned the letter that came with the check.

> *Please find enclosed an anonymous donation to provide supplemental funding for the Louisa Edwards School.*

It was signed by someone who apparently worked at the financial firm it came from.

She stared at the bold numerals and the cursive below them. Fifty thousand dollars. Fifty thousand! Oh, heavens!

She leaped up and tore out the door of her office, about to run all the way to the school to show John Adams and her dad, who was there with him. To have John Adams plan to hire another new teacher. To think of all the supplies on their wish-list they'd decided not to buy for now.

And she ran, *kapow*, right into Trent Dalton's hard shoulder, just as she had before when he'd asked if she was late to lunch.

He grabbed her arms to steady her. "Wow, you must be extra-hungry today. Something special on the menu?"

"Funny." She clutched the check to her chest and smiled

up at him. "But even you can't annoy me today. You won't believe what just came in the mail!"

"A new designer handbag? Some four-inch heels?" he asked, little creases at the corners of his eyes as he smiled.

"Way, way better. Guess again."

"A brand-new SUV?"

She held the check up in front of his face. "Look." She was so thrilled she had to gulp in air to keep from hyperventilating. "Somebody sent a check—a huge check—to the school. I have no idea who it's from, or how they even heard about us. We can serve so many more kids now. Get stuff we've been wanting, but couldn't afford. Can you believe it?"

"No. Can't believe it."

There was a funny expression on his face, a little amused smile along with something else she couldn't quite figure out. "You're laughing at me, aren't you? I can't help being excited. More than excited! Oh my gosh, this is so amazing and wonderful. Just like a gift from the heavens."

Beyond jubilant, she flung her arms around Trent's neck and gave him a big, smacking kiss on the lips, because she just plain couldn't help herself. She drew back slightly against his arms, which had slipped across her back, and could see his eyes had grown a tad more serious. The warm kiss he gently pressed to her forehead felt soft and sweet.

"I'm happy for you. You and John Adams deserve it for the work you're accomplishing in that school, and obviously your donor knows that. You're literally changing those kids' lives, giving them a fighting chance in the tough world they live in."

"Thank you. But you change lives too, you know." She stepped out of his hold, instantly missing the warm feel of his arms around her. "Gotta go. I need to tell John Adams and Dad about this."

"I'll come, too. I'm not busy right now and I'd like to see the kids again."

It hadn't rained in a few days, so the earth wasn't nearly as muddy as the last time they'd trekked over to the school. Her brain was spinning with possibilities, until a thought made her excitement drop a notch.

Maybe she shouldn't be so quick to hire another teacher or two and immediately spend some of it on teaching supplies and another couple sewing machines for the students to learn that skill on. Maybe she needed to hold onto it just in case she couldn't pay the hospital bills when they came in if the Gilchrist funding didn't come through.

No. They'd always run the hospital and the school separately: different sponsors and donors, different bookkeeping, different projects. Whoever had donated this money wanted it to go to the school and she had to honor that. It was the only fair and right thing to do for both the donor and the students.

"Did you get hold of Mike about my letter? Or am I allowed to call him now, Miss 'I'm The Director Of The Hospital And The Whole World'?" His lips were curved in a teasing smile, but his eyes weren't smiling quite as much.

"I'm...sorry if I was being bossy and...and acted like I want you to leave. I don't, really. I've just got a lot on my mind." And, boy, wasn't that the truth. "I spoke with Colleen, and apparently she does have someone lined up to come soon, but not today or tomorrow. I'm sorry about that also. I would greatly appreciate it, though, if you would stay just another few days." And all that was the truth, too, which made her feel a tad better. She wasn't being quite as deceitful as she felt.

"All right. Thanks for checking. I guess I can hang around for just a little while longer."

She drew a deep breath of relief, then glanced up at Trent's profile, at his prominent nose, black hair and sensual lips. It didn't feel like just over a week since he'd returned from the airport. As he walked next to her, not touching but close enough to feel his warmth, it seemed much longer. Oddly natural, like she should just reach over to hold his hand.

Which was not good. Not only would he be leaving in a matter of days, she didn't want to think about how shocked and angry he'd be if he ever found out about her little fibs. Okay, big fibs; the thought of it made her stomach knot.

Three figures, two taller and one small, along with a little dog, appeared up ahead on the road—obviously, her dad, John Adams, Patience and Lucky. Seeing them obliterated all other thoughts as Charlie ran the distance between them, waving the check.

"You're going to faint when you see this!"

Trent followed slowly behind Charlotte, not wanting to intrude on her moment, sharing her excitement with the two men and Patience. Though he'd been itching to leave, to move on with his life, he felt glad—blessed, really—that he'd still been here when she got the check. He'd never been around when someone received one of his donations, and it felt great to see how happy it made her. To know it would help them achieve their important goals.

He watched her fling her arms around both men, first her dad, then John Adams, just as she'd done with him. Well, not exactly the same. Her arms wrapped around their middles in a quick hug. That was different from the way she'd thrown her arms around his own neck, drawing his head close, giving him that kiss; her breasts pressing softly against his chest, staying there a long moment, her fingers tucked into his hair, sending a shiver along his scalp and a desire to kiss more than just her forehead.

"You don't know who the donor is?" her father asked.

She shook her head, the sun touching her shining hair as

it slipped across her shoulders. "No. I wish I did. I wish I could thank them. That *we* could thank them. Think there's any way to find out?"

"Not likely. But you could always contact the company it came from and ask."

"I'll do that," Charlotte said as they turned and headed back toward the hospital. "Maybe even ask if there's anything specific they want the money used for."

Trent knew his finance man was discreet and they'd get no information that could trace it back to him. "Whoever donated it stayed anonymous because they wanted to. I say just spend the money as you see fit and know they trusted you to do that," he said.

"Good point, Trent," John Adams said. "We do get the occasional anonymous donation, though nothing like this, of course. I think we should respect that's how they wanted to keep it."

"Okay." Charlotte's chest rose and fell in a deep breath, and Trent found his attention gravitating to her beautiful curves. "I'm feeling less freaked out. Just plain happy now. Why are you three leaving the school?"

"Daddy promised he would take me to the beach," Patience said. "He's been promising and promising, but kept saying it was s'posed to rain. But today the sun is shiny so we can go!" The little girl danced from one foot to the other, the colorful cloth bag on her shoulder dancing along with her.

"Mind if I come?" Trent asked. "I'll build a sandcastle with you." The kid was so cute, and he hadn't seen an inch of Liberia other than the airport and the road to and from the hospital and school. One of the things he enjoyed about his job was exploring new places, discovering new things. He turned to Charlotte. "Would that be okay? Thomas is taking care of a man needing hernia surgery, and I've already seen the patients in the clinic. The nurses are finishing up with all of them. I can check on everyone when I get back."

"Of course, that's fine. I'll see what's in the kitchen for you all to take for a beach lunch."

"Why don't you go along, Charlie?" her dad suggested. "You never take much time off to do something fun. I've been wanting to go through the information you gave me, anyway, so I can keep an eye on things while you're gone."

"Well…" Her green eyes held some expression he couldn't figure out. Wariness? Anxiety? "I'm not really a beach person, you know. And I don't want you stuck here doing my work, Dad."

"You may be the director, but I'm still a part of this hospital too, remember." Joseph smiled. "You need to get over this fear of yours. Go get your things together. John Adams and I will scrounge up some food for you all to take."

"What fear of yours?" Trent asked. From being around Charlotte just the past week or so, he couldn't imagine her being afraid of much of anything.

"Nothing. Dad's exaggerating."

"Exaggerating? The last time we were at the beach, I thought you were going to hyperventilate just going into the water up to your knees." Joseph turned to Trent. "When Charlie was a teenager back in the States, we didn't realize we were swimming where there was a strong rip current, like quite a few beaches here in Liberia have. She got pulled farther and farther out and I couldn't get to her. Her mom and I kept yelling at her to relax and not fight the current, to just let it take her. Then swim horizontal to the shore until she came to a place without a rip so she could swim back in."

"Rip tides can be dangerous." Trent looked at Charlotte and saw her cheeks were flushed. Surely she wasn't embarrassed by something that happened when she was a kid? "Scary for anybody. But obviously you lived through it."

"Yes. I admit I thought for sure that was it, though. That I was going to end up in the middle of the ocean and either drown or be devoured by a shark. So I just don't like going in the water."

"In the water? You don't even like getting in a small boat. Which has been a problem a few times," Joseph said. "You need to move past it and get your feet wet."

"Can we just drop this subject, please? I have a lot of work to do, anyway."

"Come to the beach, Charlotte," Trent said, wishing he could pull her into his arms and give her soothing kisses that would ease her embarrassment and the bad memory. "We'll work on getting you to move past your fear. You don't have to get in the water if you're not comfortable. But, you know, I did do a whole rotation in psychiatry at school. I'm sure I'm a highly qualified therapist." He gave her a teasing smile, hoping she'd relax and decide to come. Living with any kind of debilitating fear was no fun.

"Just go, Charlie," Joseph said. "It'll make me feel less guilty that I let you swim in that rip to begin with."

Charlotte gave an exaggerated sigh. "So this is about you now? Fine. I'll go. But I'm not promising to swim. I mean it."

"No promises needed," Trent said. "We can always just build a sandcastle so big that Princess Patience can walk inside."

"I like big sandcastles!" Patience beamed. "And In't care if we don't swim, Miss Charlie. Swimming isn't my favorite, anyway. We'll have fun on the beach."

"All right, then, that's settled," Joseph said. "John Adams and I will pack lunch while you get your things."

Trent grabbed swim trunks, a towel and his medical bag, which he'd learned always to have along on any excursion. Heading to the car, he had an instant vision of how Charlotte would look in a swimsuit: her sexy curves and smooth skin. Oh, yeah, he would more than enjoy a day at the beach with a beautiful woman; at the same time, he'd be glad to have chaperones to keep him from breaking his deal with her.

The thought of chaperones, though, didn't stop more compelling thoughts of swimming with Charlotte. How she'd feel in his arms when he held her close, trying to relieve her mind and soothe her fears, their wet bodies sliding together. How much he wished that, afterwards, they could lie on the hot sand and make love in the shade of a palm tree with the warm breeze tickling their skin.

Damn. His pulse kicked up and made him a little short of breath.

Chaperones were a very good thing.

CHAPTER ELEVEN

THE DRIVE THROUGH farms of papaya, mangoes and acres of rubber trees brought them to the soaring Grand Cape Mount, then eventually to the shoreline. Though John Adams had offered, Charlotte insisted on driving, of course. Trent had to wonder what made the woman feel a need to be in charge all the time. Didn't she ever want just to relax and go along for the ride?

Patience kept up a steady chatter until her father told her he'd give her a quarter if she could stay silent for five minutes. After she failed to manage that, Trent entertained her with a few simple card tricks he let her "win" that earned her the quarter after all.

They parked at the edge of the road and, as they unpacked their things from the car, Charlotte shook her head at Trent. "Is there a soul on the planet you can't charm to death?"

"To death? Doesn't exactly sound like you mean that in a nice way." Trent hooked a few beach chairs over his arm and they followed John Adams and Patience, who carried their lunches and a few plastic pails and shovels.

"Okay, charm, period. Everyone in the hospital thinks you're Mr. Wonderful."

"Does that include the director of the hospital?"

"Of course. I'm very grateful you filled in here—twice—until we can get another doctor."

Her voice had become polite, her smile a little stiff. Was she regretting that her rare time off had to be spent with him? Or could she be having the same problem he was having—wanting to take up where they'd left off at her house, knowing it was a hell of a bad idea?

As they approached the beach, Trent stopped to soak in the visual spectacle before him. A wide and inviting expanse of beige sand stretched as far as he could see, palm trees swaying in the ocean wind. A few houses sat off the shore, looking for all the world as though they were from the Civil War era of the deep south in the United States.

"How old do you think those houses are?" he asked Charlotte.

"Robertsport was one of the first colonies founded here by freed slaves. I think it goes back to 1829, so some of the houses here are over a hundred and fifty years old."

"That's incredible." He looked back down the beach and enjoyed the picturesque lines of fishermen with their seining nets stretched from the beach down into the water, about ten of them standing three feet apart, holding the nets in their hands. Several canoes sat on the shore, obviously made from a single hand-carved tree. One was plain, but the other was splashed with multiple colors of paint in an interesting hodgepodge design.

He was surprised to see a few surfers in the water farther down the beach, not too far from a cluster of black rocks in the distance. The waves were big and powerful, but were breaking fairly far out.

"I didn't know the people here surfed. I know Senegal is popular for surfing, but didn't know the sport had made its way here."

"I'm told an aid worker was here surfing maybe six or seven years ago. A local was fascinated and gave it a try. It's starting to take off, I guess, with locals competing and some tourists coming now."

"You know, we could always borrow a board from them. Want to give it a try?" he teased. The waves were pretty rough, so he knew there was no way she'd even consider it. The water closer to shore, though, was comparatively calm. Hopefully, he could get her into the lapping waves without it being too scary for her.

"Um, no. I think I'm going to be happy just beaching it, thanks anyway."

He'd have to see what he could do about changing her mind. They stopped in the middle of the wide beach and Charlotte laid some blankets on the soft sand. Patience tossed her toys and plopped down next to them. "Daddy, come help me build the castle!"

"How about we eat first, li'l girl?" John Adams said. "Miss Charlie and I brought some jollof rice, which I know you like. I don't know about everybody else, but I'm starving."

"You always starving, Daddy." The child grinned up at her father and Trent saw again what a strong bond there was between the two. The same kind of bond he'd seen grow so quickly between Chase and his son, even though he hadn't met them until the child was a toddler.

That surprising emotion tugged at Trent again, just as it had when Chase had told him about having a new little one on the way. A pinch of melancholy, knowing he'd likely never experience that kind of bond—though he knew only too well that not every family was as close as it seemed. That sometimes the chasm grew too large ever to be crossed.

After lunch and some sandcastle building, complete with a moat, Trent decided it was time to push Charlotte a little, to encourage her to face her fear. She was on her knees smoothing the last turret of the castle, and he pushed to his feet to stand behind her, smacking the sand from his hands. "Come on, Miss Edwards. Time for your psychotherapy session."

Immediately, her back stiffened. "I'm not done with the castle yet. Maybe later."

"Come on. It's hot as heck out here. Think how cool and refreshing the water will be."

"I'm going to watch Patience swim first." She turned to the little girl. "Remember you told me you wanted to learn to float in the lagoon? I want to see you."

And, if that wasn't an excuse, he'd never heard one. Obviously, it was going to be tough going getting her in the water.

John Adams grasped the child's hand and pulled her to her feet. "Good idea. Come on, let's get in the lagoon and cool off."

The child's expression became even more worried than Charlotte's. "No, Daddy. I don't want to."

"Why not?"

She pointed at the lagoon water, separated from the ocean by about fifty feet of sand. "There's neegees in there. I don't want to get taken by the neegees."

"There's no neegees in there, I promise."

"For true, Daddy, there are. They talk about it at school." She stared up at her father with wide eyes. "The neegees are under the water and they grab people who swim. They suck people right out of the lagoon, and nobody knows where they go, and then they're never, ever seen again. Ever."

John Adams chuckled and pulled her close against his leg. "Sugar, I promise you. There's no such thing as neegees. Just like there's no witchcraft where someone can put a curse on you. All those are just stories. So let's get in the water and I'll help you learn to float."

Patience shook her head, pressing her face to her dad's leg. "No, Daddy. I'm afraid of the neegees."

Inspiration struck and Trent figured this was a good time to put those psych classes he'd teased Charlotte about to good use and solve two problems at once. "Patience, you know how Miss Charlie is afraid of the rip currents in the ocean? How she's afraid to go in the water too?"

The little girl peeked at him with one eye, the other still pressed against her father's leg. "Yes."

"How about if Miss Charlie decides she's going to get in the water even though she's afraid? Then, when you see how brave she is, and how she does just fine and has fun, you can get in the lagoon with your dad and have fun too. What do you say?"

Patience turned to look at Charlotte, whose expression morphed from dismay to serious irritation as she glared at Trent. He almost laughed, except he knew she was genuinely scared.

"I guess if Miss Charlie gets in the water and doesn't get bit by a shark then I can be brave too."

"Thanks for that encouragement, Patience. Now I really can't wait to swim," Charlotte said. She narrowed her eyes at Trent, green sparks flying. "And thank *you* for leaving me no choice here. I'll be back after I get my swimsuit on."

"I'll check out the rip situation before we go in." Trent jogged into the water and leaped over the smaller waves before diving into a larger one. The water felt great and the inside of his chest felt about as buoyant as the outside. Charlotte was trusting him to help her feel safe in the water and he was going to do whatever he could to be sure she did.

Swimming parallel to the beach for a little in both directions, he didn't feel or see any major rips in the sand, though he'd still have to pay attention. Satisfied, he body-surfed an awesome wave into shore, standing just in time to see Charlotte emerge from the path that led to the car. Her beautiful body wore a pink bikini that wasn't super-skimpy but still showed plenty of her smooth skin and delectable curves. His pulse quickened and he reminded himself this little swim was supposed to make her feel safer and get past her fear. It was not an excuse to touch her all over.

Yeah, right. It was a damned great excuse, and not taking advantage of it was going to be nearly impossible.

"Ready?" He walked to her and stroked the pads of his fingers across the furrows in her brow, letting them trail softly down her cheek.

"Not really," she said under her breath. "But, since I'm now responsible for Patience not being afraid of the water for the rest of her life, I guess I have to be."

"I hope you're not mad at me. It's a good thing you're doing for her. And yourself." He grasped her hand and gave it a reassuring squeeze. "Don't worry. I'll be with you the whole time, and if you get really freaked out we'll head back in."

She nodded and gripped his hand tightly as they waded into the water, up to their knees, then her waist. In just another minute, the water was lapping at her breasts, which was so distracting he almost forgot to look for too-big waves that might be bearing down on them. He forced himself to look back at the ocean, making sure they weren't ending up in a dangerous spot, before returning his gaze to Charlotte's face. Her eyes were wide, the fear etched there clear, and he released her hand to put his arm around her waist, holding her close.

"I'm going to hold you now, so you feel more comfortable. Don't worry, I'm not getting creepy." He grinned and she gave him a weak smile in return. "In fact, why don't you get on my back and we'll just swim a little together that way until you feel more relaxed?"

"I admit I feel…uncomfortable. But I'm not a little kid, you know. Riding on your back seems ridiculous."

With that body of hers, there was no way she could be mistaken for a little kid. "Not if it makes you feel less nervous. Come on." He crouched down in the water up to his neck. "Get on, and wrap your arms around my throat. Just don't choke me if you get scared or we'll both drown," he teased.

To his surprise, she actually did, and he swam through the water with her clinging to him like a remora attached to a shark, enjoying the feel of the waves sluicing over his body. Enjoying the feel of her weight on him and of her skin sensuously sliding across his, just the way he'd fantasized.

"Okay?" he asked as a slightly bigger wave slapped into them, splashing water into their faces.

"Okay. I admit the water feels…nice."

"It does, doesn't it?" He grinned, relieved that this seemed to be working. "Ready to try a little on your own, with me holding your hand?"

"Um, I guess."

She slid from his back and, as she floated a foot or so away, her grim expression told him she wasn't anywhere near feeling relaxed. He took her hands and wrapped her arms behind his head, then placed his arms around her. Her face was so close, her mouth wet and parted as she breathed, her dripping hair glistening in streaks of bronze. He wanted, more than anything, to kiss her.

And, now that they were facing one another, pressed together, the sensuous feel of her soft breasts against his chest, of her legs sliding against his, was impossible to ignore. The sensation pummeled him far more than any wave could, and he battled back the raw need consuming him. He could only hope she couldn't feel his body's response to the overwhelming one-two punch that was delectable Charlotte Edwards.

"I…I'm not too freaked out, so that's good, isn't it?" Her

voice was a bit breathless, but of course they were swimming a little, and treading water—though his own breath was short for a different reason.

"Yes. It's good." Holding her close was good. The feel of her body, soft and slick against his, was way better than good. He wanted to touch her soft satiny skin all over. Wanted to slide his hand inside her swimsuit top to cup her breast, to thumb the taut nipple he could feel poking against his chest. To slip his fingers inside her bikini bottom and caress her there, to see if she could possibly be as aroused as he was.

The world had shrunk to just the two of them floating in the water. Intensely focused on all those thoughts, Trent forgot to pay attention to the waves. A large whitecap broke just before it reached them, crashing into their bodies and engulfing them.

Charlotte shrieked and her wide, scared eyes met his just before the wave drove them toward shore. He held on to her, crushing her against him so she wouldn't get flung loose, and her arms squeezed around him in return, tightening behind his neck. "Hold on!" he said as the surf took them on a long, rapid, undulating ride to shore.

Pressed tightly together, they rode the wave, and as it flattened Trent rolled to be sure it was his back and not hers that scraped along the sandy bottom. They slid to a stop in about five inches of water, just a short distance from the dry shore. With Charlotte still clutched in his arms, Trent rolled again so she was beneath him, shielding her from the surf. The last thing he wanted was for a wave to hit her from behind and startle her before she could see it coming. He looked into her eyes as water dripped from his face and hair onto hers. "Are you all right?"

"Yes. I'm all right." She dragged in some air. "Though I think I know how a surfboard feels now. Or a piece of seaweed."

He chuckled, then glanced up to see that John Adams and Patience were in the lagoon, the child's little body lying flat with his hands supporting her as she practiced her floating.

With a grin, he looked back down at Charlotte. "Looks like it worked. You being brave helped Patience be brave. You even rode a wave into shore!"

"Only because I was attached to you." A little laugh left her lips and she smiled at him. One thick strand of hair lay across one eye and clung to her face and lips. "I'm glad Patience got in the lagoon. Funny; I kind of forgot to be scared, too. Because of you."

"You're just a lot braver than you give yourself credit for. Hell, you're the bravest woman I know, living in that house alone, doing what you're doing here. Being afraid of a rip tide after nearly drowning in one is normal. Just a tiny, human nick in that feisty spirit of yours." He lifted the strand away from her face as he looked at the little golden flecks in her eyes, her lashes stuck together with salt water. "I'm proud of you for facing that fear. For getting in the water even though you didn't want to." Tucking her hair behind her ear to join the rest that lay flat against her scalp, he suddenly saw something he'd never noticed before.

Her ear was oddly shaped—not just different, slightly abnormal. Nearly invisible scarring appeared on and around it. Probably no one without plastic surgery experience would be able to see it at all, but he could. He pressed his mouth to it, touching the contours of it with his lips and tongue.

"What happened to your ear?"

Her fingers dug into his shoulder blades. "My...ear? What do you mean?"

He let his mouth travel down her damp throat and back up to her jaw, because he just couldn't resist any longer;

across her chin then up, slipping softly across her wet, salty lips before he lifted his gaze back to hers. "Your ear. Were you in an accident? Or was it something congenital?"

She was silent for a moment, just looking back at him, her eyes somber until she sighed. "Congenital. I was born with microtia."

"What grade of microtia? Was your ear just mis-shapen?"

"No, it was grade three. I only had this weird little skin flap that didn't look like an ear at all. We were told that's often accompanied by atresia, but I was blessed to have an ear canal, so I can hear pretty well out of it now."

"When did you have it reconstructed? Were you living in the States?"

She nodded. "I think doctors sometimes do the procedure younger now. But mine wanted to wait until I was nine, since that's when the ear grows to about ninety percent of its adult size." A small smile touched her mouth. "I still remember, when I was about five, why he told me I should be a little older before it was fixed—that it would look strange for a little girl to have a big, grown-up-sized ear, which at the time I thought was a pretty funny visual."

He gave her a soft kiss. "So you remember living with your ear looking abnormal?"

"Remember?" She gave a little laugh that had no humor in the sound at all. "Kids thought it was so hilarious to tease me about it. Called me 'earless Edwards.' One time a kid brought a CD to class for everyone to listen to, then said to me, 'Oh, right, you can't because you don't have an ear!' I wanted to crawl under my desk and hide."

He shook his head, hating that she'd had to go through that. "Kids can be nasty little things, that's for sure; convinced they're just being funny. Now I know where you got that chip on your shoulder from."

He was glad to see the shadows leave her eyes as she

narrowed them at him, green sparks flying. "I do not have a chip on my shoulder. I just believe it's more efficient for me to drive and do whatever I need to do than take ten minutes talking about it just to dance around a man's ego."

"Good thing I'm so full of myself, which you've enjoyed telling me several times. Otherwise you would have crushed my feelings by now."

"As though I could possibly hurt your feelings."

"You might be surprised." And she probably would be, if she knew how rattled he'd felt for days. How much he wanted to leave while somehow, at the very same time, wanting to stay a little longer.

Her palms swept over his shoulder blades, wrapped more fully around his back, and he took that as an invitation for another soft kiss. Her mouth tasted so good, salty-sweet and irresistible.

"Tell me more about your surgery." He lifted his finger to stroke the shell of it. "Did they harvest cartilage from your ribs to build the framework for the new ear?"

"Yes. I have a small scar near my sternum, but you can barely see it now. They finished it in three procedures."

"Well, it looks great. Whoever performed the surgery was very good at it. I bet you were happy."

"Happy?" Her smile grew wider. "I felt normal for the first time in my life. No longer the freak without an ear. It was…amazing."

Now it was all clear as glass. He pressed another kiss to her now smiling mouth. "I finally get why you built the plastic surgery wing, and why it's so important to you. You know first-hand how it feels to be scarred or look different from everyone else."

She nodded, her eyes now the passionately intense green he'd seen so often the past week; the passion that was such an integral part of who she was. "I know saving lives is important—more important than helping people view themselves differently, as you said. But I can tell you that feeling good about the way you look, not feeling like a freak, is so important to a person's psyche. And, even though I had to live for a while feeling like that, I know how blessed I was to have access to doctors who could make it better. You know as well as anyone that so many people around the world don't. And I want to give the people here, at least, that same opportunity to look and feel normal. Can you understand that?"

His answer was to stroke her hair from her forehead, cup her cheek in his palm and kiss her. From the minute he'd met her, she'd impressed him with her determination, and now he was even more impressed. She'd used a negative experience from her own life to try to make life better for others and worked damn hard to make it happen.

His tongue delved into her mouth, licking, tasting the ocean water and the flavor that was uniquely, delectably her. Tasting the passion that was so much a part of her. He was swept along by her to another place, deeper and farther and more powerfully than any wave could ever take him.

CHAPTER TWELVE

As the surf lapped over their bodies, Charlie let herself drown in the kiss, in the taste of his cool, salty lips, his warm tongue deliciously exploring her mouth. Her hands stroked down his shoulder blades and back, reveling in the feel of the hard muscle beneath his smooth skin.

She tunneled her fingers into his thick, wet hair, wild and sexy and black as Liberian coal. His muscled thigh nudged between hers, sending waves of pleasure through every nerve. The taste of his mouth, the touch of his hands, the feel of his arousal against her took her breathlessly back to their incredible night of lovemaking.

"Charlotte," he whispered, his lips leaving hers to trail down her throat, to lick the water pooled there, then continuing their journey lower until his mouth covered her nipple, gently sucking on it through her wet nylon swimsuit.

She gasped. "Trent. That's so good. I—"

The sound of Patience laughing made her eyes pop open as he lifted his head from her breast. His eyes— no longer the light, laughing blue she was used to seeing, but instead a glittering near-black—met hers. Everything about him seemed hard—his chest rising and falling against hers, his arms taut around her, his hips and what was between them.

"Charlotte," he said through clenched teeth. "More than anything, I want to make love to you right now. Right here. To wrap your legs around me and swim back into the waves; nobody would know I'm diving deep inside of you." His mouth covered hers in a steaming kiss. "But I guess that will have to wait until later."

If it hadn't already been difficult to breathe, his words nearly would have made her faint from the lack of oxygen in her brain. Even though she knew Patience and John Adams were fairly close by, she couldn't bring herself to move. The undulating water that wrapped around them was the most intimate cocoon she'd ever experienced in her life and she didn't want it to end. Couldn't find the will to detangle herself from his arms. "So I guess our deal is off."

"Our deal?"

"Not to start anything up again."

"Our deal has obviously been a challenge for me." His mouth lifted in a slow smile, his eyes gleaming. "Maybe we can come up with a slightly modified deal."

"Such as?"

His mouth traveled across her cheek, lowered to her ear. "We make love one more time. Cool down this heat between us and get it out of our systems. Then back to just colleagues for the last days I'm here so we won't have that second goodbye we both want to avoid."

The thought of one, just one more time with him, sent her heart into a crazy rhythm. "I agree to your terms. Just once."

"Just once. So—"

The sound of distant shouting interrupted him. They both turned their heads at the same time and saw a few of the surfers down the beach pulling what looked like an unconscious young man, or a body, from the water.

Trent sprinted down the beach with Charlotte on his heels.

Blood poured through the fingers of a young man sitting on the sand, holding his hand to his forehead. The group of surfers gathered around him looked concerned, and one shouted to another who was running to a mound of things they'd apparently brought with them. He returned with a shirt that he handed to the injured surfer, who pressed it to his head.

"Looks like you need a hand here," Trent said as he approached the injured boy. "I'm a doctor. Will you let me take a look?"

"You a doctor?" The young man looked utterly surprised, and no wonder. There weren't too many doctors around there, period, and it was just damned good luck he happened to be on the beach when the kid was hurt.

"Yes. I work at the Edwards Mission Hospital. This lady is the director." He smiled at Charlotte, now standing next to him, before crouching down. "What's your name? Will you show me what we're dealing with here?"

"Murvee Browne," he replied, lowering his hand with the now-bloody shirt balled up in it. "I was surfing and, when the board flipped, I think the fin got me."

"Looks like it." Trent leaned closer to study the wound. It was one damned deep gash, probably five centimeters, stretching from the hairline diagonally across his forehead to his eyebrow. The injury appeared to slice all the way to the skull, but it was a little hard to tell while it was still bleeding so much. He'd let the kid know it was serious, but reassure him so he wouldn't freak out at what he was going to have to do to repair it. "You've got a pretty good one there. But at least it's just your forehead. I took care of one nasty surf accident victim where the guy's eyelid was slit open too."

Murvee grimaced while his friends gathered even closer to stare at the gash.

"You did it good, oh!" one friend said. "You so lucky the doctor is here today."

Murvee looked worried as he stared at Trent. "What

you charge for fixing me up, doc? I don't make much. My mother makes money at the market, but she needs what I have to help take care of my brothers and sisters."

"Why don't you press that cloth against your forehead real firmly again and keep it there to stop the bleeding, okay, Murvee?" Chase said. "You don't have to worry about paying me. Miss Charlotte here pays me a lot, and she gets mad if I don't do any work to earn it."

He shot a teasing glance at her and she rolled her eyes in return, but there was a smile in them too. "We're going to have to have a little talk about your spreading rumors of what a tyrant I am," she said.

He chuckled and turned his attention back to Murvee. "Are you feeling okay? Not real dizzy or anything?"

"No. I feel all right."

"I'd like to take you back to the hospital to get you stitched up."

"No hospital." Murvee frowned, looking mulish. "I have to be home soon and I have to go to work. I can just have my mom fix it."

"Murvee…"

"How about stitching him in the jeep?" Charlotte suggested, giving him a look that said he was going to have to be flexible here. "I know you brought your bag with you. I'll help any way I can."

Trent sighed. He knew taking Murvee to the hospital and getting his wound taken care of there would take hours, and likely be tough on his family—if he could get the kid to go at all. "Fine. Since you seem okay other than the gash, I won't insist. Let's go to the car."

Murvee's friends helped him stand and the three of them headed down the beach. Trent kept an eye on the young man as they trudged to the car, and he thankfully did seem to be feeling all right, not shocked or woozy. Charlotte opened the back of her banged-up SUV and they worked together to get the kid situated inside and lying on a blanket with his feet propped up on the side beneath the window before Trent grabbed his medical bag.

"What do you need me to do first?" Charlotte asked.

"Did you bring any fresh water I can wash it out with? And are all the towels sandy, or do we have a clean one?" he asked.

"I brought extra towels. And I have water."

"Good." He turned to Murvee. "Let me see if the bleeding has stopped." The young man lifted away the shirt; the bleeding had, thankfully, lessened. Trent got everything set up as best he could in the cramped space, putting his flashlight, gauze, Betadine, local anesthetic and suture kit next to the young man. Squeezing out some of the sanitizer he always kept in his bag, he thoroughly rubbed it over his hands and between his fingers then snapped on gloves.

"Here's the water and towels." Charlotte came to stand next to him, knees resting against the bumper of the car. "What else can I do?"

He looked at her, standing there completely calm, and marveled again that she took on any task thrown at her calmly and efficiently. Including dealing with a bleeding gash that would look so awful to most non-medical professionals, it might make them feel a little faint, or at least turn away so they wouldn't have to look at it.

"You want to wash out the wound to make sure it's good and clean before I suture it? Put the folded towel under his head. After I inject the lidocaine, I want you to pour a steady stream of the water through the wound." He drew the anesthetic into the syringe. "You still doing all right, Murvee? I'm going to give you some numbing medicine. I have to use a needle, and it'll burn a little, but you won't feel the stitches."

Murvee held his breath and winced a few times as he

injected it. "Sorry. I know this hurts, but pretty soon it will feel numb."

"I don't care, doc. I'm very grateful to you for helping me."

"I'm glad we were here today." He'd felt that way on many occasions in his life, since this kind of thing seemed to happen fairly often when he was working in the field, or even like today when he was touring and relaxing. Which was why he'd become convinced that whatever higher power was out there truly had a hand in the workings of the universe.

"Am I doing this right?" Charlotte asked as she continued washing out the wound.

"Perfect." He studied it, satisfied that it looked pretty clean now. "I think we're good to go. Thanks." He squeezed a stream of antiseptic on gauze then brushed it along the wound's edges.

Trent saw Charlotte reach for the young man's hand and give it a squeeze. "Tell me about surfing, Murvee. How long have you been doing it?"

"Me and my friends surf for a year now. A guy from the UK was surfing here a while ago and he was really good. He showed some people how to surf, and now many of us do. I want to get good enough to compete in the Liberian Surfing Championships, which has been around about five years now, I think."

Trent glanced at Charlotte again as he got the suture materials together, smiling at the warm and interested expression on her face. He loved the many facets to her personality: the feisty fireball, the take-charge director, the soft and sexy woman whose love-making he knew would stay in his memory a long, long time and the person he was seeing now. She was nurturing and caring for this young man, distracting him with casual chit-chat so Murvee wouldn't think too hard about the time-consuming procedure Trent was about to do on him.

He nodded at his small but powerful flashlight and looked at Charlotte. "Will you shine that on the wound so I can see better?" They were parked within the trees and, while it was far from optimal conditions for suturing, the flashlight illuminated well enough.

She pointed the light at the wound. "Does that help?"

"Yes, great," he said as he began suturing. It was deep and would require a three-layer closure. The boy was lucky a medic was here today. While the injury would likely have healed eventually on its own, his scars would have been bold and obvious, not to mention there was a good chance the wound would have become infected, maybe seriously.

"You should see the way your head looks, Murvee. You want to check it out in a mirror, so you can watch what Dr. Trent has to do to repair that nasty gash?"

"I don't know about that, Charlotte." Trent frowned at her in surprise. Trust a non-medical assistant to come up with a wacky idea like that, though it was probably because, if she'd had a wound that required suturing, Ms. Toughness would have wanted to watch.

"I would like to see," Murvee said. "I want to tell my friends what you had to do, what it looked like."

"So long as you don't faint on me." He smiled at the young man, who gave him a nice smile in return that seemed pretty normal and not particularly anxious.

Charlotte held up a small mirror in a powder compact and Murvee took it from her, moving his head around so he could see himself.

"Please hold still, Murvee." When this was over, he was going to give Charlotte a few pointers on doctor-assisting. She'd done a great job helping the boy relax, but this wasn't helping *him*, though he had to appreciate the ingenuity in her distraction techniques. If the boy didn't get queasy, that was.

"What exactly you doing?" Murvee asked as he looked at Trent suturing his wound in the mirror, seeming fascinated, thankfully, instead of disturbed.

Since the kid asked, he figured he might as well give him the full details. "Your wound was so deep I could see some of your skull bone."

Murvee's eyes widened. "No kidding?"

"No kidding. I repaired the galea first—that's the layer that covers the bone. Now I'm sewing up the layer under the skin—we call it the subcutaneous tissue, or 'sub-Q.' You've got some very healthy sub-Q."

"Yeah, man. Fine sub-Q." He grinned, obviously proud, and Trent and Charlotte both laughed. "That's crazy-looking," Murvee said, staring into the mirror.

"The whole human body is kind of crazy-looking. One of the cool things about being a doctor is learning about how crazy it really is. And amazing."

Murvee looked at him then and Trent was glad the boy finally lowered the mirror. "Is my head going to look like this always, doc?"

"Not always." He gave Charlotte a look that she interpreted correctly, thank goodness, since she took the mirror from Murvee and tucked it into her purse. "After I finish, you'll look a little like Frankenstein, and your friends will be jealous of how cool and tough you look." He smiled, knowing from experience that boys and young men related to that and were usually amused. "But by sewing it in three steps using very tiny stitches it will heal well and, over time, the scar will become a thin line. You'll be as handsome as ever and all the girls will think you're great."

Murvee grinned at Trent's commentary, as he'd expected. "Girls think I'm great already."

The sound of Charlotte's little laugh brought their attention back to her. "I bet they do," she said. "And now you can talk to them about how you were hit by your board while you were surfing, which not many guys around here do, and ended up getting stitched up on the beach by a world-class surgeon."

"World-class?" Trent smiled, wondering if she'd really meant that, or if she was just talking to keep Murvee relaxed as he worked. Wondering why it felt nice for her to say it, when he'd always been sure he didn't need anyone's admiration or accolades.

"Are you kidding me?" Her green eyes met his and held, a brief moment of connection that warmed him in a totally different way than she'd warmed him in the water. "You're amazing. With technique like yours, you could be working as a plastic surgeon in Beverly Hills."

"Which would be your idea of having really made it, right?" Concentrating on suturing Murvee, disappointment jabbed at him that she apparently felt that way. He'd been there and done the Beverly Hills-type vanity plastic surgery and rejected it for a reason. A reason nobody understood or cared about.

"Is that a real question?" Charlotte asked, her expression one of annoyed disbelief. "If my idea of 'making it' was a Beverly Hills lifestyle, I'd have set my sights on a big hospital in the States after I got my degrees or gone to work on Wall Street. Not come to Liberia."

He looked back up at her. He should have realized her comment had just been intended as a light-hearted compliment. She was as far from a New York City or Beverly Hills socialite as a woman could be. "I know you haven't exactly chosen glamour over substance here. Except those pretty, polished toenails of yours could be considered pretty glamorous."

"Does that mean you like them? I changed the color last night." She smiled as their eyes met again and lingered.

"Yeah. I like them." He looked back down and continued the detailed suturing of Murvee's wound, trying to focus on only his work and not her lethal combo of femininity and toughness.

"Do you mind if I take a photograph of your injury, Murvee?" Charlotte asked.

When he agreed, she snapped a number of pictures and Trent wondered what she planned to use them for. Probably to put in a portfolio of the plastic surgery wing. Except it wasn't open yet.

Trent gave the young man some antibiotic tablets and instructions on how to take care of the wound.

"I know the hospital's a long way off. Any way you can get there in a week? I probably won't be there anymore, but there are several great techs who can remove your stitches. I'd also like you to have a tetanus shot."

"My family has a scooter, so I can come. Thank you again for everything." He pumped Trent's hand then reached for Charlotte's too, a smile so wide on his face you'd never have known the injury he'd just suffered if you hadn't seen the bandage on his head.

"You're very welcome. Like I said, I'm glad we were here today."

The young man headed back down the beach. Charlotte looked at Trent and the expression in her eyes made his breath hitch. He reached for her hand. "Ready, Miss Edwards?"

"Yes. I'm ready to head back."

He was pretty sure she knew that heading back to the compound wasn't what he'd been asking.

CHAPTER THIRTEEN

DARKNESS HAD NEARLY enfolded the hospital compound as Charlie pulled the car up to her house. When she'd dropped Trent off at his quarters, the look he'd given her before he'd walked away was sizzling enough practically to set her hair on fire.

Both excited and nervous, her insides felt all twisted around, thinking about her subterfuge with his release papers, the new doctor and all the things she was trying to manipulate. But all that worry wasn't quite enough to douse cold water on her plans. To keep her from wanting to relive, one more time, the passionate thrill of the night they'd spent locked in one another's arms the previous week.

Still sitting in her car with the engine off, she stared at a small impediment to that plan, all too clearly apparent in the lights that were currently burning in her house. Her dad was staying with her and wasn't leaving for another day or two.

Which meant that her house as a rendezvous for Trent and her to make love all night was out. Her mind spun with ideas of where else they might meet, though it couldn't be from now into the morning. The various possibilities, and the memories of their past love-making, had her ready to leap out of the car to run and pound on the man's door, despite the fact that she'd dropped him off only minutes ago.

Had she suddenly become a sex maniac? The thought made her laugh at herself, at the same time her anticipation ratcheted higher. For whatever reason, the secretiveness added a certain allure; why that was, she didn't know. But she wasn't going to fight the excitement she felt, because she knew she'd only get to enjoy it one more time.

The real question was, should she go inside and have dinner with her dad, take a shower to wash off the beach then find an excuse to leave again? Or just not come back until later? Her dad had encouraged her to take time off today, after all. Maybe he'd just assume they'd made a long day of it in Robertsport.

Except he'd know that wasn't true, because Patience had been with them and would be ready for bed very soon.

She shook her head at her ambivalence, reminding herself that she was twenty-seven years old and a grown woman. Her father wasn't naive or judgmental. Shoving open the car door, she decided she'd just go in and say hello, then tell him she had dinner plans with Trent; never mind that there couldn't be a candlelit dinner in a restaurant, just leftovers in the hospital kitchen.

The sound of her father's favorite jazz music met her as she opened the front door. He sat in one of the upholstered chairs she'd bought when she'd moved here, since little of the original furniture had survived the pillaging during the wars. The hospital files were open on his lap and he looked up with a smile as she entered the room.

"Did my girl get in the water today?"

"I did. I even rode a wave all the way in to shore. How about that?"

He clapped his hands. "Bravo! I'm proud of you. And not just for swimming today. For all you've done here." He gestured to the files. "I'm so impressed with what you've accomplished with the funding you have. You're making huge headway, especially considering the shambles you were left to work with."

"Thanks, Dad. That means a lot to me." When her parents had trusted her to bring the hospital and school back to life, it had been scary and admittedly daunting. But, with John Adams's help, they'd done a lot. And she had to admit she felt pretty proud of what they'd accomplished too.

"I know the plastic surgery wing is important to you, and of course I understand why." His expression was filled with both sympathy and pain. "You had to deal with a lot as a little girl."

"Things happen for a reason, Dad. You know that as well as anyone. I hope that experiencing what it feels like to look abnormal will end up helping people who have to deal with things a whole lot worse than my childhood embarrassment."

"I do know. And I'm excited about your project. But I have to ask some hard questions now, not as a father, but as a businessman. And this has to be treated like a business."

Uh-oh. She gulped, afraid she knew what was coming next. "What are your hard questions?"

"What happens if, by some stroke of bad luck, the Gilchrist Foundation money doesn't come through? Do you have a backup plan?"

She closed her eyes for a moment, wondering how she should answer. Should she tell him she'd known all along that it was a risk? That maybe it was a risk she shouldn't have taken? She forced herself to open her eyes and tell him the truth. "Honestly? No. I don't. If the foundation money doesn't come through, we're in serious trouble. I'm trying to solicit other sources of income, but none of it is for sure until we have it in our hands."

He nodded. "All right. So when will you know about the foundation money?"

"Soon. They're sending their rep here in the next few days to see if we meet their requirements."

"And I see that you've met all those requirements except for one: a plastic surgeon on site."

"I *do* have a plastic surgeon on site—Trent. I just need for him to stay until their representative gives us the green light. Then we'll have the Gilchrist check and it'll all be good."

He looked at her steadily. "Except that something tells me Trent doesn't know about all this."

For once, she wished her dad wasn't so darned intuitive. "No. He doesn't. I don't see any reason for him to know."

"Why not? Seems to me he's an important part of the equation."

"Only for a short time. He performed a brilliant plastic surgery on a boy here in the hospital and another today on the beach that I can show pictures of." She sucked in a fortifying breath so she could continue. "He doesn't want to be involved, Dad. For some reason, he doesn't want to perform plastic surgeries. But I'm still hoping he'll agree to help a few patients with serious problems before he leaves."

"He seems like a good man. You should tell him the truth."

The truth? Her dad didn't know about the lies she'd told and her stomach twisted around when she thought about what his reaction would be if he did. If he'd still be as proud of her as he said he was. "I'm handling it, Dad. It will turn out okay; we'll get the funding." And she prayed that would really happen and every problem would be solved.

"I hope you're right. Now, there's something else we need to talk about, Charlie." Her father threaded his fingers together in his lap and looked at her. "Your goals are worthy goals. Your hard work is to be commended. But have you ever asked yourself if there's more you need to consider?"

"Such as?"

"Your own life." He stood and placed his hands on her shoulders. "Have you thought about exploring a relationship with a man who lives here? Or one of the single doctors coming through? Trent has impressed me, and I've met Perry Cantwell—who's coming soon, I think you said. He's nice enough, and good-looking to boot. I know it's damned difficult to meet someone when you live and work where there aren't too many folks around. I don't want to see you give everything of yourself for this place until there's nothing left of you to share with anyone else. I've seen it happen and I don't want it to happen to you."

"It won't. I promise. I just need to get that wing open and the place running smoothly then I'll think of other things besides work. I will."

And that was the truth. Even in the midst of this serious conversation with her dad, and all the stress over the hospital's finances, thoughts of Trent were foremost in her mind, thoughts of meeting with him and finishing what they'd started this afternoon. All those thoughts sent her breathing haywire and her pulse skipping and she just wanted to end this conversation and be with him.

"In fact, Dad, Trent and I are going to have a late dinner over in the hospital. Are you okay here eating leftovers on your own?"

His serious and worried expression gave way to a big smile. "Of course. Leftovers are my favorite."

"Good." She kissed his cheek then gave him a fierce hug. She wouldn't tell her dad that the thought of giving up her freedom forever, her ability to live as she wanted and do as she wanted and run the hospital as she wanted, sent a cold chill down her spine. Or that one more wonderful night with Trent just might be enough to satisfy her relationship needs for a long, long time. "Thanks for the advice, Dad."

"Okay." He hugged her back just as fiercely. "Go on, now."

The night air embraced Charlie with a close, sultry warmth as she walked toward the hospital quarters. A huge gibbous moon hung in the sky, casting a glow of white light across the earth. Her feet moved in slow, measured steps, her dad's words echoing in her head.

Could there possibly ever be anything between her and Trent other than physical pleasure and friendship, a friendship based on both of their experiences working in developing nations and an appreciation of the tremendous need there?

No. She shook her head in fervent denial. What the two of them had experienced during their one night together was what anyone would feel after being focused on only work for months and months. What Trent no doubt felt for all the various women in his life, which if rumor was to be believed were many. He was famous in the GPC community for enjoying short and no doubt very sweet interludes until he moved on to his next job.

She could deal with that. After all, hadn't she known it from the start? Enjoying one more night of fantastic sex with a special man would be wonderful, just as it had been last week, without thoughts of tomorrows and futures and what any of it might mean.

The employee quarters loomed gray in the darkness, its roof lit by moonlight, and her steps faltered, along with her confidence. He'd said he wanted to be with her just one more time, hadn't he? She could only hope, now that they were on dry land and no longer only half-dressed, a knock on his door wouldn't bring the cool Trent who sometimes appeared. The one who had shown very clearly how little he wanted to be stuck with her in this little, forgotten place in Liberia.

A shadowy figure suddenly became visible in front of her and she nearly let out a small shriek at the apparition.

"Charlotte? Is that you?"

"Yes." She exhaled at the sound of Trent's low voice, blaming the surprise of his sudden appearance for her weak and breathy reply. "I was…coming to see if you wanted to find some dinner in the kitchen."

"Now there's a surprise—you being hungry again. Let's see what we can do about that." Through the darkness, she saw the gleam of his eyes for what seemed like barely a second before he moved fast and was there, right in front of her, his arms wrapping around her, pulling her close. Before she could barely blink, he was kissing her.

And kissing her. His mouth possessed hers in a thorough exploration that stole her breath. Not rushed, but intense and deep, giving and taking, completely different from his teasing, playful kisses of before. Every hard inch of him seemed to be touching her at once, his chest pressing against her breasts, his thighs to her hips, his taut arms against her back.

A small moan sounded in her throat as his mouth devoured hers. She wanted this: wanted this sensory explosion; wanted his kisses and touch and the heat that crawled and burned across her skin.

His mouth left hers, softly touching her eyelids, her nose, her lips, stealing her breath. "You taste so good to me, Charlotte. Way better than any food, though I have a feeling that the more I taste you, the hungrier I'm going to get."

"Me too. Food is overrated." He tasted so delicious, so wonderful, so right. His lips and tongue returned to her mouth with an expertise that dazzled, so mind-blowing that her skin tingled, her knees got wobbly and, if he hadn't been holding her so tightly, they might have simply crumpled beneath her.

She flattened her palms against the firm contours of his chest, up to his thick, dark hair that was getting a little long, and the feel of its softness within her fingers was as sensual as the feel of his body pressed to hers.

The little moan she heard this time came from him, and he pulled his mouth from hers, his heartbeat heavy against her breasts. "Charlotte." His hands roamed across her back and down to her bottom, pulling her so close that his erection pressing against her stomach nearly hurt. "Do you have any idea how hard it's been for me to keep my distance this week? Not to come into your office and lock the door and make love to you right on top of your desk?"

She might have had some idea, since the thought of knocking on the door of his quarters had crossed her mind more than once when she'd been sitting alone in her house, lying alone in her bed. "On top of my desk? It's a little small, don't you think?"

"Probably." She could see the adorable, perpetual gleam of humor behind the sexual glint in his eyes. "And the examination table is too narrow. My bed is small, too, and pretty squeaky at that. Which leaves us with finding a soft place on the ground beneath the stars tonight."

"I hope you're not thinking of making love in the mud. That sounds a little….messy."

He kissed her again, his hands moving to her waist, up her ribs, stopping for a breathless moment just beneath her breasts before moving up to cup them both. They tightened and swelled within his palms, and she wanted to be done with the talking and drag him to the ground.

"I have the place already picked out, with a thick blanket already unfolded on the ground. After I make love to you, we'll take a shower together." His lips moved to her ear, his voice a hot whisper that sent shivers skating across her flesh. "I want to taste the sea on you, lick the salt from your skin. Wash every inch of you and start all over again."

Her heart pounded so hard in her ears, she thought he just might be able to feel the vibration on his tongue as he traced it over the shell of her ear. Her breath was coming in short gasps, and she was burning up inside, wanting him more than she'd ever wanted anything in her life.

"What about dinner?" Goodness, she could barely talk. "You must be hungry."

"For you. Most definitely hungry for you." The expression in his eyes told her he wanted her every bit as much as she wanted him, and she loved that she could make him feel that way. "But I know about that stomach of yours. I have a picnic dinner all ready in my room. For later."

She managed a small laugh. "How did you find time to do all that?"

"I had powerful motivation to move fast." His lips touched one corner of her mouth, then the other, and she found herself chasing after them for a real kiss.

"So where is this blanket? If we don't go there soon, my knees will be too weak to walk."

"Not a problem." He released her and quickly swung her into his arms. A squeak of surprise left her lips and he pressed his mouth to hers as he strode through the darkness. "Quiet." His eyes, now dark, glittered with both passion and amusement. "You want somebody in the hospital quarters to investigate a possible murder? Or your dad?"

"No. Though you are about killing me here." She wrapped her arms around his neck and pressed her mouth to his throat. "How far do we have to go?"

"Are you talking about where the blanket is? It's close." His eyes, glinting, met hers. "But if you're talking about something else, the answer is, as far as we possibly can."

His words made her laugh at the same time as a wave

of hot need enveloped her. A need to experience another unforgettable night as exhilarating as the one they'd shared before.

He carried her deeper into the palm forest then stopped. She glimpsed the blanket lying open on the ground before he released her, letting her body slowly slide down his until she stood teetering slightly on her own feet, her dress bunched up to her hips where he still held on to her.

The dress bunched higher, slipping up her torso as he tunneled his hands beneath it until it was up and off of her. Until she stood in only her white bra and panties, and the misty touch of the moonlight made them seem to glow in the darkness. He looked at her, and even through the low light she could see the heat in his gaze, the tautness of his jaw, and her body throbbed for him.

"Do you have any idea how beautiful you are?" His voice was low, rough, and he lifted one hand to trace his finger along the lacy edge of her bra. "The very first moment I saw you in your office, I wanted to know what you looked like naked. And when you gave me that gift, it was more amazing than I could ever have dreamed."

He lowered his mouth to hers, one hand closing over her breast. The other cupped her waist then deliciously stroked along her ribs and down over her bottom covered in only her thin panties. She gasped at the pleasure of it. How had she managed to keep him at arm's length for the past few days? And, as his touch caressed her, thrilled her, she wondered why she had.

She broke the kiss to fumble with the buttons on his shirt, wanting to feel his skin too. Wanting to run her fingers across the hardness of his muscles, the surprising silkiness of his skin, the soft, dark hair covering it. "You know what I thought was the sexiest thing about you when we first met?" she asked.

"My amazing intelligence?" The teasing look was back

in his eyes, along with a sexual gleam that intensified the ache between her legs.

"Your hands. Those long surgeon's fingers of yours. I just had a feeling they were very, very talented. Little did I know exactly how talented, with your plastics skills and magic skills and piano skills."

"And other skills." His lips curved and with a quick, deft movement, he flicked open her bra and slid it from her arms. "I'm looking forward to showing you some you haven't seen yet."

She wished her fingers were as magical as his as she struggled to get the last of the annoying buttons undone. Finally, finally, she was able to shove his shirt from his shoulders to see his muscled chest. She flattened her hands against it, loving the feel of it, thrilling in the quick, hard beat of his heart against her palms. "Oh, yeah? Like what?"

"Showing is always better than telling." He shucked his pants and underwear until he stood fully naked, the moonlight illuminating the broadness of his shoulders, his lean hips, his strong thighs and the powerful arousal between them.

"Hmm. Is this what you wanted to show me?" Desire for him nearly buckled her knees and she decided to take matters into her own hands, so to speak. She reached for him as she kissed him, stroking him, teasing him, and she felt him respond with a deep shudder. A low groan sounded in his throat. His hands tightened on her back and his fingers dug into her bottom until it nearly hurt.

"Not exactly. Oh, Charlotte." There was a ragged hitch to the way he said her name, and in the next breath he practically pushed her down onto the blanket, kissing her, covering her body with his heavy warmth that felt impossibly familiar, considering how short their time had been together the week before.

His fingers teased her nipples, glided slowly down,

over her ribs, her belly, then lower. They slipped slowly, gently in and around the moist and slick juncture between her thighs; the sensation was most definitely magical. She couldn't control the movement of her hips as they reached for his talented fingers, sought more of the erotic sensation he gave her.

She needed more. Needed all of him. "Now, please, Trent. I want you now."

"If I could say no, not yet, I would. But, damn it, I can't wait any longer to be inside of you." Propped onto his elbows, he stared down at her. The intensity in his blue eyes held hers, mesmerized, as she opened for him, welcomed him. And, when he joined with her, it felt so wonderful, so familiar and yet so new all at the same time.

Rhythmically, they moved together, faster and deeper, until the earth seemed a part of them and the night stars seemed to burst into an explosion of light. And as she gave herself over to the pleasure of being in his arms, to the ecstasy of being at one with him, she cried out. He covered her mouth with his, swallowing the sounds of both of them falling.

For a long while, they lay there together as they caught their breath and their heart rates slowed. His face was buried in her neck. His weight felt wonderful pressing her into the soft earth, and she made a little sound of protest as he eventually rolled off her, keeping her hand entwined with his.

Still floating in other-worldly sensation, the sound of his laughter surprised her. She turned her head to look at him. "What's so funny?"

"Looks like we managed to lose the blanket." Despite the darkness, his eyes met hers, his teeth gleaming white as he grinned. "I guess we made love in the mud after all."

She looked down and realized that they were, indeed, squished down into the mud; how they hadn't noticed that, she couldn't imagine. Actually, she could. Her mind slipped back to how wonderful it had been to be with him again, and just thinking about it made her feel like rolling her muddy body on top of him.

So she did, and he laughed again as she smeared a handful of mud on his chest and stomach then wriggled and squished against him. "I think I like it. Don't people pay good money for mud baths?"

"They do. I'm pretty sure pigs like mud too."

"Are you calling me a pig?"

He gave her a lazy, relaxed smile as he stroked more cool mud over and across her bottom, which felt so absurdly, deliciously sensual she couldn't help wriggling against him a little more. "I've been around enough women in my life to never, ever say anything that stupid."

The thought of all the women he'd had in his life shouldn't have had the power to bring the pleasure of the moment down, but somehow it did. Which was silly, since she knew the score, didn't she?

Something of her thoughts must have shown in her expression, because he wiped his muddy hand on the blanket then stroked her hair back from her face, all traces of amusement gone. "I have been to a lot of places and known a lot of people." He tucked her hair behind the ear her plastic surgeon had created for her then traced it softly, tenderly, with his finger. "But you're special. I've never met anyone who is such an incredible combination of sexiness, compassion and take-no-prisoners toughness. You amaze me. Truly."

"Thank you." Her heart swelled at his sweet words and she used her one not-muddy hand to cup his cheek as she leaned down to give him a soft kiss. "You amaze me too. Truly."

"And I can tell you that, if I was going to fund a school or a hospital anywhere, I'd trust you to run it." Through the moonlit darkness, his eyes stared into hers with a deep sincerity. "I'd trust you with anything."

Damn. His words painfully clutched at her heart and twisted her stomach, making her feel slightly sick. He'd trust her with anything?

She could only hope and pray he never found out exactly how misplaced that trust really was.

CHAPTER FOURTEEN

THE DELICIOUS PICNIC Trent had put together for them, complete with a bottle of wine he said he'd tucked in his bag for the right moment, was the most intimate and lovely meal Charlie had experienced in her life. It didn't matter that they'd both been curled up on his skinny bed, towels wrapped around and beneath their muddy bodies, and that the wine "glasses" had been plastic cups.

After they'd eaten, the pleasure of the shower they'd shared—laughing as they'd washed the mud off their bodies, then no longer laughing as they enjoyed making love again within the erratic spray of water—wasn't quite enough to make Charlie completely forget his words. To forget his misplaced trust in her. To remember her conviction that the end was worth the means.

She'd hardly slept after she'd crept into her house and fallen into her bed, tired, wired and worried. And still she ended up back at her desk as the sun rose. She stayed closeted in her office much of the day, contacting every potential donor, digging everywhere she could to possibly find some cash commitments in case the Gilchrist donation fell through.

Thankfully, the hospital and clinic had been busy too so she and Trent hadn't seen one another except when he'd passed by her accidentally left-open door, giving her a sexy, knowing smile and a wink.

Deep in thought, a knock on the now closed door startled her. "Come in." She readied herself to see a tall, hunky doctor with amused blue eyes, but relaxed when her dad appeared.

"Hi, honey. Have a second?"

"Of course."

He settled himself in the only other chair in her tiny office. "I've decided to head on home tonight, instead of waiting until tomorrow. Your mom called to say a church group has sent a few members to study our school, and I'd like to be there to talk with them when they get there."

"I understand, Dad. I'm planning to come see you and Mom soon for a few days anyway, as soon as…things are settled here." No point in starting up another conversation about the hospital funding and potential problems there. She stood and rounded the desk, leaning down to kiss his cheek. "But you should wait until tomorrow morning. Why in the world would you drive at night on these roads if you don't have to?"

"I'm stopping on the way. Do you remember Emmanuel and Marie? I'm going to visit them and check out their school, which is just across the border in the Ivory Coast. I'm staying there a day, then heading home." He threaded his fingers together like he always did when he had something serious to say, and she braced herself. "Will you remember what I said about not giving everything to this place? About being open to the possibilities that may come along in your personal life? Think about giving Perry Cantwell a fair shot."

"Does Charlotte have a personal life with Perry Cantwell?"

She swung around and stared at Trent leaning casually against the doorjamb, a smile on his face. But his eyes were anything but amused. They looked slightly hard and deadly serious.

A nervous laugh bubbled from her throat. The man was leaving in a matter of days. Surely he wasn't jealous of some possible future relationship with his replacement? "I've never even met Perry Cantwell. But seems to me you've been anxious for him to get here so you could leave. Maybe I'm anxious for him to get here, too."

It wasn't nice to goad him like that after what they'd shared together last night and she knew it. But her emotions were all over the place when it came to Trent: needing him to stay until the Gilchrist rep came; wanting him to stay because she'd grown closer to him than was wise, closer than she should have allowed. This looming goodbye was going to be so much harder than the first one, as she'd worried all along it would be. And added to that was the fear that he'd somehow find out about her machinations, destroying the trust, the faith, he said he had in her.

Which shouldn't really have mattered, since he'd be out of her life all too soon. But somehow it mattered anyway. A lot.

His posture against the doorjamb relaxed a little, as did the cool seriousness in his eyes. His lips curved as he shook his head, but that usual twinkle in his eyes was still missing. "Perry's a good surgeon, but I hear he cheats at golf. Talks down to nurses. Sometimes dates men. Not a good fit for you, Charlotte."

"I'm pretty sure you're making all that up." She stepped back to her desk and rested her rear end against it. "Dad's right that I need to keep all possibilities open—except maybe not men who date men."

Her dad chuckled, which reminded her he was there. "I've got to get going before it gets any later. Will you stay with Charlie tonight, Trent? I know we haven't had any sign of burglars since before I got here, but I'd feel better if we gave it a few more nights."

"Dad, I don't—"

"Of course I will. You didn't have to ask; I would've been there, anyway."

The smoldering look he gave her both aroused and embarrassed her, and she hoped her father didn't see it, along with the blush she could feel filling her cheeks. Though she had a feeling her dad wouldn't exactly be surprised to know that she and Trent were a little more than just acquaintances and colleagues.

Her father stood. The small smile on his face told her he'd seen Trent's look and was more than aware of the sizzle between them. She blushed all over again. "I need to grab my files before I go." He looked at the various piles on her desk and frowned, lifting up one or two. "I thought they were right here. Did you move them?"

"I put them—" Oh no; he had his hands on the pile she'd shoved Trent's release papers into, practically right in front of the man! Why, oh why hadn't she buried them deep in a drawer? She hastily reached to grab them. "Don't mess with that pile, Dad. Yours are—"

And because she was so nervous and moving too fast, and karma was probably getting back at her, the middle of the pile slid out and thunked on the floor, with some of the papers fluttering around Trent's feet.

He reached down to gather the mess and she feared she just might hyperventilate. Snatching them up and acting even stranger than she was already would just raise suspicion, so she forced herself to quickly but calming retrieve and stack the files. Until her heart ground to a stop when she saw Trent had a paper in his hand and was reading it with a frown. She couldn't think of anything else that would make him look so perplexed.

"When did this come?" His attention left the paper and focused on her. "This isn't my original release from the GPC. It's dated—" he looked down again "—three days ago. Why didn't you give me this? And why didn't they send it directly to me, like usual?"

She licked her dry lips. "Because Cantwell wasn't here yet, I guess. He was all scheduled to come, which is why they sent your papers, but then something went wrong, I don't know what." Except she did know. Colleen hadn't arranged for Cantwell's travel because a certain desperate, deceiving hospital director had lied and told her Trent had agreed to stay until the Gilchrist rep came.

The end justified the means, she tried to remind herself as she stared at the confusion on Trent's face. Except it was getting harder and harder to feel convinced of that.

"You still should have given them to me. Once the GPC releases me, my vacation is supposed to officially start. I need to find out when I'm expected in the Philippines now. That might have changed."

Her heart in her throat, she forced a smile. "I'm sorry if I messed this up. I'll call Colleen."

"Don't worry about it. I'll call."

His face relaxed into that charming smile of his, which somehow made the nervous twist in her stomach tighten even more painfully. The man really did like and trust her. Thank heavens the Gilchrist rep was due here any day, then this would all be over and he could be on his way.

And that thought made her stomach twist around and her chest ache in a whole different way.

"I've got my files here, Charlie. So I'm going to hit the road."

She turned to her dad, having nearly forgotten—again—that he was in the room. How was that possible since he stood only three feet from her? His expression was serious, speculative. Probably he, too, was wondering what was going on with her and why she'd buried Trent's papers deep within a pile.

"It's been nice to meet you, sir," Trent said, reaching

to shake her dad's hand. "And don't worry. I'll take care of your daughter until I leave here."

"Thank you. I appreciate it."

"I'm standing right here, remember?" Relieved to be back to a joking mood, Charlie waved her hands. "How many times do I have to tell you two? I don't need to be taken care of."

"We know." Her dad smiled, but his eyes still held a peculiar expression as he looked at her. "We just like to look after you. Is that so bad?"

She looked at Trent, horrified at the thought that filled her head. That she couldn't think of anything better than for him to stay here a full year, living with her and looking after her, the two of them looking after each other.

She could only imagine how appalled he'd be if he somehow read those thoughts in her face and she looked down at her desk as she changed the subject. "Can I help you get your things together, Dad? I'm about to head to the house anyway."

"Already done. My car's outside, ready to go." He pulled her into his arms for a hug. "We'll see you when you come visit next month."

"Can't wait to see both of you. Bye, Dad."

With a smile and a squeeze of Trent's hand, he disappeared, leaving the two of them alone in a room that now seemed no larger than a broom closet. She felt the heat of Trent's gaze on her, felt the electric zing from the top of her head to her toes, and slowly turned to look at him.

His hand reached out and swung the door closed, and that gesture, along with the look in his eyes as they met hers, made her heart beat hard at the same time as her stomach plunged.

She was crazy about this man. There was no getting around it, and she wanted so much to enjoy every last day, every last hour, every last minute she had with him. Surely he wouldn't find out about her lies? Maybe, even, he'd decide to stay longer on his own. It could happen, couldn't it?

She stepped forward at the same moment he did, their arms coming around one another, their lips fusing in a burning kiss that held a promise of tonight, at least, being one she'd never forget.

His warm palms slid slowly over her back, down her hips and back up, her body vibrating at his touch. The kiss deepened, his fingers pressed more urgently into her flesh and, when he broke the kiss, a little sound of protest left her tingling lips.

"You sure your desk is a little too small?" His eyes gleamed hotly, but still held that touch of humor she loved.

"Yes. We already had files all over the floor once tonight." The thought of why exactly that had happened took the pleasure of the moment down a notch, but she shook it off. She wasn't going to let anything ruin what could be one of her last nights with him. Reluctantly, she untangled herself from the warmth of his arms. "I'm going to head home. Join me for dinner about seven?"

"I'll be there." He leaned in once more, touched his lips to hers and held them there in a sweet and intimate connection that pinched her heart. "Don't be surprised if I'm even a little early."

She watched him leave, gripping the edge of her desk to hold herself upright, refusing to think about how, for the first time since she'd moved here, she would feel very lonely when he was gone.

The lowering sun cast shadows through the trees as Charlie approached her house, surprised to see Patience in front of the porch with little Lucky jumping around her feet.

"What are you doing here, Patience? Where's your dad?"

The little girl's smile faded into guilt. "Daddy was in

a long, long meeting with Miss Mariam and I got tired of waiting. I came to show you the new trick I taught Lucky."

Oh, dear. John Adams was not going to be happy about this. "You know you're not allowed to leave the school and come all the way down here by yourself."

"I know. But it's just for a little bit. So I can show you. Then will you take me home?"

Charlie sighed. The child had the art of cajoling and wheedling down to a science. So much for getting showered and primped up before Trent came for their big date-night. "Okay. But promise me you won't do this again. You're not big enough to be running around all by yourself."

"I promise." The words came out grudgingly, but when Lucky yapped her eyes brightened again. "So, look! Sit, Lucky. Sit!"

The little pup actually did and Patience gave her some morsel as a reward, beaming with triumph as the dog began yapping and dancing again. "See Miss Charlie? She's really smart!"

"She is." She clapped her hands in applause, smiling at how cute and excited the child was. "And you being a good dog trainer helps her be smart."

"I know. I—"

A long, low growl behind her made Charlotte freeze, every hair on her scalp standing up in an instinctive reaction to the terrifying sound. She swung around and, to her horror, a large, feral and very angry dog stood there, its own hackles rising high on its back.

CHAPTER FIFTEEN

"PATIENCE." THE HARD hammering of her heart in her chest and her breath coming in short gasps made it difficult to sound calm. But the last thing she needed was for Patience to panic and make the situation worse. "Move very, very slowly and pick up Lucky, then quietly go up the porch steps and into the house. Don't make any sudden movements."

The child didn't say a word, probably as terrified as Charlie felt. The dog's lips were curled back in a snarl, showing every sharp tooth in its foamy mouth, and its jaws snapped together as it stared right at her. She couldn't risk turning around to see if Patience had done as she'd asked, because if it attacked she had to be ready. And it looked like it was about to do exactly that.

She glanced around for some weapon she could use to bash the dog if she had to. A sturdy stick was lying about five feet away and she slowly, carefully, inch by inch, sidled in that direction, her heart leaping into her throat as the dog growled louder, drool dripping as it snapped its jaws at her again.

Damn, this was bad. The animal had to be rabid; there was no other explanation for its aggression. That thought brought a horrified realization that this was probably the animal that had attacked and killed Patience's other dog. It was unusual enough to see feral dogs here and she knew the likely reason this one was still around was because it was very, very sick.

The sound of her screen door closing was a relief, and she prayed that meant Patience was out of harm's way. Should she try to talk soothingly to the dog? Or yell and try to scare it? She didn't know, and the last thing she wanted to do was something that would trigger it to attack her.

Sweat prickled at every pore, and her breath came fast and shallow as she kept her slow progress toward the stick, never taking her eyes off the animal. She was close. So close now. But how to pick it up when she got there? A fast movement to grab it and swing hard if the dog lunged? Keep her actions slow and steady, so she could get the stick in her hand and maybe not have to use it at all if she could just get back to the porch and in the house?

With her heart beating so hard it was practically a roar in her ears, she leaned down slowly, slowly, keeping her movements tight and controlled as she closed her fingers around the stick.

In an instant, the dog leaped toward her, mouth open, fangs dripping, knocking her to the ground, its teeth sinking deep into the flesh of her arm as she held it up in futile defense.

A scream of panic, of primal terror, tore from her throat. She tried to swing the stick at the dog, screaming again, but her position on the ground left her without much power behind the blow, and she realized the animal's teeth were sinking even deeper.

Some instinct told her to freeze and not to try to pull her arm from the dog's mouth, that it would just hold on tighter, shake her and injure her even worse. Its eyes were less than a foot from hers, wild eyes filled with fury above the jaws clamped onto her arm. It was so strong, so vicious, and a terrible helplessness came over her as she frantically tried to think how she could get away without getting hurt even worse, or maybe even being killed.

A loud, piercing gunshot echoed in the air and a split-second later the dog's jaws released her, its body falling limply on top of hers. Unable to process exactly what had happened, she grabbed her bleeding arm and tried to squirm out from under the beast.

"Charlotte." Trent was there, right there, his foot heaving the lifeless dog off her, crouching down beside her. "Damn it, Charlotte. Let me see."

"Trent." Her voice came out as a croak. It was Trent. Trent carefully holding her arm within his cool hands, looking down at it. Trent who had saved her life.

Her head dropped to the ground and she closed her eyes, saying a deep prayer of thanks as she began to absorb everything. Began to realize that the danger was past.

"Charlotte. Look at me." His gentle hand stroked her hair from her forehead and cupped her jaw, his thumb rubbing across her cheekbone. "Let me see." He tugged at her wrist and she realized she was still clutching her arm. She loosened her grip, feeling the sticky wetness of her blood on her hand as she dropped it to the ground. "You feel faint?"

"Y…yes." Stars sparkled in front of her eyes as she stared at the jagged gashes. At the oozing blood.

"Hang in there with me, sweetheart." He looked only briefly at her wounds before he yanked his shirt open—a nice, white button-down shirt, she processed vaguely—and quickly took it off. He wrapped it around her arm and applied a gentle pressure then lifted her hand up and placed it where his had been. "Squeeze to help stop the bleeding. I'm getting you to the clinic."

She could barely do as he asked but she tried. The screen door slammed behind them and Charlie became aware of the sound of Patience crying.

"Mr. Trent! Is Miss Charlie okay?"

"She's okay, but I need to take care of her. You stay in the house and I'll call your dad to come get you."

"O…okay."

The door slammed again as Trent lifted Charlie into his arms and strode in the direction of the hospital. She let her head loll against his muscled, bare shoulder, at the same time thinking she shouldn't let him haul her all the way there. She might not be big, but she wasn't a featherweight either.

"It's too far for you to carry me. I can walk."

"Like hell. For once, will you let someone take care of you? Let yourself off the hook for being in charge of the world?"

"I don't…I don't think I do that. But I admit I'm feeling a little shaky."

He looked down at her, his blue eyes somehow blazingly angry and tender at the same time. "A little shaky? You were just mauled by a rabid dog. You've lost a lot of blood. It's okay for you to lean on me a little, just once."

"Yes, doctor."

He gave her a glimmer of a smile. "Now that's what I like to hear. Keep pressing on your arm," he said as they finally got to the hospital and he laid her on an exam table. He placed a pillow beneath her head then made a quick call to John Adams. She watched him pull the pistol from his waistband and place it on the counter, wash his hands, then move efficiently to various cupboards, stacking things on the metal table next to her.

"Thank you. I…don't want to think about what might have happened if you hadn't come when you did."

"I don't want to think about it either." His lips were pressed together in a grim line, his eyes stark as they met hers. "When I heard you scream, my heart about stopped."

"Why did you have a gun with you?"

"I work in plenty of unsafe places in the world, and always pack my thirty-eight. I had it with me because you left yours upstairs last time when you were supposed to be ready for a burglar, remember?"

She thought of how the dog had been right on top of her and shuddered. "How did you learn to shoot like that? Weren't you afraid you'd hit me instead?"

"No. Even though I was scared to death, I knew I'd hit the dog and not you." A tiny smile touched his lips as he placed items on the table. "I was on the trap and skeet shooting team at Yale. Rich boys get to have fun hobbies, and this one paid off."

Rich boys? She was about to ask, but he handed her a cup of water and several tablets. "What is this?"

"Penicillin. And a narcotic and fever-reducing combo. It'll help with the pain. I have to wash out your wounds, which is not going to feel good."

He lifted up her arm, placed a square plastic bowl beneath it and began to unwrap his poor white shirt from it, now soaked in blood. Those little stars danced in front of her eyes again and she looked away. "Tell me the truth. How bad is it?"

"Bad enough. I'll know more in a few minutes." His expression was grim. "Because that dog was obviously rabid, I have to inject immunoglobulin. I'm also going to inject lidocaine because—"

"I know, I know. So I won't feel every stitch. Do it quick, please, and get it over with."

He gave a short laugh, shaking his head. "You're something else." He pressed a kiss to her forehead, before his eyes met hers, all traces of amusement gone. "Ready? This is going to hurt like hell. Hang in there for me."

She nodded and steeled herself, ashamed that she cried out at the first injection. "Sorry," she said, biting her lip hard. "I'm being a baby."

"No, you're not. I've seen big tough guys cry at this. You're awesome. Just a little longer."

When it was finally over, she could tell he felt as relieved as she did. "That's my girl." He pressed another lingering kiss to her head. "This next part is going to hurt, too, but not nearly as bad as that."

He poured what seemed like gallons of saline over her arm. He was right; it did not feel good. She thought he'd finally finished until he grabbed and opened another bottle. "Geez, enough already! What could possibly still be in there?"

"Is there some reason you have to keep questioning the doctor?" His blue eyes crinkled at the corners. "With all the technology and great drugs we have, thoroughly washing wounds like this—any animal bite, but especially when the dog is rabid—is the best treatment there is. But this is the last jug, I promise."

"Thank goodness. I was about to accuse you of making it hurt as much as you possibly can."

"And here I'd been giving you credit for being the bravest patient ever." His smile faded and he gave her a gentle kiss, his eyes tender. "I'm really sorry it hurts. Good news is, it looks like there's no arterial damage and the bites didn't go all the way to the bone. I'm going to throw some absorbable stitches into the deep muscle tears to control the bleeding then get everything closed up."

Instead of watching him work on her arm, she looked at his face. At the way his brows knit as he worked. At the way his dark lashes fanned over the deep focus of his eyes. At the way he sometimes pursed his lips as he stitched. Almost of its own accord, her hand lifted to cup his jaw and he paused to look at her, his blue eyes serious before he turned his face to her palm, pressing a lingering kiss there.

"Are you going to use a bunch of tiny stitches so I don't have awful scars?"

"I can't this round, sweetheart." He shook his head. "This kind of wound has a high risk for infection. We have to get the skin closed with as few stitches as possible, because the more I put in the more chance of infection. After it's healed completely, though, I can repair it so it looks better."

Except he wouldn't be here then. Their eyes met as the thought obviously came to both of them at the same time.

"I mean, one of your plastic surgeons can when the new wing is opened." His voice was suddenly brusque instead of sweet and tender.

She nodded and looked down, silently watching him work, her heart squeezing a little. How had she let herself feel this close to him? So close she would miss him far too much when he was gone.

When it was all over and her arm was wrapped in Kerlix, taped and put in a sling, he expelled a deep breath. "How about we head to your house and get you settled and comfortable? I'll carry you."

"I really am okay to walk." She didn't trust herself not to reveal her thoughts and feelings if he carried her, folded against his chest. "I need to."

He looked at her a moment then sighed. "All right. So long as you let me hold you in case you get dizzy."

Trent held her close as they walked slowly toward the front porch of her house and she let herself lean against his strength. The dog's body was gone, thank goodness, though there were bloodstains in the dirt. John Adams must've taken care of it. She was glad she didn't have to look at it and remember its wild eyes; see again those teeth that had ripped her flesh and held her tight in their grip.

"I feel kind of bad for the dog," she said.

"You feel sorry for the dog?" He stared down at her, eyebrows raised.

"Rabies is a pretty horrible way to die, isn't it? You shooting it was the best way for it to go."

"Yeah. It's one hundred percent fatal after it's been contracted. It's a good thing we have the vaccine to keep you safe from the virus." He looked away, his voice rough when he spoke again. "After you get settled inside, I'll come out and rake up the dirt. Don't think you want to be looking at your own blood every time you come in and out of your house."

"No. I don't." She looked up him and marveled at his consideration. "Who knew you were Mister Thoughtful and not the full-of-yourself guy I was convinced you were?"

"I'm both thoughtful *and* full of myself—multi-faceted that way."

His eyes held a touch of their usual amusement and as she laughed her chest filled with some emotion she refused to examine.

CHAPTER SIXTEEN

TRENT KNEW THE narcotics would have worn off and Charlotte would be in pain again this morning. He'd slipped from the bed and gone downstairs to make toast and coffee for her, wanting something in her stomach before he gave her more fever medication, and the narcotic, too, if she needed it.

When he came back to her room with a tray, he had to pause inside the doorway just to look at her. Her lush hair tumbled across the pillow, the sun streaking through the windows highlighting its bronze glow. Her lips were parted, her shoulder exposed as one thin strap of her pretty nightgown had slid down her bandaged arm, leaving the gown gaping so low, one pink nipple was partly visible on her round breast.

He deeply inhaled, a tumble of emotions pummeling his heart as he stared at her. To his shock, the foremost emotion wasn't sexual.

It was a deep sense of belonging. Of belonging with her.

He wanted to stay here with her. He wanted to wake up in her bed, in her arms, every morning. He wanted to see her, just like this, at the start of each and every day.

Her eyelids flickered and she opened her eyes and looked at him. She smiled, and that smile seemed to reach right inside of him, pull him farther into the room. Pull him closer to her.

He managed to speak past the tightness in his chest. "Good morning, Charlotte." He set the tray on her nightstand and perched himself on the side of the bed. He stroked her hair from her face, wrapped a thick strand around his finger. "How's the arm feeling?"

"Not so great." She rolled onto her back, her lips twisting.

He ran his finger down her cheek. "I figured that. I brought you some toast and coffee and more meds."

"Thank you." Her good arm lifted to him and her palm stroked his cheek. He wished he'd shaved already, so the bristles wouldn't abrade her delicate skin when he kissed her. "But all I want is the fever stuff. I can't spend the day all doped up. I want to know exactly what's happening."

He nodded. "If you decide you need it later, you can always take it then. Why don't you sit up and have a little bit to eat first." He started to stand, but her hand grabbed the front of his shirt and bunched it up as she tugged him toward her.

"I am hungry again. But not for food—for you."

"Charlotte." He wanted, more than anything, to make love with her. But she was in pain and the need to take care of her, to keep her arm still so she wouldn't be in worse pain, took precedence over everything. "You need to rest."

"I've been resting all night. I slept very well, thanks to the drugs you gave me." She smiled at him and pulled harder on his shirt, bringing him closer still, and he could feel his resolve weakening at the way she looked at him. It was as though she was eating him up with her eyes and he knew he wanted to eat her up for real. "I do need to feel better. And you're very, very good at making me feel better."

"Well, I am a doctor. Took the Hippocratic Oath that I'd do the best I could to help my patients heal." He smiled, too, and gave up resisting. He gave in to the desire spiraling through his body. "What can I do first to make you feel better?"

"Kiss me."

Her tongue flicked across her lips and he leaned forward to taste them, carefully keeping his body from resting against her arm. It took every ounce of self-control to keep himself in check, to touch her and kiss her slowly, carefully.

"Does it make you feel better if I do this?" He gently drew her nightgown down and over her bandages, then lifted her arm carefully above her head to rest it on her pillow. He traced the tops of her breasts with his fingertips, slowly, inching across the soft mounds, until he pulled the lacy nightgown down to fully expose her breasts.

The sunlight skimmed across the pink tips and his breath clogged in his throat as he enjoyed the incredible beauty of them. Of her. He lowered his mouth to one nipple then rolled it beneath his tongue, drew it into his mouth and lifted his hand to cup the other breast in his palm.

"Yes," she murmured. The hand on her good arm rested on the back of his head, her fingers tangling in his hair. "I'm feeling better already."

"How about this?" His mouth replaced his hand on her other breast, his fingertips stroking along her collarbone, her armpit, down her ribs, and he reveled in the way she shivered in response.

"Yes. Good."

He slowly tugged her nightgown farther down her body, gently touching every inch he could with his mouth, his tongue, his hands. He could feel her flesh quiver, felt the heat pumping from her skin, and marveled at how excruciatingly pleasurable it was to take it this slow. To think only of making her feel good, to feel wonderful, to feel loved.

The shocking thought made him freeze and raise his head.

Loved? He didn't do love.

But as he looked down at her eyes, at the softness, heat and desire in their green depths, his heart squeezed at the same time it expanded.

He did love her. He loved everything about her. He loved her sweetness, her toughness and her stubbornness and was shocked all over again. Shocked that the realization didn't scare the crap out of him. Shocked that, instead, it filled him with wonder.

He lowered his mouth to hers, drinking in the taste of her, and for a long, exquisite moment there was only that simple connection. His lips to hers, hers to his, and through the kiss he felt their hearts and souls connecting as well.

He drew back, and saw the reflection of what he was feeling in her eyes. Humbled and awed, he smiled. "Still feeling good? Or do you need a little more doctoring?"

"More please." She returned his smile, which changed to a gasp when he slipped his hand beneath her nightgown, found her moist core and caressed it.

"We need to lose this gown. I want to see all of you. Touch and kiss all of you." He dragged the gown to her navel, her hipbones, his mouth and tongue following the trail along her skin. He wanted nothing more than this. He wanted to help her forget her pain. For her to feel only pleasure.

She lifted her bottom to help him pull it all the way off, and he took advantage of the arch of her hips, kissing her there, touching and licking the velvety folds until she was writhing beneath his mouth.

"Trent," she gasped. "You've proven how good you are at making me feel better. But I want more. Why are you still dressed? I don't think I can strip you with only one hand."

He looked at her and had to grin at the desire and frustration on her face. "You want me to strip? I'm at your command, boss lady." He quickly shucked his clothes and took one more moment to take in the beauty of her nakedness, before carefully positioning himself on top of her as she welcomed him.

With her eyes locked on his, he moved within her. Slowly. Carefully. She met him, moved beneath him, urged him on. The sounds of pleasure she made nearly undid him and he couldn't control the ever-faster pace. There was nothing more important in the world than this moment, this rhythm that was unique to just the two of them, joining as one. And, when she cried out, he lost himself in her.

Curled up with Trent's body warming her back, his arms holding her close, Charlie felt sated, basking in the magic of being with him; wanting to know more about him.

"Tell me about being a rich boy. That's what you said you are, isn't it?"

He didn't respond for a moment then a soft sigh tickled her ear. "Yes. My family is wealthy and I have a trust fund that earns more money each year than most people make in ten."

"And yet you work in mission hospitals all over the world. Why?"

"For the same reason you live and work here—to give medical care to those who wouldn't have any if we didn't."

She turned her head to try to look at his face. "When did you decide to live your life that way instead of working in some hospital in the States? Or being a plastic surgeon for the rich and famous?"

The laugh he gave didn't sound like there was much humor in it. "Funny you say that. My dad and grandfather have exactly that kind of practice. I was expected to follow in their footsteps, but realized I didn't want to. When I was about two-thirds of the way through my plastics residency, I knew I wanted to do a surgical fellowship in pediatric neurosurgery instead."

Wow. She'd known he had amazing skills, but he did brain surgery too? "Did you?"

"No. I couldn't get into a program. Was rejected by every one I applied to. Then found out why."

She waited for him to continue but he didn't. "So, why?"

He didn't speak for a long time. She was just about to turn in his arms, to look in his eyes and see what was going on with him, when he answered. His voice was grim. "My mother was hell-bent on me joining the family practice. I didn't realize how hell-bent until I found out she'd used her family name, wealth and the power behind all of that to keep me out of any neurosurgery program. All the while pretending she supported my decision, when in fact she was manipulating the outcome. So I left. Left the country to do mission work, and I haven't been back since."

Charlie's breath backed up in her lungs and her heart about stopped. His mother had deceived him and lied? He'd obviously been horribly hurt by it. So hurt that he'd cut his family from his life. So hurt that he'd left the U.S. and hadn't returned.

It also sounded horrifyingly similar to what she'd been doing to him, too.

Her stomach felt like a ball of lead was weighing it down. "I'm...sorry you had such a difficult time and that you were hurt by all that."

"Don't be. It's ancient history, and it was good I learned what kind of person she really is."

The lead ball grew heavier at his words, making her feel a little sick, and she couldn't think of a thing to say. He kissed her cheek, his lips lingering there, and a lump formed in her throat at the sweetness of the touch.

"I'm going to fix you some brunch. Something better than the toast you didn't eat." He nipped lightly at her chin, her lips. "And, just for you, I'm going to perform a surgery today that I think will make you happy. But I'm not telling until after it's done."

She squeezed his hand and tried to smile. "Can't wait to hear about it." She drew in a breath and shook off her fears. He wouldn't find out. It would be okay. They'd get the donation check, the new wing would open and, when all that was behind them…then what?

She knew, and her heart swelled in anticipation. She'd ask him to stay, and not for the hospital. She'd tell him she was crazy about him, that she wanted to see where their relationship could go. The thought scared her and thrilled her; she was not sure how risky that would be. How it would feel to share her life and her world with someone. But she knew, without question, it was a risk she had to take.

By the way he'd made love to her, looked at her, taken care of her, maybe he'd actually say yes.

CHAPTER SEVENTEEN

TRENT LEFT THE OR, feeling damned pleased at the way the cleft palate surgery had gone for the child. He knew Charlotte would be happy too and couldn't wait to tell her.

The satisfaction he felt made him realize he'd been too hasty believing the skills he had were superfluous and not a good way to help people, and children in particular, as he wanted to. Working in his family's cosmetic surgery practice hadn't been what he wanted. But Charlotte had helped him see that those skills really were valuable in helping people have better lives.

While he'd done plastics procedures at many of his other jobs, it had taken her dogged persistence to make him see how important those techniques could be to those without hope of improving their lives that way except through a hospital like this one.

Striding down the hall, he couldn't believe his eyes, seeing the woman who was on his mind. There she stood, talking to John Adams, like it had been a week instead of a day since her ordeal. Hadn't he specifically told her to stay home and rest?

"What possible excuse do you have for being here, Charlotte?"

"I got bored. There's too much to do to just sit around."

"You're not just sitting around." He wanted to shake the damn stubborn woman. "Resting helps your body heal.

Gives it a chance to fight infection. Which, in case you don't remember, is particularly important after a nasty dog bite." He turned to John Adams. "Can you talk sense into her?"

"Last time she listened to me was about six months ago or so," he replied, shaking his head.

Trent turned back to her, more than ready to get tough if he had to. "Don't make me drag you back there and tie you down."

She scowled then, apparently seeing that he was completely serious, gave a big, dramatic sigh. "Fine. I'll go rest some more. Though every hour feels like five. Can I at least take a few files with me to go over while I'm being quiet?"

The woman was unbelievable. "If you absolutely have to. But no moving around unnecessarily. No cooking dinner. I'll take care of that."

"Yes, Dr. Dalton."

He ignored the sarcastic tone. "That's what I want to hear from my model patient." He noted the blue shadows beneath her eyes, the slight tightness around her mouth that doubtless was from pain she was determined not to show, and couldn't help himself. He leaned down to give her a gentle kiss, not caring that John Adams was standing right there. "I just finished the cleft palate surgery I promised you I'd do. Now I want you to give me a promise in return— that you'll take care of yourself. For me, if not for yourself."

Her eyes softened at the same time they glowed with excitement. "You fixed the boy's cleft palate today? That's wonderful! Did you take pictures like I asked you to? I need pictures to— Well, I just think we should keep a record."

"All taken care of. Now for your promise."

"I promise." She sent him a smile so wide, it lit the room. "I'll see you at home."

At home. That had a nice sound to it. He found himself admiring her shapely legs beneath her skirt, watching the slight sway of her hips all the way down the hall and out the door, and when he turned he saw John Adams eyeing him speculatively.

"So, is something going on between you and Charlie? I thought you were leaving in just a day or two. Speaking of which, did you go over everything Thomas needs to know about her stitches and the rabies vaccine course?"

He looked back at the door Charlotte had disappeared out of, and realized if he left it would be just like that—she'd disappear from his life and he'd likely never see her again.

With absolute conviction that it was the right decision, he knew he wasn't going to leave. He had to be here to take care of her, to improve the scarring on her arm after she was healed, to see exactly what a year with her would be like.

He turned back to John Adams. "I'm staying."

The man smiled and clapped him on the shoulder. "Good to hear. Welcome to the family."

Trent changed out of his scrubs, cleaned up and called Mike Hardy before going to Charlotte's so he could tell her his decision. He could only hope she'd be as happy about him staying as he felt about it. Thinking of the way they'd made love just that morning, the look on her face and in her beautiful eyes as they'd moved together, he had a pretty powerful feeling that she would be.

"Mike? Trent Dalton. How are you?"

"Good, Trent. Great to hear from you. Are you enjoying your vacation in Italy?"

"No." Had the man forgotten about all the delays? "I'm still at the Edwards Hospital in Liberia."

"You're still in Liberia?" The man sounded astonished. "Why? Perry Cantwell went there last week, so you should be long gone by now."

"Perry was delayed, so I had to stay on until he could get here." How could Mike not know all this? "I've decided I want to stay here for the next year. I'd like you to find a replacement for me in the Philippines and draw up a new contract for me."

"Trent, we never have two doctors at the Edwards Hospital. We just can't afford it."

He frowned. Mike usually bent over backwards if he had a special request, which he rarely did. Trent was one of only a handful of GPC docs that worked for them full-time, year-round. "I don't need another doc here with me. I'm sure Perry wouldn't care if he's here or in the Philippines. Ask him."

There was a silence on the line, which made Trent start to feel a little fidgety, until Mike finally spoke again. "I just found your file to see what's going on. Your release papers were sent well over a week ago. And I know Perry was about on his way when I had Colleen send them, so I'm confused. This is all a real problem, messing up your pay and vacation time and next assignment. I need to talk to Colleen and find out how these mistakes happened before we have any more discussion about you staying there. I'll call you back."

"All right."

The conversation with Mike left him feeling vaguely disturbed, but he brushed it off. He couldn't imagine there would be a problem. It probably would just come down to shuffling paperwork.

Since he had no idea when Mike would call him back, he went on to Charlotte's house. If he didn't find her resting, he was going to threaten her with something—maybe refusing to kiss her or make love with her would be a strong enough incentive, he thought with a smile. He knew that if she threatened him with something similar he'd follow any and all instructions.

He let himself in the door. Seeing her curled up in the armchair, her hair falling in waves around her shoulders, her expression relaxed, filled his chest with a sense of belonging that he couldn't remember having felt since before he'd left the States. Since before the betrayal by his mother. A cozy, welcoming old home with a beautiful and more than special woman inside waiting for him was something he'd never thought he wanted until now.

He stood there a moment, knowing he was beyond blessed to have been sent to this place on what was supposed to have been a fill-in position for just a few days. Another example of the universe guiding his life in ways he could never have foreseen.

"Hey, beautiful." He leaned down to kiss the top of her head, his lips lingering in the softness of her hair. "Thank you for being good, sitting there reading. I'm proud of you."

Her hand cupped his cheek, her eyes smiled up at him, and that feeling in his chest grew bigger, fuller. "I decided I should do what you ask, since you did that cleft palate surgery today like you promised. Not to mention that whole saving my life thing." Her voice grew softer. "I'm so lucky to have you here."

He was the lucky one. "I want you to eat so you can take some more pain medicine before that arm starts to really hurt again. Let me see what's in the kitchen."

His cell rang while he was putting a quick dinner together and he was glad it was Mike Hardy. "What'd you find out?"

"You're not going to like it." Mike's voice was grim and

a sliver of unease slid down Trent's back. "Colleen's over here wringing her hands."

"Why?"

"She sent your release papers to the director of the hospital, instead of to you, because Charlotte Edwards asked her to. Apparently she's a good friend of Colleen's, and said she'd pass them on to you. Ms. Edwards also told her not to schedule Perry's travel yet because she claimed you'd agreed to stay on another two weeks.

"According to Colleen, the hospital has to have a plastic surgeon on site when the Gilchrist Foundation rep comes there in another day or so. If it doesn't, she won't get the donation she needs and won't be able to pay the bills. I guess they're pretty deep in the hole over there, might even have to shut the whole thing down. Charlotte Edwards's solution was to keep you there—get you to do some plastic surgeries she could impress Gilchrist with and pass you off as her new plastic surgeon. After that, Colleen was going to get Perry there and you could be on your way. But it's obvious you didn't know about any of this."

With every word Mike spoke, Trent's hands grew colder until he was practically shaking from the inside out with shock and anger. Everything Charlotte had said to him spun through his mind: praising his plastic surgery skills, begging him to do those surgeries and take photos, telling him there were problems with his paperwork, delays in getting Perry there. Coming up with a fake excuse when he'd found his release papers in her office.

Flat-out lying to him all along. Manipulating his papers, his life. His heart.

It was like *déjà vu*, except this was so much worse. Because she'd obviously only been pretending to like him. She'd obviously only had sex with him to keep him there, to tangle him up with her so he wouldn't leave until after the Gilchrist rep came.

And what had Mike said? After that, Colleen had the green light to get him out of there. *Bye-bye, have a nice life, I don't need you anymore.*

How could he have been so stupid, so blind? It was all so clear now, all the plastic surgery crap lines she'd fed him.

She hadn't cared when he'd left the first time and she sure as hell wouldn't care this time.

Balling his hands into fists, he sucked in a heavy breath, trying to control the bottomless anger and pain that filled his soul until it felt like it just might rip apart.

He had to get out of there. He'd already gone over with Thomas what had to happen with the rabies vaccine. She'd be all right. And the fact that the thought came with a brief worry on her behalf made him want to punch himself in the face.

Fool me once, shame on you. Fool me twice, and I'm obviously a pathetic moron.

"Thanks for telling me, Mike. I'm going to make my own arrangements to leave."

"All right. Perry's travel arrangements are being finalized this minute, so he'll be there soon."

Somehow, he managed to finish fixing Charlotte's dinner while he dialed the airline, relieved to find he could be out of there at the crack of dawn tomorrow.

He set her food on the table, placed two pain tablets next to it and forced himself to go into the parlor. The smile she sent him across the room felt like a stab wound deep into his heart. "Dinner's on the table. Come eat, then take your pills."

As she passed through the kitchen doorway, he stepped back, not wanting to touch her. Knowing a touch would hurt like a bad burn, and he'd been scorched enough.

"Where's yours?" She looked at him in surprise, her pretty, lying lips parted.

He'd play the part she'd once accused him of, so she

wouldn't know he knew the truth. So she wouldn't know how much it hurt that she'd used him. That the pain went all the way to the core of his very essence, leaving a gaping hole inside.

It seemed like a long time since she'd told him he was full of himself and famous for kissing women goodbye with a smile and a wave. He'd do it now if it killed him.

"Colleen Mason just called to tell me I have a plane reservation in the morning, that I've been given the all-clear," he said, somehow managing a fake smile.

She sank onto the kitchen chair, staring. "What? I don't understand. I don't have… Perry Cantwell's not… I mean, that can't be right."

"It is. My vacation's been delayed long enough, and I'm meeting a…friend…in Florence." He leaned down to brush his lips across hers, and was damned if the contact wasn't excruciating. "It's been great being with you. But you know how I feel about long goodbyes, so I'll get out of here."

"But, Trent. Wait. I—"

"Take care of that arm." He turned and moved quickly to the door, unable to look at her face. To see the shock and despair and, damn it, the tears in her eyes. To know her dismay had nothing to do with him and everything to do with her precious hospital.

The thought came to him that he was running again. Running from pain, disillusionment and deep disappointment. And this time he knew he just might be running for the rest of his life.

CHAPTER EIGHTEEN

CHARLIE LAID HER head on her desk because she didn't think she could hold it upright for one more minute.

In barely forty-eight hours, her life had gone to ruin, and no amount of hard work and positive attitude was going to fix it.

She'd been a fool to think there had been any possibility of her relationship with Trent Dalton becoming anything bigger than a fling. It'd been foolish to allow her feelings to get out of control. To allow the connection she felt to him to grab hold of her—a connection that had bloomed and deepened until she could no longer deny the emotion.

She thought she'd seen that he felt it too. Had seen it in his eyes; seen it in the way he cared for her when she'd been hurt; seen it through his kisses and his touch.

Then he'd walked out. One minute he was sweetly there, the next he was kissing her goodbye with a smile and a wave, just like the first time. But, unlike the first time, he'd taken a big chunk of her heart with him.

How could she have been so stupid? She'd known all along it could never be more than a fling. Had known he was right, when he'd come back, that they should keep their relationship platonic—because, as he'd so eloquently said, second goodbyes tended to get messy.

Messy? Was that the way to describe how he'd left? It

seemed like their goodbye had been quite neat and tidy for him.

Anger burned in her stomach. Anger that she'd let herself fall for a man who'd never hidden that he didn't want or need roots. Anger that the pain of his leaving nagged at her far more than the physical pain of her torn and stitched-up arm.

And of course, practically the minute he'd moved on, the Gilchrist rep had shown up. He'd been impressed with the wing but, gosh, there was this little problem of there not being a doctor there. She'd hoped the photographs of Trent's work would help, but of course it hadn't. After all, the man was long gone, and they'd made their requirements very clear.

A quiet knock preceded the door opening and Charlie managed to lift her head to look at John Adams, swallowing the lump that kept forming in her throat.

"I'm guessing things didn't go well," he said as he sat in the chair across from her.

"No. The Gilchrist Foundation can't justify giving us the check without meeting all their requirements. Which I knew would happen."

"What are you going to do?"

Wasn't that a good question? What was she going to do to keep the hospital open? What was she going to do to mend her broken heart? What was she going to do to move past the bitterness and regret that was like a burning hole in her chest?

"I don't know. I have to crunch the numbers again, see what can be eliminated from the budget. Lay off a few employees. See if any of the other donors I've approached will come through with something." Though nothing could come close to what Gilchrist had offered. To what the hospital needed.

"There is the money the anonymous donor gave the

school." John Adams looked at her steadily. "I can put off hiring another teacher, hold off on some of the purchases we made."

"No." She shook her head even as the suggestion was tempting. "Whoever donated that money gave it to the school. It wouldn't be right to use it for the hospital. I'll figure something out."

"All right." John Adams stood and gently patted her head, as though she were Patience. "I'm sorry about all this. And sorry about Trent leaving. I've got to tell you, that surprised me. Especially since it was right after he'd told me he was staying."

"He told you he was staying?"

"He did. After he was irritated with you being in the hospital when you were supposed to be resting."

And his caring for her through all that was part of what had made her fall harder for him. "Well, he obviously didn't mean it the way most people would. Staying the night is probably what that word means to him." She tried to banish the acrid and hurt tone from her voice. After all, she'd known the reality. Regret yet again balled up in her stomach that she'd allowed herself to forget it.

Trent walked beneath the trees in Central Park to his parents' Fifth Avenue apartment on Manhattan's Upper East Side. He breathed in the scents of the city, listened to children playing in the park and the constant flow of traffic crowding the street and looked at the old and elegant apartment buildings that lined the streets.

It didn't seem all that many years ago since he'd been a kid roaming these streets, not realizing at the time how different growing up here was from the average kid's childhood in suburbia. But it had been great too, in its own way, especially when your family had wealth and privilege enough to take advantage of everything the city offered and the ability to leave for a quieter place when the hustle got wearying.

His mother had been more hands-on than most of the crowd his parents were friends with, whose full-time nannies did most of the child-rearing. He'd appreciated it, and how close they'd been, believing that the bond she shared with her only child was special to her.

Until she'd lied and betrayed him. The memory of that blow still had the power to hurt.

He thought of how his mother had tried to reach out to him during the years since then. She'd kept tabs on wherever he was working, and each time he moved on to a new mission hospital a Gilchrist Foundation donation immediately plumped their coffers. She'd sent him a Christmas card every year, with updates on what she and his dad were doing, where they'd traveled, asking questions about his own life. Questions he hadn't answered. After all, what he wanted to do with his life hadn't interested her before, so he figured it didn't truly interest her now.

She'd been shocked and seemingly thrilled to get his phone call that morning and he wondered what it would be like to see her after all this time. A part of him dreaded it. The part of him that still carried good memories wanted, in spite of everything, to see how she was. Either way, the need at the Edwards hospital was what had driven him here. Not for Charlotte—for all the patients who would have nowhere to go if the place shut down.

"Mr. Trent! Is that you? I can't believe it!" Walter Johnson pumped his hand, a broad smile on the old doorman's face.

"Glad to see you're still here, Walter." Trent smiled, thinking of all the times the man had had his back when he'd been a kid. "It's been a long time since my friends and I were causing trouble for you."

"You just caused normal boy trouble. Kept my job interesting." Walter grinned. "Are your parents expecting you? Or shall I ring them?"

"My mother knows I'm coming. Thanks."

The ornate golden elevator took him to his family's fourteen-room apartment and he drew a bracing breath before he knocked on the door. Would she look the same as always? Or would time have changed her some?

The door opened and his question was answered. She looked lovely, like she always had. Virtually unchanged— which wasn't surprising, considering his dad was a plastic surgeon and there were all kinds of cosmeceuticals out there now to keep wrinkles at bay. Her ash-blonde hair was stylishly cut and she wore her usual casual-chic clothes that cost more than most of his patients made in a year.

"Trent!" She stepped forward and he thought she was going to throw her arms around him, but she hesitated, then grasped his arm and squeezed. "It's just...wonderful to see you. Come in. Tell me about yourself and your life and everything."

Sunlight pouring through the sheer curtains cast a warm glow upon the cream-colored, modern furnishings in the room as they sat in two chairs at right angles to one another. One of her housekeepers brought coffee and the kind of biscuits Trent had always liked, and he felt a little twist of something in his chest that she had remembered.

"My life is good." Okay, that was a lie, right off the bat. His life was absolute crap and had been ever since he'd found out Charlotte had lied to him, that their relationship had been, for her at least, a means to an end and nothing more.

For the first time in his life, he'd fallen hard for a woman. A woman who was like no one he'd ever met before. Had finally realized, admitted to himself, that what he felt for Charlotte went far beyond simple attraction, lust or friendship with benefits.

And, just as he'd been ready to find out exactly what all those feelings were and what they meant, he'd been knocked to the ground by the truth and had no idea how he was going to get back up again.

"We've...we've missed you horribly, Trent." His mother twisted her fingers and stared at him through blue eyes the same color as his own. "I know you were angry when you left and I understand why. I understand that I was wrong to do what I did and I want to explain."

"Frankly, Mom, I don't think any explanation could be good enough." He didn't want to hash it out all over again. It was history and he'd moved on. "I'm not here to talk about that. I'm here to ask you a favor."

"Anything." She placed her hand on his knee. "What is it?"

"I've been working at the Edwards hospital in Liberia. They'd applied to you, to the Gilchrist Foundation, for a large donation to build and open a plastic surgery wing."

She nodded. "Yes. I'm familiar with it. In fact, I just received word that we won't be providing the donation now because they didn't meet the criteria."

"They're doing good work, Mom, and use their money wisely. I performed some plastic surgeries there and saw how great the need is. I'd appreciate it if you would still give them the donation."

"You did plastic surgery there?" She looked surprised. "Last time I spoke with you, when you stormed out of here, you told me that wasn't what you wanted to do. What changed your mind?"

"I haven't changed my mind. I didn't want to join the family practice doing facelifts and breast implants. I wanted to use my surgical skills to help children. But I've realized that I can do both."

"Are you working at the Edwards hospital full-time now? Permanently?"

"No." He'd never go there again, see Charlotte Edwards again. "It was time to leave. But I know they're getting a surgeon as soon as they can. I'd appreciate you giving them the funding check, which will help the rest of the hospital too. The people there need it."

"All right, if it's important to you, I'll get it wired out tomorrow."

"Thank you. I'm happy that, this time, what's important to me matters to you." Damn it, why had that stupid comment come out of his mouth? She'd agreed to do as he asked. The last thing he wanted was for her to change her mind, or dredge up their past.

"Trent." He looked at her, and his gut clenched at the tears that swam in her eyes. "Anything that's important to you is important to me. I know you don't want to hear it, but I'm telling you anyway—why I did what I did." She grabbed one of the tiny napkins that had been served with the coffee and dabbed her eyes. "When I went to college, all I wanted was to be a doctor. To become a plastic surgeon like my father and join his practice. I studied hard in college, and when I applied to medical schools I got in. But my father said no. Women didn't make good doctors, he said, and especially not good surgeons. I couldn't be a wife and mother and a surgeon too and needed to understand my place in our social strata."

He stared at her, stunned. It didn't surprise him that his autocratic grandfather could be such a son-of-a-bitch. But his mother wanting to be a doctor? He couldn't wrap his brain around it. "I don't know what to say, Mom. I had no idea."

"So I married your dad and he joined the practice. Filled my life with my philanthropy, which has been rewarding. And with you. You were…are…the most important thing in my life. Until I messed everything up between us." The tears filled her eyes again and he was damned if they didn't send him reaching to squeeze her shoulder, pat her in comfort, in spite of everything.

"It's all right, Mom. It was a long time ago."

"I want you to understand why, even though there's no excuse, and I know that now." Her hand reached to grip his. "I just wanted you to have what I couldn't have. I wanted that for you, and couldn't see, because of my own disappointment from all those years ago, that it was for me and not for you. That I was being selfish, instead of caring. I'm so very, very sorry and I hope someday you can forgive me. All I ever wanted was for you to be happy. You may not believe that, but it's true."

He looked at her familiar face, so full of pain and sadness. The face of the person who had been the steadiest rock throughout his life, until the moment she wasn't.

He thought about the fun they'd had when he was growing up, their adventures together, her sense of humor. He thought about how she'd always been there for him, and for his friends too, when most of their parents weren't around much. And he thought about how much he'd loved her and realized that hadn't changed, despite the anger he'd felt and the physical distance between them for so long.

He thought of how many times she'd tried to reach out to him through the cards she sent and through giving to the places he worked, places that were important to him.

As he stared into her blue eyes, he knew it was time to reach back.

"I do believe it, Mom. I'm sorry too. Sorry I let so many years go by before I came home. I don't completely understand, but I do forgive you. Let's put it all behind us now." He leaned forward to hug her and she clung to him, tears now streaming down her face.

"Okay. Good." She pulled back, dabbing her face with the stupid little napkin, and smiled through her tears. "So I have a question for you."

"Ask away."

"Are you in love with the woman in charge of the Edwards hospital?"

He stared at her in shock. She had on her "mom" look he'd seen so many times in his life. The one that showed she knew something he didn't want her to know. He was damned if the woman hadn't always had a keen eye and a sixth sense when it came to her only child. "Why would you ask that?"

"Because you've been working in hospitals all over the world for years, and I know you donate money to them. There must be some reason you came here to see me and ask me to give the Edwards hospital the foundation money, and some reason you're not donating your own." She arched her brows. "If she hurt you, I'm taking back my agreement to give them the money."

He shook his head, nearly chuckling at her words, except the pain he felt over Charlotte's lies was too raw. "She worked hard to get the Gilchrist Foundation donation. I'd like it to come through for her and the hospital."

"And?"

He sighed. Sitting here with her as she prodded him for information felt like the years hadn't passed and he was a teenager again. "Yes, I'm in love with her. No, she doesn't return my feelings." Saying it brought to the surface the pain he was trying hard to shove down.

"How do you know? Did she tell you that?"

"She lied to me and used me. Tried to keep me there just to get your donation for her precious hospital. Not something someone does to someone they love."

"I don't know. I love you but I lied and made stupid mistakes. Have you told her how you feel?"

He stared at her, considering her words. Could Charlotte have done what she did and still cared about him at the same time? "No. And I'm not going to."

"But you still love her enough to make sure she gets the donation from my foundation."

"It's for the hospital, not her." But as he said the words he knew it was for Charlotte as well, and hated himself for it.

She regarded him steadily. "I think it's for both the hospital *and* her. I made a bad mistake. Maybe she did too. Don't compound it by making your own mistakes." She stood and smiled, holding out her hand like he was still a little kid. "Come on, prodigal son. Your dad will be home soon. Stay for dinner and we'll catch up."

"I'm sorry, Colleen. For everything. I hope Mike wasn't mad that you sent the release papers to me instead of Trent." Charlie studied her online bank statements as she talked to her friend, despairing that she'd find a way out of their financial problems. With everything else a total mess, getting Colleen in trouble would make the disaster complete.

"No, he's not. I wish you hadn't lied to me, though."

"I know. I'm so, so sorry. Everything I did was stupid and didn't even solve anything."

"I bet Trent was really angry about it." Her voice was somber. "I know he left there—I arranged his travel for when he heads to Europe from the U.S. What did he say?"

"He never found out, thank heavens." That would have been the worst thing of all. Despite the crappy way he'd left, she wouldn't have wanted him to know what she'd done.

"What do you mean? Of course he did. He was telling Mike he wanted to stay there in Liberia. Be assigned at your hospital for the year. And that's when Mike told him everything you'd done."

Charlie's heart lurched then seemed to grind to a halt. The world felt a little like it was tilting on its axis, and as she stared, unseeing, at her office wall, it suddenly became horribly, painfully clear.

Trent hadn't left because he was tired of her, ready for vacation, ready to move on. He'd left because he knew she'd lied and manipulated his paperwork. He'd left because of what she'd done to him.

"Oh my God, Colleen," she whispered. Trent had once told her that trying to control the direction the world spun would end up weighing heavily on her shoulders. Little had he known exactly how true that was. At this moment, that weight felt heavy indeed.

Numb, she absently noted a ping on her computer that showed a wire transfer from a bank. Mind reeling, she forced herself to focus on business. Any money would help pay a bill or two.

But when she pulled it up, her mind reeled even more dizzily. Air backed up in her lungs and she couldn't breathe. "Oh my God," she said again, but this time it was different. This time it was in stunned amazement. "It's the donation from the Gilchrist Foundation. All of it they'd committed to us. What…? Why…this is unbelievable!"

"Oh, Charlie, I'm so happy for you! This is awesome!"

"Yes. It is. Listen, I need to go. I'll call you later." Charlie hung up and stared at the wire transfer, unable to process that it had come through, beyond relieved that the hospital wouldn't have to shut down. Once the plastic surgeon showed, they'd be able to get the wing open and operating for a long time, helping all those who so needed it.

But knowing her project would now be complete didn't bring the utter satisfaction it should have. Didn't feel like the epitome of everything she'd wanted. And as she stared at her computer she knew why.

She'd ruined the sweet, wonderful, fledging romance that had blossomed between her and Trent. Through her adamant "the end justifies the means" selfish attitude, she'd no doubt hurt the most amazing, giving, incredible man she'd ever known.

He'd wanted to stay the year with her, which just might have turned into forever. But instead, she'd destroyed any chance of happiness, of a real relationship with him.

Her computer screen blurred as tears filled her eyes and spilled down her cheeks. How could she have been so stubbornly focused on the hospital's future that she couldn't see her own, staring her in the face through beautiful blue eyes?

She'd always prided herself on being a risk-taker. But when it came to the most important risk of all—risking her emotions, her life and her heart—she'd cowardly backed away in self-protection. Afraid to expose herself to potential pain, she'd tried to close a shell around her heart, hiding inside it like a clam. But somehow he'd broken through that shell anyway.

Why hadn't she seen she should have been honest with Trent, and with herself, about all of it? Maybe the outcome would have been different if she had, but now she'd never know. Trent doubtless hated her now, and she had only herself to blame.

Her phone rang, and she blinked at the tears stinging her eyes, swallowing down the lump in her throat to answer it. "Charlotte Edwards here."

"Ms. Edwards, this is Catherine Gilchrist Dalton. I'm founder and president of the Gilchrist Foundation. I wanted to make sure you received our donation via wire."

"Yes, I did, just now." The woman was calling her personally? "I'm honored to speak with you and more than honored to receive your donation. I appreciate it more than I can possibly say, and I promise to use it wisely."

"As you know, your hospital was originally denied because it didn't meet our requirements."

"Yes. I know." And she hoped the woman would tell

her why they'd changed their minds, though she supposed it didn't really matter.

"My son, Trent Dalton—I think you know him?—he came to see me, asking me to still provide the donation. Convinced me your hospital is more than worthy of our funding."

Charlotte nearly dropped her phone. Trent? Trent was the woman's son? She tried to move her lips, but couldn't speak.

"Hello? Are you there?"

"Y…yes. I'm sorry. I'm just…surprised to hear that Trent is your son." Surprised didn't begin to cover it. He'd called himself a rich boy? That was an understatement.

"Perhaps I'm being a busybody, but that's a mother's prerogative. Trent told me he'd wanted to spend the next year working at your hospital with you, but you made a mistake by lying to him which has made him change his mind."

"Yes, that's true." Her voice wobbled. "I was selfishly stupid and would give anything to be able to do it over again. To be honest with him about…everything."

"Would that 'everything' include caring for him in a personal way? Being his mother, I would have to assume you do."

The woman's amused tone reminded her so much of Trent, she nearly burst into tears right into the phone. "You're right, Mrs. Dalton. I do care for Trent in a personal way, because he's the most incredible man I've ever known. I'm terribly, crazy in love with him but, if he cared at all about me before, I don't think he does anymore. I don't think he'll ever forgive me."

"You won't know unless you try to find out, will you? I made a terrible mistake with him once, too, tried to manipulate his life and paid a harsh price for that. Our years of separation were very painful to me, and I should have tried harder to apologize, to ask him to forgive me. I suggest you make the effort, instead of wondering. And maybe regretting."

She was right. A surge of adrenaline pulsed through Charlie's blood. She'd find Trent and she'd make it right or die trying. "Thank you. Do you know where he is?"

"He's here in New York City, visiting with a few friends. He's leaving soon. I can try to find out his travel plans, if you like."

Colleen. Colleen had his itinerary. "Thanks, but I think I know how to get them."

CHAPTER NINETEEN

CHARLIE CAREENED DOWN the muddy road, hands sweating, heart pounding, as she desperately drove to the little airport, trying to catch the plane that would take her to Kennedy Airport in New York City, which Trent was scheduled to fly out of in about ten hours. And, of course, the rain had begun the moment she'd left, slowing her progress and making it nearly impossible to get there in time.

But she had to get there. A simple phone call wasn't enough. She had to find Trent and tell him she loved him and beg him to forgive her.

As she'd thrown a few necessities into her suitcase and tried to process the whole, astonishing thing about his mother being a Gilchrist, and the unbelievable donation and phone call, she'd realized something else.

The fifty-thousand-dollar donation for the school must have come from Trent. Who else would just, out of the blue, anonymously donate that kind of money to their little school? The incredible realization made her see again what she'd come to know: that he was beyond extraordinary. A man with so much money, he could choose not to work at all. Instead, he'd trained for years to become a doctor and a specialized surgeon. He helped the poor and needy around the world, both financially and hands-on. He was adorable, funny, sweet and loved children. And if she didn't get to the airport on time, and find a way to make him forgive her, she'd never, ever meet anyone like him again.

She loved him and she'd hurt him. She'd tell him, show him, how much she loved him and make right all her wrongs.

She jammed her foot onto the accelerator. She had to get there and get on that plane. And if she didn't, she'd follow him to Florence or wherever else he was going. If she had to, she'd follow him to the moon.

Trent stretched his legs out in front of him and pulled his Panama hat down over his eyes. His flight from Kennedy was delayed, so he might as well try to sleep.

Except every time he closed his eyes he saw Charlotte Grace Edwards. Never mind that there were five thousand miles between them, and that she'd lied and obviously didn't care about him the way he'd thought she did. Her face, her scent, her smile were all permanently etched in his brain and heart.

He'd broken his own damned rules and was paying the price for it. Knew he'd be paying the price for a long, long time.

He'd been happy with his life. He liked working in different places in the world, meeting new people, finding new medical challenges. Setting down roots in one place hadn't occurred to him until he'd gone to Liberia. Until he'd met Charlotte. Until she'd turned upside down everything he thought he knew about himself and what he wanted.

He hadn't gotten out fast enough. Their one-night fling had become something so much bigger, so much more important, so deeply painful. His vacation alone in Italy was going to be the worst weeks of his life, and his new job couldn't start soon enough.

A familiar, distinctive floral scent touched his nose,

and to his disgust his heart slapped against his ribs and his breath shortened. Here he was, thinking about her so intently, so completely, he imagined she was near. Imagined he could touch her one last time.

Except the firm kick against his shoe wasn't his imagination.

He froze. Charlotte? Impossible.

"I know you're not asleep, Trent Dalton. Look at me."

Stunned, he slowly pushed his hat from his face and there she was. Or a mirage of her. He nearly extended his hand to see if she could possibly be real. He ran his gaze over every inch of her—her messy hair, her rumpled clothes, her bandaged arm.

She was real. The most real, the most beautiful woman he'd ever seen. His heart swelled and constricted at the same time, knowing what a damn fool he was to still feel that way.

"Why aren't you wearing the sling on your arm?"

She laughed, and the sound brought both joy and torment. "I nearly killed myself running off the road in a rainstorm to get to the airport, flew thousands of miles to find you, and the first thing you do is nag me?"

Yeah, she was something. He had to remind himself that single-minded ruthlessness was part of the persona he'd adored. "What are you doing here, Charlotte?"

She crouched down in front of him, her green eyes suddenly deeply serious as they met his. "I came to apologize. I came to tell you how very sorry I am that I lied to you. That I realize no hospital wing, no donation, no amount of need, could possibly justify it, no matter how much I convinced myself it did."

It struck him that she'd gotten the Gilchrist donation, and that his mother had probably meddled and spilled the beans about who he was. Charlotte must somehow feel she had to apologize, to make it right, because of the money, even though it was an awful big trek for her to catch him here. His chest ached, knowing that was all this was.

"No need to apologize. I know the hospital means everything to you."

She slowly shook her head as her hand reached for his and squeezed, and his own tightened on hers when he should have pulled it away. "No, Trent. The hospital doesn't mean everything to me. I know that now."

"Well, pardon me when I say that's a line of bull. Like so many others you fed me." She'd already proven he couldn't trust anything she said. "You've shown you'll do anything to make things go your way for the place. You've shown it's your number-one priority over everything."

"Maybe it was. Maybe I let it be. But it isn't anymore." She stood and leaned forward, pressing a kiss to his mouth, and for a surprised moment he let himself feel it all the way to his soul. He let it fill all the cracks in his heart before he pulled away.

"You're my number-one priority, Trent. You're what means everything to me. Only you. I hated myself for lying to you. After you left, I hated myself even more for letting myself fall for you, because I was sure you'd just moved on to be with some woman in Italy. That I didn't mean anything to you but a brief good time."

"What makes you think that's not the case?" Though it was impossible to imagine how she could have believed that. That she hadn't seen the way he felt about her; hadn't known what she'd come to mean to him. But, if she didn't know, he sure as hell didn't want her to find out.

"Because I know you told Mike you wanted to be assigned to my little hospital for your year assignment." Tears filled her green eyes and he steeled himself against them; wouldn't be moved by them. "When I realized you'd left because of my stupid, misguided mistakes, I knew I had to do whatever I could to find you."

Obviously, she'd come because she still needed a plastic surgeon to get the hospital wing running. "You've found me. But my plane leaves in an hour, and I really don't want to go through a third goodbye. So please just go." The weight in his chest and balling in his stomach told him another goodbye might be even more painful than the second one in her kitchen, which he'd never have dreamed could be possible.

"No. No more goodbyes. I love you. I love you more than anything, and all I want is to be with you."

She loved him? He stared at her, wishing he could believe her. But he'd learned through a very hard lesson that she lied as easily as she breathed. He wasn't about to go back to Liberia with the woman who "loved" him only as long as she needed him to do plastic surgery work, or whatever the hell else was on her agenda, then doubtless wouldn't "love" him anymore.

"Sorry, Charlie, but I'm sure you can understand why I just don't believe you."

Tears welled in her eyes again. "You just called me Charlie," she whispered. "You're the only person who always calls me Charlotte."

He shrugged casually to show her none of this was affecting him the way it really was. "Maybe because you're not the person I thought you were."

He had to look away from the hurt in her eyes. "I hope I am the person you thought I was. Or at least that I can become that person. And I do understand why you don't believe me. I deserve that disbelief. I understand you need proof that I mean every word." Beneath her tears, her eyes sparked with the determined intensity he'd seen so often. "You once asked me why I went to Liberia to rebuild the hospital and school. And I told you my roots were dug in deep there, and I wanted to grow those roots, and I'd do it no matter what it takes. But I've changed my thoughts about that."

"How?"

"I'm not willing to do whatever it takes for the hospital, because that attitude led to some terrible mistakes. But I am willing to do whatever it takes to convince you I love you. That I want to grow roots with you and only you—wherever you choose to grow them. I always told you I can find doctors to work at the Edwards hospital, but not someone to run it. But you know what? I'm sure I *can* find someone to run it, and I will if you'll let me travel with you, be with you, help you, wherever it is you're headed."

He stared at her, stunned. The woman would be willing to leave the Edwards Mission Hospital to be with him instead? As much as he wanted to believe it, he couldn't. Her lies and machinations had been coldly calculated, and he had to wonder what exactly it was she was trying to achieve this time around. "No, Charlotte. You belong in Liberia and I belong wherever I am at a given moment."

"I belong with you, and I believe that you belong with me. I'm going to work hard to convince you how sorry I am for what I did. To give you so much love, you have to forgive me." She swiped away the tears on her lashes as her eyes flashed green sparks of determination. "You said I'm sometimes like a pit bull? You haven't seen anything yet. I'll get on the plane with you. I'll follow you wherever you go and keep asking you to forgive me and keep telling you how much I love you. I'm going to quit trying to control the world, like you always teased me about, and beg you to run it with me, for us to run it together. I want that because I love you. I love you and my life isn't complete without you."

He stared into her face. Would it be completely stupid of him to believe her again?

His heart pounded hard and he stood and looked down

into her eyes focused so intently on his. In their depths, he saw very clearly what he was looking for.

Love. For him. It wasn't a lie. It was the truth.

He cupped her face in his hands and had to swallow past the lump that formed in his throat as he lowered his mouth to hers for a long kiss, absorbing the taste of her lips that he never thought he'd get to taste again.

"I love you too, Charlotte. I wish you'd just been honest with me but, standing here looking at you, I realize what you did doesn't matter if you really do love me. What matters is that I love you and you love me back." As he said the words, he knew with every ounce of his being it truly was the only thing that mattered. "Maybe if you'd told me, I would have left, I don't know. I do know that the way I felt about you scared the crap out of me."

"The way I felt about you scared me too. I knew you'd be out of my life in a matter of days, and it would be beyond stupid to fall in love with you. But I did anyway. I couldn't help it."

"Yeah?" Her words made him smile, because he'd felt exactly the same way. "I kept telling myself to keep my distance. But I found it impossible to resist a certain beautiful woman who tries to run the world." He tunneled his hands into her soft hair and looked into her eyes. "I've been running for a long time, Charlotte. I didn't really see it, until being with you made me look. But being with you made me realize that maybe, in all that running, I was really searching. And then I knew: I'd been searching for you."

A little sob left her throat and she flung her good arm around his neck. "Do you want me to come with you? Or would you like to go back to Liberia together? Will you live with me and work with me? Share my life with me?"

"I'm thinking heading back to Liberia is a good plan." He wrapped his arms around her, pressed his cheek to hers and smiled at the same time emotion clogged his chest.

"So, is that a marriage proposal? Trust you not to let me be the one to ask."

"I'm sorry." She paused. "If we go back, I'll let you drive whenever you want."

He laughed out loud. "I'll believe that when I see it. And yes, Charlotte Grace Edwards, I'll marry you and live with you and work with you for the rest of our lives." He lowered his mouth to hers and whispered against her lips. "This is the last time you have to drag me back from an airport. This time, I'm staying for good."

* * * * *

RESISTING
HER REBEL HERO

BY
LUCY RYDER

MILLS & BOON

Published in Great Britain 2014
by Mills & Boon, an imprint of Harlequin (UK) Limited,
Eton House, 18-24 Paradise Road, Richmond, Surrey, TW9 1SR

© 2014 Bev Riley

ISBN: 978 0 263 90761 2

Harlequin (UK) Limited's policy is to use papers that are natural,
renewable and recyclable products and made from wood grown in
sustainable forests. The logging and manufacturing processes conform
to the legal environmental regulations of the country of origin.

Printed and bound in Spain
by Blackprint CPI, Barcelona

Dear Reader

My parents can attest to the fact that I was always a dreamer. At age eight I wanted to be a prima ballerina, but that didn't pan out because I also loved Westerns and ran around the garden with my brother shooting everything. Then I discovered Julie Andrews and wanted to be just like her. Well, as you can see, that didn't work out either, but my love of dreaming and weaving fantastical stories in my head finally did.

A few years ago a friend showed me an article in a magazine about a Mills & Boon® writing competition and urged me to enter. With absolutely nothing to lose, I did. I didn't win, but imagine my surprise and delight when I received an e-mail from the offices of Mills & Boon® Medical Romance™ saying they loved my writing style and absolutely adored my characters, Cassidy and Sam—*especially* Sam. It was a dream come true—or rather coming true.

It's been a hard slog, getting Sam and Cassidy's story perfected, but with the infinitely patient Flo Nicoll and her expert advice it's done, and I'm *finally* able to say, 'I'm a published author.' What a thrill! Now my colleagues can stop saying, 'Why is this taking so long? Shouldn't you try something else?' And my daughters can stop rolling their eyes at me and admit I *am* Queen of the Universe—in our house anyway.

I really hope you enjoy reading about Sam and Cassidy's struggle to overcome their trust issues and admit they're perfect for each other. I also hope you enjoy your visit to Crescent Lake, with all its quirky characters. I've had such fun with them and hope you do too.

Happy reading!

Lucy

RESISTING HER REBEL HERO
is Lucy Ryder's debut title
for Mills & Boon®!

DEDICATION

I couldn't have done this without my wonderful supportive family—especially my beautiful daughters, Caitlin and Ashleigh. I love you to infinity and beyond.

A special thanks to Dr Jenni Irvine, who started it all, and to Flo Nicoll for seeing something in my writing she liked.

And lastly to my colleagues—
ladies, it's amazing how people bond through complaining.

CHAPTER ONE

THE LAST PLACE Dr. Cassidy Mahoney expected to find herself when she fled the city for a wilderness town deep in the Cascades Mountains was the county jail. She could honestly say it was the first time she'd ever been in one, and with the smell of stale alcohol and something more basically human permeating the air, she hoped it was the last.

And absolutely nothing could have prepared her for *him*—all six feet four inches of broad shoulders and hard muscles, oozing enough testosterone to choke a roomful of hardened feminists.

Draped languorously over a narrow bunk that clearly couldn't contain his wide shoulders and long legs, the man lustily sang about a pretty *señorita* with dark flashing eyes and lips like wine. The old man in the neighboring cell cheerfully sang along, sounding like a rusty engine chugging up a mountain pass while his cellmate snored loudly enough to rattle the small windows set high in the outside wall.

Pausing in the outer doorway, Cassidy felt her eyes widen and wondered if she'd stepped onto a movie set without a script. The entire town of Crescent Lake had turned out to be like something from a movie set and she was still having a hard time believing she wasn't dreaming.

Quite frankly, even her wildest dreams couldn't have conjured up being escorted to the sheriff's office in a police cruiser like a seasoned offender—even to supply medical care to a prisoner.

From somewhere near the back of the holding area a loud voice cursed loudly and yelled at them to "shut the hell up." Hazel Porter, the tiny woman currently leading Cassidy into the unknown, pushed the door open all the way and gestured for her to follow.

"Full house tonight," Hazel rasped in her thirty-a-day voice, sounding like she'd been sucking on smokes since the cradle. "Must be full moon." She nodded to the cell holding the old-timers. "Don't mind them, honey: long-standing weekend reservations." Her bunch of keys jangled Cassidy's already ragged nerves.

"And ignore the guy in the back," Hazel advised. "Been snarlin' and snipin' since he was hauled in a couple hours ago. I was tempted to call in animal control, but the sheriff said to let him sleep it off."

"I'd be sleeping too, you old crow, if it wasn't for the caterwauling, stripping paint off the walls."

Hazel shook her head. "Mean as a cornered badger, that one," she snorted, closing the outer door behind them. "Even when he ain't drunk."

Cassidy sent the woman a wary look, a bit nervous at the thought of being closed in with a bunch of offenders—one of whom was apparently violent—and a pint-sized deputy who could be anything between sixty and a hundred and sixty.

"So…the patient?" she prompted uncertainly, hoping it wasn't the fun guy in back. Hippocratic oath aside, she drew the line at entering his cell without the sheriff, a couple of burly deputies and a fully charged stun gun as backup.

"That'll be Crescent Lake's very own superhero." Hazel headed for the baritone's cell and Cassidy couldn't help the relief that left her knees a bit shaky. "He's a recent addition and a wild one, so watch yerself," wasn't exactly something Cassidy wanted to hear.

The deputy slid a key into the lock and continued as though she'd known Cassidy for years. "Wasn't a bit surprising when he up 'n left med school to join the Navy." Her chuckle sounded like a raspy snort. "Heck, 'Born to be wild' shoulda been tattooed on that boy's hide at birth."

Cassidy blinked, unsure if she was meant to respond and uncertain what she would say if she did. She'd learnt over the past fortnight that mountain folk were for the most part polite and taciturn with strangers, but treated everyone's business like public property. She'd even overheard bets being placed on how long *she'd* last before she "hightailed it back to the city."

The sound of the key turning was unnaturally loud and Cassidy bit her lip nervously when the cell door slid open and clanged against the bars. Drawing in a shaky breath, she smoothed damp palms down her thighs and eyed the "born to be wild" man warily.

One long leg was bent at the knee; the other hung over the side of the bunk, large booted foot planted on the bare concrete floor. Although a bent arm blocked most of his face from view, Cassidy realized she was the object of intense scrutiny. Her first thought was, *God, he's huge,* followed almost immediately by, *And there's only a garden gnome's granny between me and Goliath's drunk younger brother.*

"Is that why he's in here?"

"Heck, no," Hazel rasped with a snort. "Was the only way Sheriff could be sure he stayed put till you arrived. Boy thinks he's too tough for a few stitches and a couple of sticking plasters."

Cassidy hovered outside the cell, aware that her heart was banging against her ribs like she was the one who'd committed a felony and was facing jail time. Besides, she'd heard all about people going missing in wilderness towns and had the oddest feeling the instant she stepped over the threshold her life would never be the same.

Turning, she caught the older woman watching her and gave a self-conscious shrug. "Is it safe? Shouldn't we wait for the sheriff? A couple of deputies?" A shock stick?

Small brown eyes twinkled. "Safe?" Hazel cackled as though the idea tickled her funny bone when Cassidy had been as serious as a tax audit. In Boston, violent offenders were always accompanied by several burly cops, even when they were restrained.

"Well, now," the deputy said, wiping the mirth from her eyes. "I don't know as the boy's ever been called 'safe' before, but if you're wondering if he'll get violent, don't you worry about a thing, hon. He's gentle as a lamb."

Cassidy's gaze slid to the "boy," who seemed to be all shoulders and legs, and thought, *Yeah, right.* Nothing about him looked gentle and "boy" wasn't something he'd been for a good long time. Not with that long, hard body or the toxic cloud of testosterone and pheromones filling the small space and snaking primitive warnings up her spine.

Even sprawled across the narrow bunk, he exuded enough masculine sexuality to have a cautious woman taking a hasty step in retreat.

Hazel Porter must have correctly interpreted the move for she cackled gleefully even as she planted a bony hand in the small of Cassidy's back and gave her a not-so-gentle shove into the cell.

Her pulse gave an alarmed little blip and Cassidy found herself swallowing a distressed yelp, which was ridiculous, considering he'd done nothing more dangerous than sing in that rich, smooth bedroom baritone.

"Whatcha got for me, sweetheart?" the deep voice drawled, sending a shiver of fear down Cassidy's spine. At least she thought the belly-clenching, free-falling sensation was fear as goose bumps rushed over her skin beneath the baby-pink scrubs top she hadn't had time to change out of. The baby-pink top that was covered in little bear doctors and nurses and an assortment of smears and stains from a day spent with babies and toddlers.

Not exactly the kind of outfit that gave a woman much-needed confidence when facing a large alpha male.

"You get the rare steak and fries I ordered?"

Hazel snorted. "We're not running some five-star establishment here, sonny," she rebuked mildly, eyeing him over her spectacles. "You wanted steak and fries you shoulda thought about that *before* you decided to pound on Wes."

A battered lip curved into a loopy grin. "Aw, c'mon, Hazel." He chuckled, sounding a little rusty, as though he hadn't had much to laugh about lately—or had awakened from a deep sleep. "He was drunker than a sailor on shore leave. The coeds he was hassling were terrified. 'Sides, *someone* had to stop him trashing Hannah's bar. He threw a *stool* at her when she tried to intervene, for God's sake."

"Your sister can handle herself," Hazel pointed out reasonably, to which the hunk sleepily replied, "Sure she can. We taught her some great moves." He yawned until his jaw cracked. "Jus' doin' my brotherly duty, 'sall."

"And look where that got you."

The man lifted a hand wrapped in a bloodied bar towel and peered down at his side. "Bonehead took me by surprise," he growled in disgust, wincing as he lowered his arm. "Was on me before I could convince them to leave." He grunted. "Better my hide than her pretty face, huh?"

"You're a good brother," Hazel said dryly.

A wide shoulder hitched. "Didn't you teach me to stand up to the bullies of this world, ma'am?"

"*Ri-ight.*" Hazel snorted, beaming at him with affectionate pride. "Blame the helpless old lady."

The deep chuckle filling the tiny cell did odd things to

Cassidy's insides and spread prickling warmth throughout her body. Her face heated and the backs of her knees tingled.

She uttered a tiny gasp.

Tingled? Really? Alarmed by her body's response, she backed up a step until she realized what she was doing and froze. Feeling her face heat, Cassidy drew in a shaky breath and took a determined step forward. She dropped her medical bag between his long hard thighs since he took up the rest of the bunk.

So what if she was dressed like a kindergarten teacher? She was a mature, professional woman who'd spent an entire day with babies and toddlers—not some silly naïve schoolgirl dazzled by a pair of wide shoulders, long legs and a deep bedroom voice.

Well…not usually. Besides, she'd already done that and was not going there again. *Tingling* of any sort. Was out.

"Nothin' helpless about you, darlin'," the bedroom voice drawled with another flash of even white teeth as Cassidy pulled out a pair of surgical gloves. She couldn't see his eyes but knew by the stillness of his body that he was tracking her every move.

"Save the sweet talk, sonny," Hazel sniffed, amused yet clearly not taken in by the charm. "And play nice. Miz Mahoney doesn't have time to waste on idiots."

Cassidy snapped on a latex glove and opened her mouth to correct the deputy's use of "Miz" but he shifted at that moment and every thought fled, leaving her numb with shock as she realized exactly who she was in a jail cell with.

Ohmigosh. Her eyes widened. *He really was a superhero.* Or rather Major Samuel J. Kellan, Crescent Lake's infamous Navy SEAL and all-round bad boy. She stared at him and wondered if she was hallucinating. Wasn't he supposed to be a local hero or something? Heck, a *national* hero?

What was he doing in the county jail?

Besides, he'd been injured protecting his sister and saving a couple of young women from harm. And according to local gossip, everyone adored him. Women swooned at the mention of his name and men tended to recount his exploits like he was some kind of legendary superhero. And *really*. There wasn't a man alive who could do *half* the things Major Kellan was rumored to have done and survived. Well...*not* outside Hollywood.

Yet, even battered and bruised, it was clear the man deserved his reputation as big, bad and dangerous to know. Looking into his battered face, it was just as clear that one thing *hadn't* been exaggerated. With his thick dark hair, fierce gold eyes, strong shadowed jaw and surprisingly sensual mouth, the man *was* as hot as women claimed. She could only be grateful she'd been immunized against fallen angels masquerading as wounded bad boys.

Frankly, the *last* thing she needed in her life was another man with more sex appeal than conscience. Heck, the last thing she needed, *period*, was a man—especially one who tended to suck the air right out of a room and make the backs of her knees sweat.

Hazel cleared her throat loudly, jolting Cassidy from her bizarre thoughts. "Anything you need before you sew up his pretty face, hon?"

"He really should be taken to the hospital," Cassidy said briskly, ignoring the strong smell of hops and thickly lashed eyes watching her every move. "I'll need a lot more supplies than I have with me. Supplies I can only get at the hospital." Especially if the hand wound was serious. Nerve damage was notoriously tricky to repair.

"Not to worry," Hazel rasped cheerfully. "Sheriff keeps all kinds of stuff ready for when the doc's called in unexpectedly. I'll pull Larry off front desk and send him in. You'll have your ER in a jiffy." And before Cassidy could tell the woman a jail cell was hardly a sterile environment, the desk sergeant disappeared, leaving her standing there gaping at empty space and wondering if she'd taken a left turn somewhere into an alternate universe where pint-sized deputies left unsuspecting young doctors alone in jail cells with a violent offender and…and *him*.

Her heart jerked hard against her ribs and a prickle of alarm eased up her spine. The closest thing she had to a weapon was a syringe and, frankly, even tanked, her patient looked like he could disarm her with a flick of one long-fingered hand.

Frowning, she slid a cautious look over her shoulder, trying to decide if she should make a break for it, when his voice enfolded her like rich, sinful chocolate. It took her a moment to realize that she had bigger problems.

"Hey, darlin'," he drawled, "wha's a nice girl like you doin' in a place like this?"

You have got to be kidding me.

Ignoring the lazy smile full of lethal charm, Cassidy sent him a sharp assessing look and wondered if his head injury was worse than it appeared. According to gossip, Major Hotstuff—her staff's name for him, not hers—was smooth as hundred-year-old bourbon and just as potent. *That* line had been about as smooth as a nerd in a room full of cheerleaders.

Opening her mouth to tell him that she'd heard more original pickup lines from paralytic drunks and whacked-out druggies, Cassidy's gaze locked with his and she was abruptly sucked into molten eyes filled with humor and sharp intelligence. Whether it was a trick of the light or the leashed power in his big, hard body, she was left with the weirdest impression that he wasn't nearly as drunk as he seemed, which was darned confusing, since he smelled like a brewery on a hot day.

This close she could clearly make out the dark ring encircling those unusual irises, and with the light striking his eyes from the overhead fixture, the tiny amber flecks scattered in the topaz made them appear almost gold. Like a sleek, silent jaguar.

A frisson of primitive awareness raced over her skin and she tore her gaze from his, thinking, *Get a grip, Cassidy. He's the pied piper of female hormones. He seduces women to pass the time, for heaven's sake. And we are so done with that, remember?* Unfortunately, the appalling truth was that *her* hormones, frozen for far too long, had chosen the worst possible moment to awaken.

Annoyed and a little spooked, she drew her brows together and reached for his hand, abruptly all business. She was here to do a job, she reminded herself sharply, not get her hormones overhauled.

But the instant their skin touched, a jolt of electricity zinged up her arm to her elbow.

She yanked at her hand and stumbled back a step. Her head went light, her knees wobbled and she felt like she'd just been zapped by a thousand volts of live current. He must have felt it too because he grunted and looked startled, leaving Cassidy struggling with the urge to check if her hair was on fire.

Realizing her mouth was hanging open, she snapped it closed and reminded herself this was just another example of static electricity. *Big deal. Absolutely nothing to get excited about. Happens all the time.*

However, one look out the corner of her eye made her question whether the thin mountain air was killing off brain cells because Crescent Lake's hotshot hero could hardly be termed "just another" *anything*. With his thick, nearly black hair mussed around his head like a dark halo,

glowing gold eyes and fallen-angel looks, he was about as
ordinary as a tiger shark in a goldfish bowl.

Giving her head a shake, Cassidy realized she was getting a little hysterical and probably looked like an idiot
standing there gaping at him like he'd grown horns and
a tail.

Exhaling in a rush, she looked around for the missing
glove. And spied it on the bunk.

Right between his hard jeans-clad thighs.

Her body went hot and her mouth went dry because,
holy Toledo, those jeans fit him like they'd been molded
to...well, *everything*.

Tearing her gaze away from checking out places she had
no business checking out, she reached for the latex glove
and gasped when their hands collided. He picked up the
glove and held it out, tightening his grip when she reached
for it. Her automatic "Thank you" froze in her throat when
she looked up and caught his sleepy gaze locked on her...
mouth. After a long moment his eyes rose.

Cassidy's pulse took off like a sprinter off the starting
blocks and all she could think was... *No! Oh, no. Not happening, Cassidy. Get your mind on the job.*

Her brow wrinkling with irritation, she tugged and told
herself she was probably just light-headed from all the fresh
mountain air. Dr. Mahoney did *not* flutter just because
some bad boy looked at her with his sexy eyes or talked in
a rough baritone that she felt all the way to her belly.

"Excuse me?" she said in a tone that was cool and barely
polite.

"I don't bite," he slurred with a loopy grin. "Unless you
ask real nice."

Narrowing her gaze, she yanked the glove free and
considered smacking him with it. She was not there to
play games with some hotshot Navy SEAL, thank you
very much.

Setting her jaw, she wrestled with the glove a moment then reached for his hand when she was suitably protected.

"So…" he drawled after a long silence, during which she removed the blood-soaked bar towels to examine his injury, "where's the cute white outfit?"

She looked up to catch him frowning at her pink scrubs top and jeans. "White outfit?"

"Yeah. You know…white, short, lots of little buttons?" He leaned sideways to scan the empty cell. "And where's the box?"

"Box?" *What the heck was he talking about?*

"The boom box," he said, as though she was missing a few IQ points. "Can't dance without music."

What?

"I am not a stripper, Major Kellan," she said coolly, barely resisting the urge to grind her teeth. "And nurses don't wear those any more." She was accustomed to being mistaken for a nurse and on occasion an angel. But a stripper was a new one and she didn't know whether to laugh or stab him with her syringe. Instead, she lifted a hand to brush a thick lock of dark hair off his forehead to check his head wound. He had to be hemorrhaging in there somewhere to have mistaken her for a stripper. Her hair was pulled back in a messy ponytail and her makeup had worn off hours ago.

So not stripper material.

"You're not?" He sounded disappointed. She ignored him. The wound only needed a few butterfly strips and he'd probably have a whopping headache on top of a hangover. *Hmph. That's what you get for making a woman flutter without her permission, hotshot.*

His left eye was almost swollen shut and a bruise had already turned the skin around it a dark mottled red. She gently probed the area and found no shifting under the skin. No cracked bones, but he'd have a beaut of a shiner and his split lip looked painful enough to put a crimp in his social life.

No kissing in his *immediate future.*

Wondering where that thought had come from, Cassidy reached into the bag for packaged alcohol swabs. "He did a good job on your face," she murmured, dabbing at the wound.

Something lethal came and went in his expression, too quickly for Cassidy to interpret. But when he smirked and said, "You should see the other guys," she decided she must have been mistaken and finally gave in to the mental eye roll that had been threatening. Other *guys?*

Maybe he'd been listening to too many stories about his own exploits.

"And I guess the knife wasn't clean either?"

He grunted, but as she wasn't fluent in manspeak, she was unsure if he was agreeing with her or in pain. "Broken beer bottle. Talk about a cliché," he snorted roughly. "And forget the tetanus shot. Had one a few months ago... so I'm good."

Good? It was her turn to snort—silently, of course.

Her obvious skepticism prompted an exasperated grimace. "I'm not drunk."

She eyed him suspiciously. "You're not?"

He shook his head and yawned again. "Just tired. An' it's Friday," he reminded her as though she should know what he was talking about.

"Been carousing it up with the boys, have you?"

His look was reproachful. "Fridays are busy and Hannah's usual bartender has food poisoning."

"So, you were what?" Cassidy inquired dryly. "Keeping the peace as you served up whiskey and bar nuts?"

His gold eyes gleamed with appreciation and his battered lip curved in a lopsided smile. "If you're worried, you could always stay the night. Just to be sure I'm not suffering from anything…fatal."

Flicking on a penlight, Cassidy leaned closer. "I'm sure that won't be necessary, Major," she responded dryly, checking his pupil reaction. The only fatal thing *he* was suffering from was testosterone overload.

She stepped back to pick up another alcohol swab, before returning to press it to the bloodied cut above his eye. His hissed reaction had her gentling her touch as she cleaned it. "How much did you have to drink?"

"A couple," he murmured, then responded to her narrow-eyed survey with a cocky smile that looked far too harmless for a man with his reputation. "Of sodas," he added innocently, and her assessing look turned speculative. For a man who slurred like a drunk and smelled as though he'd bathed in beer, his gaze was surprisingly sharp and clear.

"I don't drink on the job," he said, hooking a finger in the hem of her top, and giving a little tug. His knuckles brushed against bare skin and sent goose bumps chasing across her skin. "Beer and stupidity don't mix well."

"Mmm," she hummed, straight-faced, turning away to hide her body's reaction to that casual touch. "Do you need help removing your shirt?" she asked over her shoulder as she cleared away the soiled swabs. "I want to see your torso."

He was silent for a few beats and when the air thickened, she lifted her gaze and her breath caught. "Your…um… torso wound, I mean." It was no wonder he had women swooning all over the county.

As though reading her thoughts, his lips curled, drawing her reluctant gaze. The poet's mouth and long inky lashes should have looked ridiculously feminine on a man so blatantly male but they only made him appear harder, more masculine somehow.

"Isn't that supposed to be my line?"

Cursing the fair complexion that heated beneath his wicked gaze, Cassidy injected a little more frost into her tone. "Excuse me?"

His grin widened and he let out a rusty chuckle. "I like the way you say that. All cool and snooty and just a little bit superior."

Leveling him with a look one generally reserved for ill-mannered adolescents, Cassidy queried mildly, "Are you flirting with me, Major Kellan?"

"Me?" Then he chuckled. "If you have to ask," he drawled, leaning so close that she found herself retreating in an attempt to evade his potent masculine scent, "then I guess I'm out of practice."

She said, "Uh huh," and reached for the hem of his torn, bloodied T-shirt, pulling it from his waistband. The soft cotton was warm from his body and reeked of beer and something intrinsically male. She hastily drew it over his head and dropped it onto the bunk, ignoring his finely sculpted warrior's body. It had been a long time since she'd found herself this close to a man who made her want to bury her nose in his throat and breathe in warm manly skin.

But medical professionals didn't go around sniffing people's necks or drooling over every set of spectacular biceps, triceps or awesome abs that ended up in their ER. And they certainly didn't get the urge to follow that silky-looking happy trail that disappeared into a low-riding waistband with their lips either.

Or they shouldn't, she lectured herself sternly, considering the last one had left her with a deep sense of betrayal and a determination not to get sucked in again by a set of hard abs and a wicked smile.

Relieved to focus on something other than silky hair and warm manly skin, she leaned closer to probe the wound, murmuring an apology when he gave a sharp hiss. Over three inches long, it angled upwards towards his pec and the surrounding area was already darkening into what looked like the shape of a fist. Wincing, she ran the tips of her fingers over the bruised area just as the outer door banged opened, slamming against the wall.

The sound was as loud and unexpected as a gunshot. In a blur of eerily silent movement, Major Kellan surged off the bunk, shoving her roughly aside as he dropped into a crouch. Deadly menace slashed the air, sending Cassidy stumbling backwards.

She gave a shocked gasp and gaped at a wide, perfectly proportioned, perfectly tanned, muscular back bare inches from her face.

CHAPTER TWO

INSTANTLY ALERT AND battle-ready, Sam barely felt the burn of his injured palm or the line of fire streaking across his belly. Adrenaline and blood stormed his system and in some distant corner of his brain he realized it was happening. Again. *Dammit.*

Not now. Please, not now.

But he was helpless to stop it—helpless against the firestorm of images that tended to explode in his brain—instantly warping his sense of reality and triggering an instinct to protect. With deadly force.

From somewhere behind him he heard a gasp, and the young deputy entering the holding area abruptly stopped in his tracks.

One look at Sam and the kid's eyes widened to dinner plates. He went sheet-white and dropped the fold-up steel table. It teetered a moment then toppled over with loud clatter. The deputy jerked back as though he'd been prodded with a shock stick.

"M-Major K-Kellan?" he squeaked, his wide-eyed look of terrified embarrassment reaching Sam as though from a distance.

"It's just m-me, M-Major Kellan. L-Larry?"

Pain lanced through Sam's skull and he staggered, clutching his head. Sweat broke out along his spine so abruptly he felt dizzy. His strength drained, along with the surge of adrenaline that had fired his synapses and instinctively turned him into a lethal weapon. It had also turned him into something he didn't recognize any more. Something he didn't like.

Sam forced back the bile that came with particularly bad flashbacks—triggered no doubt by the violence of the evening and the sudden unexpected noise. *Dammit.* He wanted to smash his fist into the wall and roar with anger and despair.

But he couldn't...*couldn't* lose control now. Not with an audience.

The blood drained abruptly from his head, leaving him clammy and light-headed. "Dammit, Larry," he growled, and sagged as though someone had cut him off at the knees.

Squeezing his eyes closed to block out the wildly spinning cell, he staggered and hoped he wouldn't embarrass himself by passing out—or tossing his cookies. He could just imagine what the sexy nurse would think about the hotshot SEAL then.

"I'm s-sorry, M-Major...it's just that I had b-both hands f-full."

He felt her an instant before her arms wrapped around him, easing him backwards, soft and silky and smelling like cool mountain air. Mortified, Sam pulled away and collapsed wearily onto the narrow bunk, slinging an arm across his face.

"Don' sweat it, kid," he slurred, and prayed for oblivion. Unfortunately, sleep always came with a heavy price and he wasn't ready to go there. The nightmares were still too real, the memories too raw, the latest flashback still too recent. So vivid he could taste the fear, hear the furious pounding of his pulse in his head.

The Navy shrinks had warned that they'd get worse

before they got better. They'd also warned that they'd last for years.

Well, hell. Just what he was looking forward to. A constant reminder of his greatest failure.

"Major Kellan?"

In the meantime he had to face Nurse…what's-her-name.

Swiping his good hand over his face, he eased open his eyes and focused on the statuesque blonde watching him warily and with more than a hint of concern.

He didn't want her pity—or anything else she had to offer. He wanted to be left alone. *Needed* to be left alone. "I'm fine," he snapped, furious with himself and embarrassed that she'd witnessed an episode. Hoping to distract his brain from the endless loop of horrifying images, Sam focused his attention on her.

Yeah, much better to focus on the nurse.

With her thick silvery blond hair haphazardly pulled off a stunning face dominated by deep green eyes and a lush wide mouth, she looked like a sexy angel and smelled like a wood sprite—all fresh and clean and earthy like the mountains in spring. Raindrops glistened in her hair like diamonds, giving her an ethereal quality that made him wonder if he *was* drunk or just plain losing it.

"No, you're not," she contradicted softly. "But you will be."

For one confused moment Sam wondered if he'd spoken his thoughts out loud before he remembered he'd said he was fine.

"Sure," he growled, clenching his teeth on a wave of grief and anger. I *will. But my friends are still dead. And the woman patching me up thinks Crescent Lake's hero is a whacked-out crazy with a drinking problem.*

Yeah, right. Hero. What a joke.

Heroes didn't let their teams down. They didn't return

home with their buddies in body bags no matter what the Navy shrinks said. But his week of detention in a small, dark hole, deep in mountainous enemy territory wasn't something he talked about. He could barely *think* about it let alone talk about the hours of interrogation and torture that had left half his team dead.

The only reason *he'd* survived long enough to escape had been because they'd found out he was a medic and wanted him to treat some sick kid. He'd tried to bargain until they let his team go but they'd dragged in the team rookie and held a gun to his head. Afterwards they'd—

No. Don't go there. Not when the horror was still so fresh in his mind that every time he closed his eyes, he was back in that hellhole.

"Major Kellan?"

Jolted from his unpleasant thoughts, Sam saw the syringe and shot out his hand to wrap hard fingers around her wrist. Other than a slight widening of her eyes, the nurse held her ground without flinching. After a couple of tense beats she arched her brow, the move managing to convey a boatload of indulgent concern. Like he was a cranky toddler up past his bedtime. He groaned silently. *Just great.*

His face heated and he narrowed his eyes but she silently held his gaze, like he wasn't almost a foot taller, a hundred pounds heavier, and a whole hell of a lot meaner.

Clearly the woman was missing a few IQ points, he decided with a mix of admiration and annoyance, or she wasn't as soft and silky as she looked. He closed his eyes on a surge of self-disgust. All he needed to complete his humiliation was for her to ruffle his hair and kiss his "owie" better.

Way to go, hotshot.

"Do I need to wave a white flag or are you a friendly?" she asked with a hint of amusement, and when his lashes rose, she indicated the hand wrapped around her wrist.

He grimaced and released her. *Jeez, could this get any worse?* Embarrassment had him muttering, "I don't hit women." He jerked his chin at the syringe. "Unless they're armed."

She followed his gaze. "Oh, this?" Her mouth curved sweetly into a smile that instantly made him suspicious *and* want to take a greedy bite of that lush lower lip. "Surely you're not afraid of a little needle, Major?" Her smile grew as though she'd just learnt his deepest, darkest secret. *Not even close, lady.* "A big tough SEAL like you?" She made a soothing sound in the back of her throat. "It won't hurt a bit. Trust me."

Sam grunted out a laugh and hauled himself into a sitting position, hissing through clenched teeth when the move sent pain radiating through his chest and burning across his belly. "That's what they all say," he growled. "Right before they stab you in the heart."

"Not to worry," she said, moving closer and wrapping him in clean mountain air. "I have no interest in your heart, Major. I'm aiming a little lower than that."

And then, as though suddenly realizing what she'd said, her cheeks turned pink and she sucked in a sharp breath while Sam choked out a stunned "*Huh?*" and dropped his uninjured hand to protect his crotch.

"Not th-that low," she stuttered with a strangled snicker. "Although I'd probably be doing the rest of the female population a favor."

He choked for the second time in as many seconds but before he could demand what she meant, the outer door banged open again and she froze, eyes jerking to his, all wide and apprehensive as though she expected him to go all psycho GI Joe on her.

Dammit. He did not go around terrorizing women. Well…not unless they were holding a machine gun on him. Then all bets were off.

Scowling, he opened his mouth to tell her to knock it off, but his brother strode into the holding cells looking all officious and in charge, and Sam turned his irritation on someone more deserving.

Unfortunately, one look at Ruben's face had Sam's annoyance abruptly fading. He knew that look. Had seen it a thousand times on his CO's face. Something was up. Something bad.

"I hope you haven't used that on him yet." Ruben tossed an armful of clothing onto the bunk. "Get dressed," he told Sam. "We're heading out."

Blondie gasped and stepped between them. "What—? No!" she hissed. "Are you insane?"

Sam ignored her outburst and rose, pain abruptly receding as his SEAL training took over. "What happened?"

"A group of hikers didn't check in after closing," Ruben said, his wary gaze flicking to the syringe, "and the weather's turned bad. Park rangers just found their vehicle up near Pike's Pass. Lake route turned up empty and they think the group took the trail leading up into the mountains."

"Elk Ridge," Sam guessed, fatigue instantly forgotten as adrenaline surged through his veins. Here was the opportunity he hadn't even realized he'd been waiting for, to get out there and do something more useful than working the taps at his sister's bar. Frankly, after months of "recuperation" he was thoroughly sick of his own company and damn tired of sitting around feeling sorry for himself.

Ruben nodded and backed away, keeping a wary eye on Cassidy, as though expecting her to use the syringe on *him*. "Can't you just wrap him up or something? My usual tracker had a family emergency and we're in a hurry."

Her eyes widened. "Wrap—? He's not a cheeseburger," she snapped, sending Ruben's eyebrows into his hairline. "And in case it escaped your notice, Sheriff, the major is bleeding, *and* he's been drinking. It would be suicidal to go climbing mountains in his condition. I'm going to insist you leave him here. Or, better yet, let me take him to the hospital."

Sam brushed past her to where Larry had set out the medical supplies. "I'm fine," he said brusquely, reaching for a wound dressing. "I told you I wasn't drunk."

Before he could open the packet she snatched it from him and shoved her shoulder into his side as though she'd physically keep him from leaving.

As if.

He would have snickered at the absurdity if he hadn't been sucking in a painful breath. Turning a scowl on her that usually had people backing off in a hurry, she surprised him with a snapped "Back it up, Major," clearly not intimidated by his big bad Navy SEAL attitude.

He gave an annoyed grunt and tried to snatch it back.

"I mean it," she warned, jabbing her finger into his chest. "Or I'll use the syringe and the sheriff will have no choice but to go without you." She narrowed her eyes at him when he continued to glare at her while contemplating letting her try.

Heck, he might even enjoy it.

"And FYI, *buddy*, I nearly got intoxicated on the alcoholic haze surrounding you when I arrived, and not five minutes ago you almost fell on your face. You are *not* in any condition to go anywhere, least of all into the mountains on S&R. Besides," she reasoned sweetly, "you're bleeding all over the sheriff's nice clean jail cell. You need stitches." She paused and dropped her eyes meaningfully to his hand and then his abdomen. "Lots of them."

Staring down at her, Sam felt his lips twitch. She was like an enraged kitten—all fierce green eyes and ruffled silver fur. For just an instant he was tempted to reach out and smooth his hands over all that soft skin and silky silvery blond hair until she purred. One look into her narrowed eyes, however, and Sam knew she would probably bite his hand off at the wrist if he tried.

He made a scoffing sound filled with masculine impatience and amusement, which only served to narrow her eyes even further. "I've had mosquito bites worse than this," he assured her, feeling unaccountably cheered by her concern. "And if you're worried about blood alcohol levels, I'm sure the sheriff can organize a breathalyzer."

For long tense moments they engaged in a silent battle of wills until she finally uttered a soft "*Aargh*" followed by "Fine" in a tone that clearly meant it wasn't, and Sam had to clench his teeth to keep from grinning. He had a feeling grinning would be bad for his health.

"Oh…and FYI, *sweetheart*," he continued, while she sorted through the supplies with barely leashed temper, "I wasn't drinking. The weasel tried to break a bottle over my head. When I ducked, it shattered against the bar and soaked into my shirt. That was *before* he tried to gut me with it."

She turned towards him with a derisive sound and raised a brow that clearly conveyed her opinion of his explanation. "I said fine, didn't I?"

"You most certainly did," Ruben said dryly, shoving his face between them. "But I'm still not seeing anything happening here, people." He waited a couple of beats as his gaze ping-ponged between them. "So if you kids could save the lovers' spat for another time, I'd like my chief tracker."

Feeling her face catch fire, Cassidy broke eye contact with the Navy SEAL to send the sheriff a long, silent, narrow-eyed look that had him backing away with his hands up.

She turned back to snap, "Lift your arm." When he did

she swiped disinfectant across the angry gash, completely ignoring the hissed response to her cavalier treatment.

After a long murmured conversation during which she cleaned and applied a few adhesive cross-strips to keep the edges of the wound together, the sheriff left. Cassidy knew the instant the SEAL's attention shifted back to her because the tiny hairs on the back of her neck prickled.

With unsteady hands she dressed his wound then cleaned and tightly wrapped his hand in a waterproof dressing, before turning away to gather the debris.

The length of her back heated an instant before a long tanned arm reached over her shoulder to snag a bandage. Cursing the way her skin prickled and her body tightened with some kind of weird anticipation, she sent a dark look over her shoulder and watched in silence as he awkwardly attempted to wrap it around his torso. After a moment she sighed and put out her hand, saying wearily, "I'll do it."

Clearly surprised by her offer, Samuel held her gaze for a long tension-filled moment. His laugh was a husky rasp in the tense silence and did annoying things to her breathing. "You're not going to strangle me with it, are you?"

Cassidy knew the taping would help him move—and breathe—more comfortably as he leapt tall mountains in a single bound. She rolled her eyes and waited while he gingerly raised his arms to link both hands behind his head.

Hard muscles shifted beneath his taut, tanned skin and she had to bite her lip to keep from sighing like a stupid female drunk on manly pheromones. She swallowed the urge to lean forward and swipe her tongue across his strong, tanned throat. As though he'd read her mind, he sucked in a sharp breath and she froze, watching in awed fascination as flesh rippled and goose bumps broke out across his skin an inch from her nose.

Heat snapped in the air between them and her mind went numb. *Good grief,* she thought with horror, *I'm at-*

tracted to him? Appalled and more than a little rattled, she lifted her gaze, only to find him watching her, the expression in his gold eyes sending her blood pressure shooting into the stratosphere. She didn't have to wonder if he was as affected by their proximity as she was.

Tearing her gaze from his, she muttered, "You're an idiot," unsure if she was addressing him or herself. In case it was him, she continued with, "And so is the sheriff for expecting you to go out like this."

"Hikers are missing," he reminded her impatiently.

She rolled her eyes. She'd treated people suffering from trauma and knew enough about PTSD to be worried about the battle-alert episodes that culminated in dizziness, muscle tremors, sweating and confusion.

"You almost fainted," she pointed out.

"Don't be ridiculous," he snapped, as though she'd suggested something indecent. "SEALs don't faint. I was just a bit dizzy, that's all. I suffer from low blood pressure."

Cassidy looked up at the outrageous lie and shut her mouth on a sigh. Clearly he was in denial. *Fine.* She was just doing her job.

Besides, he was a Navy SEAL. She reminded herself that he did this kind of thing all the time. A shiver slinked up her spine as she pictured him sneaking into hostile territory, wiping everything out before ghosting out again as silently as he'd arrived. She could even picture him—

"What?"

Yeah, Cassidy. What?

Shaking her head, she went back to binding his torso, reminding herself that she didn't need rescuing. She wasn't a damsel in distress and those gold eyes couldn't see into her mind or know what was happening to her.

Except—*darn him*—he probably did. He was no doubt an expert at making women lose their brain cells just by flexing those awesome biceps—or staring at them with that brooding gold gaze. It was no wonder she felt like she was running a fever. It was no wonder her blood was humming through her veins. Her hormone levels were probably shooting through the stratosphere along with her blood pressure.

Finally she fastened the bandage and took a hasty step back, nearly knocking over the table and its contents in her haste to escape. A large hand on her arm kept her upright and when it tightened as she turned away, she looked up. With his gaze on hers, he gently swiped a line of fire across her bottom lip. She gasped and her heart gave a shocked little blip at the unexpected contact.

"Thank you," he said, leaning towards her. And just when she thought he meant to kiss her, he snagged a plastic container of pain meds behind her. Grinning at the expression on her face, he popped the top, shook a couple into his palm.

He gave a mocking little salute and tossed the container back in the box. "Gotta go," he said, scooping up his clothing in his good hand. With one last heated look in her direction he sauntered from the cell, all long loose-limbed masculine grace, leaving Cassidy staring at the wide expanse of his muscular back and the very interesting way he filled out his faded jeans.

Fortunately, before the outer door could close behind him, Cassidy pulled herself together enough to croak, "You need stitches, Major. I suggest coming to the hospital before you get septicemia and die a horrible death."

Grinning at her over one broad shoulder, he drawled, "It's a date, darlin'," and disappeared, leaving Cassidy with the impression that he had absolutely no intention of following through with his promise.

At least, not for sutures.

CHAPTER THREE

THE SMALL TOWN of Crescent Lake had been established when traders heading north had come over the mountains and found a large crescent-shaped lake nestled in a thickly wooded area. According to Mrs. Krenson at the Lakeside Inn, it had started out as a rough fur-trading town that had gradually grown into the popular tourist town it was today.

The inn, once the local house of pleasure, had been re-modeled and modernized over the years. Rising out of a picturesque forest, with mountains at its back and the lake at its feet like a small sparkling sea, it now resembled a gracious, well-preserved old lady, appearing both elegant and mysterious. At least, that's what it said in the brochure and what Cassidy had thought when she'd arrived a few weeks before.

Now, with dark clouds hanging over the valley, the lake was nothing like the crystal-clear mirror it resembled in the pictures and Cassidy had to wish for "sturdy" rather than mysterious.

The day had dawned gray and wet and, standing at her bedroom window, Cassidy couldn't help shivering as she looked up at the mountains shrouded in swirling fog, ee-rily beautiful and threatening. She wondered if the hikers had been found.

And if she was thinking of a certain someone, it was only because he had no business being out there in the first place. He might be an all-weather hero, but he'd been exhausted, injured and on an edge only he could see. All it would take was one wrong move, one misstep and… And then nothing, she told herself irritably as she spun away from the window. Samuel Kellan was a big boy, a highly trained Navy SEAL. If he wanted to scour the mountains for the next week, it was what he'd been trained for. Heck, he could probably live off the land and heal himself using plants and tree bark.

Whatever effect he'd had on her, Cassidy mused as she closed her bedroom door and headed for the bathroom at the end of the hall, it was over. She'd had the entire night to think about her reaction to him and in the early hours had come to the conclusion that she'd been suffering from low blood sugar…and maybe been a little freaked at finding herself in a jail cell. Maybe even a little awed at meeting a national hero. All perfectly logical explanations for her behavior.

Fortunately she'd recovered, and if she saw him again she'd be the cool, level-headed professional she had a reputation for being. Besides, Samuel J. Kellan was just a man. Like any other.

After a quick shower, she brushed her teeth and headed back to her room to dress. It was her day off and she intended playing tourist. She might have come to the Cascades to escape the mess she'd made of things in Boston, but that didn't mean she had to bury herself in work. Crescent Lake was a beautiful town filled with friendly, curious people who'd brought her baked goodies just to welcome her to town.

She'd read that the Lakefront Boardwalk housed a host of stores that included a few antiques shops, an art gallery selling local artwork, a quaint bookshop and, among others, a cozy coffee shop with a spectacular view of the lake and mountains.

She hadn't had a decent latte since leaving Boston, and according to the nurses, Just Java served a delicious Caribbean mocha latte, and the triple chocolate muffins were better than sex.

Just what she needed, a double dose of sin.

A soft knock on her door startled her out of her chocolate fantasy and sent her pulse skittering.

"Dr. Mahoney?" a muffled voice called from the hallway. "Cassidy, dear? Are you awake?"

Shrugging into her wrap, Cassidy fastened the tie and shoved damp hair off her forehead. She pulled open the door as a ball of dread settled in her belly. Her landlady wouldn't disturb her unless there was an emergency.

Val Krenson's brows were pinched together over her faded blue eyes and one hand was poised to knock again. "I'm sorry to wake you, dear," she apologized quickly. "That was the hospital. They found the hikers. How soon can you get there?"

"Ten minutes," Cassidy said, already morphing into emergency mode. "Fifteen at the most." She stepped back into the room and would have shut the door but Val held out a hand to detain her.

"John Randal is downstairs, dear. Shall I ask him to wait?"

"That's okay, Val," Cassidy said with a quick shake of her head. "I'll need my car later and I don't want to inconvenience anyone." The last time the deputy had driven her anywhere she'd landed up at the jail. So not going there.

"Planning a little down time?" Val asked with a warm smile.

"It'll have to wait." Cassidy sighed. "They didn't say how serious, did they?"

"I'm afraid not, dear. Just that you get there as soon as possible." She leaned forward. "I'm glad you're here to help Monty out, dear. He tires easily these days." She shook her head. "That man should have retired years ago but not many people want to bury themselves in the mountains."

In some ways Cassidy could understand why. They were a couple of hours from the nearest large town and there wasn't much in the way of nightlife that didn't include a few bars, steakhouses and the local bar and grill, Fahrenheit's.

She might feel like a fish out of water, but she'd been surprised to discover she liked the close-knit community where people knew each other and exchanged gossip with their favorite recipes.

At least here people stopped to chat when they saw you, she thought with a smile, instead of staring right through you as though you didn't exist, or scuttling away like you were an escaped crazy. Surprisingly she was enjoying the slower pace. It was a nice change to be able to connect with the people she was treating. But long term? She didn't know.

"It's a beautiful town, Val, but I've only got a short-term contract."

Val laughed and patted Cassidy's arm. "Don't worry, dear," she said over her shoulder, a twinkle lighting her blue eyes. "I have a feeling you're going to be around a long time."

Cassidy uttered a noncommittal "Hmm" and shut the door behind her landlady. She hunted in the closet for a clean pair of jeans, underwear, socks and a soft green long-sleeved T-shirt. Dressing quickly, she shoved her feet into the nearest pair of boots and grabbed a brush that she hurriedly pulled through her wet hair before piling it on top of her head in a loose style that would dry quickly. Foregoing makeup, she grabbed her medical bag and jacket and headed for the door.

Fifteen minutes after closing the door behind the innkeeper, Cassidy pulled up beside the hospital's staff entrance. Locking her car—which everyone said was un-necessary—she hurried into the waiting room, which was already bustling with chaos and reminded her of a busy city ER.

Her eyes widened. There were people everywhere—sprawled in chairs with their heads tilted back in exhaustion, while even more hovered near the entrance, propping up the walls, slugging back steaming coffee and wolfing down fat sandwiches handed out by a group of women.

Sandwiches? Coffee? And where had all these people come from? It looked like a temporary ops center—or a tea party for big hulking men.

"Good, you're here." A voice at her elbow distracted her from the chaos and Cassidy turned to see the head nurse holding out a clipboard.

She accepted the board, feeling a little shell-shocked. "What on earth's going on?"

Fran Gilbert followed her gaze. "The town's disaster committee in action," she explained with a shrug, as though it happened every day.

Disaster—? Oh, no. Cassidy gulped down a sudden sick feeling. *Please don't tell me...!* Shaking off her pessimistic thoughts, she frowned at the older woman. "Disaster? How bad?"

Fran frowned in confusion. "Bad?" Then realizing what Cassidy was thinking, she said, "*No!* God, no. Cassidy, I'm sorry. I didn't mean to scare you." She gave Cassidy a quick hug. "I just meant that the disaster committee responds whenever the rescue teams go out. The junior league ladies take turns providing hot food and drinks. To practice they set up basic first-aid stations for minor injuries. When news came through that the hikers were being brought down, they moved operations here."

"Oh." Cassidy let out a whoosh of relief, a little awed at

the way the community mobilized when the need arose. Any disaster in a big city was met with looting and rioting.

"They say it's to practice for a real disaster but I think it's just an excuse to get out and socialize."

Cassidy nodded. "Okay, no disaster. What *do* we have?" she asked, as Fran led her towards the ER cubicles.

"Mostly minor but too many for poor Monty to cope with," the older woman said, before launching into a rapid-fire report worthy of a busy city ER nurse.

Rebecca Thornton, she told Cassidy, had slipped and fallen off the trail. She'd broken her leg and her husband had climbed down the steep embankment to get to her. He'd slipped near the bottom in the treacherous conditions and knocked himself out. Several others had then climbed down to carry the injured couple out but had found their way blocked by huge boulders. With the gully rapidly filling with water, the group still on the trail had elected to return and alert the authorities. They hadn't made it back yet and a team was still out, looking for them.

Dr. Montgomery looked up briefly from checking a young man's bruised and lacerated arm. "Glad they found you," he said with an absent smile, before turning to give the attending nurse instructions.

Soon Cassidy was swamped, treating a broken leg and collarbone, a fractured wrist and a concussion. There was a bruised and swollen knee that she suspected might be cartilage damage, a host of cuts and scrapes, and hypothermia along with exhaustion and dehydration.

And that was just the hiking party.

Once they'd been examined, treated and transferred to the wards for fluids and observation, Cassidy turned her attention to the rescue crew. Among the expected lacerations and contusions, she diagnosed torn ankle ligaments, a dislocated shoulder and a broken finger. Pretty mild considering the awful night they'd endured, she mused, sending one nurse to the suture room and another to X-rays.

She'd just left Hank Henderson propped up with an ice pack on his foot when the elderly doctor called to ask her opinion about the shoulder injury.

After examining Andy Littleton, Cassidy decided there didn't seem to be any serious ligament damage that would require surgery. She told Andy to take a deep breath and quickly pulled his shoulder back into place. He went white and swayed alarmingly before throwing up in the kidney dish she shoved at him.

Listing drunkenly while she strapped his shoulder and arm, he made Cassidy swear a blood oath that she wouldn't tell anyone he'd cried like a girl. Biting back a grin of sympathy, she squeezed his hand, and turned to find Harry Montgomery beaming at her like a proud teacher whose pupil had surpassed his expectations.

"Looks like old Howie's loss is our gain, eh?" The big man chuckled, his age-spotted hand patting her shoulder awkwardly. "He said you were a bright young thing. What he didn't say was that you have an easy way with people along with that sharp diagnostic mind." He studied her shrewdly. "I guess the old buzzard didn't want to lose you, eh?"

With heat rising to her cheeks, Cassidy looped her stethoscope around her neck. She felt like a new resident under scrutiny. Besides, one didn't have to be Einstein to pick up the question behind the compliment. The question of why she was treating runny noses and middle-ear infections in a small mountain hospital instead of running her own ER—which was what she'd originally intended.

"He's a wonderful man," she replied with a warm smile. "And I loved the daily challenges in ER." Thrusting her hands into her lab-coat pockets, she chose her words carefully. "But big city ERs are like operating in a war zone, and when you lose count of the number of ODs, stabbings and rapes you treat…" She sighed. "I realized I needed a change—to get back to basics. Howie mentioned Crescent Lake and I thought it might be the perfect place to try out something more community-oriented."

She didn't say that hearing it was deep in the Cascades and a continent away from Boston had sounded appealing. She'd been desperate to get away and work on forgetting the career-damaging fallout of treating a real-life hero injured in the line of duty. A "hero" who'd turned out to be anything but.

She shuddered at the memory. *God*, she'd been stupidly naïve and had paid a very high price. Then again, how could anyone have known the handsome vice cop wasn't one of the good guys?

The charming wounded-hero act had been just that—an act. He'd used it to lull people—*her*—into a false sense of security. He'd pursued her with flowers, gifts and romantic dinners then stolen her hospital security card, giving him access to the ER dispensary as well as a stack of prescription pads, which he'd used by forging her signature. In the end there'd been a full-scale police investigation— with her as the prime suspect.

In truth, all she'd really been guilty of had been bad judgment. She'd trusted someone who'd proved to be anything *but* trustworthy. In hindsight he'd been too good to be true: too romantic and too sensitive for it not to have been a very clever performance from a man who knew exactly what women wanted.

By the time she'd realized something was wrong, the media frenzy had crucified her, calling her professional competence into question. It had been a nightmare.

Fortunately for her, Lance Turnbull had been under internal investigation. One that had involved a dozen other women doctors around the city. Cassidy had eventually been cleared of all charges but the damage had been done. She'd suffered through snide comments and cruel jokes from her colleagues until she'd finally buckled under the stress.

"GP work is pretty boring compared to the excitement of ER," the old doctor warned, wrenching her from her disturbing thoughts. "Especially here in the boondocks."

Relieved to focus on something other than her past failures, Cassidy looked around at the controlled chaos and sent him a small smile. "I wouldn't exactly call it boring," she said, her smile turning into a grin when his deep chuckle filled the hallway.

"No, it isn't," he agreed, "especially during tourist season. But off season gets pretty quiet."

"I can do quiet. And I'm impressed with the way everyone bands together. It's wonderful knowing that there are still places where people are willing to step in and help their neighbors without expecting something in return."

"That's what's kept me here for sixty years," he said, moving to the door. "The warm community spirit. You don't find that in the city." He turned and studied her intently. "I've watched you over the past two weeks, Cassidy, and you're a very perceptive diagnostician. We could use someone like you heading up the hospital." And when Cassidy opened her mouth to remind him that she was only there for three months, he beat her to it with his parting shot, "Think about it," before disappearing down the hallway.

Cassidy watched him leave. Admittedly she was enjoying the opportunity to practice family medicine in a town where people cared about each other, but Boston was her home. And that kind of decision couldn't be made lightly.

It wasn't until late afternoon that she finally realized she'd been hanging around waiting for something to happen. It didn't take a genius to realize that *something* was a certain Navy SEAL and that she'd been waiting for him to come in to have his injuries treated.

Irritated with herself, she'd collected her purse and jacket and was on her way out when the door banged open and there he was, looking like he'd just blown in from a big, bad superheroes convention with his big, bad SEAL attitude.

When her knees wobbled and her head went light, Cassidy assured herself it was simply because she hadn't eaten anything all day. It certainly didn't have anything to do with the way his gold eyes latched onto her like a tractor beam.

Gesturing to an empty suture room, Cassidy wordlessly handed her jacket and purse to the receptionist and ignored the jitters in her belly as the sheriff half-dragged, half-carried him down the corridor and through the doorway to heave him onto the narrow bed. And just like that, every delusional thought she'd had in the early hours blew up right in her face.

"You may now stick him with as many needles as you like," the sheriff announced, shoving his hands on his hips and glaring at his brother. "In fact, that's an official order. Maybe it will improve his attitude and I won't have to toss him in jail again for disobeying a direct order."

"I said I was fine," the SEAL snarled as Greg, the young deputy who'd helped drag him into the examination room, ducked his head and made a beeline for the door.

Wise move, she thought when a string of muttered threats turned the air blue. She might be relieved he'd made it back in one piece but it had been a long day and an even longer night, obsessing about whether or not she had been imagining things. The good news was that she was sane and not hallucinating. The bad news was, Cassidy thought with a sinking sensation, he was even more dangerously attractive in the cold light of day.

And that was bad. Very bad. Because Cassidy Mahoney was done with dangerous bad boys who made women swoon. She really was too busy getting her life back to deal with two hundred and forty pounds of belligerent male.

It seemed the sheriff was too since he folded his arms across his chest and glared at his brother, clearly not intimidated by the show of aggression. "And if he gives you any trouble, make him wear a pretty pink hospital gown," he barked, ignoring the way Sam's lip drew back over his teeth in a silent snarl. "He deserves to have everyone laugh at his ugly butt after the stunt he pulled."

Cassidy watched the silent clash of wills and her first thought was that nothing about Major Kellan was ugly. She was pretty sure her staff wouldn't be laughing either. More like swooning from the thick cloud of testosterone and bad attitude that surrounded him.

A fierce golden gaze caught and held hers as though he knew what she was thinking, and Cassidy felt a flush creep up her neck into her cheeks. Besides being grossly unprofessional, picturing him naked wouldn't do a thing to convince her she'd imagined her earlier reaction to him.

The sheriff raked his hand through his wet hair, looking tired and exasperated. "Listen up, man," he growled, "I know you're a big, mean SEAL and everything, but just let the doc check you out, okay? I don't have time to babysit you or keep you from bleeding to death. You wouldn't believe the paperwork. It's a nightmare. Elections are coming up and I can't afford to have you die and make me look bad."

"I keep telling you I'm fine," Sam snarled. "Quit hovering like a girl. There's nothing Old Monty can do that I can't do for myself, so get the hell out of my face before I break your ugly mug."

"Oh, please." Ruben snickered rudely. "You can't even break a sweat without help. Now suck it up and let the doc check you out. You look like hell."

Samuel said something that Cassidy was pretty sure was anatomically impossible but before her eyes could do more than widen, Ruben turned to her with a grim smile. "Doc, he's all yours, just as I promised. He's a bit more battered and bloodied but I refuse to take credit for that. He's a hard-headed pain in the ass so you might consider sedating him." He sent his brother a meaningful glare. "In fact, unconscious would be a real improvement."

Ignoring the derisive suggestion, Sam turned narrowed eyes her way. "Doc?" he demanded. "You're the *doctor*?" His tone suggested she'd deliberately misled him. "I thought you were the nurse."

"No," she corrected smoothly. "You thought I was a stripper."

"And with that," Ruben drawled mockingly, "I rest my case." He slapped his hat on his head and adjusted the brim. "Cassidy, ignore the inscrutable death stares. Underneath all that macho SEAL *hoo-yah* attitude he's really quite sweet."

The SEAL snarled something impolite and with a deep laugh the sheriff sketched a salute and disappeared down the hallway, leaving Cassidy with two hundred pounds of seething testosterone. Sweet wasn't a word she'd associate with Major Hotstuff, she mused, moving to the supply cabinet for a towel. Just the idea of it made her want to smile. So she frowned instead.

"So," he said, taking the towel and fixing her with his mesmerizing stare, "you're a doctor."

She sent him a cool look then turned to remove disinfectant and a package of swabs from the overhead cabinet. "Is that a problem, Major, or an apology?"

His amused gaze drifted over her face and breasts to

the neat row of supplies she'd begun setting out and he drawled, "Only if you're plotting revenge."

"Fortunately for you I'm not the vengeful type, Major."

His mouth curled at one corner and he said, "Uh-huh" into the towel. Cassidy ignored the impulse to bang her head against the wall. She had a feeling it would be a lot less painful than getting caught up in the man's web.

Fortunately, her little chat with the elderly doctor had reminded her of why she was off men in anything but the professional sense. Flicking him an assessing glance, she decided the sheriff was right. He did look like hell.

"There's no one to save you from the needle this time, Major." She opened another cabinet and removed a suture kit and syringes. "In fact—" her voice was brisk as she moved closer "—I can foresee more than one in your immediate future."

Ignoring the dark eyebrow hiking up his forehead, she stepped close and pushed the soaked parka over his wide shoulders and down his arms. He shrugged and sucked in a sharp breath, before drawling, "Not just beautiful and smart, but psychic too?"

Cassidy bit back a snort and tossed the garment onto the floor, before turning to wash her hands at the small basin. "It doesn't take a clairvoyant to see that you're an action junkie looking for trouble," she replied smoothly, pulling a strip off the paper towel dispenser.

He shrugged. "Goes with the job."

"For which the free world is eternally grateful." She dried her hands and dropped the paper into the bin as she turned. She caught his eyes crinkling at the corners as though he didn't take himself half as seriously as other people did, which…surprised her. She was accustomed to being surrounded by alpha males who thought they sat at God's right hand. Discovering he could poke fun at himself had something warm and light sliding into her belly. Something that felt very much like admiration.

Telling herself that certainly didn't mean she *liked* him, Cassidy focused on his once white T-shirt, now covered in mud and blood. Shaking her head, she pulled it out of his damp waistband and grabbed a pair of scissors off the counter.

With a few snips, his shirt fell away and she quickly unwound the soiled bandage. When the move exposed fresh blood oozing from the loosened dressing, she bit back a curse.

"You're an idiot," she muttered, knowing exactly who she was addressing this time. Lifting a loose edge, she pressed her hand gently against his hard belly and ripped it off in one smooth move.

Sam hissed audibly in surprise and pain. "*Holy...!* Hell and damnation, woman, what the *hell* was that?" His fingers whitened around the edge of the bed and he looked like he wanted to wrap them around her throat.

"Sorry," she said, and meaning it. It would have been worse if she'd taken her time removing it. "It's better coming off fast."

"For you maybe... *Jeez*...does the CIA know about you?"

"The CIA?" she asked, sending him a narrow-eyed look out the corner of her eye, fairly certain he wasn't being complimentary.

"Yeah. Hear they're looking for interrogators." Definitely not complimentary. "My CO would recruit you on the spot to torture the tadpoles in BUD/S."

"Tadpoles? Buds?" she asked, pouring disinfectant into a stainless-steel bowl and filling it with warm water.

"Wannabe SEALs in Basic Underwater Demolition SEALs," he told her. "Have to knock the cra...I mean stuffing out of them during hell week to sort out the men from the boys. You'd be perfect for the job."

Apparently *he'd* managed to survive without having the stuffing knocked out of him. She wondered how he'd managed it. Sheer stubbornness most likely.

She pulled on a pair of latex gloves then ripped off a large section of cotton wool. "I'm good, but thanks anyway." She pressed a hand to the smooth ball of his shoulder. "Lie flat and lift your arm over your head."

His scowl turned into a grimace when he realized he was too big and had to scoot down the bed, ending up with half his long legs draped over the end. Growling irritably about "damn midget beds", he raised his arm and bent it behind his head. With lids lowered over his unusual eyes, he sent her a sleepy look.

"Although if you continue ripping off my clothes and making me lie down," he drawled softly, "I'll start thinking you have ulterior motives, Miz Honey."

"That's *Dr.* Mahoney to you," she said absently, carefully cleaning the area around the wound before selecting another wad of gauze to clean the wound itself. It would take about a dozen stitches to close.

"Yes, *ma'am.*" His voice was polite and subdued but a quick look caught the irreverent smirk curling his mouth. Cassidy swallowed the impulse to return that impudent grin. Or worse—kiss his battered mouth better. From all accounts he was the kind of man who wouldn't stop at kissing. From all accounts he was only interested in quick tumbles with the nearest available woman. Probably because being a SEAL precluded any kind of stable or long-term relationship.

She shivered. If she knew what was good for her, she'd shove her libido back into hibernation and stop getting all excited every time he invaded her space.

Dr. Mahoney was back in charge, she reminded herself,

and there would be no mixing her chemistry with his. On *any* level. She was going to patch him up, send him on his way, and hope like hell she never saw him again.

CHAPTER FOUR

SAM WATCHED DOC BOSTON work on his torso and wondered why he was so drawn to a woman who made it abundantly clear she wasn't interested. He tried reminding himself that he'd be heading back to Coronado soon and anything more than harmless flirting was impossible. It didn't help. Not even when he observed the competent way she wielded sharp objects.

Sure, she was beautiful but then, so were a million other women, and he'd had little problem leaving them behind. Except there was something compelling about her that told Sam she wouldn't be easy to forget or walk away from. She was smart and mouthy and didn't take his reputation as a badass seriously or treat him differently from other patients. And *that* more than anything made him like her.

Okay, he *really* liked the look of her—he was a guy, so sue him—but lately all the feminine adulation had begun to irritate him. All a lot of women saw was a SEAL with hard muscles and weird eyes. A guy they could brag about being with to their friends. He'd enjoyed that in his twenties, but in the decade since he'd seen and done things no one should see or do.

Cassidy Mahoney, on the other hand, did more of the squinty-eye thing that for some strange reason made him want to smile when he hadn't felt the urge in a long, long time. It made him want to push her up against the nearest wall and taste all that soft, smooth skin.

He thought of how she'd react if he acted on the impulse, and had to suppress a grin when her suspicion-filled look said she knew what he was thinking. His what-have-I-done-now eyebrow-lift had her eyes narrowing, as if she suspected he was up to no good. A flush rose from the lapels of her lab coat and climbed her neck into her cheeks.

If she only knew.

"I promise not to wrestle you to the ground and stab you in the throat with that," he assured her, then decided to qualify it with, "Well…maybe wrestle you to the ground…" His gaze smoothed over her breasts and up her long throat to her lush mouth. "Okay, *definitely* wrestle you to the ground. But the stabbing thing? You're safe. SEAL's honor."

She didn't disappoint him. Thrusting out a plump lower lip that he yearned to take a greedy bite out of, she huffed out an annoyed breath that disturbed the long tendrils of fine silvery hair escaping her tousled topknot. She appeared at once exasperated, embarrassed and incredibly appealing.

"Give it a rest, Major." She huffed again, shoving the needle into a vial of local anesthetic like she was probably imagining it was his hide. He covered a wince by scratching his chin. "It must be exhausting trying to keep that up."

"Keep what up?" he asked innocently, wanting her to keep talking. Even rife with irritation, he liked the sound of her voice—smooth and silky, like hundred-year-old bourbon. It intoxicated his senses and kept him from thinking about gut-wrenching guilt and things he couldn't change.

She removed the needle and flicked the syringe a couple of times before gently depressing the plunger. A tiny spurt fountained from the tip. "The seduction routine," she said, wiping an area close to his wound with an alcohol swab. "Heaven knows, just trying to keep up with it is exhausting."

"It's really no trouble," he assured her, except lately it *had* become exhausting. Most likely he was just out of practice. Life-and-death situations didn't leave much time for fun and games. "I can do it in my sleep."

She gently slid the needle into his flesh. There was a tiny pinch and almost instantly cold numbness began to spread along his side. He sighed with relief as she removed the needle and pressed a small swab over the puncture wound.

"That's the problem, isn't it?" she murmured, tossing the syringe into the nearby medical waste container. She opened the suture kit onto a strip of newly torn paper toweling. "It's meaningless."

He shrugged and this time couldn't prevent a wince from escaping. Last night he'd wrenched his shoulder hauling an injured man up a slippery cliff face. "Women seem to like it," he said on a yawn, deciding he really liked the way her wide green eyes went all squinty and irritated when he piled on the charm. It made him want to lay it on extra-thick just to see her scowl at him.

She made a noise that sounded like a snort and he had to clench his jaw to keep from grinning with satisfaction. "They probably don't want to hurt your feelings," she pointed out.

"You think so?" He tried the wounded look but he suspected she wasn't fooled.

"This is not the eighties," she informed him with a *get-real* lift of an eyebrow. "Not all women appreciate being charmed out of their panties with lines from a bad movie script."

He looked skeptical and she shook her head as though he was beyond help. Sam waited until she turned back with a suture needle and monofilament thread, before handing her needle scissors. He watched surprise flit across her face and knew what she was thinking. *What did a macho idiot know about needle scissors?* He grimaced. *Other than having first-hand experience?*

"I went to med school," he reminded her, when she made no move to take them. He was annoyed for caring about her opinion—which had been pretty obvious from the outset, thanks to the sheriff locking him in a jail cell for no good reason.

"The way I hear it," she said, accepting the instrument as well as the implied reproach with a nod, "you cut med school to play pirates." He watched her get a firm grip on the needle and press the edges of his skin together with her left hand. She pushed the needle through, released it and gripped it with the flat edge of the scissors, before carefully pulling it free.

"You shouldn't believe everything you hear," he advised darkly, talking about more than embellished stories of his SEAL exploits. He had a feeling someone had been filling her head with his youthful indiscretions—*most* of which were gross exaggerations, the rest outright lies.

Her open skepticism confirmed his suspicions. "You mean you don't wear a cape and fly around the world in your underwear, saving humanity?" Her movements were quick and confident and a neat row of stitches began closing the three-inch slash on his belly.

Sam chuckled and thanked God for BDUs. It was kind of nice having a conversation with a woman who didn't treat him like he walked on water or was there to scratch her itch. It was even better watching her full pink mouth when she talked. It made him think of long dark nights, crisp cool sheets and hot wet kisses when he hadn't thought about them in a while. It was a relief to discover he was still normal in one important area.

"You don't believe that, do you?"

She deftly tied off and started on a fourth suture. "I stopped believing in superheroes a long time ago, Major," she said absently. She looked up and caught his gaze. "So why *did* you?"

"Why did I what?"

"Join the Navy instead of finishing med school."

"I did finish," he told her, "courtesy of Uncle Sam."

"But why the armed forces when you were already doing something that would save lives?"

He fought a knee-jerk reaction to come up with some stupid macho excuse that would confirm her not so flattering opinion of him. But something held him back. Something deep inside wanted very much for her to think of him as more than a battered sailor with big muscles.

"I was in New York when the Towers fell," he said, wincing as the words emerged. He'd never shared his true reasons with anyone but for some reason found himself spilling his guts to her.

He remembered exactly what he'd been doing when his safe world had fallen apart. He'd been living the life of a typical student, concerned only with enjoying the hell out of being young, healthy and surrounded by girls and parties.

"You...you were *there*?"

Sam looked up, almost surprised to find he wasn't alone. Cassidy's green eyes were huge and filled with a compassion he knew he didn't deserve.

"A few blocks away," he said impassively. "I'd cut class and was staying in Brooklyn with a friend for a few days. We were sitting at a sidewalk café, having coffee and bagels, when...when the first plane flew into the towers." He fell silent for a couple beats before continuing. "We tried getting through but the cops stopped us. Never felt so helpless in my life. There I was, a fourth-year med student thinking I had it all."

His lips twisted self-deprecatingly. "Thinking I *knew* it all." He speared her with a haunted look. "I saw many draw their last breaths. I don't ever want to feel that helpless again. The next day Jack and I enlisted. We were determined to take a more active role in protecting our country."

"Healing the sick and saving people *is* taking an active role, Major," she reminded him, but he was already shaking his head.

"Not active enough, Doc. Besides, there are thousands of civilian doctors Stateside," he pointed out. "What about the men and women protecting our country? Protecting the free world? Who saves them?"

"I…"

"My friend's father was one of the firefighters killed that day," he continued, as though she hadn't interrupted. "I'll never forget the look on Jack's face when he heard his dad was never coming home." Sam closed his eyes on remembered devastation—of that day as well as events more recent than 9/11. "You never forget that kind of pain."

You never forget, Sam admitted silently. *And the guilt eats at you that you are alive and they aren't.*

Cassidy watched as fierce emotions moved across his features, through his beautiful eyes. She felt a little pinch in the region of her heart. Crescent Lake's hero was hurting, and the discovery that he was more than just a pretty face and a hot body terrified her in ways that she didn't want to analyze.

She'd rather think of him as a shallow womanizer who'd enlisted because men in uniform got more girls. Although, in or out of uniform, the man would attract more than his share of women.

Using her wrist to push away the tendrils of hair that kept obscuring her vision, Cassidy studied him closely. The events of 9/11 may have changed the course of his life, but she had a feeling something more recent had put that *haunted* look in his eyes. And suddenly, more than anything, she wanted them glinting wickedly at her again.

Whoa, she warned herself silently when the notion seemed more appealing than it should. *Way too intense for someone you can't wait to get away from.*

In silence, she completed another suture before asking casually, "So you didn't?"

His muscles bunched beneath her fingers and he went strangely still for a couple of beats before asking, "Didn't what?"

There was a sudden shift in the air and she felt the hair at her nape rise. Primitive warning whooshed up her spine and she sucked in a sharp breath. Lifting her head, she found his attention locked on her—laser bright and strangely intent. It was odd, feeling as though they were communicating on different levels, only one of which was verbal. And even more disturbing to realize that she didn't have a clue what it was all about.

"Cut med school to play pirates on the high seas," she reminded him, and watched, mesmerized, as his big body relaxed. His gaze lost that fierce glitter and his mouth its tight, forbidding line, even going so far as to kick up at one corner. The air surrounding them shifted again and she was left dizzied by the sudden shifts in mood.

His teeth flashed white in his dark face. "Well…technically…I suppose I did."

Cassidy sighed and concentrated on the last suture. "You're an idiot." Sam snorted, apparently as relieved as she was to lighten the tension. The band of pressure around her skull eased a little more. She really, *really*, didn't want to like him. At least, not any more than she already did. That would be so utterly irresponsible—not to mention stupid.

"That's the third time you've said that," he accused plaintively.

"I meant it before too."

His eyes crinkled at the corners. "Why? Because I like to jump out of airplanes?"

"No," she said, unlacing his mud-caked boot and dropping it on the floor, along with his wet sock. "Because you blow people up instead of healing them." She retrieved a stool from the corner and slid it under his hard calf, reaching for a pair of scissors. There was no way she was going to wrestle him out of his wet jeans to get to the thigh injury. Just the thought of him lying there in his underwear—*God, did he even wear them?*—gave her a hot flash.

"I do heal people," he said mildly as she began cutting the wet denim. "All spec ops teams need medics."

She paused and frowned at him. "Well, why aren't you doing *this*…" she gestured to the room around them "…instead of wreaking havoc and blowing things up?"

His expression clearly questioned her intelligence. "I just told you. Besides, I like blowing things up," he said as though she was a particularly dense blonde, and she wanted to smack him. She had a sneaky suspicion that had been his intention. It seemed he was as eager as she was to move away from intensely personal subjects. "And I'm good at wreaking havoc."

Cassidy rolled her eyes and said, "You are such a guy," with such feminine disgust that Sam laughed.

"And that's bad, how?"

He was so delusional that she stared silently at him for a couple of beats as though she couldn't believe what she was hearing.

Besides, the man's blood was probably ninety-nine percent testosterone and she'd been lucky to escape unscathed the first time around. Well, not completely unscathed, she admitted reluctantly, but she had a feeling if she allowed

Samuel Kellan to matter, she wouldn't be so lucky. "It's bad when you won't talk about what's bothering you."

He snorted and sent her a look that said she was delusional. "Talking's for politicians…and girls," he scoffed, and she huffed out an exasperated breath, suspecting that he was being insulting on purpose. *Sneaky.* "SEALs are doers," he continued. "They don't do a lot of standing around, talking. If they did, nothing would get done." His eyes crinkled and his grin turned wicked. "But if you want to know what I was thinking last night, I'd be happy—"

"I *know* what you were thinking," Cassidy quickly interrupted, slicing through tough, wet denim towards his knee. "Clearly your seduction techniques need adjusting."

He grinned and said, "Oh, yeah?" before waggling his eyebrows in a comical way that had her rolling her eyes. When she stopped checking out the state of her brain she found him studying her with an intensity that had her pulse hitching then picking up its pace. The man's mercurial mood changes made her dizzy.

"I'm talking about whatever it is that has you brooding when you think no one's looking," she said casually, as though she was just making conversation to take his mind off what she was about to do. "I'm talking about reacting to sharp stimuli like you're expecting a ninja attack." Something dark and haunted flickered in his gaze before his expression hardened. "Plenty of people suffer from PTSD, Major," she continued casually, as she hacked through the denim to his knee. "It's nothing to be ashamed of."

He made a rude sound. "You're a shrink now?" he drawled, and Cassidy continued as though he hadn't spoken. "I specialized in trauma medicine. People who survive traumatic experiences come through ER on a daily basis. It's very common."

"Just being a SEAL exposes you to stressful situations," Sam interrupted impatiently. "It's the job. If you can't deal, you have no business being a SEAL. So you deal. End of story." He was silent a moment and she felt the air shift again. "Besides, I like blowing things up, remember."

He clearly didn't intend to say anything more, but that was okay, Cassidy reflected. At least next time—*if* there was a next time—she could bring it up when he was in a better frame of mind. For now she'd respect his need to avoid the subject.

Lifting the denim at his knee to make the final cuts, she acknowledged quietly, "Yes, I remember."

She'd barely exposed his mid-thigh when he flinched and grabbed her hand with an alarmed "*Whoa.*" He'd clamped his free hand over his crotch and was eyeing the scissors like she was holding a live grenade.

Cassidy rolled her eyes and gently peeled away the blood-soaked denim, grimacing at the jagged gash on his hard thigh. "This is going to hurt," she said, reaching for disinfectant and cotton wool. After liberally dousing the area, she probed the wound gently, before injecting a pain-killer into his thigh.

"So," he murmured when she'd tied off the first suture and was starting on the second, "what's a big-city ER girl doing in a place like this?"

Cassidy flashed him an exasperated look and deftly maneuvered the needle scissors as she completed another suture. "We've already had this conversation, remember?"

Sam scratched his chin and the rasp of his stubble sent a shiver of awareness down her spine. It reminded her of how virile and dangerous he was to her peace of mind. "I was a little tired last night."

"Uh-huh," Cassidy said dryly, and tied off the next suture.

"You never did answer the question, though," Sam pressed, before she could ask about his sleeping habits. He looked more exhausted and drawn than a single night without sleep warranted. And with his other symptoms, he was most likely having nightmares as well.

She studied him intently. "What question?"

"You. Here in the boondocks."

Cassidy turned away from his keen gaze and sorted through a box of dressings. She needed a few moments to gather her composure. After selecting what she needed, she turned with a shrug. "Big-city burn-out. I just needed a change."

"Ahhh," Sam drawled, as she tore open the packaging with more force than was necessary.

"What's that supposed to mean?" she demanded, stripping off the backing and gently pressing it over the sutures on his belly.

He grimaced. "Romance gone bad."

Cassidy gave a shocked laugh, staggered by his perception, and dropped her gaze to his thigh. She knew what he was doing. And, boy, was his diversion effective. "Believe me, romance is *way* off base."

"Then…?"

Rattled, Cassidy sucked in a steadying breath then answered, "Let's just say I needed to find some perspective."

"Yeah," he said softly, his eyes taking on a bleak expression that had her own problems vanishing in the sudden urge to wrap her arms around him. His mouth twisted in a sad, bitter smile. "God knows, I'm acquainted with perspective."

Unsure how to respond in a way that wouldn't have her coming across as an emotional wreck, Cassidy silently went back to work. Besides, what was there to say? Fortunately, he didn't seem to have any clue either. By the time she'd finished he seemed to have slipped into sleep but when she eased away, he groaned and sat up.

A quick glance over her shoulder caught his grimace of pain. His jaw bunched and he grabbed the side tattooed with bruises as he swung his legs over the side. Having finally come off his adrenaline high, he was pale, exhausted and hurting.

"I'll get you some pain meds," she said quietly, turning away to reach into the overhead cabinet. She heard a faint sound and felt the air shift at her back an instant before heat spread along her shoulders and down to the backs of her thighs. Her pulse leapt, her chest went tight and it was all she could do to keep from turning into his big, hard body. To lean on him and let him lean on her.

A long tanned arm reached over her shoulder and he snagged a bottle of pain meds. "This'll do," he said, his voice gravel-rough and sexy. She felt his gaze and turned her head, slowly lifting her gaze up his tanned throat to the hard line of his shadowed jaw, past his poet's mouth and strong straight nose.

He was close. Too close. His gold eyes darkened and something vibrated and snapped between them. Something deep and primal. Something so incendiary she was surprised her clothes didn't catch fire.

Cassidy opened her mouth to say—*God, she didn't have a clue*—then snapped it shut when nothing emerged. The air around them abruptly heated and to her horror his eyes went all hot and sleepy. He felt it too, she realized, and all she had to do was shift a couple of inches closer…and their mouths would—

No sooner had the thought formed than Sam was moving, and before she could do more than squeak out a protest, he'd spun her around and pushed her up against the wall and the heat became a liquid fire in her blood.

She saw his lips moving but heard nothing past the rush of blood filling her ears. Her palms tingled, her body tensed in anticipation and time slowed as his head dipped. Then his mouth was closing over hers and everything… *everything*…sound, heat, sensation…was rushing at her like she'd entered a time warp and was speeding towards something destructive...and wildly exhilarating.

Shock was her first reaction, her second was *"Hmmf..."* When she realized her palms were flat against his hard belly, she tried to shove him away. She didn't want this. It was too much, too little and...*God*...too *everything*. Instinctively she knew that if she let him continue, he'd suck her into his force-field and she'd burn up in the impact. But then he lifted his head and his battered lips brushed across hers, soothingly and so sweetly, and her resistance crumbled.

With a low growl she felt in the pit of her belly, his mouth descended, opening over hers to consume every thought in her head and pull the oxygen from her lungs, leaving her senses spinning.

She heard a low, husky moan and realized with a sense of alarm that it had come from her. *God*...she never moaned. *Ever.* But, then, she'd never been kissed like her soul was being sucked from her body.

She clutched at him to keep from sliding to the floor and an answering groan filled the air, cocooning them in heated silence. This time she was certain it wasn't her.

Tunneling long fingers into her hair, Samuel wrapped them around her skull to tip her head so he could change the angle of the kiss. Instantly his tongue slid past her lips to tangle with hers. Cassidy's breath hitched, her mouth softened and her eyes drifted closed. As if she welcomed the all-encompassing heat.

And, God, how could she not? She'd never felt anything like it. It was like being suspended in a thick, heated silence with nothing but the taste of him in her mouth, the hard feel of him against her, the sound of her pounding pulse filling her head, while heat and wildness rushed through her veins.

And just when her body flowed against his and she

thought she would pass out from lack of oxygen, he broke the kiss and murmured a stunned "*What the hell...?*" between dragging desperate breaths into his lungs.

Confused by the sudden retreat, a small frown creased the smooth skin of her forehead and her eyes fluttered open to see his gaze burning into hers with a fierce intensity—as though he blamed her for the tilting of the earth.

For long stunned moments he stared at her like he'd never seen her before. Then, so abruptly her knees buckled, he shoved away from the wall and retreated, leaving her feeling like he'd drawn back his fist and slugged her in the head.

"Wh-what...? Why...?" Great, now she was stuttering. She gulped and tried again. "What the hell was that?"

Angling his body, Sam folded his arms across his chest and propped his shoulder against the wall where not seconds ago he'd had her pinned. Abruptly inscrutable, his arched brow questioned her sanity.

After a long moment his gaze dropped to her mouth again. "I had to see if you taste as delicious as you look," he drawled, as though it was perfectly normal to push someone up against a wall and suck the air from their lungs.

Infuriated with the quiver in her belly and the urge to slide back against the wall with him, Cassidy shoved at the hair that had been disturbed by his marauding fingers and glared back at him. "Look," she snapped, "I'm not some brainless Navy bunny desperate to trade passable kisses with a hot Navy SEAL. I haven't the time or the inclination and this is certainly *not* the place."

His eyes narrowed in challenge and for a second she thought he'd get mad, but finally his mouth slid into a slow, sexy grin. "*Hot?*" His eyebrows waggled. "You think I'm *hot*?"

And she wanted to slug him.

Deciding to escape before she did or said something

she would regret, Cassidy headed for the door on shaky legs. She paused with a cool look over her shoulder, as if she hadn't just had her tongue in his mouth. *Not going to think about that.*

"If you feel feverish or the area surrounding your injuries becomes inflamed and swollen," she said curtly in parting, "phone in for a prescription. Otherwise make an appointment to have those stitches removed in a week."

CHAPTER FIVE

SAM STOOD BEHIND the solid oak bar and mixed cocktails for a table of women in the corner near the dance floor. It was their second set of drinks for what looked like some kind of ritual girls' night out. Gifts were piled in the corners of the booth, leading him to surmise it was either someone's birthday or a bachelorette party.

He just hoped they didn't get out of hand and start dancing on the tables and shedding their clothes or he'd be forced to throw them out. Some of the male customers tended to get a little upset when he broke up impromptu floor shows, but even in Crescent Lake the sheriff's department frowned on that kind of behavior. The last time it had happened he'd ended up in a jail cell at the mercy of an evil blonde.

Shifting to ease the pressure on his injured thigh, Sam nodded to a few old acquaintances and poured a cosmopolitan into a martini glass.

He'd never understood how any self-respecting adult could order cocktails called orgasms or pink panthers, let alone drink them. He was a strictly beer and malt kind of guy and the thought of slugging back sickly-sweet concoctions the color of candy floss was enough to make him gag. Of course he'd also been known to toss back the occasional tequila with his buddies—but only as a matter of pride.

An off-duty deputy called out, "Hey, Sam," as he pushed

his way through the crowd, arm slung across the shoulders of a hot babe in tight jeans and even tighter tank top. Sam responded with an eye-waggle in the woman's direction and Hank grinned, calling out, "She's got a friend. Interested?"

Sam laughed and shook his head. His sister wasn't due in till ten, but until then he was in charge. It was only a little after eight and Fahrenheit's was already packed. He could hardly hear himself think over the sound of music pouring from the jukebox. The band was busy setting up but wasn't due to start until nine and the kitchen was pushing out huge platters of buffalo wings, fries and chili hot enough to singe the varnish off the bar.

He'd spent the entire week rescuing stray cattle, hauling in joyriders and dodging buckshot from old man Jeevers, who thought the deputies were aliens beamed down from the mother ship. And when he wasn't playing cop he'd worked the taps behind the bar, listening to Jerry Farnell recount his experiences in Desert Storm.

His brother had talked him into "helping out" at the sheriff's office, but Sam wasn't fooled. Ruben wanted some fraternal bonding time so he could casually talk about why Sam was home, acting like a moody bastard instead of parachuting into hostile territory and sneaking up on bad guys.

He suspected his family had formed a tag team to work on him, hoping he'd crack and spill his guts. They were clearly as tired of his bad attitude as his CO had become. Heck, *he* was tired of his bad attitude. He wanted to get back to the teams, doing what he'd been trained for.

What they didn't understand was that SEALs didn't crack under pressure or talk about their missions. What they did was mostly classified so they *couldn't* talk. Besides, he'd seen and done some pretty bad things that he didn't want to think too hard about. *Ever.* If he did he'd go crazy and end up like Jerry, propping up a bar somewhere, getting drunk while reliving his glory days.

Finally, the bozos taking up one side of the bar got tired of trying to provoke him and turned their attention to speculating about the fancy Boston babe helping out at the hospital.

He eventually stopped listening to their inventive illnesses just to have "five minutes alone with her so I can drop my shorts and show the little lady what a *real* man looks like."

Sam snorted. Doc Boston might have come to town to "get some perspective" but he suspected her *perspective* didn't include checking out the local talent. She was a beautiful, classy woman who'd probably seen countless men drop their shorts, and an idiot like Buddy Holliday would hardly impress her. Besides, her reaction to *his* kiss had told him he'd been right. Some guy had worked her over and she was taking it out on him.

Except in his experience a woman didn't always need a reason to act like a man was a pervert for pushing her up against the wall and sucking the air from her lungs. They often behaved irrationally for no apparent reason—which was why he enjoyed being a SEAL. Guys didn't mind if you scratched yourself in public, and burping was an accepted form of male bonding.

Furthermore, before she'd stormed off, bristling, with insult, she'd had her beautiful body pressed against his, her hands in his hair and her tongue in his mouth—and had enjoyed every hot minute of it, no matter what she'd said.

The good news was people suffering from PTSD didn't dream or fantasize about kissing a woman until her muscles went fluid and her breath hitched in her throat. They didn't obsess about running their hands through long, silky hair or down smooth, sleek thighs and they sure as hell didn't have erotic dreams about someone who treated them like she wanted to slide her lush curvy body up against you one minute then scrape you off the bottom of her shoe the next.

He'd be insane to even consider pursuing someone who ripped off a dozen layers of skin along with an adhesive dressing. And, contrary to popular opinion, Sam Kellan wasn't insane.

Fortunately someone called his name and Sam turned, grateful for the distraction. He'd spent way too much time thinking about her as it was.

Over the next hour he kept the drinks coming and tried to work up some enthusiasm for the trio of woman bellied up to the bar, heavily made-up eyes currently stripping him naked and acting like he should feel flattered.

He didn't. He'd learned early that women liked Navy SEALs. They liked their big muscles and hard bodies and they liked their stamina. He mostly liked women too, but tonight he wasn't in the mood to oblige them.

By the time his sister arrived for her shift, he was ready to head off into the wilderness to get away from people for a while. "Where the hell have you been?" he demanded, in a tone that had her welcoming smile morph into a confused frown.

"What are you talking about?"

"You're late."

Hannah flicked her attention to the wall clock. "Fifteen minutes. Big deal. And quit scowling like that, you're scaring away my customers." She looked over the happy crowd and noticed the group of men cozied up to the bar, scarfing down buffalo wings, and grimaced when she recognized them. "What did Buddy say to upset you?" she demanded, eyeing him cautiously, like she expected him to morph into a psycho.

"I'm not upset." *Yeesh*, what was with women lately? "Women get upset, guys get mad."

She rolled her eyes. "Fine, what are you *mad* about now?"

"I'm not mad. Listening to them yap about the length of their johns and betting on who's going to score first is giving me a brain bleed."

"So? They do that every week. Last week it was with that group of coeds from Olympia. You thought it was pretty damn funny then and told me to chill when I wanted to throw them out."

He grimaced. "It gets old real fast. You'd think they'd move on from the high-school locker room talk."

She looked skeptical. "You're talking about Buddy Holliday, right? The guy who calls himself Buddy Holly and plays air guitar against his fly?" Sam couldn't prevent a grunt of disgust. Hannah cocked her head and asked casually, "Or is it because they've been betting on a certain doctor over at the hospital?"

Sam folded his arms over his chest and flattened his brows across his forehead. "What are you yapping about now?" Except Hannah wasn't fazed by his intimidating SEAL scowl—in fact, she moved closer, as though anticipating some juicy gossip and didn't want to miss any salacious details. Sam didn't know why she bothered. They could stand at opposite ends of the bar and bellow at each other and no one would hear them over the band.

"Don't worry, Sammy. That lot are big on talk and small on action. Emphasis on small."

"And I need to know this, why?"

Hannah ignored the question. She was like a Rottweiler with a chew toy when she was on the track of something. "Ruben says she could be in Hollywood, playing a classy playboy doctor." She snickered. "I think he's in love."

And suddenly Sam felt like he was suffocating. He tore

off his apron and threw it onto the counter behind the bar, barely resisting the urge to rip the bottle of gin out of his sister's hand and smash it into the mirror behind the bar— after emptying the contents down his throat. But he drew the line at sissy drinks and knew his sister would be mad if he broke up the place.

Shoving his fingers through his hair, he bit back an extremely explicit curse. He needed air. He needed to get a grip. He needed to get away from people for a while.

"I'm out of here," he snarled, pushing past his sister. "You're on your own."

Stunned by the leashed violence tightening his face, Hannah turned to gape at him. "Wha—? What did I say? What did I do?"

Sam's snarled expletive over his shoulder died at the baffled hurt in her huge eyes. Guilt slapped at him and he let go with an angry hiss of frustration.

"Nothing," he said, wearily pressing his thumb and forefinger into his eyes to ease the headache threatening to explode his brain, along with his temper. He really needed to get a grip. Hannah didn't deserve his filthy mood. "I'm just tired and I have a headache."

"Again?" She looked concerned. "Do you need to see a doctor?" And all Sam's irritation returned in a rush.

"*No*. I *don't* need to see a damn doctor," he said wearily. "I *am* a doctor, remember?" Her expression turned skeptic and he knew what she was thinking. That he needed a shrink, not an MD.

"You never used to let Buddy bug you, so what's your problem?" she demanded, and before he could remind her he was a SEAL without a team, her eyes got big and a startled laugh escaped. "It's her, isn't it? The fancy Boston doc the guys are always talking about." Her eyes gleamed with fiendish delight, like when she was ten and she'd found him reading the *Playboy* magazine he'd found clearing out Mr.

Henderson's garage. He almost expected her to burst out with, "I'm gonna tell Mom." What came out was worse.

"It *is*." She cackled gleefully and before he could ask what the hell she was talking about, she snickered. "*You're* the one with a thing for Doc Boston. Oh, boy, this is great. It's like the time you and Ruben fought over Missy Hawkins, and came home sporting black eyes and split lips. So what's it gonna be, huh? Pistols at dawn or down-'n-dirty street fighting? Can I watch?"

Sam bit back a curse and felt the back of his skull tighten. "And they think *I'm* the family nut job." He squinted at her. "So, what are you, thirteen? I'm a Navy SEAL, for God's sake. We don't get *things* for women or fight over them. People get killed that way."

Hannah's eyes widened, she looked intrigued. "Has that ever happened?"

"*No*." *Yeesh*. "I don't fight over women. It's juvenile." Not to mention stupidly dangerous.

She stuck her tongue in her cheek. "*R-i-i-ight*," she said, like he was acting so mature.

"Yeah, short stuff. Just remember I know a hundred different ways to kill a man—or a kid sister—that'll look like they died of natural causes. Besides, I'm not interested in some fancy Boston debutante playing wilderness doctor."

Hannah looked disgusted and sent him a *yeah, right* look as she gave his shoulder a patronizing pat. She muttered something that sounded like, "Keep telling yourself that, you poor clueless moron," which he took exception to. But when he demanded she repeat it, she smirked and said, "I've got this, big guy. You go off and crawl into your man cave with your denials and delusions. I'm sure the Navy shrinks will be interested to hear you've finally gone over the edge."

Sam snarled something nasty about Navy shrinks, before turning on his heel and heading down the passage towards the back exit. He yanked open the door and slammed it on the sound of her laughter.

Hannah was wrong, he told himself, firing up the engine and shoving the vehicle into first gear. He *didn't* care if his brother had a "thing" for the fancy doctor. He'd be gone soon and didn't do relationships that lasted more than a week, tops. He was never around long enough for more. And if the voice in his head told him he was deluding himself, he ignored it since it sounded a lot like his sister. He was just tired.

Yeah, he thought with a snort of disgust. He was tired all right. Tired of sitting on his ass, waiting for his CO to call. And he was damn sick and tired of trying to convince people he was fine.

Sam had every intention of heading for the Crash Landing, a rough bar on the other side of town that catered to truckers, loggers and general badasses, but found himself pulling into the hospital parking lot instead.

When he realized where he was, he swore and scowled at the light spilling from the small ER, worried that maybe he *was* as crazy as everyone claimed. Only a crazy man would be sitting outside a hospital, staring at the glowing emergency sign and thinking of a woman whose bedside manner rivaled that of a BUD/S training instructor.

He was also a doctor, for goodness' sake. He could remove his own damn stitches. Nevertheless, he found himself killing the engine and climbing from the cab.

So he was here. Might as well get them removed. They were starting to itch like crazy anyway.

Sam entered the building, surprised to find the reception deserted. He headed for the emergency treatment rooms but found them empty as well. A little alarmed, he retraced his steps just as a door opened somewhere behind him and before he could turn, a voice called out.

"Be right with you… Oh, Samuel, what a surprise," Fran Gilbert, a friend of his mother's, said when she saw him. "Is there a problem?" She was pushing a medicine trolley and looked a little preoccupied. Sam held up his bandaged hand and watched her face clear. "Cassidy will handle that, dear. I'm doing the rounds."

"Busy?"

"Just the usual. In addition to the usual, a dozen pre-schoolers with high fevers came in earlier. We're waiting for spots to appear but in the meantime we've got our hands full with cranky little people demanding attention every second. Through that door," she said, gesturing behind him. "I made her take a break. Who knows what will happen during the night with a bunch of miserable little people." And then she was gone.

Sam stared after her for a moment, wondering if his mouth was hanging open. He hadn't had an opportunity to utter so much as a grunt. Shaking his head, he turned and headed for the privacy door she'd indicated. He pushed it open and immediately heard talking.

So much for resting up for a rough night, he thought darkly. Ignoring the fact that she was free to entertain whomever she pleased, he let the door shut silently behind him and headed down the corridor. What he found wiped all dark thoughts from his head.

Shoving a shoulder against the doorframe, Sam folded his arms across his chest and let his eyes take a slow journey up long denim-clad legs perched halfway up a ladder. Doc Boston was alone and muttering to herself about something that sounded like bedpans and floor polish as she consulted the clipboard in her hand.

She turned a page to skim it from top to bottom and then back again, before huffing out a breath and turning another page, oblivious to his presence.

"You have *got* to be kidding," she muttered with a sound

of disgust. "Who puts bedpans with surgical scrubs? This system sucks." She froze as though she'd said something indecent then shook her head with a laugh. "Yes, Cassidy, you can use the word 'sucks' without the world imploding." She exhaled as she studied the clipboard, her breath disturbing silvery blonde curls near her face. "Besides, if someone can walk around with a T-shirt saying '*Eat the Worm*' or '*Loggers do it with big poles*' in public, you can certainly say 'sucks' in private without it being followed by lightning bolts."

Sam grinned. "You sure about that, Doc?" he drawled, making her shriek and jump about a mile into the air. She grabbed for the shelf with one hand and the ladder with the other. The clipboard and pen went flying, her boot slipped and with a panicked shriek she went flying as well.

Without thinking, Sam leapt towards her. She landed against his chest with a thud, knocking the breath from them both. He staggered back against the wall and wrapped one arm securely around her back. The other he clamped around her thighs.

Planting his feet wide to accommodate his curvy armful, he grinned into shocked green eyes, conscious of lush pink lips forming a perfectly round O—which for some reason made him think of hot, wet kisses in the dark—an inch from his.

"I… You… Oh…*God*," she wheezed out, fisting her hand in his T-shirt and sounding about as coherent as Cindy Dawson in the third-grade spelling bee when Frankie Ferguson had let go with a loud burp right there on stage.

She sucked in a shaky breath and uttered one word. "*You!*" Making him wonder if she was relieved to see him or cursing him. He suspected the latter.

"Expecting someone else?" The idea did not appeal.

"I…uh… You…" She shut her mouth with an audible

snap and swiped her tongue across her lips. Then, realizing how provocative her action might appear—especially as his gaze had dropped to her mouth—she rolled her eyes and shoved against his chest. "Put me down."

"'I…uh… You'?" Sam lifted his brow, ignoring her order. "You've developed a stutter since I last saw you?"

"*Dammit*, you scared the hell out of me," she snapped, and shoved at his shoulders again.

Both brows hiked up his forehead. "*Hell*?" He was enjoying the feel of her in his arms and the light fruity scent of her hair. He was enjoying seeing her flustered when she was normally so poised. "Doc, Doc, *Doc*," he tutted, shaking his head. "First 'suck' and now 'Dammit' and 'Hell'? What's next? The *b* word?"

Cassidy froze and stared open-mouthed for a couple of beats before a faint flush rose up her neck into her cheeks. "You *heard* all that?" And when his eyes crinkled and his mouth lifted at one corner, she groaned.

"Oh, God, just shoot me."

Sam laughed. "I only shoot bad guys," he assured her, slipping his arm out from under her shapely bottom to let her slide down the length of his body while he enjoyed the friction of soft curves against hard angles. Her face flamed when she felt a certain hard angle and he bit back a groan, suddenly realizing why he'd come.

He wasn't cool with his brother putting the moves on her and he sure as hell didn't like the idea of Buddy or Jake dropping their shorts in her presence either.

Ignoring what that might mean, Sam inhaled the flowery, fresh scent of her hair and enjoyed the soft press of full breasts against his chest. Suddenly nothing mattered but putting his mouth on hers again and finding out if she tasted as good as he remembered.

As if sensing his intent, she made a sound of protest

and scrambled out of reach, her eyes huge and dark with suspicion and…was that arousal?

"What are you doing here, Major?" she demanded a little breathlessly. For a long moment he watched from beneath heavy lids before taking a step towards her, enjoying the flash of annoyance that replaced the mild panic when she found herself backed against the wall.

Blocking her escape with a palm to the wall, he tunneled his free hand beneath the soft, fragrant cloud surrounding her flushed face. He wrapped his fingers around the back of her neck and gently pressed his thumb into the soft hollow at the base of her throat. The rapid flutter beneath his touch had him lifting her face to his.

The scent of peaches drifted to him and his gut clenched. *Damn*, he thought, *she makes me hungry*. Dropping his gaze to her mouth, he feathered a knuckle across her jaw to the corner of her lips and when her breath hitched in her throat, his blood went hot.

"I had no intention of coming here," he accused in a voice rough and deep with need. "But you…make me crazy. I couldn't stay away."

With a sharply indrawn breath Cassidy fisted her hands in his shirt as though she couldn't make up her mind whether to push him away or pull him close. Sam took advantage of her indecision to open his mouth over hers in a soft kiss that stole her breath and sent his head reeling.

"Samuel," she protested tightly against his mouth.

With a deep "Hmm?" he slid his tongue along her lower lip before dipping inside where she was warm and delicious. He hummed again, this time with growing need.

God, he thought, he hadn't exaggerated the memory of her taste, or the feel of her mouth moving beneath his.

"S-Samuel," she stuttered, "this…this is a bad idea."
You're telling me. But she didn't pull away, which told Sam he wasn't the only crazy person here. In fact, she

tilted her head to give him better access and her breath hitched in her throat.

It was the sign he'd unconsciously been waiting for.

"I like the way you say my name," he growled against her lips, before rocking his mouth over hers, his control rapidly slipping. "I like the way your breath hitches in your throat when you're aroused." He pressed his hips against hers. "It makes me…hard."

"*I'm not!*" she protested. "I…don't…" Then flattened her palm over his heart, drew in a shaky breath and tried again. "You're *not*." But her words emerged on a moan when she felt exactly how hard he was, ruining her denial.

"I beg to differ," he drawled, and chuckled when she blushed and huffed out an embarrassed giggle.

"No, I'm s-serious," she stuttered, squirming away, only to find herself backed into a corner. Huffing with annoyance, she narrowed her eyes, stuck out her chin and clenched her hands as though she was contemplating taking a swing at him.

He smiled. He wouldn't mind letting her try.

"Look," she said, shoving the hair off her forehead, "I have bigger problems than your…um, ego, okay?"

Sam folded his arms and propped a shoulder against the wall, taking in the tousled, appealingly flustered picture she made. She looked about sixteen, and there was absolutely nothing cool or distant about Dr. Mahoney from Boston now.

His brow rose. "Yeah, like?" He grinned into her flushed face. "Like why bedpans are listed with surgical scrubs?"

CHAPTER SIX

CASSIDY LAUGHED. "DON'T be ridiculous," she said, rolling her eyes. Her voice had emerged all breathy and excited, like she was a teenager again, for heaven's sake. She'd been muttering about bedpans, of all things, while trying not to think about a certain Navy SEAL. Then suddenly there he was—looking like hot sin, bad attitude and way better than she remembered. And if, when she'd been pressed up against all that hard heat, she'd been tempted to get reacquainted with that awesome body, she wasn't about to admit it out loud. She'd been a little startled, that's all. She was over her attraction to him. Well, mostly.

Looking into his darkly handsome face, Cassidy admitted to herself that he was a very dangerous man. He made her forget about good sense, heartbreak and painful lessons. He made her yearn to toss good sense out with her inhibitions. Fortunately she'd come to her senses in time.

Nibbling nervously on her bottom lip, she kept a wary eye on him and focused on getting her heart rate down from stroke level, only to have it kicking into high gear again when he pushed away from the doorframe.

"Look, Major," she said quickly, throwing up a hand when he moved closer and looked like he wanted to nibble on her lip too. "I'm…busy." His chest connected with her out-flung palm and didn't stop. "*Really* busy." She squeaked and retreated, annoyed that just a minute in his presence and she was acting all girly and flustered. "Stop. *Dammit*, I don't have time for your...um...warped idea of...of foreplay. Samuel, *stop!*"

A dark brow hiked into his hairline and his mouth curled up at one corner. Great, now he was laughing at her. She huffed out a breath. Could this get any more embarrassing?

"Foreplay?"

Ignoring his question and figuring it was rhetorical anyway, Cassidy scuttled sideways and headed for the door, turning when she reached the relative safety of the hallway. *Ready to make a run for it if he made any sudden moves.*

"So what *are* you doing here, Major?" *Besides making my knees wobble and my pulse race.*

He turned, his gaze leisurely moving over her face until his hooded glance met hers, and add making her head spin to his sins. After a long moment, during which Cassidy thought she'd hyperventilate, he finally held up his bandaged hand.

"Oh." Her breath whooshed out and a small frown wrinkled her brow. For heaven's sake, she wasn't disappointed that he hadn't come to push her up against any walls. In fact, she was relieved. She was really very busy and didn't have time for games.

"Why didn't you just say so?" she gritted through clenched teeth, before spinning on her heel to head down the corridor at a sharp clip. She led the way through Reception and into the suture room, reaching for a lab coat on a nearby hook, figuring she needed the added protection against that penetrating gaze if she wanted to appear professional. Heck, if she wanted to *think*.

She fumbled for a button and was horrified to find that her hands were trembling too much to perform a task she'd mastered at five. Biting back a growl of disgust, Cassidy huffed out a breath, smoothed out her expression and turned to find him leaning against the bed, watching her thoughtfully as he slowly unwound the bandage covering his hand.

Crossing her arms beneath her breasts, she made herself focus on medical issues and not on how good he looked. "Frankly, I'm surprised to see you," she remarked, as coolly as if her pulse wasn't skipping all over the place like she was on an adrenaline rush. "I expected you to just rip them out with your teeth."

His raised brow suggested she was missing a few IQ points. "And what?" he demanded. "Use them as lethal spitballs?"

Her lips curled without her permission. "You're exaggerating."

Sam snorted. "Have you ever had nylon thread holding your flesh together?"

"No," she said, taking his hand and feeling the jolt clear to her elbow. *Whoa. Not this again.* Firming her lips, she resolutely ignored the sensation of his warm calloused skin against hers by inspecting the healing wound. After a few moments she reached for needle scissors and gently lifted each suture before snipping and tugging it free. "As a rule I avoid bar fights," she continued, looking up briefly to find his mouth tilted in an ironic half-smile.

Her chest went tight. *Yikes.* The man was living, breathing sin. *And she had a dangerous urge to...well, lick him up one side and down the other.* She frowned at her unprofessional thoughts. "And throwing myself out of moving aircraft."

The chuckle vibrating deep in his chest filled the small room and created an odd sensation in her belly. "You don't know what you're missing."

"Yes, I do," she corrected mildly, as she wiped disinfectant along the tender scar before spraying the area with a thin layer of synthetic skin. "I'm missing broken bones and you're clearly missing your mind." She covered his hand with a waterproof adhesive dressing. "Be careful with that for another few days and keep it clean and dry."

He caught her wrist before she could turn away and her startled gaze rose to his.

"Don't you want to know what it's like…hurtling towards earth at a hundred feet per second?" he murmured deeply, softly.

Cassidy swallowed hard at the expression in his gold eyes. *Holy cow.* "No, I…" *If it's anything like I'm currently feeling…terrifying.*

Without waiting for her brain to clear, Sam reeled her in until the warm male scent of him enveloped her and her common sense scattered, along with her reasons for keeping him at arm's length. In fact, she suddenly couldn't recall why she'd thought this was a bad idea. Without the slightest effort on his part he was rendering her speechless.

"Major…" She thought maybe a token protest was necessary, even though she couldn't remember what she should be protesting against.

"It's like that moment during sex," he rasped, closing the gap to her mouth as she watched, frozen with fascination, "when you realize…" his lips brushed hers and he flattened her captive hand against his chest "…there's no going back."

"Major…" she croaked again, terrified that he would feel the way she trembled. His mouth smiled against hers, as though he knew what he was doing to her. His tongue emerged to sweep across the seam of her mouth. His heart pounded like a jackhammer beneath her palm. *Or was that hers?* "And then, like a heated rush…" he murmured silkily, sending blood thundering in her ears. A breathy whimper escaped and before she could stop it her palm slid up his warm chest to his neck. "It hits you…*wham!*"

She jolted the instant his teeth closed over her bottom

lip to tug on the sensitive flesh. Hot shivers scattered from the base of her spine into every cell and Cassidy thought, *Oh, God*, as her knees wobbled.

Before she could protest again, Sam's mouth opened over hers in a kiss that instantly spiraled out of control. It turned the moisture in her body to steam and sucked air from as far down as her toes.

It felt like she'd been tossed into the center of a tornado. She told herself that if he hadn't been holding her captive she would have pulled away. Broken free. Run for her life.

At least she would have if she'd been able to formulate a single thought. Then she was being yanked up against all his hard heat, his arm an iron band across her back while he fed her hungry kisses that were all tongue and greed and stole her breath along with her mind.

Cassidy's breasts tightened and her blood caught fire. Just when she felt that insidious slide into insanity, he froze and pulled back.

Wha—?

Stunned by the force of emotions storming through her, Cassidy sucked in a desperate breath and stared back at him, wondering a little hysterically if the pounding in her head was a sign that her brain was about to explode. The man literally sucked up everything around him like a level-five twister.

His hands tightened and his eyes looked a little wild— *kind of like she was feeling*—and it took a few moments to realize the pounding wasn't in her head.

A loud *bang* was abruptly followed by yelling that had Sam shifting from sexy and sleepy to sexy and…*lethal*. Without a sound he shoved her roughly aside to move on silent, deadly feet towards the hallway, his hand reaching for…a weapon?

Awareness returned in a rush and Cassidy flung herself after him before he could launch a silent attack on some poor unsuspecting person. She grabbed for his shirt to hold him back and he rounded on her, eyes deadly and cold. It was clearly his attack SEAL face, Cassidy thought with a shudder. She could easily imagine the enemy quailing with terror. Heck, *she* was trembling.

"It's all right, Major, it's just…it's just a medical emergency." At least she hoped it was and not an invasion by paramilitary groups that gossip said hid in the mountains. Then all bets were off. And when he gave no indication that he'd heard, she shook him. "Stand down, Major, I've got this."

For long scary beats he stared at her, his expression cold and flat. Just when she thought he meant to swat her like a pesky fly, he blinked, slowly, like he was coming back from…*a flashback*?

Cassidy gulped, but then his face abruptly lost color and before she could move, he staggered. She reached for him but he threw out a hand to steady himself against the wall.

"Go," he rasped, giving her the sharp edge of his shoulder. She hesitated, watching his forehead drop against the bulge of his biceps. The muscles in his wide back bunched and turned hard. After a couple of hesitant beats she turned and took off down the hallway.

One look at the couple in ER had all thoughts of Sam's flashbacks flying from her head. The woman being propped up by a clearly freaked-out man was as white as a sheet and covered in sweat. She clutched her heavily pregnant belly, and Cassidy noticed blood and fluid staining the front of her maternity dress.

"*Help her*," the man yelled wildly when he saw Cassidy. "Help her. *Oh, God,* help her. She's bleeding. It won't stop," he croaked pleadingly. "It just won't stop and the baby…" He swallowed. "I think the baby's stuck."

Cassidy grabbed a nearby gurney and met them halfway, swallowing the urge to yell at them for waiting so long. This had all the signs of a home delivery gone wrong. So dreadfully wrong. She just hoped it wasn't too late.

"What happened?" she demanded. "Why didn't you come in earlier?"

"She wanted a home birth, but the midwife's not answering her phone," the man babbled through bloodless lips, his eyes wide and wild. "I didn't know what to do. What the hell do I know about babies? Nothing. I know *nothing… Oh, God,* what have I done?" As white as parchment, he swayed and Cassidy put out a hand to steady him. That's all they needed. Another casualty.

Before she could snap out an order for him to get a grip, the woman gave a low moan and her legs buckled. Yelling out a code blue and hoping someone would hear, Cassidy lurched forward just as the woman fell, her weight taking them both to the floor.

Vaguely aware that the man was screaming and crying hysterically, Cassidy opened her mouth to rap out an order, but the breath had been knocked from her and all she could manage was a strangled gasp.

Sam's face appeared overhead and before she could blink at his abrupt appearance he'd bent and lifted the woman off her with easy strength. Sucking in air, Cassidy scrambled to her feet.

"You okay?" he demanded in a low tone as he gently placed the woman on the gurney.

She should be the one asking but even as she opened her mouth to voice her concerns, she noted that other than a faint pallor and a hard, closed expression, Sam seemed to have recovered. His eyes were clear and sharply focused.

"Cassidy?"

She shook her head to dispel her misgivings and noticed he'd pulled on a lab coat that strained the shoulder seams and rode up his strong wrists. He'd also slung a stethoscope around his neck. He met her pointed look with a raised brow, silently telling her she had more important things to worry about. Things like their distressed patient.

"I'm fine," she rapped out. "Get her details." And took off down the hallway with the gurney, hitting the emergency button as she streaked past.

The next few minutes were a blur as she wheeled the gurney into the OR, where she checked the woman's vitals. Her concern ratcheted up a notch at the patient's labored breathing and erratic pulse.

"Dammit, dammit, *dammit*," she muttered, grabbing a pair of scissors to cut away the blood-soaked dress. She needed another experienced professional. Preferably someone who had done this before. She needed Dr. Montgomery.

By the time the night nurse burst into the OR, Cassidy had finished intubating the mother. With swift, competent movements she hooked up a saline drip and rapped out orders for drugs.

Ripping open a syringe package with her teeth, she fitted the needle and shoved it into the first vial the nurse handed to her. "Prep her for a C-section," she told the nurse briskly, injecting the contents into the port. "And then call Dr. Montgomery. I'm going to need help on this one."

"You've got help," a deep voice informed her from the doorway and Cassidy looked over her shoulder to see Sam striding into the OR.

Cassidy's eyes widened. "Major—"

"Her name is Gail Sanders," he interrupted in a voice as deep and calm as though he did this every day. "She's a kindergarten teacher. This is her first pregnancy—no history of problems." His eyes were calm and steady on hers. The silent message was clear. They didn't have time to wait for the elderly doctor or discuss *his* mental issues. "Moving her when you're ready."

Cassidy frowned and held his gaze for a couple of beats,

conscious of the look of wide-eyed apprehension the nurse flashed between them.

"Dr. Mahoney…?" Heather prompted, breaking the tension filling the room.

"Major Kellan will need the ultrasound,' Cassidy said briskly with a curt nod in Sam's direction, before moving to Gail's feet. They transferred her to the operating table as Heather rolled the ultrasound into position. Cassidy took the proffered tube of gel and squirted a thick line over the apex of the patient's distended belly.

Sam lifted the probe. "Go suit up," he said quietly, eyes on the screen as he rolled the probe through the gel. "I'll handle this."

"Major—" she began, breaking off when his golden eyes lifted. "This is…" She bit her lip and ran her fingers through her hair in agitation. "Are you…?" *Damn.* How did you ask someone if they were sane enough to handle a delicate procedure like this one was going to be?

His face darkened with impatience, and Cassidy knew he wasn't going to discuss what had happened in the hallway. Watching the expert way he wielded the probe, she was forced to admit he looked fine. More than fine. As though he hadn't had a flashback—or whatever had happened—just minutes earlier.

"I'm fine, Doctor," he snapped, returning his attention to the patient. "But *they* aren't and unless you get your ass into gear, they won't be for much longer."

Cassidy hesitated another couple of beats. "I hope you know what you're doing," she said quietly, unsure whom she was addressing.

It took her less than a minute to throw off her clothes, pull on clean scrubs and scrape her hair off her face. By the time she'd finished scrubbing Sam was behind her, holding out a surgical gown that she slipped over her arms after a searching look up into his dark face.

He must have correctly interpreted her probing look because his mouth pulled into a tight line. "This is a job for two people who know what they're doing."

"Monty—"

"Isn't here," he interrupted smoothly. His eyes caught and held hers. "We can't wait, Cassidy. And you know it."

Knowing he was right, Cassidy ground her back molars together. "You're right," she admitted briskly, moving towards the OR doors, "but *you* assist."

Heather Murray had already positioned the colored electrode pads and was fitting a saturation probe over the patient's forefinger when Cassidy hit the doors with her shoulder. Tying the surgical cap at the back of her head, she slipped her hands into surgical gloves the nurse held out.

She watched as Heather hooked Gail up to the heart monitor, a wrinkle of concern marring her brow when a rapid beeping filled the silence. Stepping closer to the ultrasound screen, Cassidy studied the strip of images Sam had printed out, before gently palpating the woman's belly. A quick examination revealed the baby lying breech, with its spine facing upward.

She felt rather than saw Sam come up behind her. "I've delivered babies in worse positions than this," he said at her shoulder.

"So have I," Cassidy agreed, "but not without an OB/GYN on standby. The bleeding is also a major concern." When he remained silent, Cassidy lifted her head to find him studying her intently. Her heart gave a little lurch. "What?"

His eyes lit with a warm smile. "You can do it, Doc. Have a little faith. Besides, I'm right here."

She was about to ask if he'd done *this* before but the monitor beeped and Heather called out, "Heart rate increasing, Doctor," and Cassidy realized they didn't have time to hang around debating his experience.

Sam shoved his hands into latex gloves while the nurse tied his gown and mask. Cassidy moved to the patient's side and hoped she wasn't making a terrible mistake. As the doctor on duty, she was about to trust a man who thought parachuting into hostile territory armed to the teeth was like making love. "Major—" Cassidy began, only to have him cut her off.

"I think we've had this conversation before, *Cassidy*," he drawled, putting her firmly in her place as a colleague now. He looked big and tough and impatient—and most of all competent. After flicking a pointed look at Heather, he returned Cassidy's gaze meaningfully. "We're good."

Biting back a sigh, she opened her mouth and said, "Let's do this."

Heather called anxiously, "Blood pressure dropping, Doctor."

Cassidy's gaze snapped to the monitor. "Keep an eye on the baby's vitals and let me know if Mom's BP drops below fifty." Sam expertly swabbed the woman's belly with iodine as Cassidy waited, scalpel in hand. The instant he was finished she felt for the correct place with her left hand and then made a clean incision with her right. The scalpel sliced through layers of skin, muscle and uterine wall. Sam gently coaxed the baby into position while she slid her hands into the exposed uterus. Within seconds the infant's head and shoulders emerged and Cassidy could see why the baby had been lying breech—and why the mother was bleeding.

The placenta had detached from the uterine wall and the umbilical cord was looped around the baby's neck and under her arm. The infant was blue and flaccid.

Cassidy's heart gave a blip of alarm. *Dammit, dammit, dammit,* she chanted mentally, getting a firm hold on the infant while Sam gently unwound the cord. He accepted the heated towel the nurse offered as Cassidy slid the infant free and handed her over. Deftly cutting the cord, she applied the clip and looked up briefly to catch Sam's intense gaze over the top of his face mask. His gold eyes were dark and solemn on hers. "She's yours," Cassidy said simply, and turned back to save the mother. Gail Sanders's time was running out.

"I've got this," he said, but Cassidy had already tuned out everything, instinct telling her that Sam really *did* have it. She didn't have to make a choice or leave the endangered infant to the nurse.

Besides, there was nothing she could do for the baby now that Sam couldn't do just as well.

Over the next half-hour she communicated with the nurse in terse bursts until she finally managed to get the bleeding under control. Heaving a relieved sigh, she wiped her burning eyes against her shoulder and ordered additional units of blood. Then she set about closing the uterus, the layer of muscle and finally the incision wound.

Lastly, she inserted a drain and stepped back to check the patient's vitals. Finding her still critical but edging toward stable, Cassidy stepped back, wondering for the first time in more than an hour if Sam had managed to save the infant.

She caught sight of him waiting just beyond the lights. For long moments their gazes held, his eyes so intensely gold and solemn her pulse gave a painful little jolt. Had she…? *Oh, God, had she imagined that feeble little cry?* Then his eyes crinkled at the corners in a rare moment of shared accord and gestured to the pink bundle in his arms.

Suddenly tears burned the backs of her eyes and she sucked in a quick breath at the blaze of emotion blocking her throat. *They'd done it,* she thought on a burst of elation that she attributed to their accomplishment and not… well, anything else.

She sent Sam a wobbly smile, rapidly blinking away

her emotional tears as she turned back to recheck the patient's vitals to give herself a minute. She clamped off the anesthetic, leaving the shunt in place. "We'll keep her sedated while we wait for the chopper," she told Heather, conscious of Sam's silent scrutiny as they transferred the patient to the gurney.

"You're not keeping her here?" he asked, as they covered Gail with a cotton spread and then a thick woolen blanket. Cassidy shook her head and went to the OR refrigerator, withdrawing a couple of vials of antibiotics.

"The hospital doesn't have the facilities for such a critical patient," she explained, hooking up another saline bag. "Besides, mother and child both need proper neonatal care. I want them in a large center with access to hi-tech facilities and equipment if anything goes wrong."

Pulling down her face mask, she took a new syringe, slid the needle into first one vial and then the other, finally injecting the cocktail into the new saline bag.

"I'll go speak to her husband," she said, when she finally ran out of things to do, her emotions suddenly as fragile as the lives they'd just saved.

Disposing of needle, syringe and surgical gloves, she quickly wrote down the details of the procedure and the drugs she'd used. With a sigh of relief she turned to leave, stiffening in surprise when long fingers closed over her shoulder.

Looking up into Sam's shadowed face, Cassidy sucked in a startled breath. Illumination from the surgical lights slid across the bottom half of his face, leaving the rest in deep shadow. It made him appear bigger and darker and... *hell*, more dangerous than ever.

Unbidden, images of what had happened in the suture room flashed through her head and she winced. *Darn*. One look into his dark gold eyes brought on a flashback of his mouth closing over hers in a hot, greedy kiss. She'd hoped to escape before he remembered that she'd almost climbed into his lap and rubbed her body against his. She licked dry lips.

"What?" she asked huskily, her throat tight with awkwardness and a sudden baffling anxiety.

"You want to see her?"

Sam watched confusion chase wariness across Cassidy's face until he gently handed over his precious bundle. She'd been instrumental in saving the infant and deserved to share the joy of that new life.

Drawn by the subtle scent of her, easily discernible even over the antiseptic smells of the OR, Sam moved closer. He'd been immensely impressed with her ability and the efficient way she'd handled the crisis. She'd never once hesitated or panicked. Hell, he'd seen seasoned soldiers panic in less dire situations and had to admire how she'd kept a cool head.

It had been touch and go there for a while, but the newborn was finally pink and glowing with life. Tiny hands were tucked against a petal-soft cheek and the infant looked, Sam thought, like a cherub praying. Huge dark eyes stared up into Cassidy's face with such mesmerizing intensity that the hair on his arms and the back of his neck rose. It was as though she knew she was being held by someone…special.

Her expression both delighted and enthralled, Cassidy gently touched a pink cheek and the tiny folded hands. "Look, Sam," she breathed, "she looks like a little angel. Like she's praying. Isn't she the most beautiful thing you've ever seen?"

For long silent moments Sam found his gaze locked on Cassidy's face, unable to utter a sound. Her expression was one he'd never thought to see on her beautiful face— soft and sweet and glowing with uncomplicated delight.

God, he thought painfully, *she really is beautiful*. And

so much more than he'd thought. Swallowing the lump blocking his vocal cords, he finally managed a raspy, "Yeah. Beautiful."

Oblivious to his chaotic emotions, she continued to murmur softly to the infant, laughing when the little rose-bud mouth opened in a wide yawn.

Feeling like he'd been shot in the chest with a high-powered rifle, Sam forced his emotions under control and moved to untie her gown. He finally gave in to the urge to brush his lips against the long elegant line of her throat as he leaned forward to murmur, "You did great, Doc."

Goose bumps broke out across her skin and a shiver moved through her as she jerked away, her face flushing as she aimed an uncertain smile in his direction. At least he wasn't alone in this unwanted attraction, he thought with satisfaction.

"You too, Major," she answered briskly, carefully avoiding touching him as she passed the infant back. She moved away jerkily, looking suddenly tired—and spooked, like she was ready to bolt.

He tucked the baby into the crook of his arm. "Cassidy?"

She paused in the process of pulling off the surgical gown and sent him a look over her shoulder, eyes wide and a little desperate.

"Yes?"

"You going to finish what you started earlier…before we were interrupted?"

Immediately a wild flush heated her face and her eyes widened as though she thought he was suggesting they finish their interrupted kiss. Her mouth opened but all that emerged was a strangled, "Uh…"

"I have another twenty-seven stitches," he went on, grinning wickedly at the deer-in-the-headlights expression that flashed across her face. Her mouth closed with a snap and her look of furious embarrassment had his soft chuckle following in her wake.

"Meet me in the ER in fifteen minutes," she snapped, and Sam got the impression she'd considered punching the smile off his face. He was suddenly glad he was holding a newborn.

Cassidy Mahoney, it seemed, was not a woman to be trifled with. And why that made his grin widen, he didn't know. Maybe he was an idiot, or crazy, like his family believed.

"What do you think?" he asked the infant staring intently up at him. The tiny girl blinked before surrendering to another big yawn, making Sam chuckle.

"Yeah," he snorted softly, "my thoughts exactly, sweetheart."

CHAPTER SEVEN

CASSIDY SENT FRAN GILBERT to the ER to deal with a hot, appealing SEAL, assuring herself she wasn't a coward. Besides, Gail's husband needed a status update.

She found Chip Sanders being fussed over by one of the older nurses on duty. The warm, motherly woman in her late fifties squeezed the new father's hand in silent support when they caught sight of Cassidy heading in their direction.

His expression was so painfully hopeful that Cassidy had to smile in reassurance as she announced that he had a beautiful baby daughter and that his wife's progress was promising.

Chip leapt up with a joyous whoop and Cassidy had to laugh when he caught her in a huge grateful hug. She briefly returned his embrace, cautioning that Gail was still critical and that she and the baby were being transferred to Spruce Ridge General.

After he rushed off to see his new family, she found herself smiling as she headed for the wards. There was nothing like making someone so happy they forgot all trauma and fear, she mused. Fortunately for Chip, everything had worked out fine.

Thanks to one overwhelming Navy SEAL. A man who seemed to have a really bad effect on her. Just the sound of his deep voice sent excited little zings into places that had no business zinging and she ended up losing a good portion of her brain.

Just as Cassidy was writing notations on the night roster, news came through that the chopper was five minutes out. After giving the night nurse a few last-minute instructions, Cassidy headed for Recovery to collect the patients for transport.

She...*they* had done everything they could to ensure Gail Sanders and her baby pulled through the traumatic incident. It was now up to the OB/GYN at Spruce Ridge General to ensure they stayed that way.

Heather was waiting for her and together they rushed the new family to the helipad, where the Medevac helicopter was already landing. While the paramedics transferred Gail and her baby to the chopper, Cassidy gave the Medevac doctor a rundown of the patient's condition and signed the release forms. With a nod, the guy sent her an appreciative smile and an over-the-shoulder thumbs-up as he loped off towards the waiting craft. Bare minutes after it had landed, the chopper was heading towards Spruce Ridge.

Beside her, Heather gave a huge sigh and sent Cassidy an elated smile. "Wasn't that just great? I love it when a bad situation turns out well, don't you?" She threw her arms around Cassidy and made her laugh with an exuberant hug. "Ooh, and wasn't the major just wonderful? With Gail's baby, I mean," she added hastily, when Cassidy drew back with a dry look. "I heard Chip was blubbering like a little girl," Heather chatted on. "Poor guy. He must have been terrified." She stopped to sigh dramatically. "Isn't he just dreamy?"

Cassidy eyed her sharply. "Who? Chip?"

Heather giggled. "No, silly. Samuel Kellan. Just wait until I tell the girls what happened. They're going to flip. Imagine, me getting to see him in action with my own eyes?" She squeaked and gave Cassidy another quick hug. Then with a hurried, "You're the greatest, Doc," she turned and disappeared into the darkened hospital.

Cassidy shook her head at the departing nurse and turned to watch as the chopper's running lights rose over the dark mountains. With the *whup, whup, whup* fading into the night, she took deep breaths of cold mountain air and slowly let the tension of the night slide away.

"Well," she said dryly to no one in particular, "it seems Crescent Lake's hero has done it again."

She wasn't jealous that Major Hotstuff was getting all the credit for the night's work, she assured herself. He'd stepped up when she'd needed him, it was true, but you'd think he'd performed a miracle worthy of sainthood.

Laughing at herself, Cassidy went to tell Fran she was taking a break. Hoping to get a few hours' sleep before the next emergency, she headed for the quiet of her office.

The privacy hallway connecting the offices was in darkness but dim light eased its way through an open doorway. Cassidy's pulse gave a little bump and she paused as the scene brought back unpleasant memories. Fear clutched at her belly until she reminded herself that Crescent Lake wasn't Boston. Drugged-up vice cops didn't break into doctors' offices in small mountain towns, looking for prescription drugs. At least she hoped not.

Besides, in the few weeks she'd been in town the most dangerous thing to happen had been when she'd been escorted to the local jail to treat a hot, attitude-ridden Navy SEAL.

No, that wasn't quite true, she amended silently. *That* had been when he'd pushed her up against the ER wall and rearranged her brain synapses.

Heart hammering, Cassidy quietly approached the open doorway. She drew in a wobbly breath and peered around the door, half expecting to find crazed druggies ripping

open drawers looking for their next fix. Her breath escaped
in a whoosh when she found everything as it should be.

She was sliding her hand up the wall to turn off the
light when she realized the desk lamp was on and not the
ceiling fixture. Heading across the room, she reached over
the desk to extinguish the lamp when a soft sound had her
wide gaze flying towards the shadows. The sight of Crescent Lake's favorite son draped over the sofa with an arm
flung across his face, gave her a weird sense of déjà vu.

Straightening, Cassidy allowed her hand to fall away.
It seemed the man couldn't find anything big enough to
accommodate his large body. She wondered absently why
he hadn't left, and took the opportunity to study him without him being aware.

He was back in the faded jeans and she took a moment
to admire the way the soft material hugged his narrow
hips and long muscular legs while cupping more intimate
places. The black T-shirt fitted even more snugly, stretching across his wide chest while straining the shoulder
seams and the sleeves around his big biceps.

It was only when she could see his lashes casting dark
shadows on the slash of his cheekbones that she realized
she'd moved across the room and was standing staring
down at him like an infatuated adolescent.

Darn, she thought, biting her lip, getting all excited
about some *guy* was the height of idiocy—especially one
who liked free-falling from high altitudes and blowing
stuff up. One who wouldn't be sticking around for long
before he was off again, saving the world.

Turning to go, she spied a blanket over the back of
the sofa and reached for it an instant before hard fingers
clamped over her wrist. In less time than it took for her
heart to jerk hard against her ribs, she was flying through
the air to land with a bone-rattling thud that knocked the

air from her lungs. She barely managed a strangled *oomph* as a heavy weight rolled her across the floor.

They came to an abrupt stop against the solid desk with Cassidy's wrists shackled over her head. A large hand clamped over her mouth, stifling her shocked gasp.

Blinking, Cassidy found herself staring up into a dark face lit with fierce gold eyes. For an awful moment she visualized him whipping out a knife and slicing her throat before she could draw her next breath.

She felt him everywhere—heat and hardness pressing her soft curves into the floor. During the tumble, one long, hard thigh had found its way between hers, effectively pinning her down. All she could do was gasp and stare into gleaming gold eyes as she waited for his next move.

One second she could see her life flashing before her eyes, the next he was cursing and rolling away to lie silently and rigidly beside her. The suddenness of the move stunned her and all she could do was try to calm her jagged pulse and smooth her ragged breathing. All she could think was, *What the heck was that?* It had been scary and…*darn it*…she hated to admit it a little exciting.

She was a sick person.

She felt rather than saw his head turn. "You okay?"

And he was insane.

Sucking in air, Cassidy lowered her arms and pushed her hair off her face before rearing upright to glare down at him.

"Are you insane?" she demanded furiously, then snapped her mouth closed when she realized that maybe it wasn't the most sensitive thing to say to someone suffering from PTSD—if that's what he had—but, *heck*, the man gave being trigger-happy a bad name.

Not surprisingly, he didn't look the least bit amused by what had happened. In fact, he looked mad—well, that made two of them—and embarrassed.

Embarrassed? What did he *have to be embarrassed about?* She *was the one who'd gone flying through the air.*

He scrubbed a hand over his face with a weary sigh and growled, "Sorry…" so softly she almost didn't catch it.

Her jaw dropped open. "Sorry? You're…*sorry*?" She was getting hysterical again and made an effort to lower her voice, even though she felt she was entitled to a little hysteria. "You can't attack people like that and just say sorry, Major."

He turned and scowled, his dark brows flattening across his forehead in a heavy line of frustration. "What the hell do you expect me to say? Besides, it was your fault."

Her eyebrows shot into her hairline. "*My f-fault?*" she spluttered, and when he smirked she had to get a firm grip on her temper before she gave in to the urge to smack it off his face.

"Hey, you were bending over me," he pointed out reasonably, as if he had women bending over him all the time. And after witnessing Heather's gushing infatuation, he probably did. *The jerk.* "What was I supposed to think? I thought you wanted to wrestle me to the floor. I was just being accommodating."

Cassidy stared at him open-mouthed for a few seconds as his words sank in then uttered a sound of disbelief. She drew up her legs and shoved her hands in her hair before dropping her forehead onto her knees. She snickered helplessly for a few beats. "You are such a liar," she said when she could talk without gasping.

He lifted the arm he'd slung over his face to crinkle his eyes at her, his poet's mouth pulled into a crooked smile. *God, that little grin was appealing.*

"Says who? *You?*" He made a rude sound. "For all I know, you *were* just looking for an excuse to roll around on the floor with me. *You* know, finish what you started earlier?"

"What *you* started, you mean," she retorted.

"Me?" He shook his head. "You have a defective memory there, Doc."

"And you're delusional. I ought to throw you out." Another mocking sound accompanied the *yeah-right* look he sent her and she narrowed her gaze. "You don't think I can?"

"Babe, I *know* you can't."

He sounded so arrogantly male that she straightened and stared at him. "Excuse me," she demanded frostily. "Did you just call me *babe*?"

He grinned and said, "Uh-huh," with the kind of look that had a bubble of laughter rising in her throat. *Darn.* She didn't want to find him irresistible, but there was just too much to like. Despite…well, everything.

Blowing out a breath, she dropped her head back against the desk, suddenly exhausted by her ping-ponging emotions. "Well, don't. It's demeaning."

"It is?" He sounded genuinely surprised. "Why?"

Cassidy snorted. "You ask that when you probably call every woman you meet *babe* because it saves you having to remember their names."

Sam was quiet for a moment, as though he was seriously considering her accusation, before finally shaking his head and saying, "That's not true. I don't call the ward sergeant at Coronado Med Center *babe*." He gave a shudder. *"Or* my CO's wife, for that matter. That's a surefire way for a guy to get court-martialed."

Cassidy caught herself smiling when she couldn't afford to. He was too big, too macho, too…*everything.* Everything she'd told herself she didn't want in a man. Everything she was finding alarmingly likeable.

She pushed out her lower lip and blew out a frustrated breath. "You're changing the subject, Major. It isn't normal for anyone to think they're being attacked in their sleep. I was just reaching for the blanket."

"That's what you say," he said, waggling his eyebrows at her when she rolled her eyes. Snagging her wrist, he tugged her towards him, tucking her body beneath his when she lost her balance. Cassidy once again found herself staring up into his darkly handsome face while his big body covered hers.

"What are you *doing*?" she squeaked, realizing his hard thigh was pressing against places that hadn't seen any action in a long while. It was mortifying to admit those places were turning liquid with heat.

"If you need to ask," Sam said, sliding his hand over her hip to rub his thumb into the crease her jeans created between hip and thigh, "you're not as smart as I thought."

She slapped a hand over his to stop him heading for forbidden territory. "I'm smart enough to know that whatever you're thinking is a mistake."

"*This*," he murmured, and dropped a kiss at the outer corner of her eyebrow, "is not a mistake." He slid his mouth to her ear. "SEALs carry really big weapons," he whispered wickedly. "Wanna see?"

Cassidy's gasp ended on a giggle at his terrible pun. *Yes, please. "No!"* She groaned silently. *No looking at his... weapon.* Or anything else.

"Major," she began, trying to sound firm, but her voice gave a little hitch as arousal sent heat skittering through her veins. "Let me up." If she stayed spread out beneath him like jelly on peanut butter, there was no telling what would happen.

His eyes had gone all dark and hot. He shook his head slowly. "I can't," he confessed, abruptly serious. Catching her hand, he brought it to his mouth, where he pressed a gentle kiss into the center of her palm. "I've tried. *God* knows, I've tried." He nibbled on the fleshy part of her thumb. "There's just no denying…*this*."

Her belly tightened and she let her fingers curl help-lessly over his jaw, rough with a dark shadow that looked a good few hours past five o'clock. The rasp against her skin sent shivers of longing and arousal up her arm into her chest and a hot yearning set up residence in her belly. "Try harder," she gulped.

His smile was quick and sinful as his big hand smoothed a path of heat down the length of her arm, over her shoul-der to her breast. "*Babe*," he drawled, brushing his thumb over the full bottom curve and drawing her nipple into a tight bud that had his eyes gleaming with satisfaction. "If it gets any harder I'll injure myself." He looked up from studying the hard tips of her breasts. "You're bound by oath to treat me then, aren't you?"

Cassidy slapped her hand over his with the intention of moving it to safer territory. "In your dreams, Major," she scoffed huskily, but her resistance was fast slipping away—right along with her mind. And she was having a hard time recalling why she should care.

"Sam," he corrected against her throat, and Cassidy lifted her chin to give him room, her eyes drifting closed with the lush pleasure of having his mouth on her. *Oh, God.* They needed to stop this before…before…

"Say it." A shiver raced down her spine, sparks burst-ing behind her eyelids as he opened his mouth to suck on a patch of delicate skin. She gave a little gasp and clenched her thighs around his, the pressure setting off tiny little explosions of sensation in forbidden places.

"Wh-what?" She tried to concentrate long enough to make sense of his words.

"My name." He abandoned her throat to kiss his way up to her parted lips. His thigh pushed harder against her. "Say it," he ordered softly, pulling back when she tried to capture his mouth with hers. A moan worked its way up from her throat and emerged as a growl before she could stop it. Tunneling her fingers into his hair, she tugged him closer and closed her teeth over his bottom lip in a punishing little nip.

"Don't make me hurt you, Major," she growled, and his answering chuckle was deep and dark and sent delicious sensations heating up lonely places. *Heck*, he was like a furnace, incinerating everything in sight—her resistance, her reservations…her *mind*—turning her to putty in his big, strong hands.

His mouth smiled against hers. "Say it," he taunted softly, applying a little hot, wet suction that made her moan. "Say it and I'll give you exactly what you want."

Cassidy heard a loud buzzing in her ears and in a far distant corner of her mind still capable of thought she acknowledged that he was right. She did want him and his name, "*Samuel*," emerged on a husky sigh.

With a growl, deep and low in his throat, he caught her mouth in a kiss so hot and raw that she felt it in the pit of her belly. He pulled oxygen from her lungs and a frantic response from her mouth. It was so good that Cassidy fisted her hands in his hair and opened her mouth beneath his, promising herself that she would stop. In a minute.

It was her last rational thought. The instant his warm hand slid over the naked skin of her belly, she lost all reason, all ability to think of anything but the sudden frenzy of his kiss. Excited thrills raced over her skin as her world narrowed and focused on his hot mouth, his eager hands. She tried to touch him everywhere at once—his shoulders, his wide back, his hard chest—as though she couldn't get enough.

She briefly acknowledged that she was in trouble— *big* trouble—when his hand slid beneath her jeans and cupped her through her panties. Thought slid away on a low moan as she arched into his touch, feeling perhaps for the first time the kind of hot, crazy desire people talked about. Too far gone to care that he was everything that was bad for her.

His touch felt too good, and the big erection pressing against her felt hard and powerful and welcome.

He shifted and before she knew it, he was whipping her T-shirt over her head. Grabbing a fistful of fabric at the back of his neck, he stripped off his own, sending both garments sailing over his shoulder into the shadows. Then he planted his big hands beside her head, and with their gazes locked he nudged her thighs apart before lowering his body slowly over hers until all that separated their good parts was denim and silk. At the press of his powerful erection into the notch between her legs he grimaced as though in pain and his eyes drifted closed.

"*Jeez*," he said, his voice so deep and rough it slid into her belly like dark sin. "*Cassidy…*" he breathed heavily, and stared down into her face with hot, glazed eyes. "You are so damn beautiful, do you know that? And I've had really carnal thoughts about your mouth for days," he growled. "It's driven me crazy, thinking about kissing you. Kind of like this." He bent his head and gave her a kiss, soft and sweet and hot. "*Oh, yeah*," he breathed against her mouth, sucking gently on her swollen lip. "It's lush and tempting and so damn sweet. It's all I can think about."

Then he opened his mouth over hers in a hard, hungry kiss that scattered her senses, and before Cassidy knew what was happening she was thrusting her hands into his hair and kissing him back, her mouth as hot and greedy as his.

Sam swept his tongue past her lips to taste the dark, sweet nectar within. She responded with a low hungry moan and closed her lips around his tongue, sucking hard.

Controlling himself with effort, Sam fed her hot, desperate kisses, tongue dueling and tangling while his hands streaked over her soft flesh, stripping off her clothing until she was left in nothing but a tiny triangle of teal silk.

Kneeing her smooth thighs apart, he settled his hips between them, pushing against her soft, wet heat until she was writhing restlessly against him.

"*Holy…*" His mind glazed over and he couldn't remember what he'd been about to say. Only knew that he wanted her more than he'd wanted anything. *Ever.*

"Samuel…" Her voice was a sweet, husky moan of desire that almost had him going off like a missile. He filled his big hands with her breasts and flicked at the hard little buds until a long, low wail tore from her throat and her back arched up off the floor.

Ignoring her entreaty, he dipped his head to scrape his teeth along her neck, nipping the delicate skin until she shivered as her palm slid down his belly. She pressed her hand against his button fly and he jolted like he'd been shot.

"*Sweet…*" he growled, grabbing her hand to pin it against the floor above her head. "Not yet, babe." He gave a rough laugh when a sound of frustration burst from her mouth. "Soon," he promised hoarsely, closing his mouth hungrily over one swollen breast. She gasped and his pulse spiked until all he could hear in the quiet room was the heavy thunder of his heart, the harsh sounds of their breathing and her soft, throaty whimpers.

She fisted her free hand in his hair and couldn't hold back the full-body shudder or the eager moan that ended with, "*Oh, my God…*"

Soothing her, he dropped a moist kiss between her lush breasts before heading south, stringing tiny, wet kisses across her abdomen. He paused to trace his tongue around her shallow navel, gently blowing against the damp skin until her belly quivered. His hum of amusement turned into a growl of pleasure.

With his mouth on her flat belly, Sam slid his hands up her long smooth thigh to hook his fingers into the narrow band of fabric at her hips. And before she could gasp out a breathless "*Wait,*" he'd slid her panties down her legs and past her toes to send them sailing over his shoulder.

Grunting, he reared back onto his heels and looked at the woman sprawled like sin before him. For a moment he savored the tempting sight then dipped his head to run the tip of his tongue up the inside of her knee, chuckling when she shivered and let out a desperate whimper.

As though sensing the direction of his mouth, Cassidy uttered a squeak of protest and tried to clamp her legs together, fisting her hands in his hair to stop his upward progress. "No, Samuel," she cried breathlessly, "I don't—"

"It's okay," he murmured, sliding his big, rough hand over her quivering belly before wedging his shoulders between her thighs. He dragged damp kisses over her hips and stomach to the soft, sweet undersides of her breasts. Alternating stinging wet kisses with little swipes of his beard-roughened jaw that made her arch and moan, Sam gentled her with his hands and lips until her muscles went fluid and lax and she gave a long, lazy hum of pleasure.

The moment he felt her body shift languorously and turn liquid he moved and closed his mouth over her soft, damp folds. She tried to tug at him, her gasp of protest turning to a cry of pleasure as he pressed closer and did something with his tongue. In moments she was flying off the edge.

The force of her climax hit hard, and, eyes wide with shock, Cassidy could only lie there shuddering and think, *Holy cow...what was that?*

But Sam wasn't finished. He uttered a rough growl and

reared up, yanking his jeans and boxer briefs down his
legs before kicking them free. Then he slid up her body,
dragging his tongue along the slick, damp flesh between
her breasts and up her long slender throat until his fallen-
angel face filled her vision. His molten-gold eyes locked
with hers. She felt the bump of him against the tender flesh
between her thighs and slapped a hand against his chest
to keep him from thrusting home.

"Condom," she gasped.

He froze and swore, surging upward to reach behind
him for his jeans. Within seconds he'd rolled the latex
down his thick shaft before he positioned himself and,
with one fierce thrust, buried himself deep.

The thick, solid invasion set off another series of explosions, sending Cassidy arching upward as her body
stretched to accommodate him. It took a couple of thrusts
but once he was buried to the hilt she let out a long low
moan of pleasure and wrapped her arms and legs around
his big body.

Softly murmuring her name, Sam slowly withdrew until
she was lightheaded with the incredible explosion of sensations. Then he thrust deeper, his mouth closing over hers
in a ravenous kiss that stole her breath and blew away what
was left of her mind.

Applying the same light suction to her mouth that he'd
used in more intimate places, Sam sucked the air from her
lungs until she was dizzy, mindless with pleasure. Then
he began to move in a slow, sweet rhythm. The sensations
shooting through her ratcheted higher and higher until her
blood caught fire and her world spun off its axis.

Before she knew it, she was straining against him, meeting his every hard thrust with one of her own, tongues tangling and clashing as her hands raced over him, greedy
for the feel of his hot, tight flesh and the steel-hard muscles shifting and bunching beneath the smooth damp skin.

Helpless with sensation, Cassidy sank her fingers into his big shoulders and clung, her third climax catching her completely unawares as it ripped a low moan from her throat. Her body bucked and convulsed beneath his, the soft growl in her ear scraping at raw nerve endings and sending more detonations exploding through her blood.

Catching her hips in his hands, Sam dug his fingers into the smooth flesh to hold her in place as he increased his pace until he was hammering every hard inch, every powerful thrust into her as though he wanted to stamp his possession onto her very DNA.

Caught up in his desperate pace, Cassidy wrapped her long legs around him, and fisting her hands in his hair was lost to his driving rhythm. Hard and fast—plunging into her deeper and deeper—until, with a hoarse cry, he came.

CHAPTER EIGHT

THE BAD THING about disastrous mistakes was that no matter how hard you tried not to think about them, the more you did. It was this vicious cycle that gave Cassidy a headache and made her cranky in the week following…well, possibly the second-biggest mistake of her life. And even if she'd managed to forget for an instant that she'd had a one-night stand with someone so completely wrong for her, she just had to catch sight of her reflection and she was groaning in mortification.

Crescent Lake's favorite son had whipped her up, given her some seriously intense orgasms and when she'd thought he was sleeping and had tried to sneak away—they had been in someone's office, for heaven's sake—he'd tightened his hold on her and said in his deep sleep-rough voice, "Where are you going? I've just started."

Even hours later her skin glowed, her eyes sparkled and her mouth was bruised and swollen from his kisses. Anyone looking at her could see at a glance that she'd had her world rocked. And if that wasn't enough, she had whisker burns and hickeys in places that made her alternately smile and blush.

Except there was absolutely *nothing* to smile about. She'd rolled around on the floor—*and* the huge sofa—with a hot Navy SEAL whose idea of a relationship probably meant a couple of nights with a busty babe before he headed off to wreak havoc in some foreign war zone.

What had she been thinking?

Clearly she hadn't given a thought to where they were or the consequences of someone walking in on them. The last thing she wanted was to find herself hip-deep in another scandal. The last thing she needed was to get all worked up over some hot alpha SEAL with "temporary" tattooed on his sexy hide in eleven different languages.

Clearly the smartest thing to do was escape. Except every time she'd tried to slide out from under his big arm, he'd tightened his grasp, his sleep-rough voice murmuring, "I'm not finished with you yet."

Finally her brain had cleared and she'd told him she needed to check the wards. His heavy arm had reluctantly slid away but not before a big rough hand had smoothed a leisurely line of fire from her naked shoulder to her knee and he'd murmured, "Hurry back…" against her throat.

Resisting the urge to arch into his touch and purr with pleasure, Cassidy had rolled off the sofa, snatched up her clothes and bolted. Standing in the shower an hour later, she'd leaned her forehead against the tiles as steaming water had cascaded over her sensitized flesh and prayed that he'd be recalled to wherever he was stationed. Because there was no way she could ever look into his wicked eyes and not remember where he'd put his mouth and how he'd done things that had made her scream.

Okay, maybe not scream, she amended, but she'd made some pretty embarrassing noises that had her blushing whenever she thought about it. But as the days passed and the gossip mill in town had him harassing bad guys and helping little old ladies across the street—when he wasn't working behind the bar and chatting up the regulars—Cassidy realized he wasn't going anywhere. *Yet.*

And when the thought of him leaving made her feel

vaguely ill and a strange ache squeezed her chest, Cassidy began to get a very bad feeling that unless she got her head on straight, she was headed for heartbreak. Besides, he hadn't called or tried to contact her, which clearly meant he was done with her.

And she was done too—*really*. So why, then, did his absence feel like a slap in the face?

But that kind of thinking was not only ridiculous but self-defeating. Samuel Kellan had "temporary" written all over him and what had seemed like more than hot steamy sex—at least to her—had been nothing but a good time for him.

In the week since he'd toppled her to the floor and brought her intimate places out of deep hibernation, he hadn't been there to rescue her from falling off ladders or to push her up against any walls. And as she left the hospital eight days later and slid into her car, she firmly told herself she was relieved. She didn't need rescuing. And she didn't need a big, strong man with a wicked smile to rock her world.

Considering what she'd endured the past year she'd be really, *really* stupid to fall for another alpha male—even one with beautiful gold eyes, awesome biceps and the ability to reduce her to a mindless mess.

Except her confusion and uncertainty grew, along with the sick feeling that her emotions were deeper than she wanted to acknowledge, and that what she'd dubbed "just sex" had been anything but.

Frankly the smart thing was to pretend nothing had happened and wait for the churning in her belly to go away. Besides, there hadn't been time to develop deep lasting feelings for someone like him.

That would have been so utterly stupid when she'd already used up her quota of stupid on a man who lived on the edge.

* * *

The following week found Sam riding shotgun while Crescent Lake's sheriff droned on and on about something or other till Sam had been tempted to drive them both off a cliff. So he'd been a bit bad-tempered. *Big deal.* Instead of doing the job the government was paying him to do, he was driving around looking for truant kids and mediating between two old codgers who'd been fighting like toddlers over a toy truck for *fifty* years. And if that wasn't bad enough, the lean, mean badass SEAL had been dumped after the best sex of his life.

Okay, so maybe a *very* small part of his surliness was because he'd thought Cassidy Mahoney would be as eager as he was for a repeat of their night of passion. Instead, she'd escaped at the first opportunity. And all he'd done since then was think about her.

Like a damn girl—obsessing about what she was doing, who she was with and if she thought about him at all. Frankly, he was behaving like a pimply-faced nerd with his first crush. She'd slid her perfect body against his, put her lush mouth and her hands on him and made his eyes roll back in his head. Then she'd calmly risen from the sofa, collected her clothes and sauntered from the room without a backward glance.

Maybe in the past he'd encouraged it, but he really hated it that Cassidy had done it to him. Maybe it made him a hypocrite, but there was just something about her that made Sam lose his mind and act like a lovesick ass. It was baffling—and downright terrifying.

So he told himself to stay away. He was leaving and had no place in his life for the kind of relationship she probably wanted. His life was perfect…except he had to listen to Ruben go on and on about seeing a shrink so Sam could get back to protecting the nation because he was giving the sheriff's department a bad name by being a jerk.

And in the next breath he was telling Sam how great it would be if he came home so they could run the department together.

Yeah, right. Like that would ever happen. Ruben liked being in charge and so did he. They would probably throttle each other in the first week.

Sam sighed—again—and wiped the already clean bar surface. Fortunately it was Sunday night and the bar was quiet except for a few die-hard regulars huddled in booths along the wall, and Sam didn't have to exert himself making conversation. Except it gave him way too much time to think—which was something he wanted to avoid like a tax audit.

The truth was he was bored. Bored with driving around harassing people during the day, only to serve them Buds and peanuts at night. So when his brother pushed through the front doors, Sam was ready to take his frustrations out on someone.

"I don't know who called you but I haven't beaten anyone up lately," he drawled, folding his arms across his chest and eyeing his brother darkly. "But I could always make an exception with you."

"No one called to complain," Sheriff Kellan said tiredly. "At least, not in the last three hours."

"Real funny. Beer?"

"God, yeah." Ruben pulled off his hat and tossed it onto the bar counter. He slid onto a stool and ran a hand through his hair. "I'm off duty. Sort of."

"How can you be 'sort of' off duty?" Sam demanded, sliding a bottle across the counter.

"I'm not here to hold up the bar and swap life stories with the barman," Ruben said tiredly, lifting the beer to his mouth.

"That's a good thing," Sam snorted. "I already know your life story, and it's about as exciting as a visit to the dentist. If you've come to nag me about my crappy attitude again I'm going to have to physically remove you."

Ruben smirked and lifted his brow in that superior big-brother way that used to drive Sam crazy as a kid. "*Right*," he snorted, and lifted the bottle in an ironic salute. "Like I'd let you." He took a couple of deep pulls before lowering the bottle an inch and fixing Sam with his dark gaze. "Got a job for you."

"In case you haven't noticed," Sam complained, "I already have a job. Hell, *three* if you count driving around in an air-conditioned SUV harassing innocent folk all day and serving beer to snarky sheriffs at night. You can do your own damn filing. Besides, I have to sleep some time."

Ruben snorted since they both knew Sam wasn't getting a lot of sleep. "Marty and Andy are back at work tomorrow and I'm tired of keeping you out of trouble. It's exhausting. Besides, with your attitude you're not exactly cut out for the sheriff's department."

Sam sent him a mocking look. "Just this morning you were telling me I should come home and join you fighting the terrible crime in Crescent Lake," he drawled. "Make up your mind."

Ruben shook his head. "Don't know what I was thinking."

"What changed your mind?"

"I need your unique skills."

Sam lifted an eyebrow. "You want me to kill someone? Blow something up? Infiltrate enemy territory?" He tutted and shook his head. "This from the man sworn to uphold the law."

"Not those skills, you moron. I'm talking about the medical degree you acquired on the taxpayer's dime. I need a doctor."

Sam arched his brow sardonically. "You sick? Your girlfriend find out she's pregnant with quadruplets?"

An irritated look crossed Ruben's face. "No, I'm not sick. And when do I have time to date?"

Sam shrugged, unconcerned with his brother's love life. "How should I know? Most days you're so busy nagging I can't wait to get away from you. Besides, the idea of discussing your sex life is just disturbing. I don't want those visuals in my head. I have enough nightmares."

"Yeah, well, I'd like to have a sex life but I'm too busy protecting the innocent people of Crescent Lake from moody badass SEALs. Besides, I have a problem only you can solve. I just got off the phone. Doc Monty was run off the road up in Spruce Ridge. They had to cut him from his car and now he's in County Gen with concussion and a shattered hip."

"*Holy...* Is he all right?"

Ruben sighed and scrubbed a hand down his face. "I think so. Anyway, we need a doctor. Like now."

"In case you've forgotten, you already have a doctor. The one from Boston? The one Hannah says you have a thing for?"

Ruben's eyes glinted and his mouth turned up in a smirk that Sam was sorely tempted to remove. Ruben shrugged. "Well, she's beautiful, single and doesn't hold up bar counters in Spruce County. What more could a guy want?" He took a drink. "In fact, I was thinking of going over to the inn later and telling her about Old Monty. Maybe ask her out." And when Sam growled a warning low in his throat, Ruben snickered. "Maybe even stay the night." Then he burst out laughing. "*Jeez,*" he gasped when he finally caught his breath, "you should see your face."

Sam folded his arms across his chest and narrowed his eyes, barely resisting the urge to reach across the bar and punch someone.

"You *do* remember I've been trained by the government to kill scum like you, don't you?" he drawled dryly, but that only made Ruben laugh even more until he was laughing so hard people from the booths in the back were craning their necks to see what was happening.

Sam ignored them and shook his head with disgust. "You're pathetic, you know that?"

Finally Ruben wiped his eyes and took a drink of beer. "No more than you," he snorted with a wide grin. "It's like you're sixteen again and mooning over Cheryl Ungemeyer."

"I did not *moon* over Cheryl. I was temporarily…um… distracted by her endowments. Especially the summer she wore that string bikini. I was young and impressionable and she was an older woman." He paused a couple of beats. "I'm neither young nor impressionable now."

"Cheryl's small fry compared to Doc Boston," Ruben told him, waggling his eyebrows. "Any idiot can see that."

"You keep your eyes, and everything else, off her endowments," Sam warned half-heartedly, pointing a finger at his brother. He knew Ruben was just yanking his chain, but it wouldn't hurt to warn the guy off. "She's a doctor, for goodness' sake."

Ruben shorted with disgust. "You should listen to yourself," he said, before finishing his beer in a couple long swallows. He set the empty bottle on the bar and rose. "I guess I'll have to look around for another medic, then," he said with an exaggerated sigh. "Maybe that guy from Redfern. The nurses all had a thing for him last time he helped out."

Sam snarled and reached over the bar to grab his brother's shirt. He yanked him close until they were nose to nose, before saying mildly, "You do that and you're a dead man." He let Ruben go with a shove. "Tell Doc Boston I'll see her in the morning."

Ruben laughed and smoothed the front of his shirt before reaching for his sheriff's hat. "Tell her yourself, stud," he said, slapping it onto his head as he turned to saunter from the bar, leaving Sam with the nasty suspicion he'd just been played.

It was past ten when a quiet knock at the door distracted Cassidy from the article she'd been reading about surgical procedures for head trauma patients. All very cutting edge and fascinating but she was having trouble concentrating.

Wondering who on earth could be visiting her at such a late hour, she tossed the journal aside and rose from the rumpled bed to pad across the floor to the door.

Expecting to see the innkeeper, she was unnerved to find a US Navy SEAL propping up the door frame, hands shoved into jeans pockets, radiating enough virility and attitude to give a woman bad ideas. Ideas she should be done with.

The shoulders of his jacket were damp and rain dotted his dark, ruffled hair. His eyes and most of his face were shadowed, leaving his left cheekbone and half his mouth and strong jaw illuminated by the hallway light.

Heat rose in her cheeks as his hooded gaze boldly swept from the top of her tousled hair to her bare feet. Her grip tightening on the door, Cassidy barely resisted the urge to slam it in his face or—worse—cover her breasts. And since he'd already seen every inch of her naked body, that, and slamming the door, would only make her look ridiculous.

It was the first time she'd seen him since he'd rocked her world and she couldn't help being conscious of her nudity beneath the thin tank top and long track pants she wore as pajamas.

"Major," she said coolly in greeting. A dark brow rose at her tone and his mouth kicked up at one corner.

"Doctor," he mocked, and after a few beats, during which he continued to study her silently, Cassidy gave in to the urge to flick her tongue nervously over her lips. His eyes went hot at the move.

Finally, when she could no longer stand the rising tension, she demanded, "What are you doing here, Major?"

"Invite me in and I'll tell you."

Wary of his strange mood, Cassidy eyed him suspiciously. "Why can't you tell me out here?"

A slow, wicked smile curved his mouth. "You want the entire floor to hear what I have to say, *babe*?"

Flushing at his reminder of the night they'd spent together, she narrowed her eyes and fought the urge to slam the door in his face-even if it did make her look like an idiot. He must have read her mind because he pushed away from the wall and stepped into her, forcing her back into the room to avoid coming into contact with his hard heat.

"Come in, why don't you?" she drawled dryly.

"Why, thank you, Dr. Honey," he mocked softly, "don't mind if I do." He angled his shoulders, intentionally brushing against her as he moved past. A shiver of awareness spread across her skin, tightening her breasts. Cassidy retreated while Sam continued into the room then turned to lean back against the door, hoping it would support her wobbly knees.

He simply took over her space with his presence, leaving Cassidy fighting twin urges to plaster herself against him or run like hell.

He shrugged off his battered leather jacket and tossed it over the back of an armchair, clearly intent on staying a while. She eyed the way his dark blue T-shirt molded to wide shoulders and a strong back and her hands tingled at the memory of running them over hard muscles covered with warm, satin-smooth skin.

Thrusting his hands on his narrow hips, Sam took his time looking around the room, making Cassidy painfully aware of her rumpled appearance and the large bed dominating the space. Glowing bedside lamps gave the room an intimate glow that had her recalling in perfect detail the last time they'd been in a room together.

He turned, catching her gaze over one broad shoulder. The hot, sleepy expression in his eyes told her his thoughts were moving along similar lines.

"You bailed." He sounded vaguely accusing, which surprised her since she'd thought they'd both wanted to avoid any "after" awkwardness. Talking about it now was not only redundant, it was…mortifying. She wanted to forget the whole incident. But if he wanted to discuss it, the least she could do was be honest.

"Look, Major, I'm not looking to start…well, anything. It…it was a mistake," she finished firmly.

His eyes darkened and his jaw flexed. "A mistake?"

Suddenly parched, she pushed away from the door and headed for the small bar fridge, determined not to let him distract her with memories of "the sofa interlude." It was over and she wasn't going there again.

She bent at the waist to grab a bottle of water and looked over her shoulder, only to catch his smoldering gaze on her backside. She straightened with a snap and "Can I get you something?" emerged on a breathless little squeak.

Unconcerned that he'd been caught ogling, Sam's brooding gaze traveled up the length of her body until his eyes met hers, heat and accusation in his expression. He shook his head. "I'm good."

Yeah, right.

She headed for the window with her bottle, hoping a little distance would help her breathe in the suddenly hot, airless room. She turned and propped her hip against the windowsill. "Why are you here, Major?" she demanded, twisting off the cap. "Are you ill? Find out your girlfriend has an STD?"

His lips twitched but he shook his head slowly, eyes

scorching and intense as he watched her lift the bottle and drink thirstily. He licked his lips, his gaze travelling from her mouth, down her throat to her tight breasts. He didn't look sick, she thought a little wildly. In fact, he looked fabulous. And hot. *Dammit.*

"Is something…um wrong?" she asked hoarsely, before clearing her throat irritably. "*Do* you need a doctor?" Her gaze checked him for blood and found none.

"Yes… No." He moved across the floor and her heart skipped a few too many beats when he came to a halt less than a foot away. His gold eyes studied her as though he'd never seen her before. "*You* do."

"I—what?" *What the heck was he talking about?*

"Monty had an accident on his way back from visiting his daughter. He's in Spruce Ridge General."

Cassidy gasped and felt her face drain of color. She tightened her hand on the plastic bottle. "Oh, God, is he all right?" She hadn't known the older man long but had come to like and respect him enormously.

"Shattered hip. He'll be out of commission for a while."

"You know as well as I do that he won't be back," she told him quietly. "After something like that the workload would likely kill him. Besides, he should be enjoying his retirement."

"He's been treating people here for the past forty-five years. Hell, he *is* the hospital."

"He still needs to enjoy his retirement."

"Tell that to him. Besides, Crescent Lake's tourism has soared over the past five years. The hospital needs someone younger who can cope with the workload." He paused. "So. You interested?"

Cassidy's heart skipped a beat but she knew enough not to read too much into his question. He wasn't asking because *he* wanted her to stay. "What about you?"

He sent her an impatient look. "I already have a job," he reminded her shortly.

"Yes," she agreed shortly. "Yelling '*boo-yah*' as you jump from high altitudes."

"That's right." His brows lowered and he folded his arms across his chest. "You make it sound like a kids' game."

"No, it's not and I appreciate that you risk your life with every mission, but you're more than a SEAL, Major. You're more than infiltration, interrogation and demolition."

"Yeah," he agreed silky. "I'm damn good at my job."

"You'd have to be. But you can't be a SEAL for ever."

A dark brow rose arrogantly. "I can't?"

Rolling her eyes, Cassidy recapped the water bottle with an irritated twist. "You know you can't," she said flatly, slapping the bottle on the windowsill with a snap. He caught and held her gaze with an intensity she felt like a burn in her gut. "Eventually you have to retire or move up the ladder."

"Or come home in a body bag."

"Don't say that," she snapped, suddenly furious with his dry flippancy. The thought of him being KIA made her queasy. She gulped, pushing her hair off her forehead with unsteady fingers. "*God*, don't say that. Just…just…*don't*."

"Every soldier, every sailor thinks about it," he reminded her gently. "It's the reality of being in any country's armed forces. *Hell*, before every mission we write letters to our families and get our affairs in order."

Cassidy felt tears burning the backs of her eyes, pressure squeezing her chest like a vice. She pressed the heels of her hands against her eyes to counteract the sudden threat of tears. "That's… *Dammit*. That's not fair."

A slow, satisfied smile lit his dark features. "Sounds like you care what happens to me," he said cockily, the masculine confidence in his voice sending her belly dipping and her temper rising. She wanted to simultaneously slug him and wrap her arms around him.

"Of course I care," she snapped hotly, before realizing how he might interpret her words. "You're…you're a valuable member of the country's special armed forces. I'd care about anyone I knew going off to fight a dangerous war."

His looked skeptical. "*Riiiiight.*" He stepped closer to plant his big boots either side of her bare feet and slapped both hands on the windowsill at her hips, effectively boxing her in. Then he leant down to brush his lips against the delicate skin beneath her ear.

"Are you sure you wouldn't miss me?" he demanded softly.

Cassidy gulped and her head spun with the warm, male scent of him. "I…uh."

"Not even a little?" he whispered, giving her earlobe a tiny nip that sent shivers of pure sensation spreading throughout her body. The back of her neck prickled, her breasts tightened and familiar heat pooled between her thighs. And when his mouth opened against her throat she moaned, tilting her head to the side to give him room. She wanted to beg him to stop one instant and the next—

"Samuel." Her voice emerged, husky and aching with a desire she could no longer deny. She wanted him. Needed the hot slide of his flesh against hers more than she needed her next breath. "This is a mistake."

"No," he rasped against her neck. "Inevitable."

She gave a breathless moan when his hands curled around her knees, pushed them gently apart to step between them until his heat and hardness pressed against where she ached.

"Admit it," he insisted softly, his hands smoothing a line of fire up her thighs to her hips. "Admit that you'd miss me if some scumbag terrorist took me out," he said against her mouth.

Dizzy with the force of her emotions, Cassidy slid her palms up his long muscular arms to his shoulders and fought the urge to clutch him close. She wondered briefly why she'd imagined she could ignore him, especially when he touched her like this. Put his mouth on her. Talked about dying.

"Yes," she breathed against his mouth, sliding her hands into his thick hair. "*God, yes*," and caught his mouth in a kiss that showed him exactly how much she would miss him. How much she'd come to need him despite her determination not to.

Sam growled deep in his throat and lifted her, yanking her hard against him. And when her legs snaked around his hips, he turned towards the rumpled bed.

"Show me, Cassidy," he growled against her throat. "Show me how much you'd miss me."

CHAPTER NINE

WHEN CASSIDY WOKE the following morning she was naked and aching in deliciously intimate places. *Again.*

Only this time *she* was alone and didn't have to scramble around looking for her clothes.

Sliding her hand over the bed where Sam's big body had heated up the sheets, she told herself she was relieved. But the truth was the hollow feeling in her chest made her feel like a hypocrite.

In the dark, intimate hours of the night she'd pressed her body to his, arched into his hungry caresses and moaned when he'd moved his hot, moist mouth over every inch of skin and thrust his body into hers. And when their ragged, harsh breathing had calmed and their skin cooled, he'd pulled her close and wrapped his arms around her as she'd slid bonelessly into sleep.

As if he'd never let her go.

He'd made her feel safe and protected as she hadn't felt in a long time—as though within his arms she'd found her shelter from the storm.

Which was ridiculous.

Samuel J. Kellan *was* the storm. He'd blown into her life when she'd been determined to hide from the world. He'd turned her inside out with his sexy smile and hot, seductive kisses that made her feel—things she didn't want to feel—and then he'd given her a glimpse of the caring, honorable man beneath the tough, broody SEAL exterior. *Worst* of all he'd made her admire him when she'd been convinced he was exactly like Lance Turnbull.

Okay, so she liked him too—a *lot*—but that was beside the point. He'd soon be back with his team, plotting mayhem and destruction in the world's hottest hotspots and she'd be…here. A world away.

Her one-night stand had just become two, and she didn't know what that meant, how she felt about it or if she wanted more. Heck, if *he* wanted more.

Fortunately, by the time she walked into the hospital she'd managed to get her wildly unstable emotions under control. Until she saw *him*—tall and darkly handsome— surrounded by animated adoring women and looking like a large hungry predator in a hen house.

As though his senses were attuned to her, Sam's head lifted and his eyes met hers across the room. The force of his gaze hit her like a sledgehammer, leaving Cassidy stunned and gasping for air because that look said he saw things she'd rather keep hidden. Things that had become painfully obvious last night when he'd talked about dying. Things she'd refused to acknowledge. Even to herself. *Oh, God.* Even with the truth staring her in the face.

Then his eyes crinkled in a private, evocative smile meant to remind her of hot, wet mouths and frantic, greedy hands. Her heart lurched in her chest before taking off like a crazed meth head fleeing from the cops.

Shocked and a little spooked by her reaction, she turned and hurried towards the hallway leading to her office, her palm hitting the door as though she couldn't escape fast enough. In reality she wanted to run for the exit and keep going until the feelings faded. But she had an awful feeling she couldn't run too far or too fast. Everything that had happened with Sam was burned indelibly into her mind— *heck*, her soul—and running would accomplish nothing.

Besides, she wasn't the kind of woman who got swept away by a couple of nights with a sexy Navy SEAL.

Was she?

Hyperventilating and angry with herself for making more of things than they were, Cassidy stormed into her office and yanked off her jacket. She flung it at the coat rack and tossed her purse into her bottom drawer with shaking hands, then gave the drawer a frustrated little kick.

What the hell was that?

"What the hell was that?"

Cassidy froze when the low, furious demand filled the room. A frisson of alarm skated up her spine as memories roared in of the last time she'd been cornered in an office by an angry man. Drawing in a steadying breath, she gathered her professionalism around her like an invisible cloak and turned to find him looking hot and annoyed and more than a little baffled.

Sam wasn't Lance, she reminded herself. And he wasn't a desperate, drug-crazed psycho.

"Excuse me?" she asked coolly, hoping he'd take the hint and back the hell off. With her emotions frayed and ragged, she wasn't up to a confrontation without exposing emotions scraped raw from panic.

Sam folded his arms across his chest, his dark brows a slash of irritation across the bridge of his nose. "You heard me."

Cassidy lifted her chin in challenge. "What was what?" She had the satisfaction of seeing a muscle twitch in his jaw. *Good,* she thought uncharitably, *I'm not the only un-hinged person here.*

"*That,*" he snapped, pointing at her. "In here. Out there. It's like you're two different people. It's confusing as hell. I never know where I am with you."

All thoughts of poise and cool professionalism forgotten, Cassidy stared back at him frostily and ignored the way her stomach clenched. "I don't know what you're talk-ing about."

"*Jeez*, Cassidy," he said roughly, his face harsh with some fierce emotion he seemed to be struggling with. "One minute you're all warm and sweet and sexy and the next… hell, you looked at me like I'm the Greenside rapist."

Wincing inwardly, Cassidy turned away, hunching her shoulders against the truth. She smoothed unsteady hands down her thighs. "You're imagining things. I was just a little surprised to see you, that's all. I'm—" She stopped abruptly when she turned to find him a couple inches away. Her eyes widened and she uttered an audible gasp. *Yikes.* The man moved like smoke.

She gulped and backed up a step. He was so close, so… *familiar.*

"That's bull."

"I beg your pardon?"

"You heard me," he growled, his deep voice scraping against ragged nerve endings. "I'm not some muscle-bound redneck you can intimidate with the frosty debutante rou-tine."

Staring into eyes fierce with a confusing mix of emo-tions, Cassidy swallowed past the lump in her throat and sighed. "It's…complicated." She shrugged helplessly. "Just old, not-so-pleasant memories. Ancient history. Really."

After a long moment he lifted a hand and brushed his knuckles across her jaw. Surprise at the gentle touch added to her ragged emotions. Emotions she didn't want or need. Emotions that made her feel fragile and susceptible and long for something she couldn't have.

"Wanna talk about it?"

A strangled laugh escaped and she finally found the strength to move away from the temptation to lean on him, draw in some of his strength and heat.

"*God, no.* It's nothing, *really.*" She drew in a fortifying breath and turned, eager to change the subject. "So, what *are* you doing here?"

His gaze narrowed, probed. "I told you last night."

"You *did*?" Now it was Cassidy's turn to be confused.

"Yeah. I told you Monty had an accident and the mayor asked me to fill in until they can get someone else—or I'm recalled." He gave a one-shouldered shrug. "Whichever comes first."

Cassidy frowned as though trying to recall what he'd said last night. "You told me about the accident." She remembered him talking about body bags and dying and then— "You never said anything about filling in as medic," she added quickly, memories of what had followed flooding her with heat. *Yeesh. So not the time to be thinking about that.* "I would have remembered."

Sam eyed her flushed face silently for a few beats then his mouth slowly curved into a smartass grin that she wanted to simultaneously smack and kiss. "You thought I was here to take up where we left off last night, didn't you?"

She flushed. "Of course not," she denied instantly, smoothing her already smooth French twist with shaking hands. "That's...that's insane," she finished lamely, trying to hide her shock at discovering they would be working closely together. *Oh, boy.*

"You *did*." His grin faded into a harsh frown and his mouth twisted. She could feel him withdrawing. "I think I get it now. Negative reaction, ancient history. I reminded you of some scumbag stalker, didn't I?" Without waiting for a response, he swore and shoved his fingers through his hair. "What the hell kind of man do you take me for?"

"Th-that's ridiculous," she spluttered and turned to reach for the clean lab coat hanging on the back of her chair to give her hands something to do. "Why would I th-think that?" Large, warm hands dropped onto her shoulders and she tensed, abruptly sucking in a shaky breath.

"Hey." His voice, deep and rough, slid inside her chest and aimed for her heart. "Is that what you think?" he demanded hoarsely. "That I would...hell...*could* hurt you?"

Cassidy looked up over her shoulder into his face and couldn't deny the sincerity behind the baffled hurt and anger. Sighing, she made herself relax and ignored the temptation to lean back against him, let him wrap his arms around her. Like he had during the night. But she couldn't. He might say he wouldn't hurt her, but he would. Not intentionally or physically. She didn't think he was capable of that. But he most definitely would hurt her. And soon.

"No, I don't," she denied, easing out from beneath his hands and moving a safe distance away. *Not really.* "A year ago I made the mistake of trusting...well, someone I shouldn't have."

She felt him come up behind her. "What happened?"

Cassidy sighed, admitting to herself that he deserved to know why she behaved like she had a multiple personality. "Lance is...*was* a vice cop. Charming, handsome..." Her mouth twisted wryly. "A hero. He...um...he was brought into ER after a drug bust went wrong."

"I sense that's not the only thing that went wrong."

Cassidy flushed with embarrassment, hating that she'd been so naïve. "He came to thank me for saving his life. An exaggeration, but he was sweet and...well—"

"Charming?" Sam demanded darkly, and when she remained silent he cursed softly. "And you fell for it."

Cassidy gritted her teeth. "I guess you could say that."

"But?"

"He had a habit of seducing women in the medical profession."

"Let me guess. He liked all the attention?" He sounded disgusted.

Cassidy shrugged. "That too."

"There's more?"

"He stole my security card and helped himself to the dispensary."

"*Holy cr*—! He stole drugs?"

"For which I was blamed. The cops were called in. Fortunately for me he was already under investigation and my testimony…well, suffice it to say he's no longer a cop."

"Good for you. I hope the bastard rots in jail." He was silent a moment. "You were exonerated?"

"Yes, but…"

"Again *but*?"

"Things got…well, *difficult* after that."

"They fired you?" He sounded outraged.

She shook her head. "No. But sometimes I think it might have been better if they had. There was a lot of gossip and jokes. Cruel jokes." She shrugged. "You know what it's like in hospitals. So…I eventually resigned and moved here." Cassidy abruptly became all business. "As I said, Major, ancient history."

A dark brow hiked up his forehead at her cool tone and his eyes darkened. "Are we back to that, *Doctor*?"

Cassidy sighed. "Look, last night was a—"

"Don't say it," he interrupted her shortly, taking a couple of long strides in her direction. Her eyes widened and she quickly moved to put the desk between them. He halted, shoving his hands on his narrow hips as he studied her, brows lowered in visible frustration.

"It *was* a mistake," she insisted, resisting the urge to roll her eyes since "mistake" was a major understatement. At least for her it was. It meant she could no longer blame her behavior on adrenaline. But he would still leave, and if she let her feelings develop, what then?

Sam was silent for so long she began to rearrange her desk to give her hands something to do. Just when she thought he'd finally taken the hint and left, a large hand covered hers.

She froze, staring down at the sight of her pale, slender hand engulfed in his. His hand was huge, tanned and broad with long skilled fingers that were capable of killing a man, bringing a baby back from the brink of death—and driving a woman out of her mind with pleasure.

The strength of it should have scared her but for some strange reason it just felt…right. *He* felt right. As though her hand had been fashioned to fit perfectly into his.

But that was a dangerous illusion and one she needed to get out of her head. He wasn't perfect, she reminded herself firmly. He was fighting demons as hard as he fought for his country. The combination wasn't healthy. For either of them.

"Why?" he demanded softly. "You didn't have a good time?"

Making a sound in her throat that was a cross between a laugh and groan, Cassidy stopped trying to escape and looked up over her shoulder into his fallen-angel face. She would like to say no, but she couldn't lie to him, not any more. So she said instead, "I refuse to answer that on the grounds that it may incriminate me."

Sam used his grasp on her hand to whip her around and tug her against him. "Then what's the problem?" His free arm snaked around her waist and his lips brushed her temple.

Cassidy pressed her palms against the hard heat of his chest and fought the urge to slide them up to cup his firm jaw, tunnel into his thick dark hair. "You. Me… Hell, I don't know. I just know it can't happen again."

His arms tightened as though he would pull her into him. "Why not?" He sounded baffled and frustrated. "You had a good time and I sure as hell did."

Cassidy sighed and pressed her face wearily into his

throat, tempted to close her eyes and burrow deep. Until she absorbed his heat, his strength. Or he absorbed all of her.

"Lots of reasons," she murmured, drinking in his clean masculine smell. "One of which is that we're now working together. I don't sleep with colleagues."

"Glad to hear it," he drawled, smoothing a hand down her back to her hip to press her closer. "I would have really hated punching Monty's lights out."

Cassidy grimaced and pushed away from him, feeling off balance like she'd entered an episode of *some adventure game show* dressed in a designer suit and four-inch heels. "That's disgusting."

"Besides, neither of us is married." He paused as though a horrible thought just occurred to him. "Are you?"

Cassidy gaped at him. "No!"

He shrugged but looked ridiculously relieved. "Then what's wrong with enjoying each other?"

"While you're here, you mean?"

He frowned and leaned back so he could look into her face. "Is that a problem?"

Sighing, Cassidy told herself she wasn't disappointed. She'd known from the beginning she was nothing more than a temporary distraction.

"I'm not built for temporary, Sam, and everything about you says your bags are packed and all you need is one phone call."

His hands dropped and she could see the truth in his eyes. Her heart squeezed, though she didn't know what she'd expected him to say. Deny it maybe?

Fortunately a voice from the doorway stopped her from humiliating herself further.

"Cassidy, Mrs. West is… Oh." Janice paused as if she sensed the tension in the room. "I'm sorry," she said, her eyes wide and curious. "I didn't realize you were busy."

"We're not," Cassidy said briskly, reaching out to snag the stethoscope she'd tossed onto the desk the previous night. "I was just on my way. Is Mrs. West in exam room one?"

"Yes, Doctor," the nurse said, wide eyes bouncing between Cassidy and Sam. "Hank Dougherty is waiting in two."

"Thank you, Janice," Cassidy said, looping the stethoscope around her neck. "I'll be right there. In the meantime, can you please hunt up a lab coat for Major Kellan and inform the staff that he's filling in for Dr. Montgomery?"

Janice beamed at Sam, and Cassidy could practically hear the woman's heart go pitter-pat. "I heard." Janice grinned excitedly. "Welcome aboard," she gushed.

And giggled when his "Thanks" was accompanied by a crooked grin.

Taking that as her cue, Cassidy headed for the door, desperate to escape before he remembered what they'd been discussing. His voice, dark as midnight and rough as crushed velvet, reached across the room and stopped her in her tracks. "I'm not him, Cassidy," he called softly, and her fingers tightened on the doorframe. She chanced a look across her shoulder.

"Not who?" she asked past the lump of yearning in her throat. A yearning she didn't want to analyze too closely.

"I'm not what's-his-name? Lance Full-of-bull."

"Today is senior citizen clinic day," she said briskly instead of replying to what was largely rhetorical anyway. "Hank Dougherty needs hip replacement surgery but he needs to get his smoking under control first. Don't let the old codger con you into thinking he's quit."

Removing the stethoscope from her ears, Cassidy smiled reassuringly at the anxious young mother hovering close.

"Chest is all clear," she announced, "but this little butter-ball has a bad fever and her ears are inflamed."

She reached for a tongue depressor. "Open your mouth wide, sweetie," she cajoled gently, "I want to check if the bad germs got into your throat."

The child gazed back with huge, tragic eyes and held out the stuffed toy she was clutching. "Elmo first," she rasped, looking on intently as Cassidy examined Elmo's throat and made some doctor noises. "Do you think you and Elmo have the same bad germs?" Cassidy asked, holding out a new depressor. The little girl nodded and obediently opened her mouth.

"Uh-oh," she said, with an exaggerated look of dismay. "Just as I thought. Have you two been sharing a toothbrush again?" Jenny giggled around the thumb she'd instantly shoved in her mouth and shook her head. "That's good because Elmo needs his own toothbrush." She tapped a little button nose and lifted the child into her arms. "And you need to suck on something other than that thumb. How about a magic lollipop?"

"Magic?" Jenny rasped shyly around her thumb.

"Uh-huh. One that'll chase away all those bad germs," Cassidy explained, reaching into a nearby cabinet. "And make your throat feel better." She held out two antibacterial lollipops. "There," she said, handing the little girl to her mother. "One for you and one for Elmo." Returning to her desk, she slid a handful of M&Ms into a small clear plastic bag and wrote "Elmo" in permanent marker on the front.

"This is for Elmo but your mommy's going to have to get your medication from the pharmacy," she explained to the wide-eyed child. "Elmo is pretty bad at taking his medicine. I want you to be a big girl and show him how it's done. Can you do that for me?"

Jenny nodded solemnly as her mother smiled at Cassidy. "Thank you so much, Dr. Mahoney. You're really good with children," she said. "Are you a pediatrician?"

Cassidy shook her head. "I specialized in ER medicine. And it's Cassidy."

"Thank you, Cassidy. And welcome to Crescent Lake."

Smiling, Cassidy sent the child a little wave over her mother's shoulder as the two left her office, and had only a couple of minutes to gulp down rapidly cooling coffee before her next appointment arrived.

A clearly harassed Cathy Howard entered with a rowdy, tow-headed toddler and sank wearily into the nearest chair. Little Timmy Howard had been one of her first patients.

"Did I ever say I wanted him bouncing around again?" Cathy asked Cassidy with a grimace. "I would give *anything* for just *one* minute of peace."

Cassidy rounded her desk and looked into Timmy's big blue eyes, catching the wicked sparkle that would one day drive girls wild. Grinning, she swooped on him before he could escape, and plopped him down on the bed.

She laughed as he tried to wriggle free. "Come here, you little monkey. I want to listen to the engine inside your chest and see if all your spots have gone."

Timmy gurgled and pulled up his shirt, exposing his little pot belly. "See," he said, tucking his chin onto his chest and peering down at his tummy. "Gone."

"Are you sure?" Cassidy sounded dubious. "I think I see one here." She tickled him, making him squirm and chortle. "And here?" The noisy raspberry she blew on his tummy made him squeal and try to squirm away, but she held him firmly. "What about here?" He gave a great big belly laugh and caught her face in his hands before planting a big wet kiss on her nose.

Cassidy laughed and brushed white-blond curls off his face. "I bet you do that to all the girls," she teased, lifting him onto his sturdy little legs. He wrapped his chubby arms around her neck and bounced happily while she listened to his chest. Satisfied that he had no after-effects of the virus, she lifted him into her arms.

Turning to hand him to his mother, she came face to face with Sam. Her heart jolted and she sucked in a startled breath. They hadn't been this close since she'd told him she couldn't get involved with him.

"Oh. Major Kellan, you…you startled me."

"You got a minute, Doc?"

Belatedly noting his shuttered expression and the grim set of his mouth, Cassidy felt a prickle of alarm. A quick examination revealed blood staining the gray T-shirt beneath his lab coat and her skin went ice cold.

"Samuel—?"

"You finished up here?" he interrupted, flashing a quick look over her shoulder at the room's occupant. "Hey, Cath," he greeted the other woman with a quick smile of familiarity. "How's Frank?"

"Hi, Sam," Cathy Howard greeted him back, her eyes alight with avid curiosity. "He's great. Thanks for asking."

"You need to come with me," he said to Cassidy, lowering his voice and backing into the hallway. "*Now.*"

Dropping a quick kiss on Timmy's curls, she handed him to his mother. "Cathy, Timmy seems fine," she told the other woman, her attention on Sam's tense back. "If you're worried about anything, don't hesitate to bring him in. Keep him quiet for another day or two and be sure to give him a multivitamin and plenty of fluids."

She murmured a hasty goodbye and hurried after Sam, calling out to Janice at Reception that they had a code blue. Fortunately it was the midafternoon lull and she was certain Fran could handle the few patients that remained.

Cassidy hurriedly caught up to Sam, her pulse a blip of anxiety as she searched for injuries.

"Where are you hurt?"

His black brows came together over the bridge of his nose. "What?"

She drew level with him and gestured to his gray T-shirt and jeans. "Blood. Where are you hurt?"

He frowned down at himself. "It's not mine. A logger's just been brought in. Bad weather caused a cable to snap. He was in the way."

"Where is he?"

"OR. I can handle it if you're busy."

Almost running to keep up with his long strides, she sent him a sideways glance. "Fran's got the clinic. What's his condition?"

A muscle jumped in his jaw. His short reply, "Bad," sent an icy chill skating down her spine.

A white-faced Jim Bowen was already lying on the operating table, his shirt and jacket wet with his blood. Heather Murray was at his side, holding a pressure bandage over the wound, while a middle-aged man held his shoulders and talked quietly to him. Another younger man hovered nearby, looking like he was on the verge of passing out. His relief when he saw Sam turned to confusion when he spotted Cassidy.

"I thought you were getting the doctor?"

Sam's brow lifted and he sent Cassidy a wry smile. "I did," he drawled. "This is Dr. Mahoney. She's an ER specialist from Boston."

Ignoring the skepticism in the young man's eyes, Cassidy moved towards the patient, noting his gray-tinged skin. She lifted her head and caught Sam's gaze. "Heather, could you please show the gentlemen out and get Spruce Ridge on standby. Major Kellan and I will handle this until you return."

Cassidy barely noticed the men leaving as she quickly shed her lab coat and pulled on a surgical gown. Tossing another to Sam, she liberally sprayed her hands and arms with disinfectant before grabbing two pairs of surgical gloves from a nearby dispenser. She shoved her hands into one pair and waited while Sam disinfected. There wasn't time to scrub.

With swift, economical moves, Cassidy cut Jim's shirt away while Sam inserted the stent and hooked up a saline drip. For several minutes they worked together in silence, cleaning the patient's chest and arm, positioning electrode disks and hooking him up to the heart monitor.

Cassidy clipped on the saturation probe and frowned as thready, irregular pulse beats blipped into the silence. Jim had clearly lost a lot of blood and was going into shock.

"He's going to need an orthopedic specialist," Sam said, tying Cassidy's face mask and shoving her hair under the surgical cap as she gently eased pressure on the dressing to assess the extent of the damage.

Jim's arm had almost been severed at the shoulder and the instant she released the pressure, blood gushed from the jagged wound. "Can't wait," she said briskly, reaching for a clamp. "We're going to have to repair this artery first or he won't make the orthopod."

"Heather," she said briskly when the nurse returned, "find out his blood type and get the status with Spruce Ridge changed to code blue. What's our blood status? He's going to need at least six units."

"Four in total," Sam said from the refrigerator, "and they're all O positive."

They shared a look and Cassidy made a split-second decision she hoped she wouldn't regret. "We'll use them all and substitute the rest with blood plasma."

Sam's brow rose up his forehead. "And if he's AB negative?"

"We'll cross that bridge when we come to it."

CHAPTER TEN

CASSIDY STARED IN dismay at the ominous storm front that had rolled over the mountains while she and Sam had been in the OR. And if that wasn't bad enough, the helicopter pilot presently running towards them was alone. He wasn't even Medevac. A Forestry Services chopper had responded to their emergency.

Just great.

"Where's the Medevac crew?" she yelled, pushing her whipping hair off her face. The icy wind roaring down the mountain held more than a hint of snow and she had a feeling the storm was closing fast.

"You're it," he yelled over the noise from the engine and rotors. "Landslides and bad weather's already caused a major pile-up on the interstate to the northwest. They're stretched thin at Spruce Ridge General and when your call came through, all Medevac were engaged. You're lucky I was in the area."

"I'll go," Sam yelled, leaping into the helicopter with familiarity and an ease born of a well-conditioned body as he grabbed the collapsible gurney and pulled it inside. He slid it into place and hung the saline bag on an overhead hook before strapping the stretcher to the floor.

Cassidy felt her stomach clench into a tight ball of terror at the thought of flying through a blizzard. She'd heard stories about the late spring storms that often tore through the Cascades and wasn't looking forward to flying into it.

Swallowing her fear, she sucked in a lungful of cold air and shook her head decisively. Grasping the open door, she pulled herself inside before she could change her mind. "I'm the responsible physician at this hospital, Major," she yelled. "He's my patient. I can't let him go until I sign him over to another practicing physician." And when his dark gold gaze lifted and clashed with hers, she added a little more sharply, "My responsibility."

For a couple of beats Sam held her gaze then he gave a curt nod. "Fine. But I'm coming with you."

Ignoring the relief that slid into her stomach, Cassidy shook her head. "Not necessary. I...*we'll* be fine. I know you have other...plans."

He sent her a puzzled, narrow-eyed look that said he didn't know what she was talking about but wanted to demand an explanation. All he said was, "Be right back," before leaning forward to talk to the pilot, who was fiddling with the panel of overhead instruments. After a couple of beats the pilot nodded and Sam clasped the man's shoulder. Moving to the open door, he flashed an inscrutable look in her direction then jumped from the helo to lope across the helipad towards the building.

The rotors picked up speed and Cassidy swallowed hard. *Oh, God.* She hoped he hurried back before she changed her mind. Besides, she'd overheard a couple of nurses discussing meeting up with him later, which meant he was probably cancelling their date—or rescheduling.

And since he'd made it clear he wasn't in the market for anything long term and *she'd* made it clear she wouldn't get involved with a colleague, there wasn't much left to say.

Was there?

So why did she feel on the verge of tears? Why did she feel as though she'd just eaten a gallon of double-cream ice cream? Was she just having a panic attack at the idea of flying through a storm in a helicopter? Or was the queasy feeling in her stomach something else? But since she refused to consider the "something else" and wasn't some damsel in distress who needed to be rescued by a big, strong man, she didn't know where that left her.

She checked Jim's vitals in an effort to calm her nerves, tugged at the straps holding the gurney in place and fiddled with his shoulder dressing. After an anxious look in the direction in which Sam had gone, she flicked at a few bubbles in the IV line, hooked up another unit of blood, and then *re*checked his vitals, aware that with every passing second their window of opportunity for flying out was narrowing.

Finally, when her anxiety was at fever pitch, Sam reappeared. Without a word, he tossed her a thick parka, extra blanket and rucksack before leaping into the chopper. He pulled the door closed behind him, abruptly shutting out the worst of the rotor roar and the first snowflakes.

Cassidy bit her lip and slid onto the bench seat, pressing a hand to her roiling belly as he leant forward to tap the pilot on the shoulder. Without turning, the man lifted his hand in acknowledgement and in the next instant the engines screamed.

Cassidy dug her fingers into the bench seat beneath her. The craft shuddered and she squeezed her eyes shut in an effort not to freak out as the chopper lifted with a sickening lurch and the ground abruptly disappeared beneath her feet.

Biting back a whimper, her grip on the bench tightened until her knuckles ached and her fingers turned white. Something dropped around her shoulders an instant before Sam's heat enveloped her. He pressed his solid shoulder close as a big, calloused hand covered hers. Once he'd pried her fingers loose, he engulfed them in a firm, warm clasp.

With his rough palm sliding against hers, he laced their fingers together and gave her a comforting squeeze. Cassidy tightened her grip when what she really wanted to do was climb into his lap and hide her face against his strong, wide chest. She'd die of mortification later, she told herself, when her feet were once again firmly on solid ground.

His cold lips brushed her ear. "You can open your eyes now," he yelled, and she shook her head, unwilling to see the masculine amusement gleaming in his eyes.

God, she'd missed looking into those gold eyes...missed him *more than she'd thought possible.*

She felt his mouth smile against her temple and shivered as hot and cold goose bumps broke out across her skin. She was unsure if it was fear, the dipping temperatures or...or a desperate need for his touch—and terrified it was a combination of all three. For some reason his proximity always seemed to trigger a confusing mix of emotions that left her reeling.

"*Babe*," he said against her ear, and Cassidy could hear the smile in his voice before he gave her earlobe a gentle nip. This time she had no trouble identifying the origin of the shivers racing over her skin. "I won't let anything happen to you," he promised deeply. "I'm a SEAL. You're absolutely safe."

Cassidy turned to yell at him for calling her babe, only to find him less than an inch away. His gaze was hot, intense and a weird sensation of vertigo sent her stomach plummeting. For the second time in as many minutes her world tilted, and she was fairly certain it had nothing to do with being suspended above the earth in a flimsy aircraft.

Every thought fled save the sudden jumble of emotions she struggled to make sense of. Blood rushed from her head. Her lungs constricted and she was forced to acknowledge that she wasn't just hanging in space with a thin layer of metal between her and the jagged peaks below. Her heart was too—for an entirely different reason.

It quivered in her chest and before she could pull back from the edge or rip her hand from his and retreat to the opposite bench—*hell, throw herself from the helicopter*—in an effort to protect herself, he lifted her hand to his lips and—*Oh, God*—pressed a kiss to her white knuckles.

A sob rose in her chest.

"I won't let anything happen to you," he repeated, with a reassuring smile that promised everything she'd told herself she didn't want and he couldn't possibly mean. And when she simply shook her head and squeezed her eyes shut, he cupped her jaw in his big, warm hand. He waited until her lashes rose before adding, "SEAL's honor."

Cassidy's heart clenched—his expression, and the heartfelt assurance, appearing more meaningful than a kiss. She sucked in a shuddery breath, suddenly terrified about what it could mean and blurted, "If we go down I'm going to kill you," as she battled with the shocking truth.

He laughed and her chest tightened painfully.

Oh, God.

She could no longer hide it from herself. She wasn't just fighting feelings for him. She was in love with Samuel J. Kellan, US Navy SEAL. A man who kept himself locked up tight, a man who didn't return her feelings, even though he wanted to be with her.

For now.

He'd wormed his way under her defenses and had settled next to her heart while making it perfectly clear she was a distraction. He didn't do long term and thinking she could matter to him was insane.

"Hey…" Sam's deep voice was laced with concern "…why the gloomy face?"

She dropped her lashes to hide her chaotic thoughts and bit her lip. Right, like she'd tell *him*. He already knew how to make her respond to him. She would rather die than have him guess how she felt.

Her pulse fluttered. He was such a beautiful man, strong, honorable and honest. He hadn't lied or made promises he knew he couldn't keep, and she couldn't imagine him taking a woman hostage after he'd been caught doing something illegal and realized he could no longer sweet talk his way out of it. He wasn't Lance Turnbull. He'd proved time and again that he could be counted on. That he was someone worthy of love. That he was worthy of her love.

Only thing was: he didn't want it.

She gave a wild little laugh and hoped he thought she was freaking out about flying. "You ask that when we're a thousand feet over the Cascades—in a tin can?"

His eyes crinkled and his mouth curled into a quick grin that had her breath catching in her chest. For the first time since that night in the jail cell he looked relaxed and… carefree. *Happy*, even.

"Isn't it great?"

Yes, it was, she admitted silently, but not the view out the window. With a sudden flash of insight she realized that he missed his team, his dangerous job. And she wondered for perhaps the hundredth time why he chose to be stuck in a small mountain hospital, treating runny noses and hypertension, instead of jumping from aircraft, yelling "*Hoo-yah*" as he took out the enemy. And if, for just a fleeing moment, she wished she'd been responsible for the dazzling pleasure lighting his gold eyes, Cassidy reminded herself that kind of thinking would only lead to heartache. Heartache she knew—with abrupt certainty—she would never recover from.

She loved him but would keep her heart safely hidden. For now she would simply enjoy the warm, masculine scent of him and the press of his body against hers, knowing it would soon be gone.

"You're insane," she yelled, and rolled her eyes when his quick answering grin flashed with wicked recklessness. And when his eyes dropped to her mouth, her blood turned hot.

An odd expression crossed his face and his eyes darkened. "Yeah," he agreed, wrapping a hand around her head to tug her close. Expecting his usual fiery mastery, Cassidy was stunned when his mouth touched hers gently in a kiss that was as sweet as it was unexpected.

And before she could remember that this was a very bad idea, she was sliding her hands up to cup his hard, beard-roughened jaw. She opened for him, tentatively touching her tongue to his, while she fought the aching need squeezing her heart.

He tasted of hot, untamed man and for once in her life Cassidy wanted to leap off the edge, uncaring where she landed. There was only *this*—this wild, exciting moment with this wild, exciting man.

Tilting her head to give him room, she traced the strong line of his jaw with questing fingers, ignoring the tiny voice of reason in her head that warned she was heading for disaster. She didn't care. She just wanted to feel what was suddenly the most significant kiss of her life.

If this was all she'd have, she would take it. But she had to remind herself they weren't alone. With supreme effort, she broke off to say, "Sam, we should stop," hoping he would make it easy for her, and hoping with equal intensity that he would not.

With a savage growl Sam leaned his forehead against hers and sucked in a ragged breath. His heart thundered in his chest like he was having a coronary, yet he felt more alive than he had in a long time. More intensely aware of his surroundings—as though electricity flowed across his skin and connected every atom in his body to the universe. To her.

Pulling back an inch, he stared into misty green eyes heavy with arousal and emotions he couldn't begin to identify, and wondered briefly what had made this kiss so different.

He was thirty-four years old, and he'd just had the hottest, wildest kiss of his life in a cold, noisy helicopter a couple of thousand feet in the air—with a woman who wasn't interested in a relationship and then kissed like she was searching for his soul.

Reminding himself that his time in Crescent Lake was running out—that this was just a fantasy interlude before he returned to his real life—Sam caught her mouth in a brief, scorching kiss. "Later," he growled, sliding his gaze over her face as though committing the soft confusion in her eyes to memory.

Damn, but she was so beautiful.

Suddenly her eyes widened and she pulled away so abruptly he cast around for the threat before he realized she was dropping to her knees beside Jim.

"He's crashing," she yelled, pulling at the straps securing the stretcher. Cursing himself for forgetting where they were, Sam leaned over to release the safety clip as Cassidy tore off the blanket to expose the patient's chest. She checked his pulse and immediately began performing CPR as Sam grabbed a headset to bark at the pilot.

Learning they were less than five minutes out of Spruce Ridge, he instructed the pilot to radio ahead with their ETA and to have a resus team waiting at the helipad. He tossed aside the headset and dug into his rucksack for the supplies he'd thrown there earlier.

He ripped off the plastic needle cover with his teeth and plunged the syringe into the vial of atropine. With a smooth one-handed move that might have impressed Cassidy if her patient hadn't been in trouble, he drew back the plunger.

"Get that into his vein," she ordered sharply, before stopping the chest compressions to begin mouth-to-mouth. The following minutes were filled with the urgency only experienced by medics concerned with saving a life, and by the time they landed and rushed him across the helipad, Jim Bowen's pulse was once again steady.

The ortho specialist was already suiting up when Cassidy followed her patient into the OR. The gray-haired surgeon's piercing blue gaze studied her over the top of his spectacles as he thrust his hands into latex gloves.

"Grant Sawyer, orthopedic specialist," he introduced himself brusquely. "Mahoney from Crescent Lake?" And when she nodded, he barked, "Fill me in."

Cassidy gave a succinct report of their intervention while the theatre staff prepped Jim for surgery. Sawyer listened and nodded as he skimmed through the patient's chart.

"Good job," he said with a brusque nod, and turned away to rap out orders for blood and instruments, leaving Cassidy with the impression that she'd just been dismissed.

She backed out of the OR, fighting the feeling that she should be doing something. *Anything* but stand around while others worked miracles.

Sam was waiting in the hallway. "You okay?" he asked, shoving off the wall he'd been propping up. Cassidy nodded absently and pushed the tousled hair off her forehead. "Why?"

"Resus says ER's swamped and could use some help. You up for it?"

"We're not flying back?"

Sam shook his head. "Storm's too bad. We're lucky we made it before all aircraft were grounded. Pilot's already gone and all roads into the mountains have been closed."

Cassidy's belly clenched. "So we're...stuck."

Sam placed a warm hand into the small of her back and sent her a crooked grin. "Just you and me, babe. Until morning."

Cassidy rolled her eyes at his use of the hated word that was strangely enough starting to grow on her. "And an ER full of accident victims."

"Yeah." He laughed dryly, steering her down the wide hallway. "And that."

Hours later Cassidy pulled off her latex gloves and made the last notations on her clipboard. Darkness had long fallen and the storm had turned the world beyond the hospital walls white and icy. Fortunately the number of casualties had dwindled to a trickle and she could finally take a break.

She was also starving.

Stretching tired muscles, Cassidy wandered out to the waiting room and handed the clipboard to the woman manning the nurses' station. "Finally packing it in, honey?" the nurse asked with a sympathetic smile.

"You're good to go," Cassidy replied, smoothing her messy hair off her face and twisting it at the back of her head, where she pinned it using a couple of pins someone had found for her. "Have you seen Major Kellan?"

"Big handsome hunk with the pretty eyes?"

Cassidy smiled at the woman's description. "That's him."

"I saw him heading towards the doctors' lounge with the ER manager about ten minutes ago," the nurse reported and eyed Cassidy with open envy. "You two...together?"

"Yes," she said with a small smile, and turned to head down the passage. They were together but not *together*. She didn't think any woman could say she and Samuel Kellan were...*together*. He didn't do together with anyone—which should have made her feel better but didn't, especially when she entered the doctors' lounge and found him surrounded by admirers.

Almost immediately he turned, a warm, intimate smile curling his lips when their gazes met and held. He quickly excused himself and headed across the room to wrap his hands around her upper arms and yank her against him. Her squeak of surprise was abruptly cut off by his open-mouthed kiss, and before she could react, he'd sucked out her brain along with her breath.

Several long seconds later Sam broke off the kiss and lifted his head a couple of inches. "Hey," he murmured, his rough, deep voice sliding against her like a heated caress.

She gulped in a shocked breath and gaped at him. "Wh-what...?" Her mouth snapped shut on her stuttered attempt at coherence. Besides, they were standing in a brightly lit doctors' lounge filled with openly staring medical personnel.

"Work with me here, babe," he said out of the corner of his mouth. Baffled by his unexpected behavior, Cassidy opened her mouth again. "What...?" but Sam was tugging her into the hallway.

"*Hey*," she complained, and tugged against his grip. "Coffee. Now. Maybe even intravenously."

Sam grimaced. "Forget about that swill. I've got something better."

Her mouth dropped open and she stared at him in shocked silence before sliding her gaze down his hard belly to his crotch. *Did he...? Could he really...?*

"*Doc!*" Sam's eyes widened but he was also battling a grin. "You have a dirty mind," he accused, and when she just rolled her eyes he spun her around and hustled her back against the nearest wall, his body following.

Surprised by the slick move, Cassidy gave a startled squeak even as his mouth closed over hers, and then he was kissing her like he couldn't wait to get her naked. She slapped a hand against his chest and made a gurgling sound in her throat.

Sam reluctantly backed off, looking a little wild. Cassidy flushed and tried to shove him away but he leaned into her and rasped out, "Give me a minute." She opened her mouth to tell him he'd had his minute when she felt something large and hard poking her belly. She froze, her flush deepening, until she was sure she was glowing like a neon sign in the desert.

"What is it with you and walls?" she huffed out, secretly grateful for the hard body keeping her upright. His gold eyes gleamed at her through thick dark eyelashes.

"If I don't take advantage of the nearest one," he growled, "you'd be practicing those sneaky evasion techniques you've perfected over the past few weeks."

Cassidy opened her mouth to reply when her stomach growled and she dropped her head back and closed her eyes in defeat. Sam chuckled and pushed away from the wall.

"Looks like you need more than coffee."

"I'm starving," she excused herself with a faint blush. "I wonder what the hospital cafeteria is serving."

Sam grimaced and stepped back, his hand sliding down to circle her wrist. "Nothing good, believe me." He gave her a gentle tug closer. "Let's go."

"Where? I'm starving."

His eyebrow rose at her petulant tone. "And I'm going to feed you," he promised. "Just not here. I managed to get us a room at a hotel a couple of blocks away."

Shock and panic moved through Cassidy. "*What?* No!"

Sam's brow rose. "No?"

"No," Cassidy said shortly. "I'm not sharing a room with you."

He sent her a chiding look. "Now, *babe*—" he began.

Only to have Cassidy interrupting with, "I beg your pardon?"

He grinned, leaving her head reeling at his abrupt mood changes. "You really shouldn't try that icy debutante tone with me, Doc."

"Excuse me?"

He leaned closer with a sinful grin that sent alarm and heat arrowing through her. "Makes me hot," he murmured against her ear, and Cassidy felt her cheeks heat. She could feel exactly how hot.

She edged away. "I can get my own room, Sam." No way could she spend the night with him and not expose herself. Her feelings were too new, too raw—and she was terrified she would just blurt them out in the heat of the moment.

"No, Cassidy, you can't." And when she scowled he smoothed his hand down to the base of her spine and tugged her closer. "And not just because you didn't bring cash or cards. The hotels in the area are all full. I checked. I was lucky, *really* lucky to get that room."

His look was carefully casual. "So, dinner and the last room at the inn?"

Cassidy sighed and made a helpless gesture. "Sam—"

He captured her hand. "Look," he interrupted quietly, "I know you don't get involved with people you work with. But we're not colleagues here. We're just a man and a woman who are attracted to each other."

She looked up in surprise. "I thought—."

He shrugged out of his parka and wrapped it around her shoulders as he steered her towards the main entrance. "You thought what?"

Looking up into his handsome face, Cassidy recalled the conversation she'd overheard earlier that day. "I know you were planning to meet up with some of the nurses later."

His stopped abruptly. "What?"

She licked her lips and exhaled noisily, hoping he couldn't see how much the knowledge hurt. "I understand. Really. It's not like we're—" She stopped abruptly and looked away, unable to continue.

Sam folded his arms across his chest. "Not like we're what, Cassidy?"

She swallowed and smoothed her tousled hair off her face, looking anywhere but at him and feeling unaccountably flustered. "It's not like we're…well, together. Or anything," she ended lamely.

His mouth compressed into a hard line and a muscle jumped in his jaw. "Well, you apparently know more than I do," he growled. "*Jeez.* You don't have a very good opinion of men, do you? Or is it just me?"

Startled by his mercurial moods, Cassidy stared up at him. "What are you talking about?

His jaw clenched. "I'm talking about the fact that you think I'd have sex with other women just because you're avoiding me."

She flushed. Okay, so that's exactly what she'd thought. "Sam—"

"Cassidy," he mocked gently, and cradled her face between his warm palms. "It's just you," he murmured, his eyes a deep dark gold that had her heart lurching in silly feminine hope. Was he saying what she thought he was saying? "Since that night in county lock-up, it's been you."

For now, she wanted to add, but didn't want to ruin the fragile mood between them. Sucking in a shaky breath, she sent him a falsely bright smile and shored up the cracks in her composure. She'd take what she could and protect her heart later. When he was gone.

"I think you promised me dinner," she murmured, and his grin was quick and white in his dark face. Leaning forward, he planted a hard kiss on her mouth. "That's just the appetizer, *babe*," he promised quietly. "We have the whole night to savor the main course."

CHAPTER ELEVEN

CASSIDY WOKE ON a surge of adrenaline, abruptly and fully alert between one breath and the next. Heart pounding in her chest, she blinked into the darkness and struggled with a sense of disorientation.

Quickly taking stock, she realized she wasn't at home in Boston and she wasn't in her bed at the inn. But she *was* naked, which could only mean one thing...*Sam!*

Fear and a gut-deep knowledge that something was very wrong had her rolling over in the wide bed just as she heard it again—harsh, ragged. There was a heavy thud and something crashed to the floor, instantly followed by a litany of snarled curses.

Pulse spiking with alarm, she lurched upright and tried to recall where the bedside lamp was situated. His abruptly yelled, *"No! No!"* sent chills streaking up her spine, and a quick tactile reconnaissance of the mattress confirmed she was alone in the bed. Was Sam fighting some psycho who'd sneaked into their hotel room?

"He's just a kid, for God's sake. Let him go... *God*, let him go."

He? Who was he talking about? Heck, who was he talking to?

A low, threatening sound vibrated deep in his throat, making the hair on her body stand on end before a babble of foreign words filled the room, menacing and a little frightening.

Launching herself across the bed, she fumbled for the light switch, rapping her elbow on the bedside table and almost knocking the lamp over in her haste. She finally located the switch and blinked against the sudden light bursting into the room.

She didn't know what she'd expected but it wasn't Sam fighting an unseen enemy. *Oh, God,* she thought. Was he experiencing a flashback or having a nightmare?

A murderous bellow had Cassidy's heart rate spiking. She watched wide-eyed as he struggled violently, arms pinned to his side, tendons, sinew and well-defined muscles straining beneath acres of sweat-slicked skin.

He was gloriously naked, but for once she failed to appreciate the perfect lines of his hard body. Her gaze was locked on his face. His shadowed features contorted with fury as he lurched around the room, crashing into everything in his path. It was a wonder he didn't wake up with all the noise he was making and Cassidy wondered if he was reliving some actual or imagined event.

He suddenly stiffened, and with a hoarse, anguished "*No!*" he jolted like he'd been struck. Then he slowly sank to his knees, his breath coming in ragged dry heaves.

Biting back the cry that rose to her lips, Cassidy pressed herself against the headboard, wanting desperately to go to him. She *needed* to go to him—especially when he thrust his hands through his hair and she got her first good look at his face. He looked completely and utterly devastated.

No longer able to keep her distance, she slid from the bed and approached him warily, desperate to comfort him. A hoarse moan tore from his throat and the desolation in the sound lifted the hair at the nape of her neck. She halted a few feet away and dropped to her knees, the sight of his wet cheeks wrenching at her tender heart. Unbearable pressure squeezed her chest in a giant fist and before she could stop it from happening, her newly exposed heart quivered...and broke.

A sob rose in her throat and she reached out a hand, her trembling fingers sliding greedily over the rounded ball of his shoulder. His skin, normally so warm, was damp and cold to the touch and her medical training took over. She wasn't a psychiatrist, but working in ER she'd witnessed enough cases of psychological trauma to know shock when she saw it.

"Samuel," she said firmly, rubbing his wide shoulder in slow, soothing movements. For long moments he remained unresponsive, the room filled with nothing but his harsh breathing—his body shaking as shudders moved through him. "Sam. Wake up, you're dreaming."

His muscles turned to stone beneath her hand as he abruptly stilled. He slowly lifted his head, turning a gaze completely stripped of emotion in her direction. He looked at her as though he didn't know her and wasn't quite sure what she was doing there.

Tension radiated off him like a nuclear blast and she braced herself for his reaction. But after long tense moments he blinked as though coming out of a trance, confusion pulling at his dark brows.

"Cassidy?" His voice emerged, hoarse and a little rusty. Her shoulders sagged and her breath escaped in a relieved whoosh that left her trembling and dizzy.

Okay, she thought, *so far so good.*

Shifting closer, she carefully smoothed a line from his shoulder to his bulging biceps and curled her fingers into his inner arm where the satin-smooth flesh was clammy. A fine tremor twitched the muscles beneath her hand. Even in the dim light his pallor was evident, as was the fine sheen of perspiration, the dazed disorientation in his eyes. She pushed damp hair off his forehead with her free hand before cupping his hard, beard-roughened jaw in her palm.

Staring into his distressed eyes, she whispered, "It's okay, Sam...I'm here," fighting the need to wrap her arms around him, to press her body close, share her warmth. Protect him from his demons. "I'm here."

After a couple of beats he lifted unsteady fingers to brush a light caress over her mouth. His tender touch, so at odds with the violence she'd sensed in him just moments ago, tore at her control, and a tear finally escaped, the accompanying sob a hot ball of razor-sharp emotions in her throat.

His eyes tracked the silvery tear before he caught it near her mouth with the tip of one long tanned finger.

"You're crying." He sounded baffled, concerned, as another tear escaped, then another.

Horrified by her slipping control, she covered his hand with hers and turned her face into his wide, calloused palm, choking back emotions that seemed to be rising faster than Biblical flood waters.

Get a grip, Mahoney. The guy needs your strength here, not tears and certainly not any declarations of love.

"I... It's nothing," she replied softly, nuzzling his hand, her gaze clinging to his as though he would vanish if she blinked. "Something happened. Tell me about it."

If Cassidy had blinked she might have missed the shield slamming down between them. Between one breath and the next his eyes cleared as he abruptly withdrew. All without moving a muscle. Then his hand slid out from beneath hers and he moved away, leaving her cold and oddly hollow.

The barrier was as tangible as a brick wall. Feeling suddenly exposed she hurriedly looked around for something to cover her nakedness. Spying his soft, well-washed

T-shirt, she grabbed it and hastily pulled it over her head, surrounding herself with his familiar scent.

He was slumped back against the bed, wrists draped over his upraised knees, head bowed, breathing heavily as though he'd run ten miles in full gear up a steep mountain slope. His face was gray and emotional strain carved deep furrows beside the tense lines of his mouth.

Wishing she could comfort him and knowing it was the last thing he wanted from her, Cassidy felt raw emotion rise like a tide from her chest into her throat. She swallowed past the lump in her throat and wrapped her arms around herself to ward off the room's sudden chill.

"What happened?" she prompted softly.

A muscle ticked in his jaw and his face settled into a blank mask that squeezed her already bruised heart. For long moments he stared silently at the floor then exhaled noisily, thrusting a hand through his hair, the jerky motion dislodging a dark lock. She had to curl her fingers into her palm to keep from reaching out to smooth it away. Smooth his pain away.

After a moment he said flatly, "The mission was jinxed from the start. It was supposed to be quick. Drop in, find the hostages, blow everything up, go home. Instead there was a welcoming committee waiting at the drop site, as though they knew exactly where we were going to be." He pressed the heels of his hands against his eyes, looking unbearably weary.

"We barely had time to dive for cover before firepower erupted around us. Back-up was still miles away and we were pinned down from all sides. I remember thinking we'd bide our time, wait them out." He broke off with a bitter laugh. "Yeah, right. We'd expected maybe a dozen armed men. What we didn't figure was that our intel was compromised. There were maybe fifty heavily armed men. All with us in their sights."

He paused, face hard, hands curled into fists, as though he was reliving that night. After a few moments of silence he added, "Back-up was also taking heavy fire and before I knew it we were out of ammo and outmuscled. Finally they rounded us up and took us into the mountains, where we were questioned. Separately. Together—hoping we'd talk."

Cassidy had a feeling "questioned" meant tortured. She went cold at the thought and pressed a fist against her mouth to prevent a sound of distress from escaping.

"Did you?"

Sam's harsh laugh scraped at her ragged nerve endings. "Honey, SEALs don't talk. Ever." He took a couple of deep breaths before continuing. "They cut us off, took out our ground support and left us with no way to contact base command. We were on our own." He fell silent. "Then one night, about a week into our capture, they came for me," he said hollowly. "I remember thinking, *This is it, time to make peace with God.*" His eyes narrowed on some point in the past and he absently rubbed his wrists.

"What h-happened next?" Cassidy prompted softly, dreading what she sensed was coming.

He gave a heavy sigh. "They must have found out I was a medic," he said flatly, dropping his gaze between his large bare feet. "I was taken to a house in the village and told to treat some sick kid. I refused unless they let my team go." He snorted. "I had to try. Turned out they were waiting for a camera crew. An entire SEAL team is good leverage when you want scumbag terrorists released." He scrubbed his hands over his face. "I eliminated two guys before they...uh...subdued me."

Sick with horror, Cassidy tightened her grip on her arms. He didn't need to tell her what "eliminated" meant. She knew. Just as she knew "subdued" meant they'd probably beaten him senseless.

"Seemed they didn't want me dead. At least, not yet.

Dead meant I couldn't save the kid, who was in pretty bad shape. I don't know how long I was out but by the time they emptied a bucket of water over me, they'd dragged in the team rookie and were holding a gun to his head. My eyes were practically swollen shut and my vision was blurring badly, but one look at him and I knew we were in trouble."

He muttered a few curses and wiped his face as though he could wipe away the memories. "*Jeez*, they'd beaten Scooter until his mother wouldn't recognize him. But at least he was still alive. Anyway, I said I'd treat the boy if they let me patch Scooter up. They argued amongst themselves for a while before finally agreeing." He laughed bitterly. "I knew…God, *knew*…I shouldn't trust them. I knew it, but I—"

He broke off abruptly, shifting restlessly, leaving Cassidy dreading the rest of the story. She could guess what was coming and braced herself, knowing that despite his training he'd been helpless to save the life of his friend.

"I asked for my med supplies and removed the kid's appendix. Took a couple of hours for his fever to break but when he finally opened his eyes, the guy with the gun on Scooter just looked me in the eye and…pulled the trigger." He sucked in a ragged breath and then for the first time since he'd begun he turned to look at her—eyes bloodshot, devastated as he relived the nightmare.

"They shot him," he said blankly, as though he still couldn't believe it. "They laughed and shot him in the head like a rabid stray." Shoving his fingers through his hair, he looked away and struggled for control as Cassidy battled against the urge to hold him close, promise things he didn't want or need from her.

After a few moments he sucked in a ragged breath and added, "I went berserk. I took out everyone and secured the kid's mother before she could rouse the whole damn village. Then I went to get my team."

"Oh, Sam," she rasped, heartsick at how unbearably sad he looked, how unendurably weary. And she could no longer ignore the compulsion to touch him. But when she reached for him he abruptly turned away, as though he couldn't bear her touch. She bit her lip against the devastating hurt of his rejection and slowly lowered her hand.

"I'd do it again," he vowed softly, his tone deadly. "They tortured and killed half my team. Good men…my brothers, my friends…and I….they were my responsibility and I failed them. If I'd made my move sooner, Scooter would still be alive."

"Or maybe not," Cassidy offered softly. "Maybe you'd both be dead."

He rounded on her with a furious snarl, a white blaze of hot fury in his eyes. "It would have been nothing more than I deserved," he snarled, rising abruptly. "I'm a SEAL. Failure is *not* an option."

He looked around a little wildly, as though he'd found himself trapped. Movements jerky with suppressed violence, he snatched up jeans, socks and boots and dressed in simmering silence. He'd shoved his arms through the sleeves of his flannel shirt and grabbed his jacket before she realized he was leaving.

"Samuel, wait." She reached out to tangle shaking fingers in soft flannel before she realized she'd moved. He stilled but didn't turn, his stiff posture broadcasting louder than words that he was barely hanging on to his control.

"Where are you going?"

"Out."

Feeling him slipping away, she did the one thing she'd promised herself she would never do. She begged.

"*Please*, Sam, don't go. Stay. Talk to me."

Ignoring her plea, he silently reached for the door, and before she knew she was moving, Cassidy slipped around his body to press her back against the door. He looked momentarily surprised, even retreated a step before his features hardened and his laser-bright gaze sliced her to ribbons.

Ignoring the aggression pumping off him in waves, Cassidy locked her wobbling knees and bravely held his gaze, aware that she was shaking inside. She had a feeling if she let him go she'd never see him again.

For a long tension-filled moment he stared at her, eyes blazing with emotions so raw and violent that she had to force her body not to step into his. "Stay, Sam...just *stay*," she pleaded hoarsely.

A muscle flexed in his jaw and she realized with shock that he was shaking too. She wanted to go to him but was held in place by the invisible *keep out* signs radiating off him. Finally he gritted through clenched teeth, "There is nothing to say. Now move out the way, Doc. I don't want to hurt you."

Doc? He was calling her Doc after everything they'd shared?

Swallowing a bitter laugh, Cassidy drew in a shuddery breath and tried not to show how much his words— heck, his attitude—hurt. "I...love you Sam," she whispered hoarsely.

His gaze sharpened as though he'd heard her but intended to ignore her ragged confession. "It's just a walk, Cassidy," he said roughly. "I need some air." And when she held out her hand, his coldly furious "I don't need a goddamn nursemaid, for God's sake. I just want some damn air. Is that too much to expect?" had her jaw dropping open in shock.

Recovering quickly, she stepped forward to flatten her palm against his naked chest, hoping her touch would somehow get through the impenetrable wall he'd built around himself. "I... Let me help you, Samuel," she blurted out before she could stop herself. "Please, don't go. I...I love you. I love you, let me help."

His reaction was swift and shockingly direct. Jerking back as if she'd slapped him, he stared at her in silence for a couple stunned beats before his expression turned into a remote mask, rejection clear in every tense line of his body.

Cassidy's heart sank and she pressed a shaking hand against the hard cold ball of misery forming in her throat. "Sam—?"

"I'm sorry," he interrupted impassively, frowning at her as though he'd never seen her before, and the cold ball of dread dropped into her chest, lodging right where her heart should be.

Two words, *I'm sorry*, were suddenly the most devastating of her life. More devastating than anything that had happened in Boston. "You're...s-s-sorry?"

He gave a heavy sigh. "Yes." His handsome face was carved with cold disinterest, his once beautifully glowing eyes flat and detached—as though she were a stranger. A stranger he didn't particularly like the look of. "I'm flattered, of course, but I thought you understood I wasn't..." He made a sound of annoyance. "Well, I'm sorry you believed otherwise. Now please step aside, I don't want to hurt you."

Cassidy didn't remember moving, could only watch as he opened the door and walked out without a backward glance. Hours later, when a firm knock sounded at the door, she flew across the room, wild hope and relief shriveling along with her heart when she opened to find not Samuel but the Forestry Services pilot.

Once the pilot left, Cassidy moved around the room like an automaton, gathering her clothing and dressing in stunned silence. She carefully washed and dried her face, ignoring the white-faced stranger in the mirror as she pulled her hair off her face and secured it at the nape of her neck. Then with her raw, bleeding heart carefully locked away behind a coolly professional façade, she left the hotel and headed for the hospital to check on Jim before taking the elevator to the helipad.

She scarcely remembered the flight back to Crescent Lake. Staring sightlessly out the window, she was impervious to the cold, the stunning scenery, the curious man at her side.

Nothing. She felt absolutely...*nothing*.

By the time the chopper touched down, Cassidy was grateful for the numbness. She even managed to aim a small smile of thanks at the pilot before alighting from the helicopter. The ground was slippery with ice as she carefully picked her way to the building.

Fran Gilbert took one look at Cassidy's face and the blood drained away from her face, leaving her pale and concerned. "What's wrong?" she demanded. "Are you okay? Is Jim okay?"

Drawing her professionalism around her like a cloak, Cassidy paused to reassure the older woman. "He's holding steady," she said. "I checked on him before I left and spoke to his doctor. He seems cautiously optimistic about Jim's recovery."

"I'll call his wife," Fran said with relief but kept her gaze sharply on Cassidy's face then voiced the question Cassidy had been dreading. "Where's Samuel?"

Cassidy wrapped her arms around herself and forced herself not to react. "I... He had to leave suddenly."

Fran looked surprised, confused. "Leave? Where did he go?"

Cassidy shrugged as though her heart wasn't a bloodied, pulpy mess. "I don't know," she admitted, pressing trembling fingers against her aching temple. "His message didn't say."

Fran digested the news in silence before saying, "You

look awful, honey, and you're frozen to the bone. Are you sick?"

Cassidy didn't believe her attempt to smile fooled the other woman but she was beyond caring. She was barely holding onto her composure as it was and Fran had just given her the perfect excuse. "I think I've caught a bug," she croaked, instantly ashamed when Fran looked concerned.

"Oh, honey, do you need someone to drive you home?" Fran asked, gently rubbing some warmth into Cassidy's frozen arms. But she had a feeling nothing would ever make her feel warm again.

She shook her head and resisted the urge to drop her head onto Fran's shoulder. If she did, she would shatter into a million pieces and she couldn't do that until she was alone.

"I can't leave, Fran," she croaked, her control slipping fast. "Now that...um..." She swallowed hard and drew in a shaky breath. "Now that the major is gone, I'll need to pull double shifts." Besides, being busy would keep her from thinking too much.

"No, you won't," Fran reproached firmly. "You'll go home and get into bed. We'll handle things today." And when Cassidy opened her mouth to argue she said, "No arguments. I promise to call if we have an emergency."

Cassidy stared into Fran's gentle blue eyes and finally pulled away. The woman knew. *Oh, God, was she that obvious?*

"I'll get my purse and jacket."

Cassidy let herself into the inn, aware that she was shaking uncontrollably as if she'd contracted some kind of jungle fever. Sweat slicked her skin and she had to wipe her damp palm against her thigh several times before she could shove the key into the lock.

Sudden dizziness swamped her one instant, the next her

stomach cramped violently and the hand that she'd flung out to grab the doorframe slapped over her mouth instead. She made a mad dash for the bathroom at the end of the hall, barely slamming the door behind her before she lost the meager contents of her stomach.

When the retching finally stopped, she dragged herself to her feet. Moving to the basin to rinse her mouth, she caught sight of herself in the mirror and couldn't hold back a horrified gasp. She was paper-white, hollow-eyed and looked like she'd just survived a major disaster. No wonder Fran was concerned, she thought, eyeing herself dispassionately. She looked like hell. And felt much worse.

Unfortunately, the numbness that had got her through the past six hours was fading and the awful truth of what had happened was finding its way through the cracks in her composure.

Her eyes and her throat burned with unshed tears and her heart felt like he'd ripped open her chest and savaged her. Hurrying back to her room before the dam burst, Cassidy shoved the door closed and she was finally—*finally*— alone.

She sank back against the door, her knees buckling as a ragged sob escaped and the first scalding tear eased over her lashes to carve a fiery path down her cheek. By the time her bottom hit the floor, keening sobs racked her body and the tight leash she'd kept on her emotions finally snapped.

It was over, she told herself. *Over*. When she'd finally admitted to feelings she'd never intended to feel.

Dropping her forehead onto her updrawn knees, she choked back a ragged cry. Samuel J. Kellan had rocked her world then walked away without a backward glance. As if she meant less than nothing.

He'd made mad, passionate love to her then coldly, dispassionately, told her he was sorry she loved him. He was flattered—*flattered*—but thought she'd understood he wasn't looking for a relationship. *I'm sorry you believed otherwise,* he'd said, slicing her to the soul. And then, when she'd stared at him, her shattered heart exposed for the world to see—for *him* to see—he'd calmly told her to step aside because he didn't want to hurt her.

He'd calmly crushed her heart…and left.

CHAPTER TWELVE

CASSIDY ENTERED BERNIE'S supermarket and exchanged a few hurried greetings of "Hello, how are you feeling today?" and "Don't forget to bring the baby in for his next check-up." As much as she enjoyed stopping to chat, she hoped she could get in and out as quickly as possible.

She had a long list of items to get for a bachelorette party, in…she quickly glanced at her watch…*yikes*, less than two hours. She also had to get back to the inn and shower and change out of her jeans and stained scrubs top.

She was heading down the snack aisle, tossing things in her trolley, when she caught sight of the sheriff's car drive past and pull in across the street. Turning away with an ir-ritated mutter, Cassidy checked the next item off her list.

She'd thought she was getting over being dumped in a Spruce Ridge hotel but then she'd heard Ruben Kellan's voice down the passage in ER. Her heart had sped up and stopped at the same time, which was not only impossible but alarming.

Her knees had turned to jelly and the blood had drained from her head so fast that Mrs. Jenkins—whom she'd been examining at the time—had shoved her into a chair and called for a nurse.

Cassidy had blamed the episode on lack of food and long hours. No one had said anything but she didn't think they believed her. Later Fran Gilbert had pulled her aside and handed her a pregnancy test. Cassidy remembered gaping at the other woman and dismissing the idea since Sam had used protection, but when she'd had a chance to think clearly, she realized she couldn't remember her last period.

So she'd panicked.

But when the results had shown up negative she'd cried, great big gulping sobs that hadn't made a bit of sense. She didn't *want* to be pregnant—at least, not like that—by a man who'd made mad, passionate love to her one minute, as though he couldn't get enough, then the next had walked out like she was nothing.

Except it had proved to be a turning point of sorts. She'd emerged from the bathroom bound and determined to get over him. She'd thrown herself into the community, introduced a monthly clinic day for the local schools and a mothers' support group that she hoped they'd continue after she was gone.

During her visit to the middle school she'd met art teacher Genna Walsch, and they'd become close friends. It was Genna's bachelorette party Cassidy was on her way to.

Whipping through the store, she piled items into her trolley before heading for the refrigeration section. She selected a few bottles of chilled champagne and then added fruit juice for pregnant guests.

Next she headed towards the deli, where she'd arranged to pick up a few roast chickens, and had to squeeze past two women studying the selection of cold cuts and chatting.

"I heard Patty Sue from the sheriff's office tell everyone he's coming back," the thirty-something blonde told her friend. "No one knows for sure if it's for good but rumor says it is. I've been surfing the net for obscure symptoms that will get me some quality time with him." She shivered dramatically. "I heard he's *real* good with his hands and I can't wait to play doc—"

The second woman caught sight of Cassidy and nudged her friend into silence, making her wonder what they'd been discussing. Or rather *whom* they'd been discussing. Just then the server turned with a welcoming smile and a "What can we do for you, Dr. Mahoney?" and Cassidy pushed the conversation from her mind.

She knew the county had hired two new doctors that were expected to start at the end of the month. She also knew she would have to make a decision about where to go once *her* contract expired.

As much as she told herself she was over Sam, Cassidy was honest enough to admit that living in the same town as his family meant it was fairly reasonable to expect him to visit occasionally. The longer she stayed in town, the greater the possibility of seeing him, and quite frankly she wasn't sure how she'd feel, or react, if she saw him again.

She'd made several enquiries and had received a couple of good offers—one of which was Spruce Ridge General—but she couldn't make up her mind. Frankly, she didn't want to leave. For the first time in her life she felt part of a community, like she was making a difference in people's lives. She liked feeling needed and appreciated, and she really liked seeing their health improve under her care. It was so much more satisfying than treating nameless masses day in and day out.

She thanked the server and turned, checking chicken off her list. And walked into a wall. Of muscle.

Opening her mouth on an automatic apology, she was instantly assailed by a masculine scent that was all too familiar. Barely an inch from her nose was a wide, hard chest covered in soft black cotton. She knew without looking up past the long tanned throat, strong jaw and poet's mouth to sleepy golden eyes, that she was inches away from the one person who was able to scramble her brain.

Samuel J. Kellan.

Her stomach clenched into a hot ball of dread and joy, and her heart squeezed in her chest. Taking a hasty step in retreat, she tightened her grip on the strap of her shoulder bag. The dimly lit aisle, the illuminated display cases behind her, the couple discussing what to have for dinner, *everything*…faded.

It was as if the universe had suddenly narrowed to just the two of them. Her skin hummed, her ears buzzed and it was only when her vision grayed at the edges that she realized she was holding her breath.

Expelling it on a shaky whoosh, Cassidy's gaze hungrily traced his handsome features. He'd lost weight and he looked tired. There was a healing laceration on his jaw and a bruise darkened his sharply defined cheekbone and the skin around one eye.

Despite his features being in shadow, he appeared tanned and amazingly fit. He looked…wonderful, even if the gaze he'd locked on her face was hooded and unreadable.

Her stomach clenched and her chest felt like a giant fist was squeezing the breath from her lungs. So many times over the past weeks she'd imagined seeing him again. Had even practiced what she would say. But nothing, *nothing* could have prepared her for the stark reality of being this close to him again after she'd convinced herself that she was over him.

Her spirits sank. She'd clearly miscalculated. And with the knowledge came a swift rise of self-directed anger. Okay, she was angry with him too. The jerk had made mad, passionate love to her and when she'd told him she loved him and *begged* him not to go, he'd ripped her heart out and told her he was sorry. Yes, well, she was sorry too—sorry she'd been stupid enough to fall for him.

Yet despite all that, she was glad to see him. Relieved he was alive and in one piece.

He was the first to break the awkward silence.

"Cassidy." The sound of his voice, as deep and rough as she remembered, brushed against jagged emotions and tugged at something deep and raw within her.

She swallowed what felt like ground glass in her throat. "Major," she said, inordinately pleased when her voice emerged coolly polite, as though they were nothing more than casual acquaintances.

His eyes narrowed and his face tightened before his features assumed an impassive mask. He widened his stance and folded his arms across his chest in a move that emphasized his wide shoulders and the bulge of his biceps straining the sleeves of his T-shirt. He was carelessly masculine in a way that made her heart speed up and her knees wobble. And it was suddenly all too painfully obvious that she wasn't going to get over him.

Ever.

She gulped. She'd been fooling herself. He was *it* for her. And nothing she did would stop this soul-deep yearning for him, this ache of knowing they weren't meant to be. That *she* wasn't meant to be—at least not for him.

And didn't that just…*suck.*

The urge to leave was suddenly overwhelming but his big, tough body blocked her way and the potent cocktail of pheromones and testosterone he exuded made her feel light-headed. Oh, wait, that might be caused by food-shopping on an empty stomach. A stomach that was suddenly queasy.

Biting her lip to keep from falling apart, she turned and had to abruptly alter her course to evade the hand he lifted. Thinking he meant to touch her, she stumbled backwards and froze. She sucked in a startled breath and her gaze flew from the hand suspended in the air between them to his face. Something flashed in his gold eyes—something that looked like pain. But he recovered quickly, a shutter slamming down over his features, and she thought maybe she'd been mistaken. His arm dropped to his side.

"How have you been?" he asked softly, and Cassidy's eyes widened. She clenched her jaw to keep it from bouncing off the floor.

He was asking how she'd been? *Really?* After he'd emotionally savaged her in a hotel room then disappeared for five weeks without a word?

She stared at him for a long moment, tempted to just walk away, but a closer inspection of his features revealed lines of exhaustion and uncertainty. Uncertainty?

Yeah, right, she thought with a silent snort, and folded her arms beneath her breasts. "Um…great," she rasped, before clearing her throat and saying with a little more composure, "I'm fine. You?"

His forehead wrinkled as though her behavior baffled him and Cassidy couldn't prevent a little spurt of satisfaction. He was baffled by her behavior? *Well, tough*, she thought, straightening her spine as though the sight of him didn't make her want to simultaneously punch him and throw herself in his arms. Besides, he'd given up the right to be baffled by anything she did.

"Um…yeah, fine," he said absently, his eyebrows pulling his face into a scowl.

Ignoring the urge to trace the arrogant arch of his brows with her fingers, she nodded. "That's…good," she said vaguely. "Your…um, family must be relieved you're home safely." And after an awkward pause during which his intense stare sent flutters dropping into her stomach, she added lamely, "Well, excuse me."

She stepped around him and escaped towards the checkout counter. This time he didn't try to stop her. Instead, he followed, looking big and bad and deliciously dangerous.

He waited while she paid for her purchases, chatting with the checkout clerk. And before she could object, he hefted her packets, announced, "I'll walk you to your car," and headed for the exit. As though expecting her to follow.

She did, quickly, trying to head him off. "That's not necessary," she told him, and grabbed for the carry-bag handle. They engaged in a brief tug of war until Sam gently removed her hand and repeated quietly, "I'll walk you to your car," his gaze as implacable as his words. His mouth tightened when she seemed about to argue, then he stepped around her, turning to wait patiently for directions.

She stood indecisively for a few moments, wondering if she should just leave her groceries and bolt. But that would only prove he still had the power to affect her.

Shoving an errant curl off her face, Cassidy sighed impatiently. "This really isn't necessary, Major," she said huffily. "I can manage a few grocery bags and I'm sure you're busy. So…I won't detain you."

He studied her silently for a few moments before transferring all the bags to one hand. The other he wrapped around her arm and steered her out into the early evening.

Hunching her shoulders against the cool mountain air and the curious looks they were receiving, Cassidy sighed and stepped through the doors. The last thing she needed was him walking her to her car. She was hanging onto her control by her fingernails as it was.

"Where's your car?"

She shifted nervously and adjusted her shoulder bag. "Major—"

"We need to talk," he said quietly, implacably, and Cassidy welcomed the surge of anger that followed his announcement. *What the hell?*

Suddenly furious with him, and with herself, she swung to face him. "There's nothing to say, Major," she said tightly, coolly. "*Nothing*. In fact, you were more than clear about your feelings the last time we…spoke. I get it. I'm not stupid, recent behavior to the contrary. I can read between the lines. Now, if you'll give me my damn bags, I'll be on my way." She grabbed her bags and yanked. This time he allowed her to take one. The others he held out of reach. Growling, Cassidy spun away and headed purpose-fully for the stairs leading to the parking lot. He snagged her arm in a tight grip.

"Cassidy…"

And suddenly she'd had enough. More than enough, actually. "*Don't!*" she snapped, ripping her arm from his grasp and turning away abruptly. She sucked in a ragged breath. "Just…*don't.*" Furious tears pricked the backs of her eyes and she swallowed past the lump of emotion threatening to choke her. She needed to escape before her rigid control snapped. "I…I have to go. G-goodbye, Major."

Sam followed silently and watched as she fumbled in her purse for the car keys. Locating them, she pressed the re-mote and even in the gathering dusk he saw her fingers tremble.

Feeling his gut clench, he reached out and closed his hand over hers. She jolted as though he'd prodded her with a shock stick. Her skin was cold to the touch and his grip tightened when she tried to yank away.

Dammit, I screwed up and now she can't even stand my touch, he thought, when that was all he wanted. He wanted to press up against her curvy body and bury his face into the soft, sweet hollow beneath her ear. He wanted to lick her smooth skin and breathe in her special fragrance—warm, slightly fruity and smelling of clean mountain air. A scent he'd craved with every breath he'd inhaled every second of every day he'd been away.

She hurriedly stepped away and waited tensely while he unlocked her car and stowed her bags on the backseat. He then opened the driver's door and held out her keys. She reached for them, careful not to touch him, and would have slid into the car if Sam hadn't abruptly pushed her back against the cool metal, knowing he couldn't let her go like this. Not after the past weeks. Weeks of hell when he'd missed her like an absent body part.

At first he hadn't understood what the hell was wrong with him. Even his commander had ripped him a new one after he'd blown off the psych eval.

He was supposed to be an invincible SEAL but he'd fallen apart—shared his nightmares and his guilt with her, for God's sake. He hated her knowing he was a cold-blooded killer. Okay, he'd killed to save himself and the rest of his team—but he'd killed in a cold rage. And he hadn't been able to bear the compassion, the sympathy in her eyes. He didn't deserve any of it. He didn't deserve her.

He didn't remember much about that night in Spruce Ridge, but he did remember what he'd said to her. And he felt ashamed.

Everyone thought he was still PTSD but Sam knew that wasn't why he'd been a basket case after that night.

Okay, he was still PTSD but that wasn't the problem, and it had taken him a couple of long weeks to realize exactly what *was*. He was missing something more important than his sanity. His heart. And *she* was his heart.

But all he could think about now was the feel of her soft curves against him. *God*, he'd missed this. Missed having her curvy body pressed against his—like he was finally home.

She made a sound of distress and tried to push him away, but Sam manacled her wrists and pressed them against the cool metal beside her head. Then he took advantage of her shocked gasp and swooped down to crush her mouth with his.

God, he thought, thrusting his tongue deep, hiding out in a desert cave, he'd thought of nothing but the feel of her in his arms, the taste of her in his mouth.

Her heart pounded as hard as his and she struggled to free herself but he wasn't letting go. Not now that he was finally where he belonged. For long moments she remained stiff in his arms, and then with a long throaty moan her body melted against him.

Heart pounding, he released her hands and abruptly broke the kiss, pressing his erection against her. *God*, he wanted—no, *needed*—her more than he'd wanted anything.

Resting his forehead against the roof of her car, he gulped in air and prayed for control, but then she whispered his name, "Samuel," and the sound of it on her lips blew him away.

He thrust his hands onto the wild silvery mass framing her face and the next instant he was devouring her with a hot, hungry desperation he'd never realized he was capable of. It burned him up, a raging wildfire that swept away every thought, every need in a wave of hot primal craving.

His emotions, unrestrained and frantic, burned hot and fierce. His hands streaked over her in a desperate attempt to feel all of her—her soft silky heat, her firm, smooth flesh—and it was a moment before he realized her hands weren't trying to pull him close but push him away.

"Stop," she cried hoarsely. "*Samuel! Stop!*"

Shocked, he froze, his chest heaving with the effort of drawing air into his lungs.

"Stop?" he croaked, not believing he was hearing right. *"Stop?"*

A ragged sound of misery escaped her throat and she flattened her palms against his chest and shoved. Sam was so surprised that he staggered back a couple steps until his back hit the neighboring car.

"Wha—?"

"Leave me alone, Sam," she croaked, and with one desperate look she dived into her car, slammed the door and shoved the key into the ignition before he could move.

The engine engaged in a roar and the car shot out of the parking lot, barely missing a battered Ford truck and a shiny new SUV parked beneath the streetlight.

The last image he had was of her white face streaked with tears, and the knowledge that he'd caused them made his gut clench in sick shock. He'd made her cry. *Again*.

Sam watched as her taillights disappeared, feeling at once numb and devastated. Gutted, like he hadn't felt since he'd let his team down. And just like that night, his rage turned outward. A red tide of primal fury he knew he couldn't let loose on the good people of Crescent Lake.

Shoving his hand into his pocket, he palmed his keys and headed towards his SUV. He might not want to let his rage loose on his friends, but he knew exactly where he *could*.

The sheriff hit the doors of the Crash Landing with the heel of his hand and strode into the bar, expecting to call in for a dozen body bags.

After a crappy week, he'd gone home armed with a six-pack and a giant pizza topped with the works, hoping to relax in front of his big-screen TV. Seattle was playing San Francisco. It was just his luck the call from Dispatch came through as Seattle slammed the first puck into the opposition's net.

Expecting to wade into World War Three, Ruben halted three feet into the bar and blinked in the dim light, aware that his jaw had dropped open. About a dozen men were propped up against the bar, tossing back tequila like they were practicing for a Mexican showdown and singing off-key enough to make tone-deaf ears bleed.

Pushing his hat up his forehead, Ruben shoved his hands on his hips and gaped at the spectacle. Sam was in the thick of things, arm slung around Chris Hastings as though they were bosom buddies when Ruben knew damn well and good they'd been enemies in high school. He'd never seen a sorrier bunch of idiots.

He strode up to the bar and pushed his way through the throng. The owner, watching the proceedings from behind the counter with an unreadable expression, nodded when he saw Ruben.

"Sheriff," he said. "Can I get you something?"

"Coffee, Joe. Strong, black with plenty of sugar."

Joe Montana lifted a brow and grinned. "One cup or two?"

"Make that two. And don't skimp on the sugar."

By the time Joe slid two coffees across the counter the men at the bar had left or wandered away, leaving the brothers alone.

"Go away," Sam growled, and defiantly lifted the last shot to his mouth. Ruben hastily removed the glass and shoved the coffee at him.

"Drink," he said shortly. "And then tell me what Crescent Lake's newest doctor is doing practicing for *America's Got No Talent*."

Sam grimaced at the cup in front of him. "Real funny."

"Not when I've been called away from a game where Seattle scored the first point against 'Frisco. Not when my *brother* is propping up Joe's bar and making people's ears bleed." Sam opened his mouth to argue but Ruben beat him to it. "Drink the damn coffee before I slap your ass in jail for disturbing the peace."

Sam scowled at him through bleary eyes for a couple of beats before he gave a heavy sigh and complied. "I was ready to quit anyway."

Ruben waited until Sam had consumed half the cup's contents before he said mildly, "Care to tell me what's going on?"

Sam shoved a hand through his hair and stared down into his half-empty cup. "Nothing." *Everything.* He'd glimpsed that flash of pain in Cassidy's beautiful green eyes and he'd gone a little crazy.

He'd shoved her up against her car and sucked her breath from her lungs and then she'd cried. The memory of her white, shocked face still had the power to make him feel like the worst kind of monster.

"Uh-huh," Ruben said mockingly.

He loved her, *dammit.* More than being a SEAL. More than his miserable life. More than he wanted to draw his next breath. And she'd told him to stop and had then fled as though she couldn't stand the sight of him.

"Nothing," he repeated wearily, shoving his hands through his hair and propping his elbows on the bar. He'd messed up and now he didn't know how to fix it.

"So," Ruben said, absently stirring his coffee, "this has nothing to do with a certain doctor you were seen practically inhaling whole in Bernie's parking lot, then?" Sam turned to glare at his brother. Ruben's sigh was as weary and heartfelt as Sam's had been a minute ago. "You're an idiot," Ruben said.

Sam straightened and opened his mouth to ream his sibling a new one, then shut it with a snap and looked away. No use denying it. He *was* an idiot.

"I messed up," he confessed roughly, swallowing past the lump of misery stuck in his throat like a burning lump of self-loathing.

"So fix it," Ruben said, his voice laced with steel and something that sounded like impatience-laced sympathy.

"Don't know if I can," Sam admitted quietly, shoving a shaking hand through his hair. "She hates me."

Ruben made a sound of irritation. "You're an embarrassment to Irishmen everywhere, you know that, Kellan?" he snapped, and when Sam's gaze flew up he added, "And here I thought your SEAL motto was 'Adapt and Overcome.'" He pointed a finger at Sam. "So get over yourself, and go do some adapting and overcoming."

"She doesn't want anything to do with me."

"You're a SEAL," Ruben reminded him ruthlessly. "Go be a SEAL. No obstacle too big and all that."

For long tense seconds Sam glared at his brother. He finally gave a sharp nod and downed the last of the godawful coffee. He slapped the cup back in its saucer and shoved away from the bar.

"Pay the man," he ordered, before turning towards the door. "I've got something to do."

Groveling sounded about right, he admitted with a grimace. *And when I'm finished she's going to know she's mine—and that I'm hers.*

Failure was not an option. Not this time.

CHAPTER THIRTEEN

CASSIDY PUSHED OPEN the glass door to the sheriff's department, recalling the last time she'd been there. And like that night, Hazel Porter was once again manning the front desk.

The deputy peered over her half-spectacles and an odd expression crossed her face. She cleared her throat loudly once, then again, and abrupt silence fell over the room as a dozen pairs of eyes swung in her direction.

Forehead wrinkling in confusion, Cassidy approached the desk, suddenly feeling as nervous as a newlywed outside the honeymoon suite.

"Evening, Mrs. Porter," she greeted the deputy. "Dispatch said you…um…had a medical emergency?"

"Glad you could make it, hon," Hazel rasped, and turned to snag a bunch of keys from the board behind her. "We have a…situation."

"A situation?"

Hazel headed around the counter and made shooing gestures at the group of young deputies watching Cassidy with big toothy grins.

Cassidy frowned. "What's going on?"

Hazel shook her head. "Ignore 'em, hon, they're just a bunch of idiots with nothing better to do than stand around grinning like loons." The last she said loudly, scowling at the deputies who instantly tried to pretend they were busy.

Cassidy opened her mouth but the desk sergeant barreled on. "It's been a real slow week and nobody in this town can keep their noses out of other people's business."

Brow wrinkling with concern, Cassidy asked, "Are you all right, Mrs. Porter? You seem a little—"

"Call me Hazel, hon," the deputy interrupted, "everybody does. And I'm fine." Then she muttered something that sounded like, "Or I will be once all the hoo-hah is over," leaving a clueless Cassidy to follow her down the hallway towards the holding cells.

Muffled laughter and scuffling sounded somewhere behind her and she glanced over her shoulder. Several deputies were pushing and shoving each other to peer around the door—like they were in junior high.

They grinned and gave her the universal thumbs-up sign. *Weird,* she thought with a mental eye-roll, and turned back to follow Hazel's diminutive figure.

"This way, hon," the deputy said, unlocking the door and gesturing as if they hadn't done something similar a few months earlier. Stepping cautiously through the open doorway, Cassidy paused, wondering why every hair on her body was standing on end like a freaked-out cat.

Biting her lip uncertainly, she looked at the deputy and found Hazel staring at her with the oddest expression in her dark eyes.

"Don't be too hard on him, hon," Hazel murmured softly. "He's an idiot, but we love him."

Alarmed, Cassidy opened her mouth, certain now that Crescent Lake's sheriff's department was under some kind of Rocky Mountain madness. "Mrs. Porter—"

"It's Hazel, hon," the deputy interrupted cheerfully, and gestured to the large lump occupying the narrow bunk—in the same cell she'd entered before. "Now, in you go, everything's already set up. Holler if you need anything."

Squaring her shoulders, Cassidy stepped into the dimly lit holding area, vaguely aware that the cell doors were all ajar—and empty. *That's odd.* The outer door slammed shut. She gave a startled squeak and told herself she was letting everyone's *weirdness* affect her.

Inhaling an unsteady breath, Cassidy tightened her grip on her medical bag and headed for the occupied cell. Stepping through the open doorway, she sensed movement behind her and whirled, using the momentum to swing her medical bag at the intruder. With a surprised curse, he ducked and lifted his forearm in a lightning-fast move that caught her wrist and sent the bag flying.

Squeaking in alarm, Cassidy scrambled backwards and stumbled over her own feet. She fell, landing hard, and for just a moment saw stars. Gasping for the breath that had been knocked out of her, she blinked and realized a man—*God, he was huge*—was bending over her...reaching for her.

She saw his mouth move but heard nothing over the blood thundering in her ears as she scuttled out of reach. But his big hands closed over her shoulders and before she could squeak out a protest, he'd hauled to her feet like she weighed nothing.

Intent only on preventing every woman's worst nightmare, Cassidy lashed out with her hands and feet, unaware that she was screaming until she heard a familiar voice calling her name.

"*Jeez*, Cassidy, stop. Stop it. *Cassidy!* Dammit. *Calm down!*"

She froze, gulping in great big sobs and stared into the dark face above her. It took her a couple of seconds to recognize the familiar masculine scent, the wide gold eyes staring at her as if she'd lost her mind.

She croaked, "*Samuel?*" and her knees abruptly buckled. He yanked her against his big warm body, hard arms keeping her from sliding to the floor.

"*Jeez,* woman," he growled into her hair, his arm an iron

band across her back as she fisted her hands in his shirt and pressed her face into his warm throat. Her heart raced at warp speed. His free hand cupped the back of her head and she breathed in the comforting scent of heat, clean male and crisp mountain air.

By the time her heart dropped from stroke level to a mere freaked out, Cassidy remembered that she was furious with him—hell, he'd just scared a decade off her life.

Acting on impulse that was triggered by fear, fury and relief, she shoved him back and rammed her knee into his groin in one smooth move. With a startled yelp, he jerked away from the unexpected attack and dropped like a stone. Suddenly free, Cassidy hastily backed up until the cold steel bars bit into her shoulders.

"*Holy...*" Sam wheezed after a couple minutes of gasping like she'd gutted him with a scalpel. "*What...the... hell...was...that...for?*"

Shocked by her own action, Cassidy could only gape at him and stutter. "You... I... *Dammit!*" Her knees gave out and she slid down until her butt hit the cold floor. When her vision finally cleared and she could speak without stuttering, she opened her mouth to apologize and "You scared the *crap* out of me, you...you *dufus!*" emerged instead.

Sam stilled for a long moment then a rough sound emerged from his throat, sounding like a mix between a laugh and a groan. Moving slowly like he was in severe pain, he sat up and sank back against the bunk, one leg drawn up tightly to his chest. In the dim light his mouth was a tight white line in his green complexion.

Appalled by what she'd done, Cassidy rose on shaky legs, took a couple of wobbly steps and dropped to her knees beside him.

"I'm...I'm sorry," she gulped, lifting a hand to brush an errant lock of dark hair off his forehead. For a moment she enjoyed the feel of cool, silky strands between her fingers before admitting shakily, "I don't know why I did that."

His rough, gravelly laugh was abruptly cut off as he sucked in an unsteady breath and wiped his face with shaking hands. After a long silence he finally opened his eyes and stared at her.

"Dufus?"

She blinked. "What?"

"You called me a dufus."

Cassidy grimaced and sat back on her heels. "Yes… well…um. It was the best I could come up with in the heat of the moment."

His mouth curled into crooked smile and the expression in his eyes made her gasp. Before she could even begin to interpret it he said, "Come 'ere," and wrapped his fingers around her wrist.

With a gentle tug he pulled her towards him. She gave a startled squeak and found herself in his lap. His arms, his warmth, his scent surrounded her and she was tempted to wrap herself around him too. Just to prove to herself that he was here. Fortunately, she recalled his behavior of the previous night and pushed away. Sam tightened his arms with a deep, rough sound of pain.

"Don't…move," he rasped in her ear. "Just…gimme… a minute."

Realizing her bottom was planted right where she'd kneed him, Cassidy froze until she remembered that she was supposed to be treating an injured prisoner. *Him?*

"Where are you hurt?" she asked quietly, resisting the urge to run her hands, her lips over every inch of him.

He stilled and there was a moment of stunned silence. Then he lifted his head to gape at her. "*Really?* You do *that* and then ask where I hurt?"

A scalding blush rose into her cheeks and she bit back

a hysterical giggle. "I'm s-sorry," she said in an unsteady voice. "But you deserved it for scaring me."

His snort told her what he thought of her apology. "I'll be lucky if you haven't permanently destroyed any chance I have of fathering future Kellans."

Reminded that he wasn't interested in making those future Kellans with her, Cassidy snapped, "That's not my problem," and tried to scramble away. He yanked her back.

"Stop that," he ordered, clamping his hands on her hips and pulling her closer. "It *is* your problem." And then he murmured something that sounded like, "Or it will be…I hope."

Confused, Cassidy pulled back to look into his face. His color had returned but he still looked a little worse for wear.

"What's going on, Sam?" she demanded, lifting her hands to examine the bruises on his face, before probing his shoulders and chest. "The dispatcher called for a medic."

"Who just about crippled me. What's with the ninja attack, by the way?"

"Sam…"

He sighed. "Look, you're right I am a dufus. In fact—"

"Sam."

"Just let me finish, okay," he interrupted quickly, his hands clenching on her thighs and sending little shivers of heat and arousal through her. "I need to say this."

Sighing, Cassidy studied him closely for signs of PTSD or at least an answer to his behavior. "All right," she said quietly, ruthlessly squelching the urge to squirm against him. "I'm listening, especially to the part where I'm right."

His mouth quirked up at the corner then tightened as he exhaled heavily. He looked nervous but Cassidy dismissed it as her imagination. He was a SEAL. The notion that he might be nervous made her want to smile. He'd survived being captured and tortured, for goodness' sake. Samuel J. Kellan didn't do nervous as much if not more than he didn't do relationships.

But something was clearly up and it was starting to make *her* nervous. "What are you doing here?" she asked quietly when the silence finally became unbearable. "Aren't you supposed to be parachuting into hostile territory and wiping out bad guys?"

"I quit," he said quietly, his gaze intense and unreadable on hers.

She blinked. "You…you…*what*? But…wh-why?"

He was silent for so long she didn't think he intended to reply but his gaze turned fiercely possessive when he finally admitted, "*You*."

"Me. *Me?*" Her voice emerged as a squeak. "*What do you mean, me?*"

Sam's mouth lifted at one corner but his eyes were serious. "I mean I was on a mission and all I could think about was you. That's dangerous, Cassidy. For me *and* the team."

This close, Cassidy could see the individual muscles in his throat as he swallowed. Not knowing where to put her hands, she smoothed them down her thighs to disguise the fact that they were trembling.

"I messed up," he admitted softly. "I was five miles above the earth in a HALO jump and closing fast when my chute failed to deploy—"

Her head went abruptly light. "*Oh, my God*," she gasped out, clutching at his shoulders and shaking him. "Tell me…" she demanded hoarsely. "Tell me you're okay." His hands reached up to grab hers before she ripped his shirt.

"*Hey.*" His grip tightened. "I'm here, aren't I?"

She stared at him wide-eyed for a couple beats then pulled a hand free and punched him—hard. "*Dammit*, don't…don't you *dare* scare me like that."

He winced and wrapped long fingers around her wrist. "If you'll just let me finish," he said gently.

Cassidy swallowed a sob and grimaced. "Sorry."

He absently lifted her hand to plant a kiss on her white knuckles in a move that stunned her. "Well, there I was," he continued, "falling at a hundred miles per hour…" Her gasp earned her a chiding look. "As I said, a hundred miles per hour, with the earth rushing up to meet me, and I thought, This is it. I even relaxed, thinking it was nothing more than I deserved for failing my team." He paused and drew in a shaky breath. "Failing you. I heard someone yelling in my head and…*hell*…I was all ready to go out in a blaze of glory. Arm the grenades and aim for the target instead of the drop site…just blow everything to hell and back."

"*Oh, God, Sam no*," Cassidy cried out, slapping a hand over her mouth to hold in the ragged sound of shock and horror. Her eyes burnt with unshed tears and he tugged her close, smoothing a shaking hand over her messy ponytail to her back. "I was reaching for my stash, voices yelling in my ears, and the next second…" He pushed her away to look into her eyes. "The next second everything faded— like I'd blacked out—and I…I heard you…yelling at me to get my butt into gear." He paused and swallowed. "Then you said…*I love you Samuel, please*…please *don't go*."

Stunned, Cassidy jerked back, fighting to free herself from his hold, but Sam's grip tightened, banding around her like steel, as though he couldn't bear to let her go. "*Don't*," he said hoarsely. "Don't pull away. I know I deserve it, but…just let me finish. *Please?*" He waited until she stilled, her face buried against his wide shoulder, tears dampening the soft, warm cotton.

"I saw your face, Cassidy," he said tightly against her temple. "As clear and real as you are to me now. And in that instant I knew… *Jeez*. You're right, I am a dufus. It

took almost dying to realize that I…that I…" He halted
and sucked in a sharp breath.

Cassidy froze and when he continued to breathe heavily
she pushed away from him and lifted her gaze past the
muscle twitching in his jaw. "That you what, Sam?"

His mouth twisted into a half-smile but his eyes glowed
with an emotion Cassidy was too afraid to interpret.

"I was on a collision course with disaster. I blamed myself for living when my friends died. And when my chute
failed I thought, *It's nothing more than you deserve.* But
you rescued me, Doc, and even though I hurt you…didn't
deserve you…I suddenly couldn't bear the thought of never
seeing you again. That I hadn't told you." He inhaled shakily. "My mind was suddenly clear, like I was finally seeing
the world for the first time. I sent up a prayer and yanked
that damn clip.

"For a couple seconds nothing happened…and then…
and then it deployed." He gave a ragged laugh and lifted
his hands to cup her face. "Other than seeing your beautiful smile," he told her softly, "it was the most welcome
sight I've ever seen."

"Oh," was all Cassidy could manage, her voice low
and raw.

"I love you Cassidy," he said solemnly. "Tell me it's not
too late. Tell me I didn't dream those words. Tell me you
didn't rescue me…my heart…only to break it."

"Oh, *Sam,*" Cassidy said again, too overwhelmed to
think past the jumble of emotions rioting through her.
"You're…sure?"

"That I love you? Dead sure—"

"Don't say that," she burst out, placing a hand over
his mouth. He paled, looking appalled. "Don't say that I
love you?"

She let out a little giggle. "No," she said, smiling, leaning in to replace her hand with her mouth in a soft, sweet

kiss. "You can say *that* as often as you like. In fact, you need to say it again."

Inhaling shakily, he thrust his fingers into her hair, his gaze falling to her mouth. "I love you," he groaned, his lips dropping to brush against hers. "God, you have no idea how much I love you."

Dizzy with happiness and wanting nothing more than to sink into his kiss, she throatily ordered, "Kiss me, then." But he pulled back, grinning at her growl of frustration.

He shook his head. "Not until you tell me."

"Tell you what?" she demanded huskily, leaning forward to catch his sculpted bottom lip between her teeth. She gave it a punishing nip and wriggled her bottom against him. *God, she'd missed this*. His scent, his touch and the taste of him in her mouth.

"Aw, c'mon, babe," he groaned, pulling back to scowl at her. "Don't keep me in suspense."

Her mouth dropped open. *"Babe?"*

He gave her a hard shake. *"Dammit,* Cassidy," he growled. "I'm dying here. Rescue me, Doc…*please.*"

Palming his tense face, Cassidy stared into his deep gold eyes, all humor abruptly disappearing. "I love you, Samuel Kellan," she murmured, her eyes soft on his before she caught at his mouth, and clung, like she'd never let go. "Don't you know? Don't you *know* yet how much I love you?"

A beautiful smile bloomed across his dark face and the next thing Cassidy found herself lying flat with his body, huge and heavy, pressing her into the cold floor. And before she could squeak out a protest, he slid a hand up her thigh to cup her bottom and pull her against him.

She thought he murmured, *"Thank God,"* and the next thing his mouth opened over hers in a kiss so hot and wet and *hungry* she nearly combusted.

Clutching at him, she sent her hands racing over his

wide shoulders and back, down his arms, reveling in the solid feel of him beneath her palms. Her eyes drifted closed in delight and she gave herself over to his hunger.

For long moments Sam's mouth ravished hers as though he was starving for the taste of her, like he'd gone years instead of just weeks without her. She hummed her own hunger deep in her throat and marveled at the lights exploding behind her eyelids.

By the time they came up for air, she was gasping, dizzy with a pleasure she'd found only with him, and frustrated that they were still fully dressed. More than anything she wanted to feel the heated slide of skin against damp skin.

It was a few moments before she was able to open her eyes, only to discover a circle of curious, grinning faces peering down at them. Clutching Sam, she gave a startled squeak and felt her eyes widen as she recognized the young deputies who'd given her the thumbs-up earlier. Then the sheriff's face appeared overhead and then another…Sam's *sister?*

Oh, my God.

A hot blush rose in her cheeks. "*Sam,*" she squeaked, ducking her face into his throat.

"Yeah," he said in her hair, his voice strangely tight. "I know."

"Do you two need a room?" Hannah Kellan asked mildly, and laughter burst around them.

Sam stiffened, finally realizing they weren't alone. "What we need," Sam growled dryly, "is some privacy."

A moment later he rolled off Cassidy and drew her to her feet in one smooth move. He yanked her back when she made a move to bolt and tucked her against his side. He shook his head at their captive audience.

Hannah propped her shoulder against the open doorway and folded her arms beneath her breasts. "Well?" she asked cheekily, her elegant dark brow lifted in a way Cassidy recognized as pure Sam.

"Well, what?" he demanded, clearly annoyed by the interruption.

"Did she or didn't she?" Ruben demanded impatiently, and Cassidy nearly giggled at the way everyone's gaze jumped from one person to another in a ridiculous parody of a tennis match.

"I haven't asked her yet."

Hannah snickered and to Cassidy's embarrassment said, "What, too busy shoving your tongue down her throat?"

Sam growled threateningly and everyone laughed. "I'll be shoving you all out the door if you don't give us some space," he told her. "*Jeez*, can't a guy propose without the whole damn zoo turning up?"

Cassidy's head whipped up. "P-propose?" she squeaked.

His gaze turned possessive but to Cassidy's amazement he flushed. "Of course. What did you think I meant?" he demanded with a scowl.

"Well…I—"

His voice dropped. "You rescued me, Cassidy. You saved me when I didn't realize until it was almost too late. I love you. You're everything I want, everything I didn't realize I was looking for."

Cassidy's eyes misted and the buzzing in her ears almost blocked out the snickers of "*Aaaaww, isn't that sweet?*" coming from Sam's siblings.

"But…but what about your job?"

"I told you I quit."

"I don't know," she said slowly, ignoring the sharply inhaled breaths around them.

Sam froze and panic flashed across his face. "What do you mean, you don't know?"

"You haven't asked me yet," she reminded him gently,

and reached up to kiss the corner of his mouth when he gusted out a relieved breath.

Turning her in his arms, he wrapped a hand around her neck and pressed his thumb beneath her chin, lifting her face to his.

"Cassidy Maureen Mahoney, will you rescue me one last time?"

Tears filled her eyes and her breath hitched in her throat. "Oh, Sam—"

"Will you marry me?" he continued in a voice deep and clear and filled with emotion. "And spend the next sixty years loving me as much as I love you? Will you raise a family with me here in Crescent Lake and work by my side at the hospital, keeping the nosy locals healthy? Especially people who don't know when the hell to take a hint."

Her breath hitched. "Oh," she sighed, staring up at him with damp eyes until he couldn't stand the suspense.

"Say something, babe," he whispered pleadingly. "You're making me look bad in front of everyone."

She giggled and a sudden hush fell as every ear strained for her answer. "Yes…" she whispered into the hushed silence, and wild emotion burst into Sam's eyes.

"Yes?"

"Yes," Cassidy said a little louder. "Yes, I'll marry you." And when he gave a whoop she put up a hand. "But…." He stilled, the panic on his face priceless. His mouth dropped open and there was a smattering of snickers. "But?" He looked suddenly nervous and wary. "But what? I have to give up a kidney? Done. My family? With pleasure."

Cassidy's mouth curled in a private smile. "I want to know all your secrets."

"All of them?" And when her eyes narrowed he said quickly, "They're yours."

"Great. Now, what's the J for?"

He blinked. "Huh?"

"In your name," she explained, curling her arms around his neck and burying her hands in his thick, silky hair. She watched as a slow, sexy smile bloomed. He leaned closer to whisper in her ear and Cassidy pulled back, wild color blossoming in her cheeks. "I don't think so." She giggled. Sam sighed then tried again and when he finally pulled back, he let his brow rise questioningly.

Cassidy rose on her toes to seal the promise with a kiss. "Samuel James Kellan, nothing would make me happier than being your wife."

A deafening cheer rose to fill Crescent Lake's jail cells. Sam ignored the loud congratulations and celebratory backslaps to wrap his arms around the woman who'd rescued him from a life of nightmares.

"I love you, Doc Honey. What do you say we find someplace more private?"

A smile lit her face with love and anticipation and she blushed adorably. "I know just the place, Major Hotstuff."

He grinned. "Lead the way *babe*."

And she took his hand.

* * * * *